**"Put this writer'**

*Scandal's Daughter*

"A spirited heroine, a scandalous past, a bewildered rake: Christine Wells gives us a charming story, rich with historical delights."

—Anne Gracie

"A touching love story . . . An impressive debut book. I thoroughly enjoyed it."

—Mary Balogh

"Romance with the sparkle of vintage champagne. A stellar debut from a major new talent!"

—Anna Campbell

"A charming romance brimming with emotion and humor. The sensual intimacy between Sebastian and Gemma mellows like a fine wine within the friendship forged long before their first kiss. Christine Wells makes the Regency as fresh and real as her characters, and I expect it won't be long before she's a favorite on every romance reader's bookshelf."

—Kathryn Smith

"Witty, emotionally intense, and romantic—Ms. Wells beguiles us in this stellar debut."

—*Sophia Nash

"A brilliantly seductive love story that belongs on every keeper shelf . . . Sizzling with sensuality."

—Kathryn Caskie

"A lovely story of best friends discovering there could be more, *Scandal's Daughter* charms and delights with humor, wit, and intelligence. An enchanting debut, *Scandal's Daughter* engages all the senses and leaves a smile on your face and warmth in your heart."

—*The Courier-Mail* (Brisbane)

"Fresh and brisk."

—*Midwest Book Review*

*Books by Christine Wells*

SCANDAL'S DAUGHTER
THE DANGEROUS DUKE

# The Dangerous Duke

CHRISTINE WELLS

BERKLEY SENSATION, NEW YORK

**THE BERKLEY PUBLISHING GROUP**
**Published by the Penguin Group**
**Penguin Group (USA) Inc.**
**375 Hudson Street, New York, New York 10014, USA**
Penguin Group (Canada), 90 Eglinton Avenue East, Suite 700, Toronto, Ontario M4P 2Y3, Canada
(a division of Pearson Penguin Canada Inc.)
Penguin Books Ltd., 80 Strand, London WC2R 0RL, England
Penguin Group Ireland, 25 St. Stephen's Green, Dublin 2, Ireland (a division of Penguin Books Ltd.)
Penguin Group (Australia), 250 Camberwell Road, Camberwell, Victoria 3124, Australia
(a division of Pearson Australia Group Pty. Ltd.)
Penguin Books India Pvt. Ltd., 11 Community Centre, Panchsheel Park, New Delhi—110 017, India
Penguin Group (NZ), 67 Apollo Drive, Rosedale, North Shore 0632, New Zealand
(a division of Pearson New Zealand Ltd.)
Penguin Books (South Africa) (Pty.) Ltd., 24 Sturdee Avenue, Rosebank, Johannesburg 2196,
South Africa

Penguin Books Ltd., Registered Offices: 80 Strand, London WC2R 0RL, England



THE DANGEROUS DUKE

A Berkley Sensation Book / published by arrangement with the author

PRINTING HISTORY
Berkley Sensation mass-market edition / September 2008


Cover illustration by Jim Griffin.
Cover handlettering by Ron Zinn.
Cover design by George Long.
Interior text design by Kristin del Rosario.



ISBN: 978-0-425-22326-0

BERKLEY® SENSATION
Berkley Sensation Books are published by The Berkley Publishing Group,
a division of Penguin Group (USA) Inc.,
375 Hudson Street, New York, New York 10014.
BERKLEY SENSATION and the "B" design are trademarks of Penguin Group (USA) Inc.

PRINTED IN THE UNITED STATES OF AMERICA

10 9 8 7 6 5 4 3 2 1

*For Cheryl,*
*my beloved mother, my rock.*

*And for Ian,*
*my father, with love and admiration.*

# Acknowledgments

Heartfelt thanks to my editor, Leis Pederson, for her understanding and her eagle eye; to all at Berkley who have worked so hard on *The Dangerous Duke*; and to my agent, Jessica Faust, whose level head and guiding hand have been invaluable.

To Denise Rossetti, cheerleader and dear friend; Anna Campbell, who sailed in to save the day when I needed her; and Anne Gracie, for never failing me when I ask for her wisdom—my everlasting gratitude. For research assistance (though any mistakes are mine) a Regency "much obliged" to K. A. Taylor, Nancy Mayer, Pam Rosenthal, and all at the Beau Monde.

This year has been a difficult one and I owe an exceptionally large debt to many people, not least my long-suffering family and friends—Jamie, Allister and Adrian, Cheryl and Ian, Robin and George, Vikki, Ben and Yasmin—thank you for your patience, love, and support.

And to a funny, bright, talented bunch of women—the Romance Bandits, my sisters-in-crime. Thank you for being you.

# One

*He will come for me, I know it. And when he does, there'll be no resistance. Only pleasure, as deep and dark and sinful as this mad desire that plagues me.*

*Will I regret the ruin that awaits? No, it will taste too sweet, I think . . .*

## London, 1817

DANGLING a man upside down by the ankles outside a London ballroom was not how Maxwell Brooke had anticipated spending his first Thursday night as the Duke of Lyle.

In fact, since he'd never expected to inherit the illustrious title in the first place, he hadn't developed expectations about the matter at all.

But if he had ever considered it, he might have anticipated a damned sight less trouble and a damned sight more comfort than he'd been granted thus far.

He'd spent four nights in a dank, draughty cavern of a house where the fireplaces belched smoke and the kitchens were so far from the dining room every meal was served cold. From there, two days' sodden journey by an antiquated and equally draughty coach had brought him to town.

And now, when finally he could look forward to a pleasurable evening seducing his fair hostess—

"Lemme up, guv! I don't mean no harm, honest." The hoarse plea barely reached Max's ears against the freshening wind, but it caught his wandering attention.

Exasperated, he frowned down at his captive. What a sorry sight! A thin, twisted body, spindly legs with wiry tufts of hair sprouting through the sparse weave of his stockings, ankles that felt like bundles of twigs in Max's big hands. The pathetic, featherweight of the man. He couldn't see the fellow's face from this angle, but he'd wager it was purple by now.

Max was tired of holding him, that was certain. He'd expected his victim to crack long before this. Someone must have paid him handsomely for his silence. Perhaps Max should beat the truth out of the fellow, but he rather thought a solid blow might kill the little ferret and he didn't want to get blood on his evening clothes.

Conscious of the ball in progress behind him, Max spoke just loudly enough for his voice to carry to his victim's ears. "My friend, do you know the penalty for treason?"

Spindleshanks kicked out in a panic, nearly freeing one leg from Max's grasp.

"Don't struggle"—Max tightened his grip until his fingers bit into the man's flesh—"or I'll drop you through no fault of mine."

The man yelped. His squirming halted abruptly. Max grunted, bracing his hips against the balustrade for extra support.

"We'll try again, shall we? Tell me who you are and what you were doing lurking in Lady Kate's gardens."

"I told you, guv. I didn't mean no harm. I've . . . I've a message for her ladyship."

Satisfaction flooded Max's chest for the first time since this business began. Instinct had told him this evening might bring him a fresh lead, and instinct had been right.

So, his hostess's saintly brother had tried to get a message to her, had he? Very clever to choose the night of a ball, when servants and guests came and went at all hours.

Did Lady Kate suspect she was being watched? Did she know that her brother, the Reverend Stephen Holt, was in prison? Clapped up in irons, allowed no visitors, no legal representation. Not even a fair hearing.

And Max had put him there.

He gave Spindleshanks a rough shake. "Tell me your message and I'll make sure her ladyship gets it."

Gasping and wheezing, the man renewed his pleas. "Aw, have an 'eart, guv! I'm to give my message to her ladyship and no one else. My business wiv the lady being what you might call personal, like."

Better and better. Max smiled grimly, scarcely aware of the burn in his shoulders and arms. There could be little doubt why such a disreputable-looking specimen should have private business with a society hostess.

*Lady Kate Fairchild.* Max knew her by sight, but since the fire and Holt's incarceration, Max had made it his business to investigate Holt's sister thoroughly. He hadn't discovered anything to her discredit. The childless widow of a former member of Parliament, Lady Kate possessed a curiously spotless reputation for a woman in her sophisticated circle of acquaintance. At seven-and-twenty years of age, she was a wealthy woman and showing little inclination to remarry, according to his aunts.

He closed his eyes, trying to shut out the memory of his great-aunts, Grace and Millicent, so fragile and shaken in the aftermath of the fire. The devastation the blaze had caused at Lyle Castle was almost incomprehensible, even to him. Max had taken charge of the household, which was in dire need of a master. He'd investigated and swiftly concluded that the fire had been deliberately set.

By the time he'd left, he'd gained control of practical matters, but he wasn't equipped to deal with outpourings of grief. And the weeping. God, the tears. Oceans of them had been sobbed down his coat in the past few days. He shifted uncomfortably, the memory of his inept attempts at consolation fresh in his mind.

Well, he wasn't good at offering sympathy—he'd rather stick needles in his eyes than wade through that emotional soup again—but he could do one thing for the bereft and grieving.

He would make those murderers pay.

At the Home Office, they called Max "the Fixer," the man they called when a job was too sensitive or too dirty to handle through official channels. He dealt with the gutter scum, the villainous, and the corrupt. He anticipated little difficulty apprehending the disorganized band of rebels who'd set fire to Lyle Castle. All he needed was for the Reverend Holt to spill his guts.

"Oh! Who's there?"

A feminine voice behind him made his head snap around. He cursed his lapse in vigilance. How had she managed to surprise him? His hearing was preternaturally acute.

The woman hesitated, as if she might draw back into the ballroom.

*Yes, go,* he thought. He couldn't release his prey, and he'd rather not explain what he was doing.

But the musical voice persisted. "Is that you, Your Grace?"

The figure shifted, and the light from the flambeaux on either side of the doorway flared over her face.

Lady Kate Fairchild.

For one frozen, unsettling moment, Max forgot why he was there. She moved forward, and the soft light behind her silhouetted intriguing curves beneath her white silk gown. Her hair was piled high, with one thick chestnut ringlet curled invitingly on her breast, and wispy tendrils escaped here and there to tickle her temples and nape. Though modestly cut, her gown showed enough of her creamy bosom to make his hands itch to explore.

Max watched her walk towards him, struck by the way she moved. Her Grecian robe stirred and rippled, caressing her slender, almost fragile body. Its skirts flared on a sudden gust of wind, allowing him a glimpse of slender ankles, crisscrossed by the straps of her gold Roman sandals.

Desire bunched inside him and rose in a powerful surge—hot and needy. Despite the circumstances, he had a compelling urge to drop what he was doing—literally—and pursue the opportunity this sudden encounter presented.

Damnation! He didn't need this. He couldn't allow a woman to distract him, even for a moment. Seduction might well play a part in his plans—certainly, seducing Lady Kate would be no hardship—but first, he must find out how much she knew and what she planned to do about it. Then he'd find a way to use her to wring information out of Stephen Holt.

Max inclined his head, the closest he could get to a bow in the circumstances. "My lady."

He continued to shield his victim from her with his body, but he didn't hold out much hope that she'd go away and leave him to finish his business with the fellow. Best to brazen it out, he supposed.

Lady Kate carried herself with unruffled grace, as if she hadn't a care in the world. Somehow, he doubted she was so sanguine. It couldn't be chance that brought her onto the terrace, where someone waited for her with a message. She must have arranged this meeting tonight.

He narrowed his eyes and focused on her face. "I thought you'd have joined your guests at the supper table by now."

"Yes, everyone is in the dining room, but I was obliged to slip out here first and repair a tear to the hem of my gown. So provoking!" She rolled her eyes and extracted a pin from her reticule. "Mr. Bellingham might be a political lightweight, but light on his feet he is not!"

Apparently oblivious to the faint grunts and groans of

his companion, she joined Max, talking all the while. "Would you mind holding my reticule? I just need to . . . Oh! I do apologize." Her gaze fixed on his hands, which were still wrapped around his victim's ankles. She peered over the balustrade. "It rather seems you have your hands full already."

He looked down, feigning surprise. "Now, how did that get there?"

She gave him a quick, oblique glance, then leaned over to see his victim better, giving Max a magnificent view of her breasts. High and round, they were, despite her fairylike figure. Not as big as his usual—

"He looks dreadfully uncomfortable," she said. "I suppose this is one of those juvenile pranks my brothers used to delight in. But the poor fellow! All the blood must be rushing to his head." She raised her voice. "Are you all right down there?"

"Help! Help me, my lady. Please!" Spindleshanks managed a feeble struggle, as if to emphasize his weakness.

She drew back, delicate fingers fluttering over her lips. "Oh, dear. I do hope you won't drop him. With the prime minister here, I mean. How would I look with a dead body in my garden and half the government in my dining room?"

Max could almost have smiled. He had to hand it to her. Cool as Gunter's ices, when she must be dying for news of her brother. "It would certainly make your party memorable."

"My parties are always memorable. I don't need a corpse in my rose beds for that." She bit her lip. "Oh, do let him up. You are making me nervous. Indeed, I shall very likely fall into hysterics."

Anyone less likely to fall into hysterics would be difficult to find. Unwillingly amused, he complied, releasing one ankle to reach down and grab the seat of the man's breeches. Max hauled him back over the balustrade and set him on his feet.

"This poor excuse for a human being says he has a message for you, my lady." He bunched the man's collar in his fist and shoved him forward. "Perhaps he will give it to you now. What's your name, fellow?"

Spindleshanks bent forward, hands on his knees, trying to catch his breath. He mumbled something unintelligible.

Max shook him. "Stand up straight when you address a lady."

"Ives," said the fellow between gasps. "Harry Ives."

Her ladyship observed the man dubiously. What an actress! Siddons was nothing to her.

"A message for me?" she repeated, the picture of bewilderment. "But why were you skulking out here? Why not deliver it the usual way?"

Before Ives could answer, she said, "Oh, never mind. Go and await me in the servants' hall. Tell the butler I sent you. I'll be down in a minute."

Ives threw Lady Kate a hostile glance, but he muttered something Max didn't quite catch and shuffled away.

Max didn't detain him. He was far more intrigued by the lady before him. After all, he'd attended this party for the express purpose of deepening their acquaintance. He'd expected Lady Kate to be another Society bore, but the mettle she'd shown so far in their encounter made him anticipate his task with pleasure.

They both watched Ives's retreating form. After a long, taut pause, Lady Kate met Max's gaze fully for the first time.

Eyes the color of French cognac, framed by an exotic wedge of black lashes, stared into his, then widened a little, as if in surprise.

He stilled, a strange shock of awareness holding him suspended, frozen in a sliver of time. It was a curious sensation, one he'd never experienced before.

He'd admired many women but he'd never reacted to any of them like this. A potent mix of emotions swept through him—desire, excitement, fascination, even tenderness. And all the while a beat in his brain said: *Not her. Not now.*

She recovered first, with a small shake of her head. Touching her temple with a hand that trembled slightly, she turned away. "I had best return to my guests."

Finally, he found his voice. "Aren't you forgetting something?"

She halted with her back to him. Her head turned slightly, so he could see her profile, limned by candlelight from the ballroom. "Forgetting something? What do you mean?"

He strolled up to her, taking his time, drawing out the moment. When he stood behind her, close enough to feel the warmth of her body, he stopped.

He saw the ripple in her slender throat when she swallowed. Her lips parted to draw in a quick breath.

Reaching around her, he closed his hand over hers and took the pin she still held. He could have sworn she shivered at his touch.

He wanted to put his other arm around her and cup her breasts in his hands. He wanted to set his lips to that vulnerable spot at the junction of her collarbone and throat, above the gold filigree necklace she wore.

But only his breath touched her there, stirring soft chestnut tendrils, before he stepped back, allowing her to turn around to face him once more.

"Your hem," he said. "Didn't you say you needed to pin it?"

Her face flushed. She lifted a tentative hand to her cheek. "Oh, yes, of course. Give it to me and I'll—"

Max smiled. "No, I insist. Allow me."

He knelt before her, running his fingers around the hem of her flimsy garment. She was so still, she might have been holding her breath. When his fingers brushed her ankle, she started and quickly stepped back, whisking the silk from his light grasp.

Max looked up and caught a wild expression in her eyes.

"Where is the tear? I can't seem to find it," he said, careful to keep any suggestion of irony from his tone.

"Rather more to the left," she replied, regaining her composure. "Do be quick about it, sir. I could have done it myself in half the time."

He found the small rent in her hem and gave a silent whistle. Score one to the lady. He had not expected to find her excuse for lingering on the terrace genuine.

He repaired the tear quickly and tweaked her skirts into place, resisting the urge to touch her again.

Straightening, he held his arm out to her. "Your guests will wonder where you are. Shall we?"

She stared at his arm as if it were a snake ready to strike her. "Oh, no. Do, please, excuse me. I must see what that fellow wanted. Go in to supper and I shall be there in a moment."

He raised his brows. "Why would you leave a party to see what that ruffian has to say? Were you expecting him?"

"Of course not!" she said lightly. "I've never seen him before in my life. But he's made me curious, and I can never rest until I have satisfied my curiosity, you know, no matter how trivial the matter might be." She gave a small hiccup of laughter that might be described as a titter. Strange. She didn't strike him as the sort of female who habitually tittered.

So she wanted him to think she was just another vapid female, did she? She intrigued him more every moment.

He could have made it more difficult for her but he decided to let her go. He would follow her and eavesdrop. One more loathsome act to chalk up on his account. He'd be glad when this business was over.

Max bowed. On impulse, he captured her hand to raise it to his lips. "I shall see you soon, Lady Kate. I look forward to pursuing our acquaintance."

If the brush of his mouth on her gloved knuckles affected her as it did him, she didn't show it. She swept him an elegant curtsey, and there was a glitter in her smile.

"No more than I, Your Grace. No more than I."

KATE hurried out of the ballroom, along the servants' corridor. Had she allayed Lyle's suspicions? She didn't think so. He was far too acute for her peace of mind. Thank Heaven Ives hadn't given her away.

Why had the duke been so rough with him? Had he guessed why Ives was there?

Stephen's incarceration was not common knowledge, but Lyle probably knew about it. The old Duke of Lyle had granted Stephen his living at the local vicarage, after all.

London buzzed with gossip about the new duke's inheritance. She seemed to recall someone mentioning that he had worked at the Home Office until recently, which made it even more likely that he knew where Stephen was and why he was held.

A most . . . *unsettling* man, the Duke of Lyle.

He'd seen her with Ives and he was intelligent enough to put two and two together. If she wasn't careful, she might end up in prison, too.

Kate shivered, remembering the way the moonlight struck his thick black hair as he bent to fix her gown. She'd known a fleeting urge to set her hand in that coarse mass and run her fingers through it. His hair was slightly longer than fashionable and brushed in no recognizable style. The new duke was no fashion plate, that was certain, though his coat was well tailored, setting off his height and his broad shoulders to perfection.

Lyle might be careless of his own appearance, but those hard, gray eyes saw too much. A dark thrill had shot through her body when his fingers brushed her ankle. And when she'd met his gaze . . . Kate shut her eyes. Despite the threat he posed to her, she was inexplicably, powerfully drawn to him, and that was even more dangerous.

She slipped down the steps, cautiously peering over the rail to the bustling kitchens below. Had Ives done her bidding or simply given up and gone away? She placed no dependence on his reliability. But then Stephen hadn't much choice but to trust the man, she supposed.

"My lady!" A hoarse whisper came from a darkened doorway to her left.

Thank goodness. She hurried down the stairs and slipped into a room where the empty preserving bottles and other odds and ends were kept.

Ives was there, waiting for her with an aggrieved expression.

"What news?" she whispered, trying to keep her skirts well clear of the dusty floor.

"You didn't oughter 'ave pretended not to know me up there, my lady. That big brute could have taken it out on my hide, what's more."

"I saved you from him, didn't I? How was I to know he'd be lurking out there in wait?"

Ives shuffled his feet and lowered his head. The light glanced off his balding crown. "Seems I deserve somefink in compensation, like. For the pain and suffering on account of that hulking fellow got the wrong end of the proverbial."

Her eyes narrowed. "You mean you want more money. Well, I won't pay you a penny more until you can convince me you have information that's worth the expense, you shifty little man."

She tapped her foot. "Come on, out with it. I don't have all night, you know. How does my brother?"

A gleam stole into the rheumy eyes. "Clapped him in irons, they have. In a cell by hisself so he can't corrupt the other prisoners. No visitors, not even a solicitor, I'm told."

Kate's blood turned to ice. "How can they do that? He has done nothing wrong!"

"C'n do anything they like to rabble-rousers these days, can't they? No questions asked."

"My brother is not a rabble-rouser. He is a man of God. Perhaps he might have spoken out against injustice, but he would never countenance rebellion, particularly a violent one." She blew out a breath. "I must see him."

Ives hunched his shoulders. "You can't. They ain't allowing no visitors."

She looked at him suspiciously. "How do you know he is in irons if no one can see him?"

Ives tapped the side of his nose. "I have me ways, I have. But I can come and go without anyone kicking up a fuss. You would stand out like a sore thumb, my lady, forgiving the impertinence. Best give me any messages you want to send him."

Kate scrutinized his face with narrowed eyes. Was he telling the truth, or finding another way to line his pockets?

The question was moot. At the moment, Ives was her only link with Stephen. She must take the risk. "I want you to get a message to him. Do you think you can do it?"

Ives thought about it. "P'raps I could at that." He fingered his chin and eyed her sideways. "It'd cost you, though. A pretty penny in bribes to the guards and such like."

"How did I know you'd say that?" She sighed. She really had no choice. "How much?"

Ives named a sum that seemed far too high, but how was she to know? Thankfully, her experience in bribing prison officials was limited.

"You can have half now, and half when I have Stephen's answer. I'll send someone down with a purse for you."

She bit her lip. "Ask him to get word to me of anyone who might help him. Tell him I have exhausted my own store of favors. No one in the government is prepared to help a man who has encouraged revolt, not even the son of a peer."

Ives rubbed his chin. "Not my place to say it, my lady,

but I'll say it all the same. It's my belief Mr. Stephen don't want to be freed. Sticking to his principles, he is. Making a protest, like."

Since this was her greatest fear as well, she cut Ives off. "You are quite correct. It is *not* your place to say it. I must go now, but don't forget what I said. Bring me that message from my brother if you want the rest of your money."

"Yes, my lady. Of *course*, my lady." Ives bowed with an unctuous smile.

No, she didn't trust him. She didn't trust him at all.

At the top of the stairs, Kate gripped the banister and breathed deeply, momentarily overwhelmed by the difficulties she faced. For a fleeting instant, she wished she could share the burden with someone. Her father was too frail to be drawn into this coil and her elder brother was in Vienna. Her sisters were wrapped up in domestic concerns; they'd be of little use in this crisis.

She could not think of anyone else in the family who would be sympathetic to her cause. Staunch supporters of Liverpool's government, every one of them, convinced revolution was set to sweep the country.

Kate blew out a frustrated breath and hurried back to her guests. Why did Stephen have to be so confoundedly noble? Instead of taking one of the many livings within their father's gift, he'd accepted an offer from the old Duke of Lyle, who was reputed to be one of the harshest landlords in the country.

Instead of an easy, pleasant life, Stephen had set his bantamweight against the might of a duke. He'd been walking on a knife's edge for two years, careful not to irritate his noble patron sufficiently to be sent away, yet shifting, persuading, cajoling, campaigning subtly for reform.

Then the old duke had died and Stephen had seen the chance for a fresh start. What had happened after that, she was not sure.

She knew a fire at the big house had killed a number of

the duke's relatives who'd gathered there after the old duke's funeral to hear the will read.

Her brother could have had nothing to do with that, of course. But there he was now, sitting in jail in the most degrading of conditions. The son of an earl, too proud to ask for help.

Was it a coincidence that the new Duke of Lyle had been on the terrace tonight and intercepted Ives? She shivered. No. Of course it was not. Nothing that man did would be anything but utterly calculated, not even the heat of passion she'd glimpsed in those stern gray eyes.

She must remember that.

AFTER supper, Kate mingled with her guests, conversing, making introductions, shepherding reluctant young gentlemen to dance.

The Duke of Lyle had been watching her all evening. She knew it the way she always knew when someone stood behind her, even if they didn't touch her or make a sound.

Kate tried to remain unaffected, neither staring back at him, nor going out of her way to avoid his regard. But the constant prickling at the nape of her neck told her he still watched, like a wolf stalking his prey. She wondered if this sensation affected small woodland creatures shortly before becoming a predator's evening meal.

But she was no shy fawn. She was the daughter of an earl, the widow of a member of Parliament. Women couldn't vote, but many still played a significant role in politics. Without her help and connections, Hector would never have risen so high.

There must be a way she could use her influence to help Stephen. With regret, her friends in the government had all refused their assistance. It infuriated her when she thought of all the advice she had given over the years, the secrets she had kept.

Her gaze focused on Peter Daniel, who had been her greatest hope. She could ruin him with a word, but he would not help Stephen. She would not forget that.

Short of lobbying the prime minister, there was only one avenue left. She must try to persuade the Home Secretary to free her brother.

Lord Sidmouth was the man responsible for the legislation invoked to put Stephen behind bars. She didn't know Sidmouth well, but perhaps he would help her, if only out of regard for her father's contribution to the party. Kate worked her way around the ballroom, seeking her quarry. Eventually, she found him.

Speaking with the Duke of Lyle.

Her heart pounded. Could the man read minds? The thought of pleading for clemency for her brother with the duke there was horrifying. She must get Lord Sidmouth alone.

She gave instructions to the orchestra, then slowly skirted the room, pausing every so often to speak with her guests, making her way by degrees to the side of the ballroom where the gentlemen stood watching the dancing.

The duke saw her coming. Despite her subtlety, he'd known she headed his way. He almost seemed omniscient, though that was an absurd fancy. She did not like the heat in his gaze. Those burning eyes seemed to read her mind, penetrate to her soul.

Bracing herself, she approached. "Duke. Lord Sidmouth." She smiled at them impartially, wondering if they'd already discussed her situation.

Sidmouth would have made a good card player. His expression betrayed nothing. "We were just discussing your triumph, Lady Kate." He gestured about him at her crowded ballroom. "Something above the ordinary run of entertainments this season. My compliments."

She couldn't care less about frivolous things like balls at this moment, but she accepted the compliment graciously.

"Thank you, my lord." Waving her fan in a leisurely way, she turned to the duke. "It is hot in here, don't you agree?"

"Very," said Lyle, his gaze insolently raking her body.

Her cheeks flamed. Confound it, how desperately she wished she did not blush! Then she realized he was trying to embarrass her, to throw her off the scent.

Kate narrowed her eyes at him. "My throat is quite parched. Would you fetch me a glass of water, please, sir?" *Preferably from the bottom of the Thames.*

Ordering a duke to fetch and carry for her was perhaps equal in insolence to his own conduct. As a duke, he might be affronted; as a gentleman, he must accede to her wishes. It was the oldest trick in the book to get rid of a man, but sometimes simple maneuvers proved the most effective.

He took the order without a blink. "It would be my pleasure, Lady Kate."

Stupidly, Kate was disappointed. He was going to give in as easily as that? She'd thought him a worthier foe.

But the duke did not take a step towards the supper room. A slight lift of his finger and one of her tiresomely efficient footmen materialized at his elbow.

Without taking his gaze from her face, the duke murmured, "Fetch your mistress a glass of water, will you, Arnold?"

She started at his use of the footman's name. "How—" No. She would not give him the satisfaction of voicing her surprise. A chill skittered down her spine. How did he know so much?

Kate glanced at Sidmouth, who looked a trifle bemused at their byplay. She would not give up. She must find a way to see him alone before he left the ball. There would be no other opportunity to speak with him privately without causing gossip.

The orchestra struck up a waltz. She'd almost forgotten she'd instructed them to do so. She must not let the duke throw her off balance like this.

Doing her utmost to ignore Lyle's disturbing presence, she turned the full brilliance of her smile on the Home Secretary. "Oh, how fortunate! I do love to dance the waltz. Dear Lord Sid—"

A hard, masculine arm clamped around her waist and swung her into the dance.

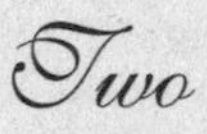

# Two

*One look that lingers a heartbeat too long. He turns his head. The crowd shifts. He is gone.*

*He steals my breath. Will he steal my heart as well?*

KATE'S heart bounded into her throat. Her stomach pitched. As the duke whirled her down the room, she even felt a little dizzy, as if she'd drunk too much champagne.

His hand imprisoned hers in a tight, unforgiving clasp. There was something almost brutal in the way he held her, though onlookers would see nothing amiss.

Panic fluttered in her chest. He couldn't keep her against her will in the middle of a crowded dance floor. She knew that, but she had to call on every ounce of self-control to stop herself from fighting to break free.

With every nerve clamoring, urging her to take flight, Kate watched other dancers slide past as if they moved behind a wall of glass. The trail of light from candles, the glittering jewels and silks went by in a blur. The noise of the crowd was muted, distant. All she could feel and see and hear was Lyle.

She tried to block him out—the arms of tempered steel, the breath that stirred her hair, the strong legs that propelled them down the room, the broad chest that seemed to inch closer with every turn. His infernal heat. She felt it, even through the fabric of clothes and gloves.

Inwardly, Kate shook herself. For goodness' sake, she was acting like some silly debutante waltzing for the first time. She had more courage than this! She would not cower before the Duke of Lyle. He might have won this battle, but she would win the war.

Lyle spoke. "You are remarkably silent, my lady. Is something the matter?"

She raised her gaze to his face. A perfect, polite, social mask. To look at him, anyone would think he was civilized. "I *shall* speak with Sidmouth, you know."

He gave her a lazy smile. "Perhaps you should thank me for a lucky escape. The Home Secretary is an execrable dancer."

"It was not for the pleasure of dancing that I wanted his company," Kate said. "But I suppose you know that."

He shrugged. "I might guess. You wish to talk him into freeing your brother."

Lyle knew Stephen was in prison, then. Of course he did. He seemed to know everything about her, including the names of her servants. "In that case, I'm surprised that you are not attempting to secure his release yourself, my lord duke. Stephen is now a dependent of yours, is he not?"

The duke gave a grim smile. "It is not my practice to condone seditious clergymen, however altruistic their motives. But I do try to intervene when I see someone wasting their time. Feminine charm will not work with Sidmouth, Lady Kate. He has a lot riding on this issue." Lyle's gaze dropped to her mouth. "You had far better work your wiles on me."

She glared, trying to ignore the hot flush stealing over her. How she itched to slap that arrogant face! "I have no intention of *working my wiles*, as you call it, on anyone."

He tilted his head. "No? How disappointing."

For Stephen's sake, she couldn't let him distract her like this. She took a deep breath and tried to steer the conversation back on course. "Sidmouth has no case against my brother, and if it weren't for these atrocious new laws, he wouldn't even attempt to hold him."

Lyle's fingers squeezed her hand so hard she almost yelped. Harshly, he said, "You don't know what you're talking about. Have you any idea what your brother has been doing these past months?"

She didn't know, but she refused to be cowed. "No, because no one will tell me! But why so secretive? Why hasn't my brother's arrest been reported in the papers? An earl's son jailed for sedition? Now *that* is news." She raised her brows. "Unless the government has reason to suppress the information . . ."

From the flare of Lyle's eyes, she knew she'd scored a hit. She followed up her advantage. "Does the cabinet really think there'll be a revolution? Or are they simply shielding themselves from fair criticism with this abominable legislation?"

The duke's austere features tautened. "I must repeat: you don't know what you're talking about. You're dabbling in dangerous waters, my lady. Go back to playing the political hostess and leave the real politicking to those who understand how these things are done."

Kate suppressed a gasp at his rudeness. Moments passed before she could master her fury. She managed to shrug. "I'd be offended by that remark if I didn't know that men always take that dismissive tone when a woman scores a telling point against them."

"I'm not interested in scoring points, madam." The duke's voice lowered to a growl. "And if you think this is a game, it shows exactly how naive you are."

Her frustration threatened to boil over. Of *course* she didn't treat securing her brother's freedom as a game.

But instead of rushing into intemperate speech, Kate

forced herself to remain silent. Obviously, nothing good could come of arguing with someone so pigheaded. He must think her a fool if he assumed she didn't take Stephen's imprisonment seriously.

Familiar though it was, the duke's condescending attitude incensed her. Over the years, she'd learned to turn off patronizing remarks with a smile, knowing she had more political acumen in her little finger than her husband, a member of Parliament, had possessed in his entire body. Why, then, did Lyle's low opinion of her intelligence rankle?

She considered. Perhaps instead of trying to correct his false assumptions, she might use them to her advantage. Men often told her things precisely because they underestimated her—politicians and peers alike. Some used her as a sounding board for ideas; others saw her as a neutral party in whom to confide.

Kate narrowed her eyes, as if to bring the past into perspective. Come to think of it, she knew an awful lot about the members of the present government.

"I mistrust that look," murmured the duke. "What scheme are you cooking up now?"

"Scheme?" She smiled. "Oh, nothing of the sort. My mind simply wandered, that's all. I was thinking how interesting my years as Hector's hostess were. You know, I really owe it to posterity to publish my memoirs." She darted a look upwards, and saw that the duke's face had hardened to sharp planes and angles.

"*So* many fascinating stories," she continued. "And a few, *tiny* peccadilloes here and there to spice up the brew. Well, rather more than a few, actually, and some of them not so tiny." She fluttered her eyelashes. "I think it would make interesting reading, don't you?"

He searched her face, and maddeningly, she sensed him relax. "You wouldn't do it. You don't have it in you to create a scandal like that. Not the proper Lady Kate."

That mocking mention of her good reputation fueled

her fury. "I would do *anything* to get my brother out of that place. Don't cross swords with me, my lord duke, or you will see what I have in me to do."

She saw that his disbelief wavered, so she went in for the kill. "In fact, I've kept a diary of these fascinating anecdotes. Written in code, of course, no names mentioned. But it will be a simple thing to turn the diary into something more readable. I don't know why I never thought of it before."

She almost quailed at the duke's murderous expression. She wouldn't be surprised if his hands closed around her throat to choke the life out of her in the middle of her own ball. But his violent reaction showed her ploy might work.

It took all her courage to face him when a lively sense of self-preservation told her to break from his hold and run. Forcing a lightness into her voice that she was far from feeling, she added, "Of course, if my brother were free I could easily forget there ever was a diary. In fact, I—"

"Shut up, you little fool!"

The dance ended before Kate could summon a retort. She longed to fight Lyle with all guns blazing, but out of regard for propriety, she made herself sink into a deep curtsey.

He bowed, still holding her hand tightly enough to crush her fingers. She winced and shot him a fiery look, but he ignored it. His features had returned to their customary impassiveness, though his gray eyes blazed under hooded lids.

She would have pulled away then, but his grip made it impossible. He drew her hand through the crook of his arm and compelled her to move with him through the crowd.

Furious, she tried to disengage herself but he held her captive. Any more effort to get away and this would soon turn into a tussle. She gritted her teeth and went with him, searching for an opportunity to escape in a dignified fashion.

Out of the corner of her eye, she saw Lord Sidmouth bow his head to listen to something a soberly dressed young man murmured in his ear. Quickly, Sidmouth nodded and headed to the door in the young man's wake.

He wasn't leaving? Kate's heart pounded as she moved through the crowd at the duke's side. When would she gain another chance to speak with the Home Secretary? It was not as if she, a lone female, could call on him the next day. She must see him now.

A voice behind her made Kate jump as if a gun had gone off in her ear. "Dear Lady Kate, don't run away. You promised the next dance to me."

The duke halted, allowing her to turn around. Her husband's old friend Peter Daniel held out his arm to her in a clear act of chivalry. Had her distress been so obvious? She darted a quick look around but no one else seemed to take any notice.

Kate snatched at the chance for escape. "Of course, Mr. Daniel. How could I forget?"

Daniel gave her a fat wink and watched as she tried to free herself from the duke.

"Daniel," said the duke, stepping forward. His tone was a warning. "Go away."

Fat chuckles boomed out. "Oh, come now, Lyle. You can't keep the greatest beauty in the room to yourself. Lady's promised to me! Do you wish to fight me for her? Pistols at dawn, eh?"

Daniel raised his quizzing glass to observe Lyle's tight grip on Kate's wrist. Kate marveled at his courage. She held her breath to see what Lyle would do.

His gray eyes burned into Daniel's. His grip relaxed on her wrist. He didn't release her, but Kate lost no time in tugging her arm free and sinking into a curtsey. "Do excuse me, sir. The sets are almost made up."

Lyle had no choice but to let her go or risk a ludicrous scene. He bowed, and with a look that told her he had not yet finished with her, he walked away.

Kate blew out a breath of relief, watching him melt into

the crowd. Now she needed to escape Daniel. There wasn't a moment to lose. Sidmouth might have left already.

Daniel quirked a brow. "His Grace appears put out. What have you been saying to him? Stinging him with that tongue of yours, my precious little wasp?"

Kate regarded him coolly. She didn't want to discuss the duke or their disagreement, and she still hadn't forgiven Daniel for refusing to help Stephen.

However, she acknowledged he'd done her a service in rescuing her from the duke.

He waved away her thanks. "Oh, don't mention it, my dear. I'm far too old for dancing, but for you, anything."

Kate glanced to the door. "Then would you mind terribly if I excuse myself, sir? We are about to run out of claret cup and the old tabbies will be up in arms if there is none to be had."

Without giving Daniel a chance to reply, she left him and hurried in the direction she'd seen Sidmouth take.

A cursory search of the parlor where refreshments were laid out told her Sidmouth was not there. He wasn't in the card room, either. Had he left? She questioned the footman stationed at the front door, but he hadn't seen Lord Sidmouth depart.

"I think you'll find him in the green drawing room, my lady," said her butler, the epitome of quiet efficiency. "I saw his lordship go in not five minutes past."

He must have slipped away with the younger man for a private discussion. Some urgent government business, perhaps. If she weren't so desperate, she wouldn't dream of interrupting, but given the circumstances, it was a perfect opportunity.

Kate hurried back upstairs. Instead of turning right at the top to head for the ballroom, she turned left and slipped along the corridor. She tapped on the door to the green drawing room, then opened it.

A large hand shot out and clamped over her arm, yanking her inside. It wasn't Sidmouth's.

The duke spun her around and kicked the door shut behind him. "Looking for me?"

She glanced wildly about. Sidmouth wasn't here. They were alone.

Her heart lurched, then plummeted to the pit of her stomach. The shadows made his features more pronounced—the aquiline nose, slightly crooked, as if he'd once broken it; the hooded eyes, with their thick, straight brows. The uncertain light leached the color from his face until he seemed a creature of jet and marble and ice.

"I was looking for Sidmouth."

Lyle's jaw hardened. "You won't learn, will you?" He pulled her hard against him, jerking her head back with the force of it, and the resemblance to anything cold and inanimate vanished.

Flesh and blood male pressed against her, hot and vital. She hadn't been so close to a man since long before Hector died, and never like this. Lyle looked as if he might devour her whole.

"Let me go!" Her words fell too loudly in the empty room. To her annoyance, they held an edge of panic. Why had she sparred with him? She'd suspected this duke was no gentleman, yet she couldn't resist.

They were alone. If anyone found them, her honor would be compromised. She couldn't scream. That *would* cause a scandal. It would be undignified to struggle. Not that she could have done much. She could barely move without rubbing her body against his.

"Take me back to the ballroom, sir!"

He laughed. "Oh, I don't think so."

And then he kissed her.

There was nothing gentle or gentlemanly about the duke's assault. Strong arms tightened around her, one hand cupping her head, fingers thrust into her hair, holding her steady against his brutal mouth.

She gasped and his tongue surged in to tangle with hers. The shock of it almost stopped her heart. No one but Hector had ever kissed her on the mouth, and his kisses had been dutiful, tight-lipped, and brief.

*But this man* . . . Lyle's kiss ravaged her until she was breathless and her lips felt bruised. And like some witless debutante, she stood there practically swooning in his arms. She should struggle. She should scream. The kiss was a punishment and a warning, nothing more.

Yet the heat stabbed her loins and her heart pounded and arousal streaked through her body like lightning through a summer sky. His scent was a subtle mixture of sandalwood and man, his lips hot and dry and firm. Every breath, every touch excited her more. Who could have guessed the mouth that had sneered at her so contemptuously in the ballroom could elicit such a fever of desire?

This must not be happening. She detested him, didn't she? And she'd thought the feeling was mutual. But despite the promptings of her brain, her body yielded, softened, molded itself to his.

He shifted and his torso dragged against her breasts, making her nipples tingle and ripen. Fierce, mad yearning welled up inside, so intense and unexpected that she gripped his lapels to anchor herself.

Lyle murmured something and the hand at her nape gentled to a caress. His mouth slowed to a leisurely exploration, as if he knew she'd surrendered, as if he'd won. She sensed his satisfaction in the softening cling of his lips, in the confident stroke of his tongue, in the slight relaxation of his embrace.

Suddenly, reason clawed to the surface. What on earth was she doing? She'd been returning his kiss!

Furious with herself, Kate twisted in his arms, struggling to break free, but that only made him tighten his hold, trapping her hands between their bodies. She stamped on his instep, and when that produced nothing but a low grunt, she used the only other weapon she had—her teeth.

She bit down viciously on his lower lip until she must have drawn blood. Kate winced at inflicting such pain on him, but Lyle didn't even flinch. When she finally unclamped her teeth, the duke lifted his head, still holding her hard against him.

"Vixen," he said, the trace of a laugh in his voice. "Next time, I'll bite you back."

He trailed a finger down the sensitive skin of her throat and pressed just above her collarbone. "There." And he bent to kiss the spot.

Kate's knees nearly buckled. Shuddering, she jerked her head away. She tasted the salt of his blood on her tongue, and the intimacy of it horrified her.

In this short encounter, Lyle had done to her what no other man had dared. And he'd thrown her into utter confusion.

"There won't be a next time." She could have killed herself for the querulous note that came into her voice. "I shouldn't have allowed it to happen once."

He tilted his head. "You think you had a choice in the matter? Well, that is refreshing."

She hated him, but no more than she hated herself for such weakness. She could have stopped him if she'd wanted. For heaven's sake, there were hundreds of people in the ballroom a few yards away who would have come running if she'd screamed.

She should scream now.

But she wouldn't.

Oh, but he was dangerous. They'd barely met and look what she'd let him do to her! The fire of shame flooded her cheeks, where there'd only been a flush of excitement before. It was as if she'd completely lost control of herself, a terrifying thing to contemplate.

She wished he had not chosen to exercise this strange

power over her, especially now, when she needed a clear head . . .

Oh, God, *Stephen*. Guilt flooded her. She'd forgotten him! This was no time for allowing herself to be distracted. There was too much at stake.

She spoke between gritted teeth. "Release me, if you please."

Before she'd finished the sentence, she was free.

Kate stepped back and saw that the duke breathed hard and fast. For a bare instant, she caught a feral light in those gray eyes, but it was quickly doused, leaving them the usual shade of polished granite.

She wished she possessed as much command over herself. Just remembering the feel of his fingers tangling in her hair made her breathless and hot.

She wrestled with her embarrassment. "Don't *ever* do that again!"

"I could think of few better occupations for that mouth of yours." He raked a hand through his hair. "Do you know how many ears were flapping in the breeze as you outlined your little plan?"

"Don't be absurd. No one else could have heard me. Everyone was moving around too much."

"Your conversation bordered on treason, ma'am. What will happen when your victims find out you intend to expose their dirty little secrets? I would not give a penny for your life if that got about."

She swallowed hard. He was right. She courted danger by speaking her threats so openly. She'd not thought of that, principally because she'd never intended to publish the memoirs. The diary was utterly fictitious. She had more sense than to commit such sensitive information to paper.

On the defensive, she matched his biting tone. "If you'd simply explained that to me instead of manhandling me in this fashion, I might well have listened. Did that occur to you?"

"It did." He smiled. "But speaking would not have been nearly so pleasurable."

"For you, perhaps! I am not accustomed to being treated like this."

His eyes gleamed. "No?" he said softly. "Poor Lady Kate."

The understanding in his expression horrified her. She must get away from him. He saw far too much.

Still smiling, the duke advanced towards her. She backed away, but he advanced until her shoulders pressed against the wall.

There was nowhere to go, and she wasn't entirely sure she wanted to run. God help her, this man fascinated her even more than he frightened her.

He nodded slowly, as if he sensed her reaction and understood.

"Lady Kate, your brother knows where the rebels who set fire to Lyle Castle are hiding. He will be released *if* he cooperates and tells the authorities what they wish to know. If not—" He shrugged, leaving the rest to her fertile imagination.

So that was the root of it all! She knew Stephen could not have been directly involved in the uprising.

"But how do you know he has this information?" she countered. "It seems unlikely these arsonists would tell my brother where they were going."

"My dear, he has admitted it," said the duke, almost gently.

Oh, *Stephen*! She could have howled at his naivety. He'd as good as hanged himself with that admission.

The duke traced her cheek with one fingertip and her skin shivered at his touch. "Perhaps you could persuade him to do the right thing. I might arrange for you to see him, if you promise me you will try."

She held still, trying to ignore the sheer power of that light caress. She needed to think, not feel.

The realization dawned on her. He expected her to take his side against her own brother? He must rate his attractions highly.

She stared coolly into his eyes. "Whatever he has done, sir, my brother has my full confidence and support."

But she lied. She didn't give a fig about Stephen's principles. She would do *anything* to get him out of prison. But Stephen wouldn't bend to pressure or threats if he thought he was doing right. Her persuasion would count for nothing.

Lyle's palm cupped her cheek, and a strange light entered his eyes. Not tenderness. Perhaps compassion?

For the second time that evening, Kate felt as if something had sucked the air out of her lungs.

He was going to kiss her again, and the worst part was she longed for that complete possession almost as much as she feared it. She could have screamed with frustration at her helplessness. Usually, she had not the slightest difficulty making men keep the line.

Her gaze fixed on the trace of blood where she'd bitten him, a dash of crimson against the duller red of his lip. As he moved closer, the image blurred and swam. She closed her eyes until his breath brushed her mouth, willing herself not to lean in to him.

At the last possible moment before they touched, he drew back.

He laughed softly. "I can almost see the cogs whirring in that busy mind of yours. I'd like to know what you're thinking, Lady Kate. But since I'm not certain whether you're in earnest about publishing these memoirs, let me give you some advice. Destroy the diary and forget you ever knew those secrets. Knowledge can be a dangerous thing."

The next moment, he was gone, closing the door behind him with a decisive snap.

The sound dislodged the thick haze of desire that clogged her brain. Her mind sprang into action, working furiously.

With the duke's disclosures in this room, all hope of persuading Sidmouth or anyone else in the government to help Stephen was gone.

Stephen's arrest hadn't been based on a misunderstanding, as she'd wanted to believe. By his own admission, he knew the whereabouts of wanted criminals, arsonists who had staged a violent insurrection against the family of the Duke of Lyle.

No one would sympathize with a man, even a vicar, who aided such felons. Perhaps Stephen believed in their innocence, or perhaps he did not want to send men to their deaths by informing on them. Either way, if he hadn't been persuaded by imprisonment, there was no chance he'd listen to her.

So, no help through official channels. Nor would Stephen help himself. It seemed now she had little choice but to use the only weapon she had left.

The duke had turned wild in the ballroom when she'd mentioned writing her memoirs. The mere threat of publishing them had acted on him like a spur to a stallion's flank.

He was desperate to stop her seeing Sidmouth. Perhaps even as Lyle had kissed her so passionately, he'd been deliberately delaying her search until Sidmouth left. Confound the man! And confound her for letting him dupe her. She didn't doubt she'd missed her chance.

Anger at the way he'd used her ripped a strangled cry from her throat. She bit her lip hard, almost as hard as she'd bitten his, trying to bring her emotions under control.

Calm. Calm. She'd save her fury at his tactics for later.

Now, it was enough to judge that her instincts had been right. Knowledge might be dangerous to her, but she could also use it as a powerful weapon. If wielded judiciously, it might save her brother.

Even if Lyle was right and she put herself at risk by threatening the government, the risk would be worthwhile if it meant Stephen might walk free.

She narrowed her eyes and started to plan.

Oh, yes. Knowledge could be a *very* dangerous thing.

MAX spent the rest of the evening in the card room, but his mind couldn't have been farther from the play.

He brooded over that scene with Lady Kate. Why had he let her goad him like that? Why hadn't he restrained himself? Instead of taking her in a slow, smooth seduction, he'd frightened her with force and hungry kisses.

He had rather disconcerted himself, if it came to that. He'd almost made a scene, stealing that dance from Sidmouth, something he'd never felt remotely tempted to do in his entire life.

Fortunately for him, his hostess was a consummate lady. She hadn't betrayed her fear or her fury to anyone watching. Only he had felt her go rigid beneath his hands, seen the pulse that beat in her throat, heard the little gasp she gave when he took her in his arms to dance.

He had to admit it. He'd been jealous. Jealous of Sidmouth!

Not a rational reaction, but when Lady Kate had smiled at the Home Secretary like that, and almost commanded him to waltz, the need to keep her to himself had overtaken him. He'd almost punched Daniel in the face when he'd claimed his dance. The older man's suggestion of pistols at dawn had struck him as far too civilized. What the hell was wrong with him?

He was a professional. There was no excuse for rushing his fences like that. He couldn't afford to let passion rule him. He couldn't afford to make a mistake.

But he'd already been soft with her, hadn't he? The most efficient way to get the information he wanted was to abduct Lady Kate and hold her to ransom against the brother's cooperation. Had he not found her so likeable and appealing, he wouldn't have hesitated.

And he couldn't even plead the likely consequences that deterred him from carrying out the plan. He could abduct her without fear of reprisals. Lady Kate would be anxious to maintain her spotless reputation, so she'd hardly raise a hue and cry about her kidnapping once he set her free. In condemning him, she'd ruin herself, and Lady Kate was a woman who prized her honor highly.

When the hand of cards came to a close, Max scanned the room, surprised to find it almost empty. The other gamesters must have departed for their clubs. He saw his cousin Romney lounging in the corner and made his way to him.

He jerked his head. "Come on. We're leaving."

With an acquiescent grunt, Romney followed. As they reached the landing, he cocked an eyebrow in Max's direction. "Did you speak with her?"

"Lady Kate? Yes, I did." He paused. "She is far more trouble than I'd expected."

Romney's mouth quirked up appreciatively. "Gave you curry, eh? Easy on the eye, though, ain't she? Brains, too, if you like that sort of thing."

Max barely suppressed a growl. In spite of himself, it seemed he did like precisely that sort of thing. More than liked it, in fact.

He shouldn't have been so rough with her, but the way she'd babbled on, getting herself deeper and deeper into hot water, he had been fierce with fear on her behalf. Anyone could have overheard those thinly veiled threats.

Suddenly, he wondered if Daniel had heard them. Was that why he'd come to Lady Kate's aid in the ballroom? It was a possibility he couldn't ignore. He'd deal with Daniel later.

Besides the danger she posed to his own cause, Lady Kate was a danger to herself. If she made good her promise of blackmail, one of two things would happen—either Sidmouth would cave in and free Stephen Holt, an outcome that would throw Max back to square one in his investigation, or Sidmouth would refer the matter to Faulkner, head of covert operations.

Faulkner would have no compunction. If Lady Kate posed a threat to the security of the realm, he would order his men to silence her.

Either way, it was imperative to stop her getting to Sidmouth. He'd been successful tonight. Tomorrow, Sidmouth left London to attend a house party, so that would give Max time.

He needed to think of a more final solution. In the meantime, he must find that diary. Max was not so naive as to think Lady Kate would follow his advice and burn the damned thing. In any case, it might be best to find out what she knew. He'd read the diary and then decide how to dispose of it.

Max glanced around. No time like the present.

The crowd had thinned considerably and there was a steady stream of guests flowing downstairs. He and Romney joined them. When they reached the door, Max accepted his hat and coat from a footman and stepped into the cool air outside.

When they stood in the lee of his barouche, Max stopped. "Romney," he murmured, still holding his accoutrements.

"Aye."

"Take the carriage. I have business here tonight."

Romney threw him a quizzical look, but he nodded. "Right.

"Here." Max handed Romney his hat and coat. "Send the carriage back to wait for me at the King's Arms, will you? I've no idea when I'll be finished here."

Romney tugged an imaginary forelock. "Whatever you say, Your Grace."

Max shot him an irritated glance and melted into the

shadows. He had reconnoitered the house the previous evening, but he hadn't guessed how soon he'd need to know the lie of the land.

The house stood on its own grounds, reportedly a gift to Lady Kate on her marriage from her father, the Earl of Stratham. Max skirted around to the west wall and slipped through the shrubbery to the small, paved courtyard at its heart.

Gravel paths radiated outwards from the courtyard like spokes of a wheel. Screened by this well-ordered wilderness, he'd hear anyone else's approach long before they knew he was there. He'd sit on the ornately carved stone bench that graced the small space and wait until the household was abed before making his move. Max hoped the dawn wouldn't catch him or he'd be obliged to return the following night.

When he told Lady Kate to beware of eavesdroppers, he'd been sincere. He had assumed responsibility for inquiring into the fire at Lyle, but he wasn't naive enough to believe he was the only one with an interest in the investigation's outcome.

In fact, he sensed someone had been shadowing him for days. Possibly one of Faulkner's minions. Max didn't trust anyone, not even his esteemed head of operations. Faulkner hadn't fought his way to the top by taking chances or taking anything on faith.

Remembering he'd brought a flask with him to the ball, Max pulled it from his pocket and unscrewed the cap. He took a sip of brandy, and the ferocious sting in his lower lip brought his mind back to the reason he was there.

Lady Kate and her mouth.

Heat flashed through his body. He hadn't played that scene in the parlor very well, but he couldn't regret kissing her. All he regretted was that circumstances prevented him taking their passion further.

He wondered how soon he could persuade her to bed. Just thinking about it made him hard as the stone bench he sat on.

Why must he want her so much? In all the years he'd worked for the Home Office, he'd never allowed his personal interest to hold sway. He'd been confident he could approach the Lyle Castle fire in the same detached way he approached all his cases.

He'd read the reports from the coroner and the local magistrate, viewed the charred remains of the poor souls who had died so horribly, inspected the seat of the fire, interviewed tenants and staff at the big house.

Sensing his presence was needed, he'd stayed at Lyle longer than he'd anticipated. But he'd been incapable of offering comfort to these strangers, the family and dependents of the old duke. He'd never excelled at that emotional palaver. If only his brother, the silver-tongued Alistair, had been there to help him, he would have soothed the natives in no time.

But Alistair was in Paris, nursing a broken heart. All Max could do was assure the grieving he would find the perpetrators of this horror and make them pay. And then do his duty by the legacy that should never have been his.

The noise of linkboys and carriages clattering over the street cobbles finally quieted. More time passed before the lights were doused, one by one, throwing the house into darkness.

He was about to move when he heard gravel crunch, so softly, it could have been a small animal rustling in the bushes.

But he didn't think so. He tilted his head to pinpoint the sound. It had come from the path to his right.

Silently, Max rose and moved to a place shielded from the path by a high hedge.

He heard nothing more before a figure stepped cautiously into the clearing.

Max couldn't tell whether the man was armed, but he wasn't going to take any chances. He launched forward, and as the figure heard him and turned, Max's fist clipped his chin.

The man crumpled where he stood.

# Three

*From nowhere, he appears. A dance? Deep as the darkest forest, his voice echoes through my soul.*

*He clasps my hand. The startling touch rips through me like a gunshot. A flash of heat and light.*

MAX gripped the man's shoulder and rolled him over. Perry. What was he doing here?

Darting a quick look around, he dragged the young man's unconscious body to the stone bench and hauled him onto it. He reached into his pocket for his flask.

Damn the boy! Until now, he'd tolerated Perry's slavish devotion, his awkwardness, his habit of getting in the way at critical moments. But it was one thing for Perry to accompany Max on jobs, observing and learning the ropes. Quite another to spy on him without his knowledge.

Was he spying for Faulkner?

Fear punched Max's gut. If Faulkner found out about Lady Kate's veiled threats, he'd stop at nothing to silence her. Max glanced down at the open, youthful features of the man who remained unconscious on the stone bench, laid out like an effigy.

Perry was not the tool he'd have chosen to shadow a hardened operative, but then perhaps Faulkner thought Max less likely to suspect the inexperienced youth. If Perry were under orders to keep an eye on his mentor, it begged the question—why? What did Faulkner have riding on Max's investigation?

He shook Perry, who groaned and rolled his head from side to side. Max shook him again and the boy's eyes opened to stare at him blankly.

"Get up." He yanked Perry upright and put the brandy flask to his lips.

Perry choked and spluttered as if he'd never tasted the stuff before. Half the brandy dribbled down his chin. What an innocent! Not for the first time, Max wondered what had made Faulkner employ the lad in the first place.

"Perry, what the hell did you think you were doing?" He kept his voice low, but Perry couldn't have mistaken his irritation.

The young man wiped his mouth with the back of his hand. "Looking for you. You said you'd let me help you with the investigation."

Relief swept through Max. Lady Kate might still be safe. Perry would report back to Whitehall, of course, but at least Faulkner hadn't sent him.

Still, the last thing he needed was this youngster nipping at his heels like a boisterous puppy. He'd already given him a job to do. "You were supposed to befriend the maid."

"I have." Perry winced and rubbed his chin. "Thinks I'm sweet on her, stupid little bitch."

Max frowned. "Haven't I taught you to be more respectful to women than that?"

Perry shrugged. "She's only a maid."

"Even so." Max glanced up at the house, swearing under his breath. He didn't have time for this.

He gripped the young man's elbow and helped him stand. "Go home. I'll have work for you in the morning."

"Can't I help now? I could keep watch. I could—"

"That won't be necessary." Max sighed. If he didn't

throw him a bone, Perry would continue to pester him. "Go and wait for me at the King's Arms. I'll have something for you when I return."

"All right, I'm going." The young man shrugged off his hold and turned to leave. No longer troubling to keep his voice down, he added, "Oh, and Mr. Faulkner wants to see you tomorrow, first thing. Cheerio, then."

Max swore viciously under his breath. He watched Perry until he was out of sight, then moved quickly. Perry could double back and follow him and ruin everything, but he'd have to take the chance.

So, the head of operations wanted to see him. Summoned him as if he were still an underling and not a newly minted duke. Max grimaced. Faulkner couldn't know about the diary, but he'd already expressed concern about locking up Lady Kate's brother, since his family had such powerful connections in the government. If Faulkner found out about Lady Kate's threats, she'd face a greater danger than the kidnapping Max planned.

Max shut down these speculations and brought his mind back into focus. He'd think about how to deal with Faulkner once he had that diary in his hands.

KATE couldn't sleep. She lay among tangled covers and sheets, staring at the full moon that shafted milky light through her window. Listening to the sounds of the night, she breathed deeply, in and out, trying to calm her racing mind.

But the clamor in her brain refused to quiet. She thought of Stephen, lying cold and alone in a dark cell, manacled to the wall like the most dangerous criminal. She thought of Sidmouth, her last hope in the bid to win Stephen's freedom. Of Lyle, bent on stopping her.

She thought of that incendiary kiss . . .

A reminiscent shiver skipped down her spine. She'd never experienced such passionate heat, not even in the early days of her marriage, when she'd believed herself in love with Hector. What a cruel disappointment their union turned out to be.

To Hector, Kate embodied wealth, position, and most important, political connections. All she'd wanted was a man to love, one who'd love her in return.

Hector had made it clear he'd never be that man. So, she'd created one. In a small journal bound in calfskin, Kate wrote about a dark, mysterious lover, someone she could welcome to her bed each night without guilt or consequence.

She'd filled that journal with her wildest fantasies, the deepest longings of her heart. Admittedly, Kate possessed little experience of lovers, dark and mysterious or otherwise, so she'd improvised quite a lot. Sometimes, she'd write. Other times, she'd read over the entries, and they'd warm her the way a hard, male body might warm her in her bed.

Now, when her mind endlessly ticked over all the day's events, the temptation to retrieve her journal from its hiding place tugged at her. Writing in that small book usually comforted her, transported her to another realm, another life, leaving her worries and the aching loneliness of her existence behind.

But she doubted even her phantom lover could occupy her thoughts now. Stephen's predicament and Lyle's strong presence loomed too large.

What she needed was a plan of attack.

She must speak with Sidmouth. If she sent for him to call on her, would he come? Or had Lyle warned him of her threats? She might work through an intermediary, but she couldn't endanger someone else by involving them in what was tantamount to blackmail.

A letter was out of the question, clear evidence against her if she were prosecuted . . .

*Prosecuted.* For the first time, the gravity of the undertaking she contemplated chilled her. She'd spoken to Lyle without considering the consequences. Did she really have the courage to pursue that idle threat?

But it need not amount to open blackmail. She didn't have to put it quite so crudely when she spoke to Sidmouth. She knew well how hints and innuendo could convey volumes to a politician. And without witnesses, he wouldn't be able to prove a case against her.

So, subtlety was the order of the day. If it seemed like a chance meeting brought them together, that would be best.

How could she find out Sidmouth's schedule? He attended many of the balls and parties to which she was invited. They might meet in the next day or so. If only she could be sure.

Oswald was bound to know. She would call on her sister and brother-in-law in the morning and find out.

And after she'd made her position clear to Sidmouth, what then? What if Sidmouth told her to do her worst? Would she go ahead and publish her tell-all memoirs?

No, that would achieve nothing but a scandal for the government and her own disgrace.

But she couldn't let Sidmouth call her bluff. She needed to raise the stakes. She needed to show him exactly what it would mean to those politicians to have their dirty linen aired.

Kate sat straight up in bed. She needed to write those memoirs.

MAX made his way through the shrubbery to the side of the house, where an iron trellis against the wall supported a climbing rose. Looking up at the window he meant to use, he took off his gloves and shoved them in his pocket. Then he set his hands on the trellis and climbed.

Unfastening the second-floor window was child's play to

one who hadn't wasted all the time he'd spent in London's rookeries. He moved through the empty bedchamber—the master suite, if he wasn't mistaken—and cautiously opened the door.

The corridor outside was dark, save for the light from a few candles guttering in their wall sconces. He eased out the door, liberated one of the candles, and looked around.

As soon as he saw the slice of light under her bedchamber door, he knew he'd arrived too soon. Better to have chosen a night when she was out, but he couldn't afford to wait. Not with Faulkner on the scent.

He needed to steal that diary. Of course, Lady Kate could reconstruct her notes from memory, but it would take her much longer than if she cribbed from a detailed journal. If he delayed the execution of her plan, it would give him time he needed to arrange her abduction. He no longer doubted he'd have to spirit her away, if only to keep her safe.

Max felt a glimmer of interest in the diary's contents on his own behalf. He would not stoop to blackmail, of course, but it would be interesting to know . . .

Balked of his first port of call—a lady would usually keep something so intimate in her bedchamber, surely—he raised his candle and jogged lightly down the marble staircase to the first floor. These were private family apartments, by the looks of it. He made a cursory search of the rooms, but none offered an appropriate hiding place.

Silently opening the door at the end of the passage, Max's candle illuminated rows and rows of volumes in what looked to be a small library. A smile spread slowly over his face. Where better to hide a book?

He stepped inside and shut the door behind him. The more he considered, the more likely it seemed that if Lady Kate had not already relocated it after their argument that evening, the diary would be here. In her bedchamber or sitting room there was always the chance of a servant or visitor noticing it. If she wanted to keep such an important document secret, unremarkable, she might well hide it here, in plain sight.

The heavy curtains were drawn and no one stirred on this floor. There was little danger of being detected, but he'd have to watch the time. Only an hour or so before the skivvies would be creeping about, lighting fires and preparing for the day.

Max used his candle to light a lamp and set to work.

After a long, fruitless search, he stopped and sat back on his heels. He'd worked his way through the classics, botany, and history, but an entire wall of shelves remained to be searched. How could he approach this more scientifically?

Lady Kate had said she'd kept the diary throughout her marriage, hadn't she? Then she might have wished to keep it secret from her husband also. In that case, of course she wouldn't choose the book room. Hector Fairchild had rather fancied himself as a scholar.

Max rose and dusted himself off, muttering an oath. He looked around. What a waste of— Hang on!

Novels! He'd bet his life that dry stick Hector Fairchild had never read a novel.

He scanned the shelves until he found them. An entire collection of the things ranged along two shelves, bound in dull green morocco, with what appeared to be Lady Kate's monogram tooled in gilt on the spine. Not a trace of dust on those shelves, either, which argued the books had been read recently. Max yanked each volume from its place and leafed through.

Finally, he found it, and blew out a breath of satisfaction. Inside the cover that should have contained *The Castle of Wolfenbach* lay a slim, handwritten book, bound in calfskin.

He couldn't see very well in the dim light of a solitary candle, but it looked like many of the pages were dated at the top. A diary, certainly. But was it the one he sought?

He'd have to take the chance. Slipping the book into his

waistcoat, he shoved the empty cover and the rest of the romances back into place.

He ran his fingertip over the monogram on the spine. An image rose in his mind of Lady Kate, sitting up in bed writing in her journal, her hair unbound . . . He shook his head. Damn it, she wasn't even here and she distracted him! The sooner he solved this case and left London for Lyle, the better.

Max glanced around the room to make sure he'd replaced everything, then extinguished the light.

Lady Kate would know someone had been there when she discovered the diary missing but she'd keep the news to herself. He didn't want the servants raising hue and cry if they found something out of place.

She'd probably guess he was the culprit. He smiled to himself as he silently made his way along the corridor. Score one to him.

Final victory would be sweet.

KATE set down her candle on the library table. Its small, flickering light cast misshapen shadows on the wall. The surrounding quiet seemed almost oppressive after the noisy gaiety of the ball. She had the wildest urge to scream.

Oh, she was as twitchy as an unbroken filly! For the hundredth time, she imagined Stephen in his cell, cold and alone.

She hoped he didn't catch some terrible disease before she could get him out. She wondered how he could bear such conditions. But Stephen was big and strong and healthy, his trust in the Almighty unshakeable. Even if he wouldn't give in and cooperate with the authorities, he would never despair.

Her gaze wandered to the shelves of Minerva Press novels tucked in the bottom corner of the library.

Her journal . . .

She hadn't touched the journal for some time, perhaps not since last winter. Now, the urge to return to the familiar thrill of her imaginary lover propelled her across the room.

Kate reached out for the volume that hid her illicit prose, but snatched back her hand just as her fingertips touched the leather spine. Tonight, of all nights, she should not delve into those fanciful meanderings. She should think only of Stephen.

Biting her lip, she marched over to her escritoire and sat down to write the first chapter of her political memoir. That would put her mind to more effective use.

It would also take her mind off . . . irrelevancies. Like the hot, velvety smoothness of the duke's lips when he'd kissed her throat. Like the dual feeling of security and terror when his arms had banded around her that first time.

*Stop it!* Really, the last thing she needed at the moment was this complication, this . . . distraction.

Kate shivered. The library was cold and she hadn't brought a shawl. She would collect the necessary implements to make a start on her memoirs and take them back to her bedchamber.

She selected paper, pen, and ink, then picked up her candle and left the library.

A creak on the stair made her jump. Without thinking, she hurried along the corridor and out to the landing, her candle's flame flickering wildly. She looked up the staircase, but saw no one amongst the shadows.

It took moments for her heartbeat to slow. Foolish! The house always creaked in the night. As a light sleeper, she should know that very well.

She hurried up the stairs to bed.

A glow on the staircase made Max duck back into an empty bedchamber and ease the door so it was almost shut.

Was it Lady Kate? He couldn't resist hoping as he watched through the crack.

The glow headed his way, and in moments he glimpsed her elfin figure, clad in flowing white, with that lovely chestnut hair cascading down her back.

Temptation gnawed at his bones like a ravenous wolf. He burned to go after her, to sweep her into his arms and carry her back to bed. If he could wait that long. Once he touched her, they might not make it as far as her door.

Reason told him he'd have all the time in the world for seduction once he'd taken her somewhere safe. But the heady element of risk heightened his sensual need, clamoring for precedence over his logical brain.

With a struggle so violent it was almost physical, he made himself stay hidden. He was a professional, damn it! He needed to stop chasing skirt long enough to make a dent in solving this case.

It was vital that he secure the diary without his friends at the Home Office knowing. Then, he'd have time for everything he wanted to do with her.

He couldn't delay. Dawn threatened and Faulkner would expect him to report his findings in the morning. He needed to get back to that master bedchamber and escape the way he'd come.

When he heard the door snick shut, Max left his hiding place. He stepped out into the corridor . . .

And came face to face with Lady Kate.

She must have closed her door from the *outside*.

He was upon her before she'd opened her lips to scream. Covering her mouth with his hand, he used his body to pin her to the door, crushing her breasts against his chest.

In the semidarkness, he saw her eyes grow wide and frantic. She pummeled his arms and pushed at his shoulders, to no avail. Her breath came hard and fast and hot on his palm.

She choked and cried out, but his hand muffled the sound. Twisting and bucking, she tried to get free, but she was no match for him. All her squirming achieved was her own frustration and his escalating arousal.

Fighting his body's reaction, he pressed his lips against her ear. "Don't be alarmed," he breathed. "It's Lyle."

Abruptly, her struggles stopped. Then they started again with renewed vigor.

Max spun her around and clamped her against him with his forearm locked between her breasts, his hand still covering her mouth. With the other hand, he fumbled for the door handle. She jammed her elbow into him just as the door gave way and they stumbled inside.

Pain exploded in his ribs. With a grunt, he let her go. She staggered backwards, her fingers pressed to her mouth.

"Careful," he said. "You know how it'll look if you scream." Without taking his eyes off her, he straightened and closed the door behind him gently with his heel.

She was panting, which did wondrous things for her breasts, even covered by that crisp, white nightgown. Her hair clouded about her face in thick, glossy waves. He wanted to plunge his hands through that soft mass and wind it around his fingers.

Max's gaze roved her elegant, gently curved body and snagged on her feet. Only one of them wore an embroidered pink slipper. She must have lost its mate in their struggle. That naked, vulnerable appendage with its toes curling into the carpet held a fascination all its own.

She'd caught him. He wasn't sorry. Perhaps he'd wanted to be caught. He didn't even need to think of an excuse for being there. She was reason enough.

"Get out of my bedchamber." Her voice trembled with rage, or fear, or passion, he couldn't tell which. "Get out of my house."

She didn't think he'd meekly do her bidding, did she? He moved towards her. "Not until I have what I came for."

"Oh! This is unpardonable! *This* isn't about my brother—"

"I wanted to see you." It felt like the truth. He couldn't get enough of her. And there she was, naked under that modest night rail, with her hair tumbling over her shoulders and a large, inviting bed behind her . . .

Desire blazed inside him, fierce and consuming. It was far too soon, but he couldn't help himself.

"See *me*?" Her eyes widened. "You cannot seriously think that I—that we . . ." She trailed off, swallowing convulsively. "No."

He took another step. "No?"

She backed away, looking about her, perhaps searching for a weapon. "You—you wouldn't force an unwilling woman."

The uncertainty in her tone sent another rush of blood to his loins. He'd never forced any woman, but he was so hot for her there was no telling what he might do. He'd never felt like this before.

Closing the distance between them, Max caught her chin in his hand. "But you're not unwilling. Are you, Lady Kate?"

"Yes, I . . ." She trailed off, her eyes large and luminous. She didn't seem to want to fight him anymore.

Triumph surged inside him, but some remnant of civilization stopped him ravishing her on the spot. He'd make it as good as he could for her, but in his present state, he doubted he'd last long. At least, not the first time.

Moonlight traced the pure outline of her features, and he remembered her vaunted virtue, the strange innocence of her kiss.

Forcing himself to slow down, he rubbed his thumb along the seam of her closed lips, coaxing them to part, then dipped inside. His breathing hitched as he invaded the moist, enveloping warmth of her mouth. His heart thundered in his chest. This was going to be extraordinary.

The voice of reason in his head sent a warning—he'd meant to leave her alone tonight, just take the diary and go—but the jungle drums in his blood drowned reason out.

He had to have her now.

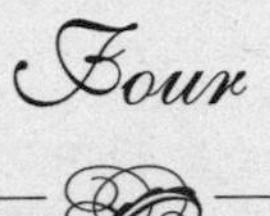

# Four

*The dance is not a waltz. He does not embrace me. But his gaze holds me, entranced.*

*I falter a step.*

*And he smiles.*

KATE closed her eyes, overwhelmed by the intense desire that seemed to radiate from Lyle like heat from a blaze. She was shaken, off balance, not thinking clearly. Not thinking at all.

There'd been moments before he'd identified himself, when she thought she was going to be hurt or even killed by this large intruder who attacked her without warning. And her only thought beyond breaking free was what a waste she'd made of her life.

Knowing who perpetrated the assault hadn't calmed her. Even now, her heart raced and her breath came in short pants. She wanted to run but she was caught in his sensual snare.

Almost in a daze, she felt urgent, deft fingers work at her night rail, tugging at the ribbon that closed the gathered bodice.

Each brush of his skin against hers burned like a brand. A

large hand, with a latent strength, a roughness that was somehow right but unexpected, slipped inside and skimmed over the swell of her breast.

She gasped, and he said, "Open your eyes," but she didn't want to, because she didn't want to accept that this was real. Then she'd have to pull away. Then she'd have to tell him to go.

His hand cupped her breast and his mouth found hers and this time, she kissed him back. There was no need to resist, because he wasn't really there. It wasn't Lady Kathryn Fairchild who was doing these things, it was the dream version of herself, and she was safe.

His palm flattened and rolled over her nipple. She shuddered and her lips clung to his as if she was drowning and he her only source of air.

"Open your eyes, Kate." He breathed the words, hot and soft into her mouth.

She made a muted, negative noise in her throat and turned her head aside. She wished he wouldn't talk so much.

Lyle's fingers worked her nipple, pinching and tugging it, shooting darts of fire through her body, inflaming her desire.

His mouth found her throat, kissing and licking. And he held her while she shivered with a feverish, thrilling hunger.

She wanted to throw her head back and invite him to feast. On her neck, her breasts, all those sensitive places that had never known a man's touch. She wanted to feel him, skin to skin, she wanted to wrap one leg around him and press him so close they were almost joined. She wanted to do the most shameful, brazen things . . .

*Only whores behave like that . . .*

"No!" Gasping for air, Kate recoiled and gave Lyle an almighty shove. She must have taken him by surprise, because he released her, eyes glittering, hard mouth softened with kisses.

The next instant, he reached for her again, but she swung up her hand to slap him. He caught her wrist, his eyes burning into hers, signaling a silent battle of wills between them.

Then suddenly, he looked up, beyond her and dropped her hand.

Instinctively, Kate glanced over her shoulder, scanning the bedchamber, then turned back to stare at him.

But she was looking at empty space.

A string of oaths ran through Max's mind as he moved silently along the corridor. He'd heard a noise that sounded like it came from the master suite. It might have been a member of the household, but he doubted it. He should have known that damned boy wouldn't obey him and go home. He ought to have hit him harder.

But whether or not the intruder had been Perry, he was gone by the time Max arrived. Max peered into the darkness outside, trying to discern movement amongst the greenery, but there was none.

He turned to contemplate the empty corridor. He didn't expect Lady Kate would welcome him back.

Desire still simmered in his blood, but he knew better than to attempt to persuade a furious woman to bed. And if he'd stop thinking with his nether regions for five seconds, he'd admit he'd already lingered here too long.

Max set one leg over the windowsill and almost groaned aloud. He'd very nearly had her. The element of surprise had certainly worked in his favor. Next time, her guard would be up. A pity, but then he'd always relished a challenge.

In moments, he'd escaped the way he'd arrived, with only a tear in his shirt cuff, which had caught on a rose thorn on the way down the trellis.

He fingered the ragged linen, and automatically, his finger moved to his ragged lip. A bolt of pure lust shot through him at the thought of those small white teeth of hers sinking into his flesh. He actually turned back and set one foot on the bottom rung of the trellis before he realized what he did.

Swearing, he pushed away from the wall. How did she do this to him? He'd always considered himself rather more civilized than the general run of men. He had lusty appetites, it was true, but he'd never allowed them to rule him. Lady Kate stirred primal instincts he'd never known he possessed. He didn't like it. He didn't like it at all.

Max let himself out the back gate into the alley that ran between Lady Kate's house and the houses behind. Buttoning his coat, he strode in the direction of the King's Arms, where his carriage awaited him. The brisk morning air would clear his head and, hopefully, calm his body so he could think.

Reflecting on what he already knew of Lady Kate, he expected the diary would be everything she'd threatened. She possessed that rare combination of beauty, warmth, and intelligence, the kind of woman men admired, but one in whom they also found it possible to confide.

She'd said the diary was coded but he didn't expect any trouble deciphering it. Presumably, Lady Kate's code would be primitive at best.

But he wouldn't make the mistake of underestimating his adversary in any other respect. She was astute, she was experienced in political life, and she would know how to wield this power she held.

She'd expressed herself clumsily to him in the heat of battle. She would be more delicate when she made her threats to Sidmouth, but Max didn't intend to let her get that far. Stephen Holt would not go free until he had informed on those rebels. Max would make certain of that.

He'd found the diary. The devil of it was that he had not yet decided what he was going to do with the damned thing. Hand it over to Faulkner, his superior at the Home

Office, and he'd substitute one blackmailer for another. Faulkner was in a position to do far more harm with the information than Lady Kate ever could.

Max certainly didn't intend anyone to use these ministers' peccadilloes against them. If the diary contained any serious misdemeanors, he'd be obliged to pursue the matter through official channels. But he didn't think Lady Kate would have kept secrets that might amount to criminal acts. Despite her threats, she wasn't corrupt.

Might the diary contain information of a personal nature about Lady Kate herself? He quickened his pace, conscious of the slim volume pressing against his chest. He'd rent a room at the King's Arms and read it. Suddenly, he couldn't wait until he got home.

As he rounded a corner, a sixth sense made Lyle turn.

No one there. But he'd had the impression of movement all the same.

Slowly, he took his white evening gloves from his pocket and tugged them on. Loudly, succinctly, he said, "All right, Perry. You can come out now."

Silence answered him.

Max considered confronting his shadow but thought better of it. No need to borrow trouble, after all. Not with the diary in his possession.

Instinctively, his eyes sought cover, in case someone should open fire. He didn't have a pistol with him, though he wasn't entirely defenseless if it came to a fight.

He didn't question this alertness. Instinct had saved his hide on more than one occasion in the past. He wouldn't shrug off this creeping sense of unease lightly, even if there was no solid evidence to support it.

Despite his vigilance, nothing untoward occurred and he arrived at the King's Arms in one piece. Max crossed the yard and entered the inn, eager to get a start on reading the diary.

He found his manservant enjoying a tankard of ale in the noisy taproom.

George glanced at him without apparent recognition, a habit borne of caution.

On Max's signal, he drained his tankard unhurriedly, then tossed a gruff quip to the tapster before shambling over to the table where Max sat.

"Something brewing, eh, guv? I seen that look on your face afore, I 'ave."

"Perceptive of you, George," Max murmured. "We shall stay here yet awhile. In fact, I might as well rack up for the night. Get me a room, will you? And make arrangements for yourself and the horses. I've work to do."

"Right you are, guv." George rubbed his hands. "There's a pretty wench of a landlord's daughter—"

"I don't want to know. Just make sure you're not caught with your breeches around your ankles if there's trouble afoot. I might need you."

George tipped his hat. "Right you are, guv'nor."

Max sighed. "Is there any chance you might bring yourself to call me 'Your Grace'? I am a duke now, you know."

The blue eyes twinkled under shaggy brows. "Not hardly. You wants bowing and scraping, you can get it from one of those fancy-pants new servants of yours. You won't get it from me."

Max snorted a laugh and put a hand on George's shoulder. "Good man."

"Your Grace!" Max turned to see Perry. Damn the boy, he'd forgotten he'd told him to wait.

"Ah, Perry. I'm glad you're here."

The blue eyes glowed. Wasn't the boy getting too old for this kind of hero worship? Well enough when he was fourteen, but now it had become . . . unsettling.

Max hesitated, trying in vain to think of a task he trusted Perry enough to carry out.

Suspicion dawned in that sulky, angelic face. "You said you'd have orders for me."

Something trivial. Something that would occupy him, keep him out of Max's way for a while. Something simple. Max clicked his fingers. "Ah, yes. I do have a job for you. I want you to go back to Lady Kate's house and keep watch. If anything untoward occurs, I want you to report back, understand?"

Perry seemed to expand with excitement. "Yes, sir! Your Grace. I'll go at once."

"Yes, do that," murmured Max. "Come and see me at midday to report your findings." He nodded. "You may go."

"I won't disappoint you, Your Grace."

As his expectations weren't high, that wouldn't be difficult. Max smiled, a trifle wearily. "No, I know you won't do that."

He watched Perry go. The boy needed weaning.

But the estate Max had inherited demanded his immediate attention. As soon as he'd finished with this arson business, he'd return there to stay for the foreseeable future. He couldn't afford the time to accustom Perry to the idea of his absence. Besides, a clean break might be best for the boy.

Perry's father had run a series of prostitution rings, the worst of them involving children. Max had been triumphant when he finally secured the evidence to prove his suspicions, but Perry's father was a member of an old, powerful family. Faulkner, the sycophant, had tried to sweep the whole affair under the carpet, but Max had used every ounce of influence he possessed to force it into the open. Perry's father had stood trial and been sentenced to hang. The villain had used all of his influence to get his sentence commuted to transportation, but he had died on the voyage to Sydney.

The man's crimes had been heinous enough. Worst of

all, he hadn't limited his evil to strangers. He'd debauched his own son.

A familiar surge of impotent rage and deep pity doused the last embers of Max's exasperation. Punishing the blackguard couldn't erase the damage he'd done his son. However irritating Perry became, Max could never forget what a terrible childhood he must have endured.

Something ought to be done for the boy when Max left London for good. Now, however, Max needed to put that sad history out of his mind and concentrate on Lady Kate's diary.

A modest room awaited him upstairs, which suited his purpose well enough. As soon as George had removed his boots and left, Max slipped out the diary and turned it over in his hands. An unassuming little book to hold such power.

Something made him hesitate. He had the strangest feeling that reading this small, elegant volume would change his life.

Trying, for once, to ignore his instincts, Max poured himself a bumper of brandy, sat in a comfortable armchair by the fire, and opened the book.

KATE stood in the middle of her bedchamber, flushed and breathless, for too many moments before she realized.

He wasn't coming back.

She strode to the door and wrenched it open, scanning the corridor.

But it was empty, the house quiet. Some objects on the floor caught her eye and she hurried to retrieve them. Her ink bottle, pen, and paper still lay on the floor where she'd dropped them when he'd surprised her. Her slipper lay quite a distance away, as if she'd kicked it there during their struggle.

She found her candle and used her fingernail to scrape up the wax that had dripped and hardened on the floor.

Gathering up her implements, she took them back to her bedchamber, and spilled them with a clatter onto a piecrust table.

Trembling, Kate gripped the table's edge and bowed her head. "Oh, God!"

The old, familiar humiliation welled inside her, sickening and hot. Cringing at the memory of her wanton behavior, she clutched her gaping night rail together and sank onto the nearest chair.

How did this keep happening? She had almost . . . She shuddered to think how close she'd come to throwing her virtue to the winds.

Stupid, stupid, stupid! And he hadn't even cared enough to stay in the room with her while she did it! Poor, overzealous, love-starved Kate.

What must he think of her? Why had he left so abruptly? What had she done?

Her gaze fell on the bed, and she squeezed her eyes shut as the heat flooded her face and pricked behind her eyelids. She hovered on the verge of tears, a weakness she hadn't indulged in for years.

But to have guarded her precious virtue so well for all that time, only to throw it away on a man who by rights she should treat as her enemy!

And she didn't even *like* him.

She should be utterly thankful he'd left before she'd let him do more.

Kate could not pretend, even to herself, that she would have said no to him. What a terrifying thing to contemplate, that she should forget her morals and plain common sense as soon as an unscrupulous man took advantage of her. They had only just met!

Waves of embarrassment crashed over her as she

thought of how she must have looked when he left her. Hair a wild, slatternly tangle, breasts exposed, eyes dazed. She'd panted for him like a bitch in heat.

If he hadn't meant to go through with her seduction, why had he returned to the house in the first place?

*Stephen.* That was it. That could be the only explanation. He'd come to try to seduce her into acquiescence, or perhaps even into helping him. The mystery was why he'd left before he could achieve his aim.

Perhaps . . . She swallowed past the lump in her throat. Had he found her so repugnant he couldn't bear to touch her, even for the sake of his investigation? Ugh! She wished she'd resisted him, as any sensible woman would have done.

It couldn't be helped. She'd been rash and stupid, but there was no going back.

She needed to calm down. She needed to take deep breaths. Far, *far* more important than the Duke of Lyle was getting Stephen out of jail.

She would not let the duke distract her from her purpose. She would write the first chapter of her memoirs so that she had something to bargain with. If it was true she courted danger by making these veiled threats, she needed insurance.

Nerves twanging with tension, Kate tied the strings of her night rail together and braided her hair into a severe plait. Arranging paper, pen and ink on a small table, she sat down to write.

PERRY knew how to move silently through the darkness when he needed to. One of the many things he'd learned from the duke.

*His Grace, the Duke of Lyle.* Perry savored the title his mentor now held. *Duke.* The highest rank of nobleman in the country. Wealth and power beyond most men's wildest dreams.

He'd known Lyle would resign from the Home Office on inheriting the dukedom, of course. Why would anyone who'd landed such a bounty remain in the employ of the government, under the authority of a man like Faulkner?

As head of operations, Faulkner was methodical and unimaginative, subtle as a battering ram. Self-satisfied, too. He saw Perry as his own instrument, but Perry's allegiance was—and always would be—to Lyle.

He owed Lyle his life, and a great deal more than that besides.

A rustle of leaves heralded the one he awaited.

"Mr. Perry." An excited, young, female voice.

He cursed under his breath. Turning, he saw her, all plump eagerness, with her big, cow eyes and the equally bovine abundance of her breasts.

So womanly and curvaceous. She made him want to vomit.

But he would do it.

For Lyle.

"I thought you weren't coming. You're never late." Louisa Brooke turned back from dismissing her groom and studied Max from beneath the brim of her hat.

The black gelding beneath her snorted and tossed his head. He looked like a temperamental brute, too strong for most ladies, but Max knew better than to offer assistance. His sister rode as if she'd been born in the saddle and never took kindly to a suggestion that she might not be able to manage for herself.

"My apologies. The delay was unavoidable."

He hadn't yet been to bed. He'd spent the rest of the hours before dawn and beyond trying to translate Lady

Kate's diary. Written in Italian, damn her. He knew Latin and Greek—he'd learned them at school—but not more than a smattering of Italian words, most of them lewd. What he'd managed to extrapolate from the Latin he knew didn't seem to make sense at all. He couldn't take the diary to an official government translator. He didn't want the Home Office to know the diary existed. He couldn't immediately bring to mind anyone else he trusted enough with the task.

Max had meant to catch a couple of hours' sleep before presenting himself at Whitehall, but then he'd recalled the engagement to ride with Louisa in Hyde Park. It was too late to cancel the outing. Then he remembered that many women of his class knew a little Italian. Perhaps Louisa might help him translate the diary.

He glanced at her, sitting straight-backed on her horse, precise to a pin with her blond hair tied back severely from her face and a rather ugly hat that he supposed must be the high kick of fashion on her head.

He made his sisters a generous allowance. The more extravagant they were, the more it pleased him. He needed to make up for the lean years following his father's death.

"You learned Italian at school, didn't you, Louie?"

"After a fashion, yes." She glanced at him, a flash of intense blue. "I learned more from Mademoiselle Renaud." At his enquiring look, she added, "Our governess was half Italian. Don't you remember?"

He frowned, searching his memory. "Was she pretty?"

"Not particularly."

"Then I wouldn't remember her."

She snorted. "You're atrocious!"

"No, my dear. Just a man." He smiled, unabashed at her outrage, and it felt like the first time he'd smiled in years.

So, Louisa was fluent in Italian. He could trust her with the diary, but if he did give it to her to translate, would he jeopardize her safety, too? He might be watched even now, though he hadn't sensed anyone trailing him.

At least the park wasn't crowded at this time of the morning. He and Louisa could speak freely without the danger of being overheard.

"I'd like you to translate something for me," he murmured. "Could you do that?"

"Something in Italian? I expect so. Is it to do with—"

"My work. Yes. That secret government work that you know nothing about."

"Oh, that. Yes, of course. I'd like to help." She sighed. "We are so prosperous these days that I hardly know what to do with myself. I shall relish the challenge."

"Wait until you see your new home," murmured Max. He studied her. "Don't you have several hundred balls and parties to go to this season? I'd thought you were living a life of frivolity and dissipation."

Louisa shrugged, glancing away from him. "I am nine-and-twenty, my dear brother. Neither debutante nor matron. An old spinster of no account. And all of those balls and parties become the same after a while."

She grimaced and then laughed. "That makes me sound unforgivably maudlin, doesn't it? Suffice it to say that I will enjoy this task you have set me far more than any social engagement."

He guided her into a small grove of trees where they'd be screened from observers and reached into his coat pocket.

"Here." He handed over the diary. "Now, you might find some of its content shocking, but I count on you to translate it faithfully. I need to know everything, right down to the last syllable. Keep it somewhere safe and send for me as soon as you're finished."

Louisa put out her gloved hand to accept the small diary. Her horse remained obediently still while his mistress buttoned her short jacket over the precious volume.

"I doubt I'll begin until this evening," she said. "Mama has every minute of my day planned. But I shall plead a headache and stay at home tonight."

She glanced at him, and in a voice that seemed a little hard, added, "You needn't worry that I can't keep a secret. I can."

He smiled down at her. "I'm not worried about that." He reached over to her and took her hand, giving it a small shake. "Thank you, Louie."

Louisa smiled. "It is good to be useful."

"I came as soon as I could, yer ladyship." Ives wiped his mouth with the back of his hand and shifted his feet. His beady eyes gleamed as he scanned the bookshelves that lined the room.

Trying not to show her revulsion for her unprepossessing go-between, Kate asked, "And how fares my brother?"

"Moved him to another cell, they have. Has a proper cot and a blanket and water to wash with and boiled mutton for his dinner. All the comforts he could wish. He says to tell you he is quite easy and you need not bother your head over him."

Kate rolled her eyes. "He did not tell you who might help us free him?"

"It's as I said to you before, my lady. The man don't want to be saved." Ives shrugged and spread his hands. "What could I do? Weren't nothing the likes of me could say to persuade him."

It seemed fantastic, yet, knowing Stephen, she could well believe it. Stubborn, muddle-headed fool!

"Does he know he is being held for sedition?" she demanded. "Does he know what the penalty for that is?"

"Aye, he knows all that, but he says they won't try him seeing as how he ain't done nothing wrong. They're just holding him so he'll spill his guts about that fire they had at Lyle."

Yes, the duke had mentioned it. Kate narrowed her eyes. "So if he tells where those men are hiding, he can go free. He knows that?"

"Yes, my lady. But he vows he won't, and he's got a will, has our Mr. Holt."

"He has, indeed," said Kate, thinking of her bullnecked, righteous, darling of a brother. "All right, you may go." Kate handed Ives a purse containing the rest of the money she owed him.

He stopped and began to count it. Kate blew out an exasperated breath and swept from the room.

With the first chapter of her memoirs safely dispatched to her solicitors, Kate paced the floor of her drawing room, considering her next step.

She'd already decided she needed to approach Sidmouth casually, in a social setting.

Perhaps her brother-in-law might be persuaded to invite the Home Secretary to dinner . . . She folded her arms and gazed blindly into the gardens below. Oswald was a staid, unimaginative fellow, loyal to the government. He'd already refused to help her free Stephen; she could well imagine his reaction to the news that she planned to blackmail Lord Sidmouth.

Fingering the velvet curtains, Kate watched a swallow dart and swoop in the street outside and a sudden longing for a similar freedom beat within her. The burden of sole responsibility for Stephen's plight seemed almost too heavy to bear. Did she really have the courage to take on His Majesty's government?

For Stephen's sake, she would have to try.

As a solicitor's clerk of the finest caliber, Mr. Tibbits appreciated order and method. Upon the death of his former employer—a man almost a decade younger than Mr. Tibbits himself—he'd been fortunate enough to secure a position with Mr. Crouch. That gentleman possessed an equal appreciation for order and method and so many wealthy and distinguished clients, it was a wonder he could keep pace with them all.

Happily engaged in enumerating the manifold pleasures of his occupation, Mr. Tibbits dipped his quill in the inkstand, preparing to draft an affidavit in his neat, looping hand.

Before he set pen to parchment, a large shadow fell over his desk.

He nearly jumped out of his chair. His gaze flew upwards. A tall, dark man loomed over him.

He put a hand over his racing heart. "Good heavens, sir! You scared me."

He didn't know this stranger, but from the fine quality of his garments to the arrogance of his bearing, he was Quality, through and through.

Large, white, elegant hands settled on his desk. The stranger leaned in. "Tell your employer I wish to see him."

The clerk's heart pounded harder. There was distinct menace in the stranger's stance and in his glittering dark eyes.

Still, Mr. Tibbits knew his duty and he was conscious of the younger clerks around him who had raised their heads to watch the exchange. "Do you h-have an appointment, sir?"

"An appointment?" The man's teeth gleamed. He barked a laugh, turned, and ran lightly upstairs to the gallery floor, where Mr. Crouch's office lay.

"Sir! You can't go up there without an—"

The office door opened and slammed.

"—appointment. Oh, dear!" Mr. Tibbits hurried up after the man, fear lending wings to his heels.

Oh, dear. Oh, gracious. Mr. Crouch would be ever so angry if this man arrived without an appointment and Mr. Tibbits hadn't stopped him.

Puffing, Mr. Tibbits reached the office door, knocked briefly and turned the handle.

The door was locked.

"Mr. Crouch, sir!" He raised his voice and spoke through the keyhole. "Are you all right?"

He listened at the door, but the voices were too low for him to make out what was said.

In less than a minute, the door flew open, and Mr. Tibbits almost fell into the stranger's arms.

The stranger gripped him by the elbows and set him back on his feet. "Steady, old man."

With a flash of that devilish smile, he was gone, tucking a sheaf of papers into his waistcoat as he jogged down the stairs.

Mr. Tibbits took a deep breath and opened the door wider, preparing himself for a reprimand.

His employer sprawled in a chair, his usually neat cravat askew, gasping for breath.

"Sir!" Mr. Tibbits bustled into the room. "Are you hurt? Shall I send for a doctor? Call for the constable?"

Mr. Crouch shook his head, his eyes troubled. His mouth worked.

"No, Tibbits. I beg you to forget this incident altogether. But you must send word to Lady Kate Fairchild. I must . . . I must see her. *Immediately!*"

FAULKNER'S secretary showed Max in promptly. No kicking his heels in the waiting room as he'd been obliged to do so many times before.

If Max had cared to flaunt his new ducal dignity, he would have refused the summons and issued one of his own. He couldn't abide such posturing, however, so he complied with Faulkner's request. He needed Faulkner's cooperation and he was more likely to get it if he didn't ruffle the old man's feathers.

For many moments, his presence in the inner sanctum went ignored. Max gave a sardonic smile. Things hadn't changed so very much, after all. The head of operations sat behind his huge oak desk, leafing through a report with the calm deliberation of someone who wanted to set his guest at a disadvantage. That was all part of the game, and it had been many years since Max had let the tactic intimidate him.

He stared at the precise line of scalp parting the thinning strands of Faulkner's grizzled brown hair and wondered how long it would take his sister to translate Lady Kate's diary.

The silence stretched. Max was half-tempted to leave. He needed Faulkner's help, however. He needed to keep Stephen Holt in jail.

The click of an interconnecting door opening made Max tense, all senses alert.

Another player walked into the room, and suddenly, the rules changed.

Jardine.

Black hair sprang back from his forehead to form a widow's peak, and the eyebrows beneath flexed like arrowheads, giving him a rakish, almost devilish air. He looked as if he'd be good for nothing but self-indulgence and vice, but Max knew the façade of decadence masked a Machiavellian brain and remorseless determination.

They'd been rivals of a sort ever since Eton, but whereas Max had needed the Home Office work, needed the money, been obliged to toe the line, Jardine came and went as he pleased.

Jardine chose this life, returned to it again and again like an addict, while Max had always felt more akin to a slave. A slave on the verge of freedom.

Not long now . . .

"Did you get it?" Jardine came straight to the point,

dark eyes glittering with mockery. Max could almost believe he knew everything that had transpired last evening. But of course, that's what Jardine wanted him to believe.

Faulkner glanced up, forehead creasing like a bulldog's.

Max wouldn't give Jardine the satisfaction of showing discomfort. He sat without an invitation and lounged back, apparently at his ease, while his brain teemed with speculation. Perry must have passed on the details of their encounter last night. But the lad hadn't known what Max sought.

He raised his brows in mild surprise. "Get what?"

"Oh, come now, *Your Grace*," murmured Jardine. "The boy told me you broke into a certain lady's house last night. What were you looking for?"

Max gave a saturnine smile. "I would have thought you, of all people, might guess the answer to that, Jardine."

"Ah. The fair Lady Kate. Boasting of your conquests, Lyle?"

"Hardly. I've made no secret of my object regarding Lady Kate. I'm trying to persuade her to use her influence with her brother to make him see reason."

"And was your, ah, *persuasion* successful?" purred Jardine.

Max repressed a wry smile. "Unfortunately, I was interrupted. Someone else broke into the house while I was there." He spared a scathing glance for his former superior. "You should keep a tighter leash on that cub Perry, Faulkner. He's a damned liability."

A glance passed between Jardine and Faulkner, so swiftly, he might have imagined it.

"He's your protégé," Jardine pointed out.

"He's nothing of the kind," Max said. "Faulkner recruited him. Against my advice, if you'll recall. I'll not take responsibility for that. If I've tried to keep the lad out of trouble and given him enough skills to keep himself alive, it was out of compassion. I never wanted him mixed up in this."

"We've been watching her ladyship," said Faulkner as if Max hadn't spoken. "Seems to us she's going off half-cocked about this brother of hers. Begging most of the cabinet to intervene in the matter. Much more agitating on her part and we might have to do something to keep her quiet."

Jardine interposed, watching Max. "Of course, we could simply act as she wishes. We could let the brother go."

Max glared at him. "He's our only link with the Lyle arsonists. We'll just have to break him sooner, that's all."

"Work on the woman," growled Faulkner. "You're a smooth bastard, Lyle. You should know how to get her to dance to your tune."

Jardine snorted and turned away. So that affair still rankled, did it? A faint glow in his chest told Max he wasn't quite above petty triumphs when it came to Jardine.

"I'll take care of it, one way or another." He frowned. "Does Sidmouth know about Lady Kate's campaign? I thought it best not to mention the subject to him yesterday evening."

Faulkner shuffled his papers, looking disinterested. "Of course not. He's nervous enough as it is, what with all the unrest in the country. Man's starting to believe his own rhetoric."

"What is really going on?" Now he'd leaped the hurdle of the diary, Max relaxed a little. "Despite the scaremongers I find it difficult to believe we're on the brink of revolution."

Jardine shrugged. "We have our sources, of course, but they're far from reliable. Sorting the wheat from the chaff, I'd say there are pockets of unrest all over the country, but hardly on a scale that's likely to sweep the nation. Certainly, the situation is less dire than Sidmouth would have the English public believe. But that is strictly *entre nous*, of course."

"Oh, of course," murmured Max.

Faulkner grunted. "That's not to say we can tolerate the kind of trouble Lady Kate is capable of causing. Regardless of how volatile we believe the situation to be, the fact remains we can't afford to let the mob get hold of anything damaging. The story of a country vicar imprisoned for sedition without trial is just the kind of tidbit our detractors will latch onto and distort for their own ends. It could spark a nasty rebellion, if not outright revolt."

Max doubted it but said nothing.

"Keep her quiet until we've wrapped up the arson case, Lyle. I don't care how you do it. Scare her, seduce her, use the brother. Do all three. Whatever it takes."

"And afterwards? What happens to Lady Kate?" Max tried to keep his voice completely neutral, but the tautness in his body must have alerted Jardine.

The black eyes gleamed, and Max was uncomfortably aware that Jardine had sniffed out his . . . partiality for Lady Kate. Well, nothing startling in that. He'd made it clear at the ball he admired her. But he couldn't let Jardine see just how important she'd become.

"If she's a good little girl and gives us no further trouble, nothing at all," said Faulkner.

Somehow, Max doubted Lady Kate would take the loss of her diary meekly. She possessed intelligence and a fair degree of subtlety, but driven by fear for her brother there was no telling what she might do. She was a powder keg, ready to ignite.

If only that damned brother of hers would cooperate, Max could have him released and remove the imperative driving Lady Kate to blackmail.

"And if Lady Kate persists?" he inquired, knowing the answer.

"Then, my dear fellow, we must eliminate her. An accident to her carriage, perhaps." Faulkner flicked a glance at Jardine. "I'm sure I can trust you with the details."

# Five

*Stolen moments, now. Caution demands too high a price.*

*He is everywhere. In my mind, in my heart, in the deep, midnight sky among the stars. I teeter on the verge of something dangerous . . .*

*Longing for the fall.*

"A word with you, if I may." Jardine strolled out of Faulkner's office close on Max's heels.

*What now?* thought Max.

"Of course." He drew on his gloves in a leisurely fashion, as if he had all the time in the world. He couldn't let Jardine sense his urgency. There were a thousand things to attend to before he could put his plans in place and he only had a few hours before Lady Kate left.

Jardine waited until they were outside. He put on his hat and gestured for Max to walk with him.

Finally, he said, "You might be interested to know that a document was delivered to Oddling and Crouch Solicitors this morning. The first chapter of a certain lady's memoirs. With instructions to make the writings public if anything happens to the lady."

Good God! The little fool . . .

Those ridiculous eyebrows flew upwards. "You didn't know?"

Silently, Max shook his head. Damn him to hell, Jardine was enjoying this. He shouldn't be so surprised that Jardine also had an informant in Lady Kate's household. What riled him most was that Perry hadn't brought him the news first. When he found that boy, he'd string him from the nearest lamppost.

Max didn't allow his fury to show. "And how did you discover the document's contents? Surely the lawyer claimed privilege?"

"Threatened to rape his wife," said Jardine flippantly. "Oh, don't look at me like that. I wouldn't have done it."

Max considered Jardine with unwilling fascination. "Your methods have always been direct, haven't they?"

"It saves a considerable amount of time," Jardine drawled. He sighed and went on. "A little bird tells me your Lady Kate is bound for Richmond this afternoon. What do you make of that?"

Max shrugged. "I would have thought that was obvious. She's running our esteemed Home Secretary to ground so she can blackmail him with these memoirs of hers."

"And thereby put her neck in the noose," murmured Jardine. "Such a pretty neck, too."

Anger ripped through Max at the personal remark. Anger tinged with alarm. It was one thing for Jardine to sense Max's interest in the lady. Quite another for him to express interest on his own account.

But instead of reaching down Jardine's throat and ripping his lungs out, Max replied evenly, "You and I both know she'd never be tried. Even if it weren't for the political implications, a jury would acquit her in the blink of an eye." He paused. "But Faulkner won't let it come to that. He'd kill her first."

Jardine flicked lint off his sleeve. "Of course. Wouldn't you? There's no telling how much she knows. Even if she knows nothing at all, the merest hint of her intentions in one of the broadsheets would set the public baying for blood. Faulkner couldn't afford the publicity of a trial. I imagine the lady knows that."

They walked on in silence. What did Jardine want? He'd said nothing that wasn't already clear to all concerned. There must be something else, some vested interest apart from Lady Kate. But what?

After a few minutes, during which Max knew Jardine studied him, his companion spoke. "You've grown soft, Your Grace."

The mocking words stung. At one time, Max had prided himself on his cold-bloodedness, his willingness to do whatever was required to get the job done. But to assassinate a gently bred lady desperate to save her brother from incarceration was beyond anything he'd ever contemplated.

Jardine was not so squeamish. And if it came to a fight between them, who would win?

"There might be an alternative," Jardine said. He glanced speculatively at Max. "Our head of operations is not the man he was. He is looking towards retirement and such considerations inevitably change one's perspective. There have been . . . lapses in judgment, shall we say?"

Max digested this. Clearly, Jardine wanted the top job and he was prepared to help Max protect Lady Kate. In exchange for . . .

Max hissed out a breath of disgust. "You want the memoirs."

Jardine bowed. "In a nutshell. I can put the information to better use than Faulkner ever would. The man's vision is remarkably limited in scope." Jardine showed his teeth. "Oh, I assure you, my motives are pure. What was it you always said? The end justifies the means?"

Max would have preferred Jardine to stay out of it, but the man knew too much. Admittedly, there were certain strategic advantages to keeping his old rival in plain sight.

He glanced at Jardine's chiseled profile. "I'll see what I can do."

AT noon, Max hadn't yet finalized his preparations. He jogged down the steps of his Mayfair house and strode off in the direction of Piccadilly, where his friend Lord Vane ran a private boxing establishment even more select than Jackson's.

"Your Grace! Your Grace!"

Perry. Clenching his jaw, Max halted, struggling to contain his fury. Perry's failure to keep watch on Lady Kate's house that morning meant that Jardine now held incriminating evidence against her. Exasperated with himself for trusting the boy that far, Max pinched the bridge of his nose. Why didn't he just tell the young fool to make himself scarce? In truth, he owed Perry nothing.

But he could never forget that he'd taken the young man's father away, condemned him to the hangman's noose. Nor that Perry had suffered cruelly at his father's hand. Max took a deep breath and did his best to keep his temper.

Turning around, he said, "Ah, Perry." Max took out his watch and glanced at it. "I did say I'd see you now, didn't I?"

Perry trotted up to him and fell into step as Max turned and walked on. The young man tried his patience at the best of times, but today his buoyant eagerness made Max want to strangle him.

"You said you'd have a job for me."

"How rash of me," murmured Max, drawing on his gloves. "Give me a moment. I'm sure I'll think of something for you to do."

He looked about him, letting Perry's chatter form part of the background, like the clop of horses' hooves and the shouts of costermongers plying their wares in the busy street.

Though London was its usual noisome self, spring

pervaded the air in subtle ways. A gentle warmth. The faint, sweet scent of flowers from the basket of a passing maidservant. Unremitting birdsong and a mellow quality in the light.

It was a time of tender new growth, heady optimism, and the madness of young love. Or, if you were a member of the Upper Ten Thousand, it was the Season, an endless round of balls, musicales, visits to the opera, the theater, even to the museum if some fashionable exhibit like the Elgin Marbles was on display.

For many years that gaiety had passed him by. Oh, he'd always had the entrée to that world. His blood was as good as anyone's and very few knew of the dirty work he did for the Home Office. His acquaintance assumed he was a desk Johnny and he'd never seen fit to correct them. Even the excuse of lack of funds didn't answer because most gentlemen of his age punted on tick until their creditors set the bailiffs on them.

He'd cast himself out, he supposed. At eighteen, he'd suffered the crushing discovery that the father he worshipped was not only an inveterate gaming addict, but bankrupt into the bargain. In one fell swoop Max's future, his brother's army commission, his sisters' dowries, his mother's jointure all disappeared.

Shortly afterwards, his father died in what the local magistrate euphemistically called a shooting accident. The old Duke of Lyle refused the family assistance, and if Max had known his mother had intended to plead with the old tartar, he'd have forbidden her to go anywhere near Lyle. The family was Max's responsibility and no one else's.

Max had come down from Cambridge and an uncle had found him a place in the Home Office. Before Max had spent a fortnight in that job, Faulkner pounced, recruiting Max to his secret division with the promise of more money and more excitement. If Max had known what lay in store for him, he would have flatly declined.

Now, having inherited a fortune and position beyond his wildest dreams, it was time to settle down. He'd throw off the mantle of shame he'd carried with him for over a decade and begin life anew. Perhaps, this Season, he might even find a suitable wife.

But the fire at Lyle had left him with responsibilities he couldn't shirk. The first step in dealing with them was to disarm Lady Kate.

"I say, Your Grace—"

"Perry, I have asked you several times to call me Lyle. I can't abide being 'Your Graced' every other minute."

"You are very good, sir. But I hardly think it sits well with your consequence to eschew the niceties—"

Max looked down at him in amusement. "Are you actually presuming to tell me I'm not high enough in the instep, boy?"

"Well, sir, it is not my place to censure you, that's true, but—"

"Oh, save your breath," Max snapped, exasperated. "One day, you will learn that position and wealth have little to do with character, and which to value more."

The late duke had been one of the most reprehensible men of Max's acquaintance, and that included the many criminals he'd put to justice.

Past grievances were needless burdens. He must concentrate on the present. And the near future. And the question of Lady Kate.

He glanced at Perry and wondered if he'd regret this. "I do have a job for you, as it happens. A small matter of kidnapping . . ."

BY late afternoon, Kate sat with her maid Sukey in a hired post chaise bound for Richmond, where the Home Secretary would spend the week. Under her apparently idle questioning, her brother-in-law had let that detail slip.

She'd received the invitation to Mrs. Digby's house party but politely declined it on the grounds of previous engagements.

Now, the rest of the world could go hang. She needed to see Sidmouth before it was too late. She'd dispatched a note to Mrs. Digby apologizing for her late change of plans. Kate didn't doubt her hostess would welcome her; the Digbys had been friends with her family for generations.

"Will your duke be there, d'you think, my lady?" said Sukey.

Kate looked at her, startled. Had she and the duke become fodder for backstairs gossip?

"If you mean the Duke of Lyle, I wouldn't be at all surprised if he is there." Guarding Sidmouth like a bulldog, no doubt.

*Blackmail.* An ugly word. In the heat of argument with Lyle she'd made hasty threats. With the opportunity to reconsider in the cold light of day, she wasn't sure she had the stomach to go through with them. What if they tried her for blackmail, or even treason?

But wouldn't that be alerting the world to the reason for the blackmail? That there were, indeed, secrets she kept that would damage the government if they became known?

No, Lyle was right. They'd deal with her quietly. They'd weigh the consequences of her carrying out her threats against the evils of setting Stephen free. Once he was released she would never consider making those secrets public. They must know that.

But what if making these threats merely opened Pandora's box? What if they no longer trusted her to keep her mouth shut? Perhaps she really was in danger, as Lyle had said.

Well, she wouldn't take any chances. The first chapter of her memoirs would go to print if anything happened to her. She would have to make that clear to Sidmouth and anyone else with an interest in the affair.

Kate swallowed, and her hand trembled as she fiddled with the strings of her reticule. The insurance was useless if no one knew about it. Until she could communicate her plan to Lyle and his minions, she was at risk. She had hired outriders for the journey and made sure they were armed. Still, she could not rest easy.

"Are you all right, my lady? You look a bit pale."

"I'm perfectly well, thank you." She averted her face and stared out at the lowering dusk. "Just a little fatigued from last night, that's all."

True enough, she thought ruefully. Though it hadn't been the ball that had tired her, but all that had followed.

The carriage lurched, throwing them both forward. Before Kate could recover, a shot exploded through the air.

"Stay down!" Kate grabbed Sukey's wrist and yanked her to the floor between the seats. She crouched as best she could in her petticoats, with the hard wooden busk of her corset digging into her midriff.

They'd come already. They were going to kill her. She couldn't breathe. *Oh, think! Think!* Were there pistols inside the carriage? She saw that Sukey gazed upwards at the empty holsters a second after she did. They both blew out disgusted breaths.

"Never fear. There are four men outside who are bound to protect us," said Kate, forcing herself to sound confident.

"Hired men," fretted Sukey. "They'd turn tail and run at a mouse's squeak. Mark my words, my lady."

Kate hoped to Heaven Sukey was wrong. She looked wildly around the carriage. "Is there *anything* we can use as a weapon?" If only it were winter, and they carried hot bricks to warm their feet, that would have been something, but no. The carriage was bare of anything useful.

"Only this." Sukey held up her reticule.

"Unless you have a pound of shot in there, I'd say we're sunk. We shall have to rely on the men. That's what they're paid for, after all."

Shouts rang out from the coachman's box and one of the footmen standing behind gave a strangled cry. A horse screamed and the carriage jolted and shuddered, throwing them against one another.

Gasping for air, Kate braced herself against the seat, hoping the coachman had the beasts under control. The men must be putting up a fight. But how would they, two lone women, defend themselves if her hired servants were overcome?

The carriage door flung open, and a masculine figure filled the doorway. Kate screamed at the top of her lungs but no one came to their assistance. The man reached in, caught Sukey about the waist, and hauled her through the opening.

With a flurry of skirts and limbs, Sukey fought like a wildcat, thrashing and kicking, but the man ignored her cries and threw her over his shoulder. He carried her off as easily as a sack of meal.

"Sukey! No!" Still yelling for help, Kate scrambled up, but the door slammed shut and the carriage bounded forward, throwing her back onto the seat.

Immediately, she yanked on the check-string, but the chaise hurtled on at a breakneck pace. She wrestled the window open and stuck her head out to shout to the coachman to stop.

But the man tooling the carriage was not the coachman she'd hired.

Deaf to her pleas, he hunched over his reins and whipped up the horses. Kate had to grip the windowsill to stop herself falling again. She reached for the hand strap and sat down with a thump as the carriage bounced over the uneven road.

What had they done with the men she'd hired for the journey? Where were they taking her? Kate's palms were clammy and her pulse raced. She made herself take deep breaths, trying to calm down enough to think of a way out.

They rounded a bend too fast, and she hung on to the strap with all her might to stop being thrown. She could have sworn two wheels came off the ground.

Her heart beat so hard she could hear it, even over the rattle of the carriage and the pounding of hooves. Was someone trying to kill her? It was a strange way to go about it if they were. And what about Sukey? Why had they taken her away?

"Oh, God!" she whispered. "Please keep her safe."

Forcing down her fear, Kate tried desperately to think. Green fields whizzed past in a blur. They'd left London far behind, and somehow, she didn't think their destination was still Richmond.

Surely they must slow down at some point, but this coachman stopped for nothing, not even a yellow bounder that lumbered along the narrow road towards them. They passed the stagecoach with inches to spare.

Kate began to feel a mad kind of hope. Perhaps they'd crash and she could run away in the confusion. No, they'd catch her. How far or fast could she run, hampered by her petticoats, wearing thin slippers on her feet?

Where were they taking her? A suitable spot to kill her and dispose of her lifeless body? She started shaking, realizing that whatever the case, she was dealing with men who balked at nothing to achieve their aims. Not even murder.

She should have listened to Lyle.

The carriage horn blasted a warning and the vehicle slowed a little. Kate put her head out the window to see what had forced the driver to abate their pace.

In the distance, a shepherd was driving a large flock of sheep across the road.

Their pace slackened further, to a more normal speed, and determination clenched Kate's jaw. She must get away. A jump from a moving carriage was likely to end in bruises and sprains, but the alternative would be worse if her surmises were correct. Even if she broke every bone in her body to do it, she had to get out of this carriage.

She spied a cottage by the road she could run to for help. She might even appeal to the shepherd, who now whistled to his dog to hurry his flock.

It was a slim chance, but the best she was likely to get.

Bracing herself so she wouldn't tumble out before she was ready, Kate reached through the open window and found the door handle. Keeping an eye on the commotion up ahead, she eased the door handle around.

The sheep weren't moving fast enough and the carriage drew ever closer. A shot rang out, and she realized the coachman had fired it over the sheep's heads, trying to clear a path.

Was it her imagination, or had the carriage slowed a little more?

Another shot fired and the sheep scattered in all directions. The shepherd waved his hands and shouted while his dog barked in a frenzy.

The road was clearing due to the coachman's heavy-handed tactics and soon they'd hit full speed again. It was now or never.

Kate turned the handle and the door flew out of her hand, swinging wildly. She watched the ground flow past beneath her and bile rose in her throat.

Fighting the urge to close her eyes, she took a deep breath and jumped.

The wind flew out of her when she landed. She tumbled and rolled down the grassy embankment, crying out as a sharp pain stabbed the back of her head.

The last things she saw were stars, swimming against a leaden sky.

KATE woke to the sound of vicious swearing. Some of the words were ones she'd never heard before, but they were uttered with such venom, she knew they weren't polite.

Vaguely, she thought she ought to be afraid, but her head pounded with a vicious intensity that left little will for anything except trying to bear the pain without weeping. She felt as if a giant hand was crushing her skull and setting fire to it at the same time.

A small moan escaped her. Fighting the agony in her head, she dragged her lids open. And looked straight into a familiar set of hard gray eyes.

"Oh, you," she mumbled, letting her lids shut. "Go away."

"You'd be in a fine mess if I did. Come."

Hands slid beneath her shoulders and waist, and a pair of strong arms lifted her, effortlessly swinging her up against his chest.

One of his coat buttons dug into her side, but she hardly noticed. The pain and his warmth and strength overwhelmed everything else. A glimmer of reason said she shouldn't trust him, but somehow, she simply felt safe.

Safe, but far from comfortable. Every movement was like a blow to her brain, and she felt unspecified aches all over her body. But for some reason, it seemed vital not to complain or betray her weakness. She gritted her teeth and didn't so much as whimper as he carried her to a chaise—presumably the same one she'd been traveling in.

She let her eyes drift shut again once they were inside. Was Lyle her rescuer or her captor? The situation was too overwhelming for her confused brain to analyze. It seemed best to avoid dealing with it until her strength and reason returned.

He deposited her gently beside him on the banquette seat, arranging her limbs with impersonal efficiency, propping her against him. His arm slid around her. His hand settled at her waist.

A tap of his stick on the roof and the carriage leaped forward.

Kate couldn't help crying out at the sudden knifing pain the jolting caused. Why couldn't they slow down? She certainly wasn't going to try jumping out of a moving carriage a second time.

Another starburst of agony made her moan into his big shoulder. She wished she hadn't done it. She squeezed her eyes shut and bit her lip and tasted blood.

Until dizziness swarmed over her, and consciousness slipped from her grasp once more.

MAX paused in the doorway, watching her, as he'd watched her all night from the chair by the fire. Lady Kate's constitution was not as fragile as her ethereal appearance might suggest, but she'd taken a severe blow to the head as she tumbled from that carriage.

He'd seen it happen. He'd been riding behind the carriage since they left London, reluctant to let her out of his sight now that Jardine knew about the diary. He'd thought of every contingency, hadn't left anything to chance.

Except the determination of one foolish, headstrong woman.

Still, she hadn't killed herself, and that was the main thing. He hadn't liked to make her travel too far after her accident, so instead of the comfortable house he'd arranged for her, he'd been obliged to take the cottage George found for them a mile or so from where the accident occurred.

Once he'd loosened her stays and unpinned her hair, she'd slept peacefully enough, helped along by a small dose of laudanum lacing the warm milk he'd given her to drink.

Now, as the morning sunlight filtered through the curtains of the cottage's sole bedchamber, Lady Kate lay on her side, one hand forming a loose fist beneath her smooth-skinned cheek, a faint crease between her finely arched brows.

He watched her, soft-lipped and dreaming, and wanted her with an intensity he'd never felt before.

This cottage was hardly an appropriate setting for the seduction he'd had in mind. He wondered how soon she'd be fit to travel again.

With a cynical smile at his impatience, Max picked up a pitcher and poured water into the matching basin. He was splashing his face with shocks of ice-cold water when he heard Lady Kate stir.

He reached for a towel and wiped his face with it, then ran his fingers through his hair. In lieu of a comb, it would have to do. All his kit had been sent to the hunting box he intended to use as a safe house. When he turned, he saw her stare at him with an expression of dawning horror.

The utter revulsion in her gaze touched him on the raw. "What were you thinking, jumping out of a moving carriage? You could have been killed."

Max hadn't meant to raise his voice or use that scathing tone. He thought he'd calmed down overnight, but seeing her fully regain her senses for the first time, blaming him—fearing him—inflamed him anew.

Lady Kate winced, and her delicate hand fluttered to her brow. "Don't shout. I can't bear it."

A weight lifted from his chest. She'd taken a nasty knock to the head, and for a moment or two when he'd first come upon her, he'd thought she was dead. He never wanted to relive those few moments, didn't even want to think about his violent reaction.

Dappled sunlight played over the pillow next to her cheek. A bird burst into song nearby, breaking the silence. Carefully turning her head, Lady Kate glanced out the window.

Her eyes flared in alarm and her gaze shot back to him. "Have I been here all night? With *you*?"

There was a tremor in her voice. Fear? Or something else? Coolly, he nodded. "I thought it best to let you sleep. You were in no state to travel."

She clutched the lacy tucker at her bosom in a defensive

gesture and tried to sit up. With a fretful moan, she sank down again. "Sukey. She was taken. What did you do with her?"

"Your maid is quite safe. She was conveyed back to your home in London."

"She'll raise the alarm. She'll send my people to look for me."

"She will not." Perry would see to that. If there was one thing Max could count on Perry to do, it was to twist the plump little maid around his finger. Women adored his angelic good looks, and it seemed Lady Kate's maid was no exception.

"The world believes you've traveled to Scotland to nurse your aunt, who has suddenly taken ill." He grew serious. "If your relations know what's good for you, they will support that story."

She stared at him for a long time, her hazel eyes dark in her pale face. "I'm ruined. I have spent the night alone with you in this cottage. The damage is done."

*Better ruined than dead.* He didn't say it. She wasn't ready to hear the truth yet.

"You are not ruined. I have arranged matters most carefully. When this is over, I will provide you with a plausible account of your whereabouts that none will call into question. Don't worry. You'll return home without a mark on that lily-white reputation of yours." He raised his brows. "Why would anyone question the word of the virtuous Lady Kate?"

Tears filled her remarkable eyes, and if his heart hadn't been fashioned from marble, he might have felt sorry for her. Tears were the lowest form of feminine warfare, in his experience. But clearly, Lady Kate was in tremendous pain and trying valiantly to suppress her emotions. It must gall her for him to see her like this.

"Don't cry," he said roughly. He handed her a glass of water. "Here, drink this. You must be thirsty."

She took the water from him, slender fingers wrapped around the glass. Sunlight danced across her chestnut curls as she lowered her head to sip.

She looked up. "Why have you brought me here?"

Instead of answering, he picked up a plate on which he'd assembled bread, cheese, and some pickle he'd found in the larder. Plain fare, not at all what she was used to, but filling.

"Eat first. Then we'll talk." On the command, which was more akin to a threat, he left.

KATE breathed, as if for the first time since she'd woken and seen Lyle at his morning ablutions. She had no intention of eating. She needed to escape.

Slowly, she raised herself on her elbows. So far, so good. She could even sit up without fainting, though her head ached as though someone beat it with a cudgel.

She swung her legs and set her feet on the floor. Gingerly, one palm on the bed, she transferred weight to her feet and prepared to stand up.

Pain sliced through her ankle. She overbalanced, but caught the bed in time to stop herself falling.

Confound it! She wasn't going anywhere that day. She sank back and closed her eyes, trying to focus on mastering the pain.

"What do you think you're doing?" Lyle's voice came from the doorway.

Her gaze flew up and her heart commenced a steady pound.

"I must have hurt my ankle. I was testing to see whether it was a sprain or something more serious." At his skeptical look, she added, "My nurse always said the best way to heal a sprained ankle was to walk on it."

He tilted his head, considering her, then moved into the room.

There was an air of the uncivilized about him this morning. Even though his clothes were arranged neatly, his cravat was not quite perfect, suggesting he hadn't changed his raiment since the night before. His dark hair remained tousled despite the finger-comb he'd given it earlier. He must not have shaved, because stubble covered the lower part of his face. The roughness over the skin surrounding his mouth seemed to make his lips appear softer, more sensual. Suddenly, the bedchamber seemed very small.

The duke lounged towards the bed where she sat, and her throat tightened, excitement surging through her body. Every inch of her reacted to this man and came alive. She no longer felt bruised and battered and weak. Alertness raced through her. She felt as if she could run a mile.

"You weren't thinking of going anywhere, were you?" His deep voice seemed to reverberate through her.

She didn't answer. She seemed to have lost the power of speech.

He stood within touching distance, looking down at her, and she fought the craven urge to draw back. Her only path of retreat lay in moving deeper into the center of the bed. He might consider that an invitation.

The duke smiled, as if he knew her thoughts. "Because if you are well enough to attempt an escape, no doubt you're sufficiently fit for some other . . . activities I have in mind."

"No." Real fear gripped her. Despite this surge of energy, she was far too weak to fight him. Part of her didn't even want to. That frightened her more than anything.

The expression in those merciless gray eyes showed serious intent, and she turned her head away so he wouldn't read the anguished indecision in hers. She'd never thought to end her years of celibacy like this.

But his hands cupped her head, threading fingers through her unbound hair. Thumbs stroked the tender skin beneath her eyes, sweeping outwards along her cheekbones with infinite gentleness.

Almost against her will, her eyelids fluttered closed. His fingertips moved through her hair, lightly massaging her scalp. As his thumbs gently circled her temples, she felt the pain and the tension flow out of her.

He increased the pressure to a deeper massage, and she had to grip the bedclothes to stop swaying into his touch. Against her will, a small moan of pleasure escaped her.

Abruptly, his hands left their task. She opened her eyes, conscious of disappointment and a tidal wave of relief. A moment later, she realized her headache had abated, though it hadn't disappeared entirely.

She looked up at him, and his eyes blazed like winter fire.

"Lie back, Lady Kate."

# Six

*He comes to me in the night. A firm step sounds on the terrace. A whisper of my name. Half dreaming, half unwilling, I'm drawn beyond the door.*

*Into the moonlight. Into his arms . . .*

HER face must have reflected her fear. Impatiently, he said, "I'm not going to ravish you. It's clear you're still unwell."

Relief swept over her, but she rallied swiftly. "So you'll wait until my health returns to ravish me? How magnanimous!"

From the flaring look he shot her, Kate knew she played with fire.

"My lady," he answered softly, "when I take you, ravishment will have nothing to do with it."

*That's what I'm afraid of.* Her mouth went dry. For once, she couldn't think of a witty rejoinder. Her heart pounded in her throat.

She was wholly in the duke's power, and nothing she'd seen of him thus far indicated there was any softness or compassion in him. Instinct told her pride would not allow him to take her by force, nor to attempt seduction while she felt poorly. But she couldn't forget the evening of the ball, when he'd kissed her in spite of her struggles and made her like it far too much.

For an instant, she wished she was someone else. Someone who could joyfully, willfully follow her inclinations without guilt or fear.

Lyle saw everything, that was the devil of it.

She slid back farther into the bed, and for the first time she realized her stays were loose. At some point, he must have taken off her gown.

Cheeks burning, she pulled the counterpane up to her chin. Along with her embarrassment at his exploration of her person, she was conscious of a purely feminine wish for a looking glass and some hairpins. If he appeared rakishly disheveled, *she* must look a fright.

His lips turned up a little. "That's better. Now, I'll tell you why you're here, and perhaps you'll reconsider your plan to escape." He paused. "Someone is trying to kill you."

Kate's mouth fell open. She'd feared that the men who stole her carriage were government agents, but that was at the height of her terror. That Lyle had taken her for his own purposes made more sense. Since discovering the identity of her kidnapper, she hadn't rested easily, but she'd dismissed the threat of assassination.

"*Kill* me?"

With a curt nod, Lyle glanced away. "The Home Office knows about your memoirs, don't ask me how. You knew you'd cause a flurry in the government dovecote with that small piece of blackmail. Well, you have. You're a danger to the peace of the realm and they want you eliminated."

Slowly, the idea sank in. "The government is prepared to murder to keep me quiet," she whispered. She could hardly believe it. She'd banked on them not wanting to bring her to trial because her allegations were so sensitive. Despite Lyle's warnings, she'd never expected they would take such decisive—such *final*—action against her.

Lyle ran a hand through his hair. "Yes."

She couldn't put her finger on it, but something about this story didn't ring true. "Why didn't you explain this to me before? I might have come away with you willingly."

"Is that so?" His tone reeked of skepticism.

"Well, at least I might have formed my own scheme to get away." A scheme that didn't involve staying, unchaperoned and vulnerable, in a small cottage with the Duke of Lyle.

He frowned with impatience. "There wasn't time for argument. Even now, they hunt you."

She blinked. The notion that someone wanted to kill her was simply too fantastical. She should have hysterics or cower under the covers and refuse to come out. Of course, her pride wouldn't allow her to do either, even if she were so inclined, but still . . .

Mentally, she shored up her defenses. The idea that she might be in danger wasn't new. She'd prepared for this eventuality, hadn't she? She'd sent the first chapter of her memoirs to her solicitor with instructions to publish it if anything happened to her. But still, a sense of unreality pervaded her, perhaps the only thing that stopped fear incapacitating her reason.

She licked her lips. "Can you get a message to these government people?"

His entire body tensed with alertness, like a pointer on the scent. "I expect I could."

"Then tell them I have given the first chapter of my memoirs to someone for safekeeping. Someone I trust. His instructions are to make them public if anything happens to Stephen or to me."

Something flickered in his eyes. He hesitated, then said, "I'll tell them, yes."

Lyle took her hand, an electric touch. Startled, she tried to tug free. His smile held a trace of bitterness as he released her fingers.

"Try not to worry. You have no reason to trust me, it's true, but I'll ask you to do so, all the same. I am . . . experienced in these matters, and I've pledged myself to protect you." Lyle rose to go. "Sleep now, but we cannot delay too long. Tomorrow morning, if you're fit, we'll leave."

He paused. "It would be best if you don't complicate matters by trying to escape. Flinging yourself from the frying pan into the fire will not be helpful, and I should certainly resent any more time spent looking for you." He leaned forward. "Just as I would certainly resent any more injury to your person."

She refused to meet his eye. His effect on her was far too compelling for her peace of mind. Why did she almost think she'd rather take her chance with those government assassins than brave Lyle's plans for her?

She called after him as he reached the doorway. "How do I know this isn't an elaborate ruse to stop me seeing Sidmouth? How do I know I can trust you?"

Lyle turned back. "That's not the question you should ask, my lady. The question is, can you afford *not* to trust me?"

SUKEY had always thought it must be enormously romantic to be abducted, just like a heroine in those novels her ladyship liked so much. And Mr. Perry was exactly as she had imagined her own hero—tall and fair, with the pure, stern face of an angel.

But after the initial excitement of being plucked from the carriage, thrown over his shoulder, and carried off—she could be an actress on the stage, the way she'd pretended to scream and fight and kick—Mr. Perry had left her in this smelly old barn.

She drew a breath and it rattled in her chest. Her throat thickened. She hadn't experienced this tight, scratchy feeling since she was a child.

If only Mr. Perry would come back! She'd wanted to wait for him outside, but he'd ordered her not to show herself.

What kept him? He'd promised to drive her back to

London. She was to stay with her sister's family until Lady Kate returned safe and sound.

Sukey's eyes itched and watered. This dratted barn! Soon, her cheeks would stream with tears and her nose would be red. A fair sight for her Mr. Perry to clap eyes on.

Something that sounded like a carriage rumbled to a stop outside. It must be him!

Quickly, she primped her hair, letting its flaxen waves fall, unbound, and lay back on the hay, arranging herself in a romantic pose for her hero's return.

A heavy tread grew closer. Sukey gazed upwards, studying the chinks of sunlight in the broken roof slats, trying to control her breathing, trying not to inhale the scent of cow dung and hay.

The footsteps stopped. Out of the corner of her eye, she glimpsed him, a tall silhouette by the door. Watching her.

An almost panicked thrill ran through her at the thought. But before she could call to him, her physical discomforts overtook her. Her throat closed over, so she had to drag in every breath. And each one of those breaths seemed to stretch her lungs close to breaking point.

"Help!" she gasped, sitting up, clawing at the strings of the light cloak she wore. Her chest felt so tight. If she just loosened the ties a little . . . but that didn't work.

"Help me, please!"

The figure didn't move. Who was it? It couldn't be Mr. Perry. He was her hero. He would come to her aid.

She turned her head to look at him fully and blinked in hurt surprise. "Mr. Perry," she forced out. "*Help* me!"

But he simply watched her struggle for breath.

BY dusk, Max couldn't stand it anymore. He needed to get out.

"I'm going to scout around. Make sure no one's watching."

He tossed the words to George over his shoulder as he mounted his horse.

"Oh, and next ye'll be telling me how to clean the tack and all," muttered George.

Max sighed. "Don't be daft, man. I need to get away for a bit. Look after her for me."

A knowing gleam stole into George's eyes. "Aye, she's trouble, that one. Knew it as soon as I clapped me oglers on her." He clutched the gelding's bridle. "Take my advice and swive her tonight, guv. Get it out of your system, like."

Max had been thinking on much the same lines, but that didn't make George's comments acceptable. "Save your impudence for someone who appreciates it, George. Stand aside."

George grinned and released the bridle.

Once he came to open ground, Max urged Thunder into a gallop, savoring the feel of riding prime horseflesh, something that had been a rarity in the lean years after his father's death. His one personal extravagance since he'd inherited the dukedom had been buying this hunter. He'd cost all of five hundred guineas and it was money well spent.

As the twilight faded, he slowed his mount and picked his way more cautiously. He'd intended to work off some of his frustration, but the ride had exacerbated, rather than dulled his mood.

God, he wanted her. Even in the midst of planning for her protection and securing an amnesty from the government, he wanted Lady Kate with a gripping intensity he'd never known before.

Refraining from taking her when she lay on that bed so pliant and receptive to his touch had taxed his powers of restraint to the extreme. He had to keep wrenching his mind into focus, bringing it back to the very real problem of keeping Lady Kate from trying to escape. And making sure her brother stayed in jail.

Quite simply, she fascinated him. He'd never met an

aristocratic lady with quite that combination of intelligence and daring. Physical courage, too.

Jumping from that carriage must have required backbone, foolhardy though the attempt was. But then, perhaps not so very foolhardy. She hadn't known who kidnapped her, after all. She must have been desperate.

He'd expected that once he told her of the threat against her life she'd instantly become more malleable. He'd have no further trouble with her once she knew the danger she was in.

And he prided himself on being a good judge of character!

Despite a situation that would throw most females into fainting fits, she'd coolly told him she'd already considered and dealt with the likely consequences of her plans to blackmail the government.

While his mind applauded her cleverness, in reality, the maneuver had only increased the danger. With that tactic, she'd progressed from distressed female ready to do anything to save her brother to professional blackmailer—a woman who knew exactly what she was about. A troublemaker who might not confine her activities to this one occasion. Someone who needed to be eliminated.

Jardine had lost no time in appropriating the opening chapter of her memoirs that she'd so cunningly sent to her solicitor for safekeeping. She would be very fortunate if Jardine decided to keep the information to himself.

Max snorted. He should have known as soon as he met her this assignment wouldn't be easy.

EXHAUSTED by her painful efforts, Kate sank into her pillows, panting. Running away was out of the question. Her ankle wasn't sprained, but she could barely walk. Added to that, she didn't know where she was and she had neither money nor transport. If someone really wanted to kill her, she suspected she was better off with the duke than on her own. He might try to seduce her when she recovered, but his restraint that morning showed he was not entirely without scruples.

Kate put plans for escape out of her mind for the moment, but she couldn't stop thinking about Stephen. Without her to campaign for his release, how would he win free?

Her brother was a grown man and two years older than she. As far as worldly knowledge went, however, he was like a babe in the woods.

Lyle said all Stephen had to do was tell the Home Office the whereabouts of a handful of criminals and all would be forgiven. That quiet, stubborn refusal was typical of Stephen. He had a rather tiresome sense of righteousness that would never be swayed by self-interest or greed.

*Oh, Stephen! Why did you have to get mixed up in this?*

And why did she still feel responsible for him, after all these years?

A door slammed. The sounds of Lyle moving about the adjoining room caught her attention.

It was Lyle's estate, his house that had been burned by those rebels. Not only that, but he was a duke, a powerful man. Perhaps he could have Stephen released. Perhaps she might work on him, even as he sought to manipulate her into helping him change her brother's mind.

But how?

A dart of apprehension shot through her, but she shook her head. No. Not *that* way. A woman never really won if the victory meant compromising her virtue, she was sure.

But she was very good at charming people, at making men feel comfortable with her. Perhaps the duke might be persuaded . . .

PERRY could have left her there. She'd lain among the straw, bright pink in the face, sides heaving, like a sow delivering a litter of piglets.

But he had orders from Lyle, so he lifted her and carried her into the fresh air outside.

He pulled out a flask—an exact replica of the one Lyle had given him to drink from the previous evening—and raised it to her lips.

The maid choked and wheezed. Her nose ran. What an appalling sight! But soon, her breathing slowed and quieted. She took out a handkerchief and dabbed at her nose, gazing up at him with puffy, worshipful eyes.

"Come on," he said. "I'll take you home."

THE next morning, Kate paused in the doorway, watching Lyle. The duke sat at the only table in the cottage with a handsome traveling desk open before him. He might have dispensed with a change of raiment, but he'd carried writing implements on this rescue mission. Interesting.

His dark head was bent over a letter he was composing. He didn't look up, though a flicker of his eyelids indicated perhaps he sensed her presence, the way she always sensed when he was near. He wrote without falter or pause for thought.

She couldn't see what he wrote, but she could tell from the decisive movement of his hand across the page that the script would be strong and bold. Like the rest of him.

Only when he'd signed the document, folded it, and chosen a wafer to seal it, did he look up.

He rose at once and bowed, letting his gaze run over her. "You seem more like yourself this morning."

Careful of her sore ankle, she dipped a curtsey, still aware of the letter that remained unsealed on the table. She burned to know what was in it, but of course she was too well bred to ask.

Good breeding had become excessively inconvenient of late.

He made no attempt to enlighten her, slipping the letter,

unsealed, back into his traveling desk and setting the desk on a spare chair.

"Would you care to take some breakfast before we go? I sent my man to the village for a basket. And there is coffee, too."

His manner was perfectly polite, but strain tightened the lines bracketing his mouth and darkened his eyes.

Had he slept last night? Where had he slept? There was only one bed in the cottage, and she certainly would have known if he'd lain down beside her.

He indicated the coffeepot. "Will you pour?"

"Of course." She sat opposite him at the small wooden table and wished for the soothing warmth of tea, rather than the pungent, thick coffee that poured sluggishly into the tin mugs he provided. It looked like mud. She didn't know if she could bring herself to drink it.

However, she opened the basket and found slender bread rolls, strawberry jam, and a pat of pale, creamy butter.

"Nothing like the scent of fresh bread, is there?" she said, hoping he would not see through her chatty tone to the breathless anticipation beneath.

It was like walking a knife's edge. Danger to the left and right, and a niggling suspicion that the worst danger of all lay squarely on the path she now trod. She only knew what Lyle told her, after all.

He hadn't harmed her yet. On the other hand, the Home Office's rather final solution to her threats bore the ring of truth.

Should she believe him when he said she was in danger? What had Lyle to gain from kidnapping her, after all? He couldn't be so uncertain of his talents as to think he needed to steal her away to seduce her. She'd shown herself shamefully willing on the night of the ball.

An unpleasant fluttering in her stomach made her take a sharp breath. At least she would not be so foolish as to succumb to him again.

She glanced up briefly from her bread and butter and saw him watching her with that curious cold fire in his eyes. It was a struggle to smile at him and appear unconcerned, as if that heated encounter after the ball hadn't occurred.

Lowering her gaze, she took a swift sip of coffee. She gulped and fought the urge to choke. The hot slurry burned its way down her throat; she felt its heat all the way to her uneasy stomach.

"Is the coffee to your taste, Lady Kate?"

Her eyes watered with the effort of suppressing a cough, but she managed it. "Oh, yes. Very, er . . . pleasant."

Kate was renowned for never losing her aplomb, even in the most fraught situations. For some reason, it had become a point of honor with her to remain in complete control of herself when the duke was near.

Defiantly, she took another painful sip of the brew.

"You like George's coffee?" He lifted his mug to scrutinize its contents. "How extraordinary. I find it almost undrinkable, but unfortunately I've had to make do with his services on this journey. The man's culinary skill scarcely compares with his discretion, but the latter is far more valuable to us at present."

Kate cleared her throat. "Where are you taking me?"

"To a hunting box in the shires. An almost forgotten part of my holdings. My great-grandfather was never fond of hunting, so he leased the house each season. This time, it will be leased to us, a Mr. and Mrs. John Wetherby."

Husband and wife? She ought to have known he would try a trick like that. "Why not say we are brother and sister?" she said evenly. "It would make more sense."

A gleam in his eye told her not to push the matter any further. Swiftly, she changed the subject. "You don't look at all like plain Mr. Wetherby."

An inscrutable expression came over his face. "And yet, a bare fortnight ago I was plain Mr. Brooke."

She gave a wry smile. "Somehow, I doubt anyone would describe you as plain, whether you were a commoner or a duke."

There was an arrested look in his eyes. He glanced away. "It hardly matters. At this season, we're unlikely to be troubled with neighbors."

He smiled, returning his gaze to hers. "In fact, we will be quite alone."

# Seven

*His kiss is warm velvet and sliding ecstasy.*
*And the world falls away . . .*

LOUISA Brooke pressed her palms to her heated cheeks. Even the night air that wafted through the open window didn't cool them.

How could a lady write such . . . *intimate* thoughts, even in the privacy of her journal? And why did they make her, Louisa, feel so breathless and jittery and warm? As if *she* were the one experiencing this dark lover's touch.

Louisa knew what her symptoms meant, of course. She was not as naive as a spinster lady ought to be. Not only that, it seemed she was far too vulnerable for one who'd spent her adult life shoring up her defenses.

This journal represented danger. It explored an erotic realm forbidden to unmarried ladies like her. Perhaps it was right and proper that realm was denied to innocent spinsters. Better to remain ignorant than to burn with longings destined to remain unfulfilled.

But for this well-born, unmarried lady there was no escape from that confronting text. She had a duty to perform.

She couldn't turn away from the ardent words that wove sinuously, like tendrils of a vine around her mind. Clinging, twisting, gripping until she thought of little else but that small volume and the wealth of passion it contained.

Heat flared through her body as she recalled a particularly evocative passage. Max had said she might find the journal's contents shocking. Did he know the author of this work? And why did he want it translated? What did one woman's sexual odyssey have to do with national security?

She shouldn't think about it. She should simply do as he asked: translate the journal and return it to him as quickly as possible. Perhaps, if she tried very hard, she might make her mind translate automatically, without consciously considering the information at all.

Louisa smoothed her trembling hands on the skirts of her muslin gown. She picked up her pen and dipped it in ink. She bent her gaze to the page and tried to fortify her mind against this strange sensual offensive.

But the shadowy figure of this lady's lover loomed large. The act of translation, expressing those thoughts and feelings in her own words, using the pronouns "I" and "my," seemed to intensify her reaction to the text.

*Boldly, I ran my palm along his flank and covered his male parts while he slept. He did not sleep much longer . . .*

Louisa gasped and her pen sputtered ink over the page. She reached for a blotter and pressed it down to remove the excess ink.

How could she write such a thing? She'd never be able to look her brother in the eye again.

She pushed away from the table, repressing a wild urge to scream. It was too much! He couldn't expect this of her. Surely, if Max knew what the journal contained he'd never have asked her to translate it.

The blatant eroticism of the text was one thing, but beneath it ran familiar undercurrents of frustration and longing.

And loneliness. God, yes, the loneliness was so sharp she

could taste it. She'd experienced those emotions too many times on her own account to wish to relive them through someone else.

She rose and paced restlessly to the window, kneading her nape with her ink-stained fingers, digging without mercy into the knotted tendons beneath straggling wisps of blond hair. The pressure and pain came as welcome relief. She'd sat too long at her task.

Far longer than she should have. She ought to get word to Max that she could do no more. When he discovered the nature of the journal he would understand, surely. He would take the journal away, to someone else who could read and write Italian, most probably a man . . .

No, she couldn't allow that. Strangely, she felt a kinship, a loyalty even, to this unknown authoress. The possibility that this lady's secret life might become fodder for an insensitive man's amusement appalled her. The thought propelled her back to the table again.

She touched the small book, softly running her fingertips over the page.

Someone had written this. A lady, much like Louisa. So like Louisa, in fact, that it might have been her own words she translated. Those experiences became hers; she *became* the woman in those pages.

And the dark lover took on a face she knew too well.

"My dear Louisa. All alone?"

The unwelcome voice jerked her out of her thoughts. She turned swiftly, and an even more unwelcome figure stood there in all his dark-edged masculine glory.

Smiling at her, rot him. Lord Jardine had the most devilishly attractive smile. Thank God it no longer affected her the way it had when she was a naive seventeen.

*Too late now,* a voice inside her whispered. *You are lost.*

Louisa forced her tongue to work. She managed to say in her usual, calm way, "The family is from home this evening. But I'm sure the butler told you that at the door."

He inclined his head. "Astute of you. Yes, I believe he mentioned some such, but I wasn't attending. The mere sound of your name obliterates all else from my mind. But why so pale, m'dear? Surely, you expected me."

He paused, then said softly, "Aren't you going to ask me to sit down?"

"No," she said. "If I'd known you were here, I would have refused to receive you. I suppose you bribed your way in."

"Greased old Finch's palm with a couple of yellow boys," he agreed. Then he frowned, those quick, dark eyes searching her face. "Why are you hiding from me? I've looked for you all week since I heard you were in town."

Her control almost slipped her grasp. "You are scarcely of such significance to me that I would put myself to the trouble of avoiding you."

He gave a crack of disbelieving laughter. "My love, you will have to do better than that."

She scowled. "I've been unwell, if you must know. In fact, it's very likely an infectious complaint, so you'd best leave me before you catch it."

His brows snapped together. He strode forward and took her chin in his hand. Slowly, Jardine turned her face to the light with a deft, delicate touch as if he were an expert examining fine porcelain.

She tried not to flinch.

"But no," he murmured. "You're not pale at all. You are flushed, in fact." His frown deepened. "If you have a fever, why aren't you in bed? Why isn't someone attending you?"

A fever? She almost choked. That described her condition precisely. She stared into his face, with its angular lines and dark velvet eyes. The spoiled, rich, beautiful mouth that begged to be . . . *kissed.*

It took every ounce of her will to resist the standing invitation of that mouth. She batted his hand away and stepped back. "Your concern is touching but unnecessary, my lord. I am well enough, as you see. Why are you here?"

He stared at her, quite as if he guessed the reason for her reddened cheeks. Slowly, he smiled. "Do you know, I have quite forgotten?"

She couldn't stop her hand from reaching up to fidget with the fichu that shrouded her bosom. He watched her nervous gesture, then turned away with a quirk to his lips.

The second his eye alighted on her work was a second too late. Her heart leaped to her throat, beating madly. She'd forgotten to cover the journal. And worse, the translation, written in her own hand, lay there for anyone to see.

Curse the man! His mere presence scrambled her wits.

Wildly, Louisa searched for some form of distraction. She could only think of one thing.

Despising herself, she put the back of her hand to her forehead and swayed.

"Oh! Oh, help me! I—I think I'm going to faint."

"AND how do you like Derbyshire, sir? I hear it is excellent country for raising sheep."

Kate had managed to keep up a polite, prosaic flow of conversation for most of the journey to the hunting box. Lyle indulged her, as a parent might indulge the hopeful chatter of a child striving to postpone bedtime.

An apt analogy! Bedtime with the duke was something she, too, was determined to avoid.

His lips twitched. "I confess, I hadn't thought about it. I inherited Lyle Castle less than a fortnight ago, you know."

He stretched one long, booted leg before him, and she couldn't help noticing the flex in his thigh muscle, so close to hers. He had the thick, powerful thighs of a sportsman.

Thighs she should not think about at all.

Kate tore her gaze away, hoping he hadn't noticed her scrutiny. This carriage was far too small. How had she never noticed the lack of room inside these vehicles before?

The duke seemed to take up every spare inch of space. She was obliged to sit up very straight, keep her knees rigidly together, hand clenching the strap to avoid brushing any part of him with any part of her as the badly sprung carriage lurched and swayed on its way.

The strain of keeping so rigidly upright made her limbs burn. After a while, her body began to tremble. Eventually, she lost feeling in her left foot, but she allowed nothing of her physical discomfort to show in her demeanor. Then he would win this round. He'd won far too much from her already.

Though she carefully avoided physical contact with the duke, she felt his heat. She could smell him—the masculine scent of horses and leather unadulterated by the expensive pomade or scent that most gentlemen of her acquaintance used. Of course, he didn't have his kit with him to freshen whatever cologne he might wear ordinarily. He'd sent all of it ahead to the hunting box.

She thought of her own luggage strapped to the roof of the carriage. At least she had a change of clothes—several of them, though perhaps they might be too formal for life in exile. It was fortunate she didn't have to make do with what she stood up in. She was covered in mud and grass stains from head to toe.

Oh, confound it! Her unwise actions had put her in danger—she accepted that. But why did her rescuer have to be Lyle?

"I can't make out where we are," she said, peering through the travel-grimed window at the scenery. Deep green fields bordered by lush hedgerows undulated down to scattered wooded copses, then swelled to gentle hills in the distance. A cottage dotted the landscape here and there. She didn't recognize the country or any of the landmarks that might identify it. She didn't think she'd been here before.

They'd stopped at an inn, but the duke hadn't allowed her to alight for more than the time it took to use the necessary.

He hadn't granted her the opportunity to ask where she was or even deduce her whereabouts from her surroundings.

"We're in Leicestershire. It's probably best you don't know exactly where," said the duke indifferently.

How she wanted to hit him! She turned her head to look at his straight-nosed profile. "Best for whom?"

"For me, of course. Your ignorance will hinder you if you try again to escape."

"There's plain speaking! I mean to wait until my ankle heals before I attempt another mad dash for freedom. So for the moment, we may both rest easy."

A gleam stole into his eyes. "Somehow, I doubt I shall *rest easy* tonight."

"Oh?" She raised her brows, pretending innocence. "I would have thought you'd be fatigued from the journey. I know I shall sleep like the dead."

Before she knew what he was about, he took her chin in hand, tilting her face to the light. "Almost, I am convinced," he said. "And yet, you've behaved like a cat on hot bricks since we left the cottage." He smiled. "Tell me—" He smoothed a stray curl behind her ear. "Do you think I'm going to ravish you in a moving vehicle?"

Most of the air left her lungs. She forced out, "On past experience, I should say it's very likely." Her skin tingled where his fingers brushed it. Why wasn't he wearing gloves?

"But so uncomfortable," he replied, withdrawing his hand with a faint smile at the reaction she hadn't been able to hide. "Unnecessary, too, when all the delights of a soft bed and a cozy fire await us. Perhaps even some decent coffee. A hot bath . . ."

She shivered. The prosaic setting for seduction he painted was far more enticing than a promise of silk sheets and fine wine.

Mr. and Mrs. Wetherby. Oh, yes, he knew what he was about.

The duke's character couldn't be further from that of

the considerate lover who pleasured her so sweetly between the pages of her journal. What Lyle wanted, he took. Would he even care how much pleasure he gave?

No. She would *not* speculate about how adept a lover Lyle might be. She'd no ambition to become his mistress.

"I beg your pardon?" The duke's deep voice interrupted her thoughts.

She blinked. "Nothing. I didn't say anything."

"On the contrary. You snorted."

"Snorted? I? I would never do anything so vulgar."

His lips twitched. "No? Oh, my mistake. Perhaps it was merely a sniff, then."

With dignity, she acknowledged, "It might have been a sniff. I could very well have sniffed. In a purely disdainful manner, you understand."

"And what, may I ask, has merited such disdain on your part?" Lyle seemed to enjoy idle conversations.

She smiled sweetly. "I was thinking about men and their overweening conceit. One man in particular."

The duke's lips twitched. "Anyone I know?"

She took a deep breath and blew it out. Ordinarily, she could spar with the best of them, but the duke unsettled her, kept her perpetually off balance. She risked saying something that might give him a clue to how she felt.

She needed to change the subject. "How long will you keep me in that place?"

"At my hunting box? Until one of two things happen. Either you convince me you will not publish your diary or your memoirs—a difficult thing to do because I'm not easy to convince and I never trust anyone's word—or until your brother tells the authorities where to find those rebels. You will never be safe until we can convince the authorities you are no longer a threat." His gaze dropped to her lips. "And I can't immediately think of any other eventuality that would induce me to release you."

"So you are prepared to commit some considerable time

to this venture, then," Kate said in a constricted voice, aware that he watched her mouth with intense concentration she found quite unnerving. "I might warn you, Lyle, that one thing—perhaps the only thing—my brother and I have in common is that we are both excessively stubborn."

The duke smiled, his head drifting closer. "Ah, but then neither of you have experienced my unique powers of persuasion. Shall I give you a taste? Yes, I think I shall . . ."

She braced for an assault on her lips, but his mouth bypassed hers, to settle in that vulnerable place on her neck. All power of speech melted away. In a heated reminder of his promise that night of the ball, the promise to bite, he let his teeth graze her skin, ever so gently. Just once. Then his lips turned soft, tantalizing, as they drifted over her throat, trailing heat in his wake.

Beyond words, Kate tried to keep still, tried not to react, though she longed to fling back her head to allow him better access. She didn't want to be bitten—her dark lover had never attempted such a thing—but somehow, the wordless threat of that bite seemed to heighten her pleasure.

She almost wished he would . . .

"No. Stop!" she whispered. But he already had.

He smiled and sat back and the carriage rolled on.

"*THIS* is the hunting box?" Kate stared out the carriage window. She'd never been to Melton country before, but she couldn't believe many hunting boxes were as grand as this.

The Jacobean house was substantially larger than the pied-à-terre she'd imagined, though certainly not as large as the country estate where she'd been raised. Still, the warm redbrick contrived to make it appear cozy and the park in which it stood was immaculately kept.

Kate let relief overwhelm her jittery reaction to the duke. She wasn't certain whether this house was a haven or a prison, but at least the neat exterior augured well for what lay inside.

A comfortable bed and clean sheets beckoned. Not to mention a hot meal. Sukey always told her it was indecent for such a slight woman to have such a healthy appetite. Certainly, her hunger had assumed indecent proportions since she'd been confined in a carriage with the duke all day.

But first, a long, hot bath. After the tumble out of that carriage and her long ride inside it today, she ached everywhere, though at least her ankle seemed to have mended.

She glanced at the duke as he joined her. She wouldn't mention her discomfort to him, or he might suggest quite another way of tending to her hurts.

The memory of his skilled, gentle touch when she'd suffered the headache the day before made her insides melt in reminiscence.

But she couldn't afford to let him get that close to her here. She no longer had the excuse of indisposition to save her from seduction. And her resolution was not as strong as she would have liked.

"A tidy little place, isn't it?" Lyle nodded, preparing to alight. "I've never stayed here, but anyone who hunts knows it well."

He turned to hand her out of the carriage, and even that prosaic act nearly brought a flush to her cheeks. She needed to take hold of herself.

"Mrs. Wetherby, welcome to Quenton Hall," he said softly, for her ears alone.

He slid an arm around her waist, gazing down at her with open adoration. What a magnificent actor. If she hadn't known him better, she might have wilted on the spot.

But the pointed reminder of her new identity left her in no doubt that this sudden burst of tenderness was feigned. Well, she could act a part, too.

She resisted the urge to kick him in the shins. They were supposed to be man and wife, but that didn't mean he had to be so provokingly demonstrative. He was behaving more like a lover with his mistress than a gentleman with his wife.

But what was sauce for the goose . . .

Instead of pulling away, Kate sent the duke a melting look under her lashes, her lips curved into a sultry smile. Just because she'd been celibate all these years didn't mean she'd forgotten how to make a man turn a little hot under the collar.

His false smile faded and his arm tightened around her. He swung her to face him, his head bending to hers as if for a kiss.

So much for taking him at a disadvantage! He didn't seem to notice the servants who had come out to bid them welcome.

She managed the breath of a laugh. "You forget yourself, sir! You will shock these good people." She glanced meaningfully towards the retainers who awaited them.

He stopped, but the gray eyes retained their heat. She stood there, heart pounding, her mind an inconvenient blank. He held her gaze, and it was moments before he turned his head. Seeing the servants, he slackened his hold, and she slipped from him, hurrying across the drive to the front steps.

A middle-aged man and woman, both smiling calmly, waited for them at the door. They showed none of the trepidation one might have expected when meeting a new master—a ducal one at that—but then Kate remembered: They were not Lady Kate and the Duke of Lyle here. They were Mr. and Mrs. Wetherby.

She jerked out of her thoughts when she caught the word "honeymoon" pass Lyle's lips. He'd caught her arm through his once more and now he pressed her closer to his side.

She held on to her smile, though she longed to yank her arm free. Would she have to pretend to be in love with the duke the entire time she was incarcerated here? Couldn't she simply have married him for his money?

He seemed to have no trouble with the charade. As the butler and housekeeper showed them to an oak-paneled hall, Lyle kissed her hand with easy grace, as if it were the most natural thing in the world. "My love, you must be fatigued from the drive. Go upstairs. I'll be with you shortly."

His gray eyes held menace mixed with sensual promise, and she didn't know which frightened her more. Kate repressed a shiver and turned to follow the housekeeper to her quarters.

# Eight

*He loves me with unrelenting gentleness. Sweet, tender pleasure, murmured endearments. Such wonders of heat and touch.*

FINISHED. Louisa dusted sand over the final page of her translation and shook it off, blowing the excess grains away.

She closed her eyes and took a deep, shuddering breath. *Thank God!*

Incredible that a mere book could affect her so profoundly. She'd be glad to see it leave her hands.

Yet some wicked, rebellious part of her would mourn its loss.

She drew Max's letter out of the secret compartment of her desk and read the significant passage. "I shall visit our cousins at Hove next week. Give the package into Romney's keeping until then."

Romney and Fanny planned to leave London for the country in the next couple of days, citing Fanny's imminent confinement.

Louisa smiled and shook her head. Romney was, indeed, a changed man if he'd agreed to leave the pleasure haunts of London at the height of the Season for rural domesticity and the squalling of a newborn babe.

Romney. Her cousin had about as much sensibility as an elephant. She couldn't bear him to read the journal. Supposing he *could* read, which was a thing she'd always doubted.

No, she would not give the journal to her cousin, as Max directed. She'd keep the journal and the translation with her. She would accompany Fanny and Romney home and hand the documents to Max herself.

A stay in the country would be good for her. It would get her away from *him*.

Louisa frowned, banishing the thought immediately. She'd stopped running from Jardine years ago. He would always find her. The man was a natural predator. And she'd learned, to her cost, that the hunt only excited him more.

Strangely, he hadn't lingered on the night of his most recent visit. As soon as he'd rung for her maid and given the poor woman a bitingly sarcastic lecture for not taking better care of her mistress, he'd left the house. As far as she knew, his gaze hadn't turned in the direction of her desk and the sensitive material on it again.

She couldn't tell whether Jardine had read the translation. Uneasily, she wondered if he was fluent in Italian. She didn't think he'd ever mentioned it, but one could never tell what talents Jardine hid up his sleeve. He might well have read and understood the original diary.

And if he had . . .

She didn't know which might be worse—that in one swift glance he'd assimilated the truth of the situation, or that he might think *she* was the author of those passionate chronicles.

At times, she told herself he couldn't have seen enough to draw any conclusion, but she knew his quickness, his finely honed instincts. She couldn't make herself believe it.

Carefully, Louisa stacked the pages of her translation.

She tied them in a sheaf and locked them in her desk with a key she kept on a small chatelaine at her waist.

She ought to tell Max what had happened. It might be important. But Max would kill her if he found out she'd had anything to do with Jardine.

No, she decided. She'd avoid reviving that old animosity at all costs. It might end with one of the stupid oafs killing the other, and she couldn't bear that. As long as no one knew the truth, she could hold on to her calm existence and to her self-respect.

She wouldn't wait for Jardine to make the next move. She'd leave quietly, beg a seat in Fanny's carriage rather than taking her own.

God willing, by the time Jardine knew she'd left, she'd be rid of the troublesome diary and the translation as well.

FOR a mad instant, Max had believed the part he played. He'd believed she was his wife. A deep, savage, possessiveness had overwhelmed him. He'd wanted her too badly to wait.

Then reality surfaced. The spell broke and he focused once more on the job at hand. Lady Kate was a job, delightful and intriguing though she might be.

He'd never failed in a mission and he wouldn't start now. But he could have his cake and eat it, too. As long as he shut out any foolish tenderness he might feel for Lady Kate, he could get the job done. And enjoy himself while he did it.

He'd sent his own form of blackmail to the lady's brother. If he didn't care about his own freedom, Stephen Holt would certainly care about his sister's.

But despite Max's anxiety to resolve this case, he hoped Stephen Holt wouldn't succumb straightaway. A few days with his counterfeit wife in this sylvan setting would be no hardship.

He jogged up the stairs and strode along the corridor to

the bedchamber the butler had assigned to Lady Kate. Knowing he couldn't push matters too far all at once, Max had requested separate bedchambers.

Bedchambers separated by a connecting door.

He paused with his hand on the doorknob and briefly fantasized about what he might find if he were a very lucky man. Lady Kate, reclining on a day bed in dishabille, or better yet, gloriously nude, standing by the window with the sunlight glinting gold in her hair.

He knocked and entered without waiting for her permission, as was a husband's right. Lady Kate was standing at the window—fully dressed, devil take it—and clearly wanting him gone. Of course. He'd warned her he'd be up shortly, hadn't he?

He took off his gloves and laid them on an occasional table, very much at home. "I was serious about resting. You must be tired after all you've been through."

Her gaze flickered to his gloves and back to him. "If we are to share this room I shall sleep on the floor."

He smiled. "Oh, you needn't do that. Mr. and Mrs. Wetherby are a sophisticated couple. My bedchamber is next door."

The relief that swamped her face told him she hadn't yet discovered the discreet panel that connected the two chambers.

She wouldn't remain ignorant for long.

"I've given orders for a bath to be drawn for you," he said. "One of the manifold comforts of this house is that it boasts a separate bathroom."

He let his gaze drift over her body, knowing it was a liberty, an insolence he wouldn't ordinarily offer to a lady. "Would you like me to help you undress?"

The mention of the bath made her eyes fill with longing, but wariness swiftly succeeded it. She half turned away. "I am sure one of the maids will do that."

She placed her palm on the table beside her as if to

steady herself. "You will grant me privacy, Lyle. Give me your word."

He raised his brows. "But of course. If that is your wish." He infused his tone with doubt and had the satisfaction of seeing that familiar blush stain her cheeks and the fair skin of her throat.

She still looked uncertain, as if she didn't trust him, yet good breeding prevented her doubting him openly.

He paused, clasping his hands behind his back and looking thoughtful. "It might be difficult to keep my word, however."

Her gaze flew to his. "You wouldn't!"

He continued to look thoughtful, ignoring her nervous interjection. "I am here to protect you. What if the house catches fire? What if government agents break in and kidnap you, or worse? No, on second thought, I cannot give you my word to stay away from your bath. In fact, the more I think about it, the more I'm persuaded it's my duty to stay with you."

She looked as horrified as a virgin on her wedding night. "No!"

"I'd turn my back, of course," he went on, playing with her. "And believe me, that would tax my powers far more than yours."

Her nostrils flared. She took a step towards him, hazel eyes shooting sparks. She looked like she might actually strike. Now, that would be interesting.

A lady to the last, she clenched her hands into fists and controlled her impulse. "If you refuse me privacy, I won't bathe at all."

"Cutting off your nose to spite your face, aren't you? I'd be ready to wager you're longing for a bathe after that tumble you took. So soothing, the hot water sliding over your skin . . ."

Her freezing gaze made him want to strip her and haul her over his shoulder to the bath. The hot water would soon warm her. And if that didn't work, he could certainly assist the process.

Between rigid lips, she said, "I can make do with the wash stand. Now, go away!"

The tiniest break in her voice caught him by surprise. A pang of remorse struck him. Of course, this had been a game to him, and a delightful one, but she was a woman and completely in his power. She'd had a difficult time. Reluctantly, he acknowledged it was unfair to taunt her.

He held up his hands in a conciliatory gesture. "Very well. I give you my word I shan't enter the bathroom with you in it. Even if flaming rafters fall around my ears, I shall leave you to burn before I break my vow. Satisfied?"

She watched him for a moment, her eyes still wide. Then she nodded.

"I'll leave you to bathe, then." At the door, he turned back with a smile. "And I won't even imagine what you look like while you do it."

He closed the door on her outraged gasp.

*BLISS.*

Kate lowered herself into the bathtub and breathed a long sigh of relief. The water cushioned, soothed, and warmed her body. Her many aches and pains after that ill-advised leap from the carriage had plagued her throughout the morning's drive, though she'd done her best to conceal her discomfort.

Typical Lyle. He'd noticed and offered her an inducement she couldn't refuse. When she got out, she'd think about how to get back to London. Right now, she'd simply sink into peace.

She smiled at the maid who attended her, a quiet girl, far more efficient than Sukey. "You may go. I'll call when I require assistance."

Kate slid down further, watching the linen shift she wore lift and balloon with water. Ordinarily, she wouldn't choose to wear a shift while bathing, but she didn't quite trust Lyle to stay away.

She sighed. Never mind that now. The duke's image receded as she abandoned herself to sensual pleasure of an innocent kind.

The bathroom was small and cozy, with a thick, patterned carpet on the floor and a bright fire in the hearth. She could stay there for hours and not get cold.

Such luxury! She'd see about installing a room like this at home. Now there was piped water to be had in London, separate bathrooms were the rage in wealthy households.

She laid her head back and contemplated the calico curtain surrounding her. An ingenious invention, designed to ward off stray drafts. Lavender-scented steam rose and furled upwards, funneling through the small opening at the top of the tentlike structure, to curl around the moldings in the plaster ceiling.

She parted the curtain a little way with a languid hand. On a small table beside the bath stood a glass vial of oil—presumably the lavender scent that seemed to exercise such a calming effect on her senses—a scrubbing brush, a small cake of soap, and a flannel.

Kate took the soap and ran it idly up her arm, watching the bubble-edged lather trail along her skin. On her shoulder, a purple-and-red bruise bloomed around the strap of her shift.

After all the worry of the past few days—over Stephen, the kidnapping, the sick anticipation of Lyle's next move in this seductive game they played—a drugging weariness spread through her limbs. She would think about how to escape the duke tomorrow. First, she needed to recruit her strength for what might lie ahead.

Ah! She was exhausted. She could almost . . . fall . . .

Even as her eyelids drifted shut, Kate sensed someone's presence. She opened her eyes a crack, dreamily expecting the intruder to be the maid with a can of hot water.

But the shadow rippling across the calico curtain was too large to be a maid.

MAX smiled to himself. He'd pushed his luck a little too far in Lady Kate's bedchamber, perhaps. If he made any more jokes about guarding her from harm, she might soon realize that she wasn't in danger at all.

He stood at a window and gazed out at the rolling green countryside, now hazed with a light fall of rain. He'd know what to do with this place once this business was over. He enjoyed hunting—the physicality, the exhilaration of it. The thrill of the chase. Ah, yes. Hunting, spying, and women—all pursuits he'd enjoyed at one time or another.

Would he know what to do with himself when it was all over? Well, he would have the estate to occupy him and all of the other holdings he'd inherited according to the entail. That was a challenging enough responsibility for any man. The Duke of Lyle had fingers in many pies, from coal mines in Wales to this gem in the heart of Melton country.

How long would he keep Lady Kate here? An interesting question. He'd dispatched his ransom note to the Reverend Holt with Perry on the boy's return from delivering Lady Kate's maid back to London.

What if the answer he sought arrived tomorrow? Would he leave Lady Kate while he investigated Holt's information, or let the reverend gentleman rot in prison a day or two longer than necessary while he got to know his captive better?

His lips twisted with rueful self-knowledge. He was no saint, particularly where Lady Kate was concerned. Perhaps he needn't choose. Holt might hold out a little longer. Percy might be delayed.

He started as a sudden burst of rain clattered like a handful of pebbles thrown against the window. As the fat drops hit the glass and drizzled down the pane, he imagined the cascade of steaming water down a slender, white back . . .

He'd said he wouldn't picture Lady Kate in her bath, hadn't he? Max shrugged with a sense of inevitability.

He'd lied.

But he was well punished for such indulgence. The images that flitted across his mind merely tantalized him. They wouldn't harm her because she'd never know of them anyway. He'd no intention of breaking his word to her about giving her privacy. Until she started to trust him a little he'd get nowhere with his plans for her.

Still, there wasn't much time. He'd only have Lady Kate to himself for a few days. If he didn't move quickly she'd go back to her settled, sophisticated, oddly spotless life and forget he existed. Uneasily, he realized he'd have a far more difficult time forgetting her.

Restless, he turned from the window and glanced at the ormolu clock on the mantelpiece. He was hungry; he should take steps to make himself presentable and join Lady Kate in the light meal he'd ordered for her when she emerged from her bath.

Another image flashed across his mind—Lady Kate, rising from the tub like Venus, water cascading over those firm, high breasts, streaming down her lithe flanks. The urge to join her there, to fulfill every sensual promise he'd left unspoken, gripped him in a way that demanded immediate response.

From the beginning of their acquaintance, he'd wanted her, and the desire had grown to outright need.

He'd given his word he wouldn't disturb her.

*Word of a gentleman.* He growled, moving towards the door.

It had been a long time since he'd considered himself a gentleman.

LYLE! Gasping, Kate hugged her body, covering the essential parts where the fabric of her shift clung and revealed her shape.

Her heart bounded, kicking her pulse to a frantic pace. In the space of a few seconds, contradictory emotions passed through her. Outrage that he'd invaded her privacy, alarm, apprehension, and a perverse, terrified excitement so intense it almost sickened her.

She heard the swish of the curtain parting behind her. She made as if to turn around, but large hands bracketed her head, holding it still with gentle but insistent pressure.

A large presence loomed behind her. She sensed his weight and substance, though she couldn't see.

Kate wanted to cry out, but her voice wouldn't cooperate. He didn't speak, either, just cradled her head in his large hands, letting her anticipation build.

Was this some kind of game? She didn't like it, but her body reacted. Heat pooled low in her belly. Her breath stuttered and came in short pants.

*"No!"* But the word passed her lips as a whisper.

His grip on her head shifted lower, She tried to scramble up, reaching for the calico curtain to cover herself, but he slammed her back against the high lip of the tub.

Her shoulders took most of the impact but pain lanced her head where it connected with the metal. The shock of such brutal force paralyzed her.

Hands descended to her throat, caressing it almost lovingly, as if he hadn't hurt her at all. Shame swept over her. For a few instants, this encounter had excited her, but no more. Tears started to her eyes.

She couldn't look at him, too humiliated to cry out for help. What would they do, anyway? They thought he was her husband. He could do what he liked to her and no one in this household would dare interfere. Foolish to come to this place as his false bride. Foolish not to try to escape.

Desperately, she whispered, "Don't. Please don't."

As if her words acted as the trigger, his hands tightened around her throat.

*It's not Lyle.*

The instant she realized, panic swept over her in a blinding rush. She screamed, struggling and flailing her arms. She knocked the table flying and the glass vial smashed on the floor as the hands gripped her.

Jagged agony ripped through her throat. She gasped, desperate to drag air into her lungs, but those merciless hands slowly constricted her air passage. Kate clawed at them, desperate to ease their grip, but in vain.

She kicked and thrashed harder, twisting and sliding in the water, commanding all her strength to fight certain death. Her lungs heaved and the blood drummed a deep tattoo in her head. Her vision blurred, washed with a thousand pinpricks of light.

This was it, the end. Nameless regret flooded her, an emotion so powerful, for an instant it overwhelmed her physical pain.

Blackness edged her vision, pulling her under. Unimaginable pain. Her lungs were about to burst.

Suddenly, the chokehold on her throat vanished. She flopped like a rag doll into the water, barely retaining the strength to keep her head above the sloshing waves.

Lyle erupted into the room, moving faster than she'd ever seen a man move before.

His sharp eyes swiftly assessed her. "Are you all right?" At her slight nod, he added, "Which way?"

Gasping, unable to speak at first, she shook her head. She hadn't seen where her attacker had gone. She didn't care.

"Lyle!" she croaked. But she spoke to thin air.

Tenderly, she brushed her fingertips over the painful spot on the back of her head. There was a lump. Her throat felt like it was filled with shards of glass. Every swallow was agony.

She sat, trembling uncontrollably, her mind flashing with scenes of the attack. The water had grown tepid. She'd soaked in this bath for a long time, yet she didn't feel clean.

Cupping shaking hands together, she scooped up some water and splashed her face, then buried it in her hands. She needed to get out, but she was shaking so hard and so drained by her fight with death that she didn't know if she had the strength.

It took a long time to summon the will to move. Gingerly, she lifted herself out of the tub, shivering despite the fire and the room's warmth. She felt weary, like an old woman, wrung out.

*Someone had tried to kill her.*

She wrapped a towel around herself and sank to the floor, shaking. She couldn't stop.

When Lyle returned, Kate was still huddled in the corner of the room, hugging her knees. And very, very cold.

He took one look at her and scooped her into his arms, as if she weighed nothing at all. His warmth barely penetrated her icy skin, but his arms around her felt strong and safe.

He strode out and down the corridor to her bedchamber, setting her down gently on the hearth rug by the fire.

"You've had a shock," he said. "Here, drink this."

His deep, quiet voice steadied her a little. She opened her eyes, which were now level with a pair of highly polished top boots and trailed her gaze upwards.

She saw that he held out a silver flask to her, but she couldn't lift her hand out of the enveloping towel to grasp the neat little container. He knelt beside her and raised the flask to her lips, placing his free hand behind her head to steady her. She winced.

"Don't worry, it's only brandy."

"No, it's my head," she whispered hoarsely.

His fingertips tilted her head forward, gently searching her scalp through her hair. "A nasty bump. We shall have to see what we can do about that. In the meantime, drink. And then we shall have to get you dry or you'll catch your death by cold rather than strangulation."

Kate was in no condition to quibble, so she obediently took a series of slow, painful sips of the fiery liquid from the duke's flask.

It burned her throat almost unbearably, but the warmth stole through her body, tracing a path down to her stomach and spreading along her limbs to her fingertips and toes.

The pain in her head intensified, as if something beat a cudgel inside her skull. She winced, repressing a whimper.

Lyle spoke. "I'll ask the housekeeper to prepare a tisane. In the meantime, let's get you dry."

"No." But she was far too weak and numb to put up a decent fight. Gently, but with a determination that allowed for no argument, the duke helped her to stand.

"Tell me what happened." He set about toweling her dry, or at least, drying the parts of her that weren't covered with a sopping wet shift. "I'll work as quickly as I can."

Kate tried to remove her mind from the room, tried to pretend it was Sukey drying her legs with such brisk efficiency, rubbing the towel with firm pressure down her arms, traveling with gossamer lightness over the bruises.

But he was too large a presence, both figuratively and literally, to imagine away. Those big hands, so gentle. The concentration with which he performed his task.

Kate clenched her teeth to stop them chattering. Part of her wanted Lyle to go away. But she needed to get dry, as he said, and she didn't want a stranger with her now.

Lyle made an impatient noise and pinched a fold of her shift between finger and thumb, peeling it away from her leg. "I shall have to take this off you."

She twitched it from his hand. "Do it . . . myself."

Kate swallowed hard and reached for the towel. But when he gave it to her, she was shaking so much, she dropped it on the floor. She gave a hoarse cry, frustrated at her uselessness.

"Did you catch him?" she whispered.

MAX picked up the towel and shook his head. He had a hard time looking her in the eye. "George is scouring the grounds, but there are any number of hiding places and avenues of escape. Pretty cool, to come right into the lion's den. He must be mad or foolhardy, and I don't know which would be worse."

Thank God he hadn't listened to the promptings of his better self and stayed away from her. She'd very nearly . . .

He closed his eyes, clamping his lips together so he wouldn't let out a roar of guilt and shame.

He'd managed to deal with the situation with his customary efficiency, but blind fury still raged under his calm surface. At this unknown assassin, but mostly at himself, for failing to prevent the attack.

He didn't make mistakes. The way one stayed alive, the way one got the job done in his line of work was to keep ahead of the adversary every step of the way. How had he missed the signs?

Was his desire for this woman dulling his instincts? Blinding him to everything but the need to lure her to his bed?

If he'd treated this like any other case, the attack wouldn't have happened. If he'd been able to control his lust better, she wouldn't be sporting those livid marks around her graceful throat.

He took a deep breath, trying to calm himself.

God, he was a beast. Even now, he wanted her. That lovely body still quivered with distress, and all he wanted to do was to make it quiver with an entirely different emotion.

He watched her, trembling from head to foot, her hair darkened by damp and hanging in rats tails around that piquant face, and a sickening wave of shame broke in his chest. Her eyes were slightly dazed with the aftermath of fighting for her life. Soon, real terror would set in.

The trained professional said now was his best chance to question her, but the man was strangely reluctant.

Another nail in the coffin of objectivity. He couldn't treat Kate like any other witness, no matter how much he wanted to block these ridiculous feelings he had for her.

He could pinpoint the exact moment the reality of her near escape came home to her. She gave a sobbing gasp. A shudder ran through her frame. He saw her shoulders tense as she fought it. She was trying to maintain the appearance of calm in front of him, but it was damnably difficult. Her sheer courage was worse reproach than tears and recriminations.

Lyle wanted to hold her with every fiber of his being, but he hadn't the right. He hadn't quite reached that level of hypocrisy. He was responsible for her distress. And he was responsible for her safety now.

*He'd nearly lost her today.*

"I didn't believe you." Her voice was a husky breath.

"Pardon?"

She turned her head slightly, as if she heard, but she didn't look at him. "I didn't believe you when you said I was in danger. I was stupid. I thought . . ."

Her teeth sank into the plump cushion of her lower lip, and she gave a small choking sound that wrenched his guts.

"I thought you had fabricated the whole thing to keep me quiet. I was biding my time until I could get away." She swallowed hard, and her hand lifted involuntarily to touch the welts on her throat. "I should have listened when you said you wanted to guard me while I bathed but I . . ."

She flushed and he knew what she'd thought. She'd thought correctly. He'd had no other purpose than to seduce her. Not a thought in his thick head for her safety.

She lifted her chin, and for the first time, met his eye. "I am sorry."

Oh, Christ. Max shoved a hand through his hair. She'd seen through his lies with her clear, quick gaze. She'd been correct in her assumptions. And now, when he'd failed her, *she* was the one expressing remorse!

But the lie had become truth now, and it would be safer for her never to know how he'd deceived her. He needed her to trust him or she'd be in greater danger than ever.

Saying nothing, he steered her closer to the fire.

"I'm cold. Even standing in front of the fire, I'm c-cold."

He'd finished drying all the parts of her he could without taking off that sodden shift.

Now came the hardest part.

Trying not to stare—though she'd scarcely notice if he did, she was so cocooned in shock—he peeled the wet fabric upwards, revealing lithe, shapely legs and the triangle of pubic hair between them. Her stomach was flat, with an enchantingly neat navel. He bunched the fabric and lifted it higher. She raised her arms and he pulled off the wet shift. Her breasts . . .

*Don't think about her breasts.*

With a deep breath, he set about drying her damp skin with broad, impersonal strokes.

He tried not to look at her. God, he tried. For seconds, all he did was brush the towel over her skin, down the slope of one slender arm, then the other, holding her limp, cold hand in his. Controlling his breathing, praying she wouldn't see how rampant he was with lust.

He closed his eyes as he worked but that only heightened his other senses. She might be shivering, but he could feel her womanly heat, and the scent she'd used in the bath tantalized and beckoned.

He tried not to notice the firm thrust of her breasts or the way the towel snagged slightly on her sweet, pink nipples as it fell. Along the curve of her torso, over her flat belly, down her thighs, avoiding the place between them as too great a threat to his self-control.

He knelt to dry her thighs, and only then permitted himself a prolonged glance at those slender limbs with their delicate ankles and the pretty feet he'd glimpsed that first night in her bedchamber. That night seemed long ago.

She stood mute and unresisting as he worked the cloth over her body, until he reached around her to make a last swipe down her back. The small amount of force made her trip forward a little, dangerously close. It took every ounce of will he possessed not to wrap his arms around her, set his lips to hers, and warm her in the most intimate ways.

Max clenched his fists around the towel until his knuckles turned white. By God, he'd wronged her, and he paid for it now.

He took another deep, calming breath and unclenched his hands, finger by finger, then he grasped her upper arms and set her away from him. The effort nearly cost him his hard-won composure. Thankfully she was too overwrought to see how much he wanted her.

"That will have to do." His voice sounded harsh. He snatched up a wrapper he'd taken from the bathroom and draped it over her shoulders.

She clutched the wrapper around her, hiding her from his gaze.

Gently, he turned her and guided her towards the bed. "Get into bed now, and I'll send for the maid. And you'll want some ointment for those bruises."

Almost without volition, his hand lifted. Softly, he traced the livid necklace with a fingertip. The discoloration was turning a nasty purple.

Kate didn't answer, but she still shivered as if she could never be warm again. Hard-hearted bastard that he was, he felt sick to the stomach that such a brave, bright woman could be brought to this.

He wanted to wrap his arms around her. He wanted to warm her with his body and his kisses. He wanted to protect her, to make her feel safe.

But there was no time for indulging in such foolish tenderness, and besides, Lady Kate was a job now. Every good operative knew the dangers of becoming emotionally involved in a case. He should have remembered that from the start. If he had, this might never have happened.

"Do you—do you know who did it?" Her husky voice held a distinct tremor.

He gave her the truth. "No, I don't." That troubled him more than anything. The most likely candidate was Jardine, but somehow, Max didn't think so. The man might be ruthless, but he had no reason to kill Lady Kate—at least, not at this juncture.

And Jardine wouldn't have failed.

Icy rage swept through Max at his own naivety. Damn him for a smug bastard, he'd taken everything Faulkner had said at face value. He should have known better than to trust that man. He should have been vigilant from the beginning. Faulkner might well have planned this all along.

From now on, he wouldn't let her out of his sight. And he'd damn well keep his hands off her into the bargain.

"Get some rest," he said curtly, knowing how callous he must seem. It couldn't be helped. "And tell the maid to pack your things. As soon as you're well enough, we're leaving."

# Nine

*The madness continues. Every night now, and he stays with me until dawn.*

*Can my heart contain such secret joy? I wade through misery each day 'til he is here.*

"IT'S getting dark and there's no moon tonight," said Lyle. "We'll have to wait until daybreak."

Kate had spent hours in a dreamless, deep slumber, foiling Lyle's plans for a fast getaway.

He didn't look at her, but Kate's gaze followed him hungrily as he moved around the room, checking windows, examining the lock on the door.

She needed the kind of warmth and comfort that a fire and a featherbed couldn't provide. For once, just this once, couldn't she have someone to hold her? Her phantom lover would not be remotely enough company tonight.

How ironic that she should desire warmth and flesh and blood from Lyle, the most uncompromising man she'd ever met. The sane part of her mind had registered the expression on his face when he'd found her, naked and shivering in the bathroom. A dark, primal look of sheer rage, swiftly cloaked with ruthless intent.

He'd moved like a predator, stalking her faceless attacker. He prowled now, restless, waiting. Perversely, stupidly, she wanted him to forget about her safety and concentrate, quite simply, on *her*.

Foolish! But her usual staunch self-discipline had been stripped away in that attack, revealing a core that was all need and passion and pure, feminine desire.

More than anything, she did not want to be alone tonight.

"Do you need anything? I'll send a maid up," he said indifferently, as if she'd spoken her thought out loud. As if she were just anyone.

Pain flooded her. Humiliating, this craving for his touch, but she didn't have any resources left to fight it.

She brushed her forehead with a shaking hand. "I don't want the maid."

He sent her an impatient glance, and his gaze snagged on the tray next to the bed where she lay. "You haven't eaten."

He approached the bed purposefully, as if he'd feed her with his own hands. Part of her thought that might be interesting.

"I tried," she said in a scraping whisper. "But my throat—"

"No, of course." He stared down at the tray and shook his head, clearly irritated. "I should have known. I'll have them send up something more suitable. Something soft that will ease your throat."

He reached out and touched her bruised skin, letting his fingers drift down her throat with exquisite gentleness that seemed at odds with the sheer size of him, the strength in those well-shaped hands. His eyes smoldered as he contemplated the damage the unknown assailant had caused.

She caught her breath, willing him to explore her further. But slowly, as if it cost him much, he drew his hand away.

He started, as if woken suddenly from a trance. "I'm sorry. Did I hurt you?"

She shook her head. "Lyle, I—"

"I have things to attend to." He turned to leave. "I'll have that food sent up, and then you'd best get more rest. You'll need your strength for the journey tomorrow."

Without a backwards glance, he closed the door quietly behind him.

Despair swept through her. She didn't want him to go. She wanted . . . *him.*

Kate shifted restlessly, trying to persuade herself it was better this way. She was shaken and weak, not herself at all. She might want him now, but it would be far better for her in the long run if he left her alone. He'd chosen not to take advantage of her vulnerable state. She ought to be grateful. Instead, she felt cheated, rejected, and so alone.

Angrily, she punched her pillow. *Oh, buck up, you stupid, sniveling female! This is not the time to feel sorry for yourself. How are you going to help Stephen now?*

Obviously, if someone wanted to kill her, she must accept Lyle's protection and stop looking for ways to escape.

That said, how might she yet campaign on Stephen's behalf? Would Lyle help her? It seemed that he, as the inheritor of the estate on which the arson occurred, should have some say in the matter of Stephen's freedom.

Perhaps she could persuade him to use his influence on Stephen's behalf?

Truly, she was not thinking straight. On the morrow, after a decent sleep she might be calm and well enough to plan. For the moment, she needed all her strength to get through the night.

All kinds of terrors awaited her once darkness fell. She was prone to nightmares, and that horrifying attack lent itself to reenactment in her dreams.

Kate stared at the canopy over her soft, luxurious bed

and wondered when she'd be able to swallow again without feeling like she forced a jagged rock the size of a cricket ball down her gullet.

When the maid came in bearing a tray, her throat contracted in anticipated agony, but she dragged herself up and allowed the girl to bank the pillows behind her back and place the tray across her knees.

Smiling her thanks at the maid, she nodded a dismissal. When the door closed behind her, Kate picked up a silver spoon and prodded the gelatinous syllabub, watching it quiver on the plate.

She spooned it into her mouth and let the alcoholic custard slide down, rich and soothing.

After one mouthful, she realized she was ravenous, and finished the syllabub in short order. Checking under the second cover, she inhaled the fragrant steam of chicken broth. Her stomach grumbled and she smiled at its rude insistence.

Having demolished every last morsel of the supper Lyle had so thoughtfully ordered her, Kate put the tray aside and sank back into the pillows with a replete sigh.

The meal had worked wonders. She almost felt like her old self. Except she'd never felt this alone before.

Of course she'd been lonely. Hector hadn't touched her for years before he died. Hence the phantom lover, the man she'd fabricated to take the edge off her pain.

The pain had been general, a dull ache, a desire for company—male company—but she'd never wanted anyone in particular before.

Now, the yearning centered on one man, but it seemed she was too late. Had she succumbed to the duke's wiles that morning, or even if she'd accepted his teasing offer to watch over her bath, she would have him now, to hold her and soothe her with those magical hands when she needed him the most.

Once again, she bent her knees to her chin and hugged them, wondering when they'd managed to dress her in one of her ridiculously staid night rails. Nothing like the scandalous garment she'd worn that time she'd made her final attempt to seduce her own husband. Her eyes squeezed shut with renewed humiliation.

*Think about something else.*

Perhaps Lyle avoided her because he thought she needed more rest. But she'd *had* rest—hours of it—and shouldn't she be the judge of whether she was fit enough for company?

Kate blew out a breath in frustration. Lyle couldn't wait to be alone with her that morning. And now she needed him, he pulled away. He was hot one minute, cold as black ice the next. Was he playing some sort of game with her?

Hector had displayed similar ambivalence early in their marriage. There must be something wrong with *her*.

MAX paced his bedchamber restlessly while Lady Kate slept on. He needed to act. He hated leaving others to do his work but he wouldn't trust anyone else to guard her now, not even George.

A low whistle signaled George's approach. From the look on his servant's face, Max knew the news wasn't good.

"Anything to report?" Max subjected his groom to a piercing stare that usually cowed lesser men. George took it without a blink.

He shook his head. "Silent as the tomb out there, guv. You oughter get some shut-eye."

"I will in a moment. Do we know how the fellow got in the house?"

George shrugged. "No muddy footprints anywhere, which suggests he might have walked in through a door. Off the terrace, mebbe."

It scarcely mattered. The place wasn't a fortress. Though the servants had locked up for the night, there were any number of ways an intruder might get in.

Well, he would stay on watch tonight. Then he'd take

Lady Kate to Hove and lock her in the tower where no one could get to her.

And, equally important, where *she* couldn't get out.

Despite the scare she'd received, he wouldn't trust the woman to keep herself safe and stay out of sight of her own free will. Her apparent fragility hid a tiresome streak of independence. She was liable to get herself into further trouble if he didn't restrain her adventurous spirit. Lady Kate was one of the bravest woman he'd ever met, and one of the cleverest, but she simply didn't know what she dealt with. The ruthlessness of those in his business far surpassed anything she could imagine.

George cleared his throat. "Any notion who done the deed, guv?"

Max frowned. "No, and that's the devil of it. A gently bred lady can only have so many enemies, after all. My first thought was Jardine, but the fact her ladyship is still alive seems to discount his involvement. Unless . . ."

Faulkner himself? Now, there was a thought.

He dismissed George and sipped his brandy, swirling it around his glass. Firelight danced and flickered in the amber liquid. He took another swallow, refusing to let it remind him of Lady Kate's eyes.

*Concentrate on the matter at hand*, he told himself. *Faulkner.* Max frowned. Hadn't Jardine mentioned something about Faulkner losing his grip? What had that been about? The head of operations had seemed his usual abrupt, soulless self at Whitehall the other day.

Internal wrangling had never interested Max, but perhaps he ought to take an interest in this case. He wondered if Perry knew anything. He'd always been a favorite with their head of operations.

There were endless possibilities. Perhaps a member of the government had discovered Kate's intentions. Had she mentioned them to a friend or acquaintance? Someone with a secret they'd do anything to hide?

Hopefully, Louisa had translated the diary by now. When he read the translation he'd be in a position to assess how dangerous Lady Kate really was, and to whom.

Max stretched his arms above his head in an attempt to revive his cramped muscles. Using an armchair was a good tactic if he wanted to sleep lightly, but it played merry hell with his back.

It was highly unlikely that the unknown assassin would strike again so soon after his failed attempt. His very nearly successful attempt, Max corrected himself.

He'd never forget the pure, white-hot terror that gripped him when he'd heard the sounds of struggle from the bathroom. Thank God he'd been nearby. Thank God.

His gut twisted every time he thought of Lady Kate sitting in the bath, blank-eyed and trembling.

He should have stopped to help her, but faced with crisis, his brain and body fell back into habit—catch the criminal and let others care for the victim. Only this time . . .

How had she managed to crawl under his skin in a matter of days? Protecting her wasn't just a job. It was far more than that.

Damn him for a fool! Getting sentimental about a woman was the worst thing he could do. Emotion clouded one's judgment. The first thing he'd learned at the beginning of his career was to keep his feelings out of a case. If he was going to keep Lady Kate alive until the threat passed, he'd need to quash this foolish obsession.

And what was so special about her anyway? What did she have that a hundred other women didn't share?

So very many things, honesty compelled him to admit. The sparkling intelligence in her eyes when she challenged him over her brother in that ballroom, the daring that led her to use her knowledge as a weapon, her staunch physical courage when she threw herself out of that carriage, and again, braved that hideous assault in the bathroom. And that lovely, lithe body . . . Max shut his eyes. Even while she was trembling, cold, and bedraggled from the shock of the attack, his baser self had noticed all kinds of things about her as he toweled her dry.

Delicately turned ankles and narrow feet. He could spend hours just thinking about those pretty feet, and her legs, long and slender, just as he'd imagined them. The curve of her bottom, so round and womanly, the sweet, firm weight of her breasts.

He thought of the ugly collar of bruises that now ringed her neck and launched out of his chair.

For the forty-fifth time that evening, he opened the connecting door between their bedchambers and looked in on her.

She lay on her back, rumpled and abandoned, one arm crooked at the elbow, wrist lying on the pillow above her head. The other arm was flung wide, as if to say, *Come to me*. In other circumstances, he wouldn't hesitate to accept the tacit invitation.

As he moved further into the room, her lips parted on a lilting sigh, as if she'd heard his thoughts and expressed her disappointment.

With a muffled groan, he let his fingers brush the counterpane that covered her. She'd wanted better comforting than he'd offered her that afternoon. But he couldn't even touch her hand without needing to touch her everywhere else.

She'd already suffered once because his focus on her had obliterated everything else, dulled his instinct for danger. He wasn't about to jeopardize her safety again. The only way to keep her alive was to maintain his distance and do the job he was trained for.

He turned down the bedside lamp and quietly left.

KATE woke on a shuddering gasp, swimming up from a nightmare she couldn't recall. As soon as she opened her eyes, she knew she wouldn't get back to sleep that night.

The snick of a door opening broke the silence. Terror

gripped her anew, sending her pulse into a frenetic race. Had the assassin returned? Her gaze flew to the bedchamber door but it was shut. A shaft of pale light caught her eye, and she swung her gaze to the wall opposite. Then she remembered Lyle's mention of a connecting door.

The duke's large form filled the doorway, his shadow projecting forward into the room. Relief flooded her body. Thank Heaven, it was Lyle.

He didn't speak. In the dim light, she couldn't discern his expression. She wondered if he'd heard her cry out as she woke.

Lyle hesitated, as if taking a silent surveillance, or perhaps listening for regular breathing.

She couldn't breathe. She couldn't make herself draw the slightest wisp of air. Her heart pounded in her ears as she willed him to say something, silently begged him to come to her.

He paused a few moments more, head to the side, listening. Then he turned and disappeared the way he came.

Kate flung onto her side and smacked her pillow in disappointment.

She didn't see him until he loomed at the bedside. He found her hand and pressed it around a glass tumbler.

"Drink this. It will help you sleep."

Nerves jangling, she took the glass and sipped, choking a little on the strong liquor.

"More brandy?" She made a face but she took another long sip.

The fiery liquid burnt out the pain in her throat, leaving it pleasantly numb.

"Steady." Amusement tinged his voice, but she ignored him and drained the glass in one last, inelegant gulp. *Dutch courage.* She held the glass out for more.

He hesitated, then took it. "Well, I suppose it doesn't matter if you're a little drunk," he said softly, as if he spoke to himself. "At least it might ease the pain."

Lyle left her. From the adjoining room she heard the mellow glug of brandy pouring. Returning to the bedside, he handed her the glass. "Now, sip that slowly and then see if you can sleep."

He patted her shoulder in the most irritatingly fraternal way. With a scowl, she raised her glass and drank deep. A small ball of fire burned pleasantly in her belly, but a sense of injury nagged at her mind.

Kate licked her brandy-moistened lips and said to his retreating back, "I suppose you're just going to leave me here, unprotected."

Determined to challenge him, she reached over and turned up her bedside lamp. She'd no intention of sleeping yet.

Lyle halted. "I am next door, within earshot," he replied evenly. Slowly, he turned back.

"Well, quite honestly, I don't think that's good enough." Kate eyed a drop of amber liquid that clung to her brandy balloon. Enunciating her words grew difficult. Perhaps it was a side effect of her sore throat.

She sank back into the pillows, holding out the glass with a limp wrist. He stepped forward and scooped it up before it dropped to the floor.

Another silence, as if he struggled with himself. "I think you ought to let me be the judge of how best to protect you, Lady Kate."

"As you were this afternoon." It slipped out before she could stop it.

He sucked in a sharp breath. If she could have cut out her tongue, she would have. *It wasn't his fault.*

"I'm sorry," she faltered. "I didn't mean it. You tried to protect me but I wouldn't let you."

He sighed. "No, that's not—"

"I want you to stay." She blurted it out, cringing at her forwardness, vaguely aware she would never have started this conversation had it not been for the brandy and the loneliness that stretched before her as vast and wide as the Atlantic.

"That would not be wise." Lyle's voice sounded constricted.

"Just hold me," she whispered.

"You know it would be more than that."

Perhaps she did. Perhaps that's what she wanted. "Please, Lyle," she said quietly. "I don't wish to be alone tonight."

She tried to think of something that would clinch her argument, but he spoke first.

"I can't do it. I can't just hold you." Lyle's voice thickened. "There are no half measures with you, Kate."

He wanted her. A sense of feminine power flared in her breast, fueling her reckless courage. She might never have such a chance again. Until now, she'd marked time in her diary with her phantom lover. But the flesh-and-blood man standing before her, rugged and raw, radiating sexual passion like a furnace blasts heat, was infinitely more desirable than her dream.

She sought his eyes and gazed steadily into them. "Then don't take half measures," she said. "I want it all."

His nostrils flared, and she noticed his fists clench at his sides. "That's the brandy talking. Go to sleep."

Hot blood suffused her face. She'd as good as propositioned him, yet he refused her. "I'm not foxed," she said with quiet desperation. She would not beg a man to share her bed. Not after Hector. Never again.

He exhaled a shuddering breath. She sensed his tension, as if it cost him much to deny her, or perhaps guilt placed him under such strain. He was angry at himself for failing to protect her. She realized that now.

"For Christ's sake, don't do this to me, Kate! Do you know why I'm not going to sit here and hold you and kiss your fears away?" His jaw hardened. "Because when I take you, I want to give it my full attention. I don't want to be watching for government assassins out of the corner of my eye." The wealth of feeling behind his words thrilled her. He sounded as if he were on the edge, as if he might explode with pent-up desire.

"Whatever lies between us, now is not the time to explore it." He ran a hand through his hair in frustration, and the mess he made only heightened his raw appeal.

The beginnings of a beard shadowed his jaw. She wanted to touch, to run her fingertips over that rough stubble on his chin, to rake her fingers through the wild tangle of his hair.

"Stay," she said again.

He looked down at her, clearly tempted. The pull between them intensified, until she thought she might scream just to break that awful, nerve-wracking silence. But he was strong. He tore his gaze from hers, turned from the bed, and walked away.

Kate watched his figure melt into the darkness of the bedchamber next door. After a few moments, the faint glow in the doorway intensified, as if he'd turned up a lamp.

She stared at the light for a long time, until it flickered and swam before her eyes.

She shook her head. No. She was not going to let him go.

MAX picked up a poker and stirred the fire. A soft footfall behind him made him turn around.

She stood in the shadows, her hair streaming around her, feet bare, like a fairy creature, not the sophisticated Lady Kate.

She hesitated in the doorway, as if debating whether to enter the lion's den.

Without taking his eyes from her face, he replaced the poker.

She licked her lips, and his cock gave a hard twitch at

the nervous gesture. She looked young and uncertain, and he realized that the poised Lady Kate was not mistress of herself in every situation.

His blood heated. His heart thumped. This was the worst idea in the world.

"Don't come any closer," he said, fighting to keep his speech even, to regulate his breathing.

She gave him a wide-eyed stare. "Why not? I only want to talk to you."

"Not even you are that naive, Lady Kate. Step over that threshold and I won't be answerable for the consequences." He shot her a glare and turned away, hoping that would be the end of it.

But as he stared into the flames, he sensed her, hovering on that final step.

"I keep going over and over it in my mind," she whispered. "There was a point when I thought—no, I *knew* I was going to die. And I felt . . ."

She trailed off but he could guess what she was going to say. Terrified. She'd been frightened out of her wits. Anyone would be. And it was all his fault.

". . . regret," she finished. "My thoughts were far from clear, but I'm fairly certain I remember regret. I wished I'd *done* things, rather than written about them."

She said the last sentence almost to herself. What was she talking about?

He heard her move forward and muttered an oath under his breath. He should have locked the communicating door.

The carpet hushed. He turned around and she stood there, watching him, with a strange mixture of questioning and yearning in her eyes.

Her arms lifted, as if she'd hold them out to him.

In two strides, he'd caught her up and crushed her to him, ravishing her mouth in a kiss that was part punishment, part desperation.

And anger. Fury that he couldn't resist her, even though he needed his wits about him, even though he hadn't lied when he said he didn't want to lose himself in her and make them both vulnerable to attack.

But he couldn't stop. The softness and fragrance and the sheer, delicate power of her drew him, compelled him. She was like quicksilver in his arms, darting her tongue into his mouth, caressing him with light touches of those elegant hands. Inflaming him, burning his noble, practical resolutions to ash.

All recollection of her injury flew from his head. He pushed her against the wall, so her back was plastered to the wainscoting.

Rough treatment, but she didn't object, meeting him with a boldness she hadn't shown before. Her hands ranged over his back. Her lips tasted so sweet, for an instant, he was ashamed of taking her against a wall like a harlot.

But she gasped when his hand closed over one firm, high breast, a shuddery breath that spoke only of pleasure, and suddenly, he wanted to shock her. He didn't want this to be the tender encounter she'd craved. It was a warning, pure and simple. A warning not to play with fire or she'd get consumed in the flames.

Abandoning preliminaries, he bunched her night rail in his hand, lifting it past her thigh. She made an incoherent sound of protest, but he was lost in the feel of the silky skin beneath that modest garment, lost in the womanliness of her, and he let his hand drift and circle upwards, until he touched the place he wanted most.

She stiffened and tried to squirm away, but he held her there, touching, circling, building the rhythm, and soon she relaxed slightly into his questing hand.

She was so small, so very much smaller than he. Usually, he liked his women big and buxom. He felt he might break Lady Kate if he wasn't careful.

And part of him wanted to break her, bend her to his

will. Possess her, despite her constant assertions of independence. Or, perhaps, because of them.

He slanted his mouth over hers in another, endless, drugging kiss and used the distraction to slide one finger into her.

Hell, she was tight! He could almost believe her a virgin, but for those years of marriage. Max groaned. He was hard as a poker, and absurdly, he wasn't sure if she could take him.

He rubbed his thumb over the small nub of flesh above her entrance, and she gave a gasp that almost seemed of surprise. Beating back his own desire, he pleasured her there until she cried out and trembled and warm moisture slicked his hand.

"Oh," she gasped. "I think—"

"Don't think. Don't talk." He leaned his forehead against hers, still working her, riding the crest of those waves of pleasure. "For God's sake, Kate, don't talk now."

Max saw in her eyes that she wanted to say something and he knew it was dangerous to hear it, so he covered her mouth with his while he fumbled with the fall of his breeches. He quickly brought his erection to her entrance, eager to distract her.

Distracted was one word for it. Her eyes widened as he slowly impaled her, easing through her tight passage.

He began to move, bracing her against the wall, stroking upwards, holding her hips and pulling her down onto him. As if by instinct, she wrapped her legs—those slender, shapely legs—around his waist, sheathing him to the hilt.

If she said anything after that, he didn't hear her. His senses were so focused on the exquisite sensation of her surrounding him, warm and moist and welcoming, drawing him in.

Long, leisurely strokes, until he thought he might go blind with need. Unable to wait any longer, he increased the pace, and her pants and sighs escalated. Suddenly, she clenched around him and threw her head back, mindless in release.

As she came apart, he lost control, soon following her over the edge. The wonder and power of the pleasure exploding through him nearly obliterated caution. He just managed to shift her off him before his seed pumped in hearty spurts down her belly.

He set her down, steadying her with his hands at her elbows as her legs gave way. She looked up at him. The lips he'd devoured so ravenously parted as if to say something, then closed again.

Lady Kate, bereft of speech.

He huffed a shaky laugh, triumphant as an adolescent bedding a woman for the first time. He slid his hands up and down her arms.

"Wait here."

Max moved to the wash stand and wet a towel in the basin. Still mute, leaning back against the wall, she watched him, looking dazed and utterly sated. A purely masculine sense of satisfaction flooded his chest. It might be wishful thinking, but she looked as if she'd never experienced such pleasure before. With Hector Fairchild as a husband, perhaps she hadn't.

She took the towel from him, but her hand dropped to her side and she made no move to use it.

"It's for, er . . ." He gestured at the wetness around her thighs. Wasn't she experienced in the bedroom? Did he need to explain?

"Oh, here, I'll do it." He set to work on her, wiping gently, then threw the towel into the fire.

"You'd better get some sleep now," he said.

She simply nodded, so he steered her back to her bedchamber and put her to bed like a child. He resisted the good-night kiss. One touch of those lips and he'd be inside her again. His cock twitched, clearly ready to oblige.

Taking a deep breath, he stifled his baser urges. "Get some rest. We drive out early in the morning."

The last thing he saw were those wide, amber eyes before he turned his back and made himself leave.

# Ten

*I could gaze on him for eternity, but where is the joy in only looking? A statue would do as well.*

*I'd no idea a man's skin could be so soft . . .*

WHO would have thought? Kate lay in the dark, twirling one lock of hair around her finger. Who would have thought it could be like that?

Her body tingled with life. She'd never felt less like sleeping. She wanted to dance. She wanted to run a mile.

Forget tisanes and syllabub. *That*—what he'd done to her—was as good a cure as any for her aches and ills.

Well, obviously, Hector hadn't known the first thing about what he was doing. Which shouldn't have surprised her, since he was so incompetent at everything else.

Or perhaps what she had with Lyle was special? Even in her wildest dreams of her phantom lover, it had never been like *that*. Those big hands . . . She shivered pleasurably at what those hands had made her feel.

Would Lyle marry her now? A gentleman would, but she wasn't so certain this particular duke was civilized enough to be called a gentleman.

This was all so sudden and new. She wasn't even sure she wanted marriage. Not with the duke, not with anyone. Did she really wish to give up her independence? Hector had been weak-willed and easily manipulated, except in the bedroom, where she exerted no charms for him at all. Lyle was a man accustomed to command. She would not find him so malleable.

Best to ignore the whole thing, pretend it had never happened, until she could decide.

*But those hands . . .*

No. She would not act like some foolish chit with stars in her eyes. If what the duke said was true, no one need ever know that she'd spent this time with him. As long as she didn't become pregnant . . .

She bit her lip. A week ago, the possibility of getting with child would have deterred her from an encounter like this. But her very close brush with death had shown her that this half-life she'd led since her marriage could not go on. No more writing in a diary instead of experiencing the real thing. From now on, she would embrace life.

She'd deal with the consequences if and when they arose. For the moment, she would enjoy all that Lyle had to offer.

Anticipation humming through her veins, Kate turned over, feeling the pain in her throat for the first time since she'd entered the duke's bedchamber. She made herself as comfortable as she could and closed her eyes. She'd put the uncertainty about Lyle out of her mind and try to sleep.

But those big hands roamed her body, even in her dreams.

"I'VE been thinking, Lyle."

Max looked up. Lady Kate's eyes sparkled with determination.

"Have you? How terrifying," he murmured. He'd wondered how she would behave after the night before.

Crashing embarrassment, he'd expected. Shyness, yes. But not this bright-eyed goddess, full of purpose.

She narrowed her eyes at him. "I've been thinking I ought to learn how to defend myself."

If she'd stuck a knife in his ribs and twisted it, she couldn't have reproached him more effectively for his neglect. "You don't need to. I'm here."

She left the obvious unspoken. He hadn't been there the previous afternoon. He hadn't prevented that ring of bruises around her throat.

"But don't you think it would be a good thing for me to know? For instance, you could teach me to shoot."

"No."

"Why not?" she demanded. "Many ladies shoot. Why, I've heard your own sister is proficient at the art."

"It's not an art, it's a skill, and it takes more than a few days to master. Besides, I am not letting you loose on the countryside with a pistol."

"You make it sound like I would go around shooting indiscriminately. And why do you say a few days?"

He paused, eyeing her. She didn't miss a trick. He ought to be more careful what he said around her. "I anticipate it won't be more than a few days before your brother capitulates. It follows that you will have no further incentive to publish these silly memoirs of yours, ergo, the government agents who are trying to kill you will cease and desist. And we will all live happily ever after."

She observed him with speculation in her eyes, and he realized his tone had taken on a bitter edge. He swung away from her and stared out the window.

"What about hand-to-hand combat, then?" she pursued, coming up behind him. Lord, she was like a terrier with a bone. "Aren't there any tricks you might teach me to defend myself from—"

He turned and took her by the shoulders, none too gently. She winced a little, and the reminder of her injuries inflamed rather than gentled him. He gave her a small shake.

"Listen, Lady Kate. I am here to protect you and that's the end of it. You do not need to shoot pistols; you do not need to know any physical tricks."

Her eyes widened. "No swords, either?"

He gritted his teeth. "No swords."

"Well, yes, I suppose they are out of fashion nowadays. And it would be rather troublesome to carry one about with me all the time." Her face lit. "I know! What about a dagger? A pretty little silver stiletto I could fit in my reticule, or—"

There was nothing for it. He pulled her to him and kissed her, dimly aware he couldn't stop her mouth any other way.

But that motivation soon went up in flames as her lips clung to his and her arms snaked up around his neck.

He shouldn't do this. He needed to put distance between them. Yet she felt perfect in his arms, so soft and warm and scented.

He crushed her to him, careful of her injured throat, but at the same time too urgent to treat her with delicacy.

She didn't seem to mind, returning his kisses with drugging passion.

He drew back, looking down into her eyes, which were dazed and shining. Something shifted inside him, a dangerous, life-altering shift. This woman was too significant, too important to lose.

He pulled away. "Don't. Kate, I—"

She stepped over to him and reached up to cup his jaw with her hand. "It wasn't your fault. Yesterday afternoon. You did as I asked. You couldn't have known he'd—"

Shame stabbed his gut. "Thank you. You need say no more." The harsh words and his dismissive tone made her recoil. She stepped back, letting her hand fall.

Good. That was how it should be.

He fed his anger with more words, like an engineer feeding coal into a furnace. "You've been nothing but trouble from start to finish, meddling in what doesn't concern you. I should have let you go your own way when you tumbled out of that carriage. I should have let you get yourself killed. But I've sworn to protect you and that I'll do until this tiresome business is over. Until then, you do as I say or you won't like the consequences."

She'd been shocked by his outburst, but when he finished his tirade, she surprised him. A curious smile flitted over her lips.

"Oh, dear! And they say we women are delicate creatures. I'm so sorry to have wounded your pride, my lord duke. But I never asked you to protect me, to take me away from my home and my friends. If I had wanted protection, I would not have asked for it from you. But now we are in this tangle, let me make one thing clear. I won't tolerate being treated as if I am some troublesome chit who is importuning you to help her. I never wanted your help. And I'll be—I'll be *damned* if I'll obey you when your orders are so nonsensical. Any number of situations might arise where you can't be with me. I'd feel much more confident if I had some rudimentary knowledge of self-defense."

She looked at him straightly. "I am quite aware I'm no match for a man, but surely there might be ways to at least gain myself time to scream."

He held tight to his temper and spoke slowly and clearly. "You will not need to scream. No one will get within a hundred paces of you. Not on my watch."

Knowing Kate, if he armed her with fighting skills, she'd only become more daring. Foolhardy even. He couldn't afford to let her gain confidence or she'd discount the danger that surrounded her, flout his orders, perhaps even jeopardize his plans to keep her safe.

For a moment, she regarded him in silence, a faint smile

tugging at her lips. "Do you know, Lyle, it's rather thrilling when you come over all masterful." She stood on tiptoe, placed on hand on his shoulder, and touched her lips to his. If concern for her safety hadn't been uppermost in his mind, his resolution would have dissolved there and then.

He drew back and saw a purposeful glint in her eye. The little minx! He shook his head. "Cozen me all you like. You'll not get your way in this, m'dear." He removed her hand from his chest, ignoring her look of chagrin. "Be ready to leave in ten minutes, if you please, ma'am." He bowed, and strode out of the room.

As he shrugged into his greatcoat, he thought of the conversation they'd had and fought a smile. How many women would immediately search for a way to fight back? How many women would weep and cling rather than provoke him until he kissed her senseless? Life would never be dull with Lady Kate.

"FANNY, don't be absurd. You are *not* a whale," said Louisa. "The merest suspicion of a bump, that is all, and you must be six months gone at least."

"My dear, you are too kind." Fanny sighed. "But I daresay I outweigh the Prince Regent by now. Romney hates my being so fat."

"You know that's not true." Since Louisa's big cousin doted on his wife in the most slavish and sickening way, Fanny could only be indulging in her high sense of drama to make such a foolish statement.

Fanny shrugged her shoulders pettishly. "Oh, I'll grant you, he's jumping out of his skin with excitement over the new baby. He's convinced it's the son and heir. I hope," she said pensively, "that it is a girl."

"Either way, the child will be well loved," said Louisa quietly.

A familiar pain stabbed her heart. How she longed for a

child of her own! She was years older than Fanny and piercingly aware that the time to bear healthy children was running out.

She'd tried to tell herself that some things could never be, yet a part of her had always hoped for . . . well, a miracle, she supposed. In the meantime, she'd be the best aunt and cousin the children in her family could wish for. She glanced at Fanny. At least she would not have to worry about her figure thickening.

The thought should have cheered her, but it did not. Her flat, almost concave stomach seemed lacking next to Fanny's swollen belly. *This field lies fallow . . .*

Louisa took a deep breath and tried to put the matter out of her mind. The more pressing concern was to return the diary and the translation to her brother.

As Fanny continued to rummage disconsolately through her extensive wardrobe, Louisa risked another surreptitious glance at the small watch that hung from a fob on her bodice. She needed to get away from London, but the way things were going, Fanny might never decide what to wear for the journey, much less what to pack.

"What about the blue cambric? That's pretty," said Louisa. *Please wear the confounded cambric!*

Fanny sent her a sharp-eyed look. "Is something the matter? You seem on edge today."

A commotion downstairs saved Louisa from answering.

"Oh, that will be Romney," said Fanny. "He's as mad as a bear this morning. He hates being holed up in a traveling carriage with me when he'd prefer to ride."

Louisa didn't answer. Her mouth dried so quickly and completely she could barely swallow. Her pulse raced and her breath shortened, the way they always did when—

Heavy steps sounded on the stairs, and she knew, just *knew* whose steps they were.

Gripping her hands together, she trained her eyes on the door.

It flung open and he stood there, the great, sleek brute with grim purpose behind the devilish smile. That detestable smile.

"Lord Jardine!" Fanny gasped as he kicked the door shut behind him. "What are you *doing*?"

He leaned his shoulders against the oak panels, ignoring the shouts and hammering of the footman who'd chased up the stairs after him. "I am settling an old score."

How very apt! "He has come for me, Fanny," said Louisa quietly. "Do not be alarmed."

"I don't care who he has come for. Romney will kill him if he finds him in my boudoir."

Genuine amusement flickered across Jardine's features. He shrugged. "Stranger things have happened." He turned, locked the door, and pocketed the key.

Fanny gasped, planting her hands on her hips. "Lord Jardine, this is *outrageous* behavior. I demand you leave at once!"

He held his gloves in one hand, slapping them on his palm in a rhythmic, meditative, and wholly insolent way that nearly drove Louisa mad. How was it that his mere presence, his slightest gesture could overset her so?

To Louisa, Fanny's scandalized tirade faded into background noise. The world had narrowed to just her and Jardine, the slap of his gloves, the rasp of her ragged breathing, and her heartbeat, pounding in her ears.

Ignoring Fanny, Jardine strolled towards her, and it took every ounce of self-possession for Louisa to remain where she was.

He halted before her, too close. "If, by some miracle, Romney *did* succeed in killing me, would you be sorry, Louisa?" Leaning down, he murmured, "Or would you rejoice in your . . . freedom?"

All the warmth drained from her face. She tried, but she couldn't hold his gaze. Her lashes lowered.

She didn't wish him dead. It was an agonizing

possibility—a likelihood—she endured every day. And he hadn't the slightest idea what it cost her or he wouldn't have asked that question.

His fine, black brows arched. "Ah. I think I have my answer."

"Really, Jardine! What is this about?" Fanny's voice sounded less scolding now and more intrigued. Her black eyes snapped with curiosity.

Louisa shot her a quelling glance and drew a steadying breath. "My lord, if you wish to speak with me, I suggest you call in Mount Street. It is scarcely appropriate—"

"I've called in Mount Street. Several times," he answered with another of those smiles. "And now I discover you're here, on the point of leaving for the country."

How had he found out? She'd sworn her mother to secrecy. "I'm not obliged to advise you of my movements, Lord Jardine." She looked him straight in the eye and said the words clearly, daring him to argue. *"You have no claim over me."*

Utter fury flooded his countenance. Inwardly, she quailed, but she managed to maintain her surface calm. The least sign of weakness and he'd take full advantage of it. Jardine was a ruthless killer and master manipulator. It took strength, determination, and guile to get the better of him in any encounter.

He held her gaze, and suddenly, his face softened, his beautiful mouth taking on that sensual curl that never failed to fill her with hopeless yearning. She tore her gaze away.

In command of himself once more, he slapped his gloves on his palm. "I'll follow you."

*"What?"* She gave a startled laugh, though nothing about his assertion was remotely amusing. "You most certainly will not!"

Jardine strode to the door and turned the key. "Just try and stop me."

Yanking open the door, he stepped back fluidly, causing the footman he'd eluded to stumble into the room.

Jardine's hand shot out and grasped the man by the cravat. He pulled the footman up so they were nose to nose and spoke very succinctly. "You let a strange man walk into your lady's house, right up to her boudoir." He twisted his fist, and the footman gulped for air. "Don't. Let it happen. Again."

He released the footman, who slumped, dazed, against the doorjamb. Then with a flamboyant swish of his driving coat, Jardine left.

Louisa waited until the footman scrambled out of the boudoir and the street door slammed shut. Then she sank into the nearest chair.

Immediately, Fanny flew to her, pelting her with questions.

Louisa made no response. She didn't know the answers. She couldn't even begin to guess. Jardine pursued her as relentlessly as he'd ever pursued the most hardened criminals. Why now, after all these years?

When they'd first fallen in love, Max had forbidden the match—as well he might, for he'd witnessed first hand the dark side of Jardine's character, the ruthlessness that lurked beneath the polished surface. Young, headstrong, barely eighteen, Louisa hadn't heeded Max's warning that nothing mattered to Jardine more than his dangerous profession. Until the day Jardine sacrificed *her* in the line of duty.

Never again. Never again would she trust him with her heart. Never again would she call him her love. At least, not out loud.

Years had passed since she'd sent him away. What had made him renew his campaign to win her in spite of it all?

Louisa shivered. Jardine always caught his quarry in the

end. She couldn't let that happen to her. She'd known deep down that running away was not the answer.

She must gather the courage to fight back.

THE short journey to Hove was accomplished largely in silence. Swaying with the movement of the carriage, Kate stole a glance at Lyle. He slouched in the corner, apparently at ease, but his vigilance showed in the tense line of his jaw and the glint of watchful gray eyes under his hat brim.

Between kissing her with such incendiary passion and handing her into the carriage, Lyle had assumed the air of a soldier on a mission—impersonal, uncaring, brusque to the point of rudeness.

As if he hadn't made furious love to her last night. As if he'd resolved to succeed in his appointed task at all costs—even at the expense of whatever lay between them.

Rather sourly, Kate admired his single-minded determination. By contrast, every cell of her body clamored for the feel of him—surrounding her, covering her, inside her. Even when she closed her eyes, she smelled him, sensed his taut, expectant energy. His presence filled her senses utterly. Every breath she took, she breathed him in.

Lyle's restless tension had nothing to do with desire. Protecting her, finding the rebels, was serious, dangerous business. She wished her wayward, treacherous body would understand that, instead of yearning for his touch. His words at the ball came back to her: *"This is not a game . . ."*

Kate battled to marshal her scattered wits. Lyle had the right of it. She needed to regain her focus, too. Far more important than her passion for the man beside her was her brother's predicament. Lyle had the power to arrange for Stephen's release. She needed to persuade him to exercise it. And if that meant annihilating whatever fragile trust had built between her and Lyle, so be it. Stephen was her kin, her blood. His safety was paramount. It had to be.

She respected Lyle's reasons for hunting those men. But surely there was another way to find them besides locking up her brother?

Having rehearsed what she'd say in her mind until she was word perfect, Kate cleared her throat. "Lyle?"

His gaze flickered to her and out the window again. "I'm sorry. I haven't been a congenial traveling companion, have I?" He hesitated. "I was thinking of the fire."

Her prepared speech withered on her lips.

Lyle blew out a breath. "There were four in line for the dukedom before me, did you know that? They all died that day."

Kate swallowed hard and remained silent. Expressing sorrow or regret seemed wholly inadequate.

Lyle stared at the countryside that passed steadily by, until it seemed he wouldn't continue. Kate started when he spoke. "Please don't imagine it affected me in a personal way," he said. "They weren't my immediate family. In fact, I'd never met any of them before."

Sensing that he wanted to speak of it, perhaps unburden himself in some way, Kate asked, "How did it come about that so many died that day?"

His lips tightened. Moments passed before he opened them. "Those who expected a legacy from the old duke gathered in the muniments room for the will reading, while the rest of the family waited in the drawing room in another wing of the house." He blew out a breath. "All who heard the will read died. Every one of them."

Kate gasped. "How awful." She hadn't realized what utter devastation the fire had wrought.

"I wasn't there. I . . ." He looked down at his hands. "I detested the old duke. It would have been hypocritical for me to attend his funeral. My brother was abroad, thank God."

His bowed head struck her heart. She wished for the courage to smooth that unruly black hair from his brow, to draw him into her arms. "You don't blame yourself for your absence, surely?"

He turned his gaze to hers. With a bitter smile, he said, "No. Even I am not so conceited as to believe I could have stopped the fire. Most likely, I would have perished along with the others. But . . . one feels a sense of, oh, I don't know. Guilt? Responsibility? Certainly, it's my duty now to see those rebels brought to justice. I owe it to the dead, but I also owe it to the survivors. Their lives will never be the same."

A grand Elizabethan manor house loomed in the distance, beyond a handsome park. The carriage bowled past the imposing gates and continued down the road a little way, before turning into a lane.

"That fire changed your life, too," Kate said softly. "Now, you are a duke." She wondered how he would adapt to the transition. "How strange Fate is."

His brows snapped together. "It wasn't Fate's hand that set that fire, Lady Kate. It was a very human one."

"And you are determined to see justice done. Yes, I understand." She paused, gathering her courage. "Similarly, *you* must understand that my brother has done nothing to warrant being locked up for sedition. He doesn't condone violence. He never has. Never! If you only knew—" She felt her voice rising and fought to control her emotions. Emotional display would get her nowhere with Lyle.

"He will be free soon enough. You have my word."

Lyle sounded so certain, but he didn't know Stephen. Kate cleared her throat. "These . . . methods of persuasion you spoke of . . ."

He turned his head to look at her and she couldn't stop the heat that rose to her cheeks. *Those hands. Those big, magical hands.* "I—I meant your methods to persuade my *brother*. I don't see how they could be more persuasive than his sense of right."

When he merely looked skeptical, she said, "My dear sir, my brother is a saint. He would, indeed, go to the scaffold rather than betray another man to his death. He has all the conviction of a martyr. You will not sway him."

Lyle considered her for a long time, his eyes clear and perceptive.

"What is it?" She brushed at her face. "Have I a smut on my nose?"

"No. I was trying to decide when you are most beautiful," he replied. "When your brow furrows a little—" He traced the spot with his fingertip. "There. Or when your lips curve in that soft, pensive smile." He cupped her jaw in one hand and brushed her mouth with the pad of his thumb. "Ravishing."

She sat still, in wondering fascination, her breath coming faster. "I asked you a question, Lyle."

"Yes?" He bent towards her, angling his head, as if for a kiss. "What was it? I've forgotten."

Words stuck in her throat as his face filled her vision. She closed her eyes on a small sigh. For an instant, his warm breath caressed her lips. Then his mouth took hers.

It was an open, carnal kiss that shocked her, just as his unfettered possession of her body had shocked her the night before. Here was no gentle, respectful lover, but a man taking everything he wanted, giving no quarter.

She placed her palms on his chest, then slid them up to grasp his lapels. The force of his kiss drove her back against the squabs and she sank into them, pulling him into her. She kissed him back as if her life depended on it, with a raw sensuality she'd never shown another man. Ravenously, like a beggar at a feast.

And oh, hadn't she starved all these years?

"A tower." Kate stared up at the crenellated structure that stood next to a barn some distance from the house. It looked like the final remnant of a medieval castle. "You're locking me in a tower?"

"For your own protection. Come on." Lyle took her elbow and hurried her up the path to where a sturdy door barred the way. He produced a key to unlock the door and they stepped into a dark, round room with a central staircase that wound in a tight spiral to the floor above. They mounted the steps and emerged through a trapdoor in the ceiling into a room fitted out with rich red hangings and carpets and a large tester bed.

Kate eyed the chamber in amazement. "What *is* this place?"

Lyle bowed. "This will be your quarters for the next few days, my lady."

Her eyes widened. "You're going to lock me away in here, all by myself?"

He smiled down at her. "Some of the time," he answered, trailing his gaze down her body. "But I think I'll be able to keep you . . . reasonably entertained while you're here."

She hated that an anticipatory shiver ran through her and hated even more that he saw it. She thought about the previous night and wondered how soon they might repeat the experience.

"Books, for example," he continued, with an innocent expression.

Kate started. "Er, books?"

"Yes, books are very entertaining, don't you agree?" said Lyle. "And I'm sure there is some needle and thread somewhere, should you wish to sew."

She choked. "I'm more likely to scratch your eyes with the needle and garrote you with the thread!"

"Oh, and you may take your daily exercise in the barn."

His lips twitched at the glowering look she gave him. So he thought this was amusing!

Lyle glanced around. "I must make sure everything is secure. In the meantime"—he gestured at a pile of heavy-looking tomes—"there are the books."

He tipped an imaginary hat and disappeared through the trapdoor.

LEAVING George to guard the tower, Max strolled across the manicured lawns to the house. He walked through an open French door and immediately heard sounds of a disturbance.

"I won't have it, sir!" Small feet tromped along the corridor.

"You'll damned well have it and like it, madam!" Romney's unmistakable roar and stomping followed, attended by a soothing murmur he recognized as his sister's. Surprised, Max considered the meaning of her presence. Hadn't she trusted Romney with the diary? Perhaps she hadn't finished the translation yet.

The door to the drawing room in which Max stood flung open and a very pregnant lady erupted into the room, closely followed by her irate husband. On seeing him, they stopped short.

"Max!" Fanny's eyes lit and she moved forward to take his hands. "How delightful to see you. Do sit down and I'll ring for tea. Louisa, your brother," she spoke over her shoulder unnecessarily.

"Hello, Max." Louisa smiled and gave him her hands also, but strain shadowed her face. The diary. What secrets had he burdened her with?

He shot her a questioning glance and she nodded slightly, as if to confirm she'd accomplished her task. Then Romney was upon him shaking his hand and offering him something stronger than tea.

Romney ran his finger between his collar and neck.

"Good thing you turned up, old fellow. She wanted to redecorate the house. Immediately. That one might have been ugly."

Max shook his head at Fanny in mock exasperation. The Romneys delighted in their arguments and wouldn't know what to do if they ever found themselves in perfect harmony.

"I have brought a guest to stay in your tower," said Max. The two ladies looked intrigued.

"Snaffled her, did you?" Romney raised his brows as he poured them both a drink.

"Snaffled?" said Louisa, straightening. "Do you mean you have constrained this lady to accompany you here?"

"Of course not, Louisa," said Max, sending a warning glance to Romney. "The lady is here for her protection." He paused. "Someone is trying to kill her."

Louisa gasped. Fanny's face lit up. "That sounds vastly exciting. Better than a play! When can we meet her?"

"You, madam, shall go nowhere near the tower," her husband warned.

Fanny opened her mouth to retort, but Louisa intervened. "He is perfectly right, you know, Fanny. Though not perhaps, as *tactful* as he might be." She sent their cousin a withering glance then turned back to Fanny. "You know you couldn't manage the stairs."

"Well, perhaps this mysterious *she* can come to us?" Fanny looked enquiringly at Max.

Max shook his head. "Out of the question. Just curb your curiosity for the moment, puss, and let the lady be." He cocked an eyebrow. "Louisa? A word in private, if I may."

"Yes, of course. We should go to the library, perhaps."

Graceful, as always, Louisa led him from the room.

As they walked the corridor in silence, he noticed a tension in the air about his sister, as if she were holding very tightly to her composure.

Once they reached the library, she immediately went to an oak chest beneath the window. She opened the lid and took out the diary and a sheaf of foolscap—her translation, he supposed—and clutched them both to her chest. She didn't speak.

He closed the door behind him with a loud click, shattering the silence.

"How will you use this information?" Louisa blurted out.

"That is government business. I'm afraid I can't say."

"But how can it be—" Louisa began, but caught herself. She searched his face. "You don't know what is in this book, do you, Max?"

"Not precisely," he admitted. "I wouldn't have needed you to translate it if I did, would I?"

"Oh. Yes, right." Louisa still made no move to hand the documents over.

"I'll have them now, if you don't mind," he said, stretching out his hand to her. Suddenly, his hand shook. The answer to what kind of threat Lady Kate posed lay between these pages, and perhaps even a clue as to who wanted her dead. But more than that, the diary was hers, her thoughts, a part of her. He was almost sick with apprehension about what it might contain.

"Do you know who wrote this?" Louisa asked. "Is—is it the lady in the tower?"

"No." Max felt honor-bound to protect Kate's identity, even from his sister. "Now, give me the diary and your notes, please, Louie."

Her face worked, as if she were trying not to burst into tears. What was the matter with the girl? She shoved the papers and the diary into his hands, then brushed past him and wrenched open the door.

"I give you joy of them," she whispered and closed the door behind her.

Max was left gripping the papers, staring at the unresponsive door. Why was Louisa so distraught? Did she object to him reading someone else's private papers? The morality of it troubled him, too, but for the sake of Lady Kate's safety it had to be done.

*Women.* He shrugged and sat down to read.

# Eleven

*I want to give him everything, pleasure him as he has delighted me. Curse my confounded, chaste ignorance! I know there is more . . .*

LOUISA approached the tower cautiously, looking about her to check that no one saw.

She stopped short when she got inside. George sat there on the bottom of the winding staircase, gnawing on a chicken bone.

"Lady Louisa." He straightened to full attention, attempting to hide his drumstick behind him.

"Do go on with your meal, George," said Louisa, smiling at him. "I came to make the acquaintance of the lady upstairs. My brother said I should see to her comfort."

She hardly ever lied, but in a good cause, she could be very glib. Nodding to him, she swept past, giving him no opportunity to gainsay her.

Pushing up the heavy trapdoor was a feat in itself, and Louisa tried several times before it lifted and swung back. She popped her head through the opening and saw a woman above her, standing in an aggressive attitude. "Oh, don't run me through with your hat pin, I pray!" laughed

Louisa, scrambling through the opening and rising to her feet. "I'm quite harmless, I assure you."

The woman eyed her doubtfully, but she put the pin down on an occasional table. She looked a little wild, with her hair coming lose from its tight coil, her chest rising and falling as if she'd had a fright.

"I hope I didn't scare you. I'm Louisa. Lyle's sister, you know."

A moment passed before the woman relaxed. "Lady Kate Fairchild," she responded, returning her smile. "Please call me Kate. Do sit down. I'm delighted to make your acquaintance, only what you must think of my being here like this, I can't guess!"

Louisa took the chair Kate indicated. Waving away Kate's embarrassment, she said, "My brother told me only that your life is in danger. That is enough for the present."

Kate made a wry face. "It is true, though it sounds so melodramatic when you put it like that."

Something about this lady—her manner, her humor perhaps—made Louisa almost certain she was the author of that diary. Suddenly nervous, Louisa launched into speech. "Well, I can see you would much rather rest, so I'll leave you. I just came to see if there was anything I could do to secure your comfort while you're here. Are you quite famished? I'll send up a basket. Oh, and books! Do you read? If you are to stay here any length of time, you must let me bring you some books. I—"

*I read your diary and it felt like you'd written my life.*

No, she couldn't say that, not in a thousand years. But she stood there with a powerful longing in her breast for connection. She wanted so much to talk with this woman, ask her, oh, all kinds of things. But one couldn't force intimacy, particularly on the first meeting, and she'd no intention of blurting out that she'd read Kate's diary. How intrusive and embarrassing Kate would find that. She'd be horrified.

Kate smiled. "You are so kind. I admit, I am hungry and

I would like some books to read." She glanced at the pile of serious-looking tomes on the table. "That is, do you have any novels? I confess I'm partial to them."

"Oh, yes. My cousin Fanny has tons of them," Louisa said. "She is quite addicted."

"In fact, I feel a little like a heroine in a novel at the moment," said Kate, grimacing. "Or at least one of those maidens in a fairy tale. The princess in the tower."

And she did look rather like a fairy princess, with her slightly tip-tilted nose and wide hazel eyes. "I suppose Max put you here because this tower is most easily defended," said Louisa.

"I'd like to be able to defend myself," answered Kate, glowering a little. "Your brother won't agree to teach me. He likes to think he is my sole protector, that I shouldn't need to learn any defense techniques myself. But look—"

To Louisa's astonishment and horror, Kate unpinned the fichu from around her neck, revealing yellowing bruises that bloomed and darkened like a crude necklace against her milk-white skin.

"Someone tried to strangle me."

Louisa sat down abruptly on a nearby chair. Her fingertips brushed her own throat, and suddenly, she had difficulty swallowing. "Who?" she managed.

Kate shrugged. "Your guess is as good as mine. Well, actually, that's not quite true. It seems I have annoyed someone in the government."

Louisa gasped. "I cannot believe that in a civilized society such as ours the government could have a lady of quality killed because she had 'annoyed' them."

Sighing, Kate said, "Well, I have done a little worse than annoy them, actually." Her gaze flickered to her hands, which twisted in her lap. "You see, my brother is in prison because he won't tell the government where suspected arsonists are hiding. He is a simple country vicar, no danger to anyone at all."

"In prison?" said Louisa. "How dreadful." Arsonists? Did she refer to the fire at Lyle? No wonder Lady Kate had been desperate. And no wonder Max refused to help her brother. He was determined to track down the rebels who had burned the family pile.

Lady Kate said, "And the worst of it is, they don't need to bring my brother to trial under these new laws. They can hold him indefinitely. You see why I was desperate. I've threatened to expose certain members of Parliament for the rogues they are if they don't release my brother."

What a story! And what courage Kate must have to confront her brother's persecutors like that. "You are very brave. I wish I had half your courage," said Louisa. "So that's why Max put you in this tower."

"Yes, but I feel . . ." Kate rubbed her arms and shivered. "I feel even more vulnerable here. Like a sitting target."

Staunchly, Louisa said, "My dear, Max will not fail you. He is experienced in these matters, and to my knowledge, no one has bested him yet." She stood. "I'll leave you now, but I'll be back with a basket of food and those books."

AFTER reading one page of that diary, all the blood left in Max's brain. He could barely see straight. These were the writings of the virtuous Lady Kate?

A red mist descended over his eyes as he read on. This mystery lover—who was he? Somehow, Max had been convinced Lady Kate was faithful to her dull dog of a husband, yet it seemed she'd played him false from the beginning.

Max flicked through to the end. The entries were sporadic, covering many years and they stopped a few months earlier. Had she begun another journal? Or had she given her lover his congé?

He lowered the sheaf of papers to his lap and tipped his head back against the chair, breathing deeply. He was so torn between unbridled lust and raging jealousy, he didn't know if he could keep reading.

This couldn't be the diary she'd spoken of, the one in which she'd recorded sensitive government information. He passed the members of the cabinet through his mind. No, he couldn't imagine any of the present government in the role of this mystery lover.

But something impelled him to go on. Knowing it was a violation, knowing that if she discovered what he'd done she'd never forgive him. He needed to read it. He needed to know.

He turned the page and lowered his gaze.

The library door wrenched open. "By God, I'm going to strangle that chit one day."

Romney stormed in and headed straight to the drinks tray.

*Oh, hell!* Max flipped over the papers and laid them in his lap, hiding an erection of truly massive proportions. Damn it, he should have gone to his bedchamber for some privacy.

Crystal clinked as Romney poured himself brandy. "Want some?" he barked over his shoulder.

"Please." Maybe brandy would take the edge off him. He needed something to calm him down, that was certain.

Romney handed him the drink, and Max's hand shook as he took it. Fortunately, Romney was in one of his rages and didn't notice.

Thick eyebrows lowered, his overly long auburn hair flying in all directions as if he'd tried to yank it out, there could be only one cause for Romney's fit of temper.

"What has Fanny done now?" Max resigned himself to the inevitable.

"Wants to go back to town," Romney grunted. "The whims of pregnant women! She's supposed to be resting, for God's sake, and she wants to go back to London. She's bored here, if you please! We've only just arrived."

Max made sympathetic noises, letting his cousin fume about the iniquities of his wife. Fanny and Romney were never happy unless they were fighting, so Max wasn't unduly concerned.

He tried to think of a way to extricate himself from the conversation so he could continue his reading. "I'm sure Fanny will see reason. Just let her calm down a bit." He put down his brandy glass and gathered up his papers, making as if to rise. "Now, I really must g—"

"She says I'm smothering her." Romney sighed, rubbing his forehead. "M'mother died in childbirth, you know."

Smothering a groan, Max eased back in his chair. He regarded his cousin with sympathy. "Fanny is healthy as a horse. She's had an easy pregnancy. There's no reason to fear."

Romney breathed deeply through his nostrils. "Yes, you're right. But I won't take any chances. She's not going back to London. I've made that clear. Ordered her to stay."

"And did that work?"

Romney sipped his brandy. "She's packing her bags as we speak."

Max could well imagine. "Romney, tell me. Is it important to keep her in the country?"

"Lord, yes. The doctor recommended quiet and fresh country air for her confinement. She's been queasy, you know, and another journey in a closed carriage back to town won't do her any good."

"Then, my friend, you will have to practice diplomacy," said Max. He held up his hand before Romney could argue. "I know it's unfamiliar territory, but you need to think of your wife's well-being. Don't command her. *Ask* her to stay. Tell her you are worried for her health. You might even confide in her about your own mother. Be assured, her tender heart will melt at your concern."

Romney turned a little green. "*Ask* her to stay?"

"I know this will be a novel experience, but you can do it," said Max encouragingly. "You might even plead."

"*Plead?* Are you mad? If I back down on this, she'll walk all over me like an old carpet for the rest of our lives. She'll lead me around by the nose like a performing bear. She'll—"

"No, she won't. Who will be getting their way if she gives in to your plea? You will."

"At the expense of my pride," grumbled Romney.

"What's more important? Your pride or your wife's health?"

Romney muttered into the dregs of his brandy, then tossed them off and set down his glass with a decisive snap. "You're right. Damme if I ever thought I'd be taking marital advice from you, coz, but stranger things have happened."

Max smiled rather grimly. "I'm certainly wiser about other people's affairs than I am about my own. Go to her now. You don't want to have to drag her back from London."

Romney launched himself out of his chair, looking like a sulky lion. "Plead, you say?"

"On bended knee. She'll fall all over you, I guarantee it."

"Oh, all right." At the door, Romney thought of something and looked back. "The mysterious female in the tower. Lady Kate, I take it?"

Max grunted. "Yes." He fingered the papers that burned his hands. "I'll tell you the details later. Go on. Do your duty like a man."

With the deep breath and set shoulders of someone marching into a losing battle, Romney left the room.

The second the door closed behind him, Max leaped up and turned the heavy key in the lock. He didn't relish any more interruptions.

Max settled back into his chair and found his place. He swallowed a healthy dose of brandy and continued to read.

By the time he'd finished, he'd realized two things—first, this mysterious lover was a figment of Lady Kate's imagination; and second, he was as hard as a block of wood with wanting her.

He felt inordinately relieved about the first revelation. It hadn't been difficult to detect. One night, the lover would come to her in London; the next, they would make love on a gondola in Venice. There was no way they could travel so quickly between the two cities. And no flesh and blood man could possibly be that perfect.

The writer of this erotic journey had let her imagination run to the realms of fantasy but something told Max she had little real experience between the sheets. And the combination of innocence and blatant, inquisitive eroticism made him wild for her.

Max swallowed the last of his brandy. Lady Kate's sensual world had so enthralled him, he'd left his glass untouched at his elbow for some time.

He rubbed his eyes and pinched the bridge of his nose. As the sky had darkened, he hadn't even interrupted his reading to light a lamp, he'd been so engrossed. How long had he sat there?

Lady Kate's form rose in his mind. She was up in that tower now. He needed to go to her, not least because she would be hungry and bored, wondering where he was.

He left the library, lengthening his strides, clutching the diary and Louisa's translation. *Louisa!* Now he understood her reaction. No doubt the task had appalled her.

Max groaned. He ought to speak to her, apologize for making her translate a text that no maiden lady should see. The awkwardness of that forthcoming conversation was enough to make him blanch, but it had to be done.

He jogged upstairs to his bedchamber to hide the diary and the translation. Pray God he could return the diary to Lady Kate's house before she discovered it was missing. She'd be mortified if she knew he'd read it.

Even as he thought it, Max knew he would keep the translation.

He ought to burn it. A gentleman wouldn't have read it in the first place.

Well, he'd never pretended to be a gentleman.

He left his chamber and let himself out a side door to walk over to the tower. He wished there was a convenient fountain he could dive into to relieve the hard, hot ache in his loins. He needed to calm down before he saw her again, regain mastery over his emotions. It was clear from her diary what Lady Kate liked in a lover—someone smooth and gentle and polite.

He was none of those things. He'd been rough with her last night. He winced at the memory of taking her like some common doxy against a wall when there was a perfectly good bed they could have used. He should have been kind and gentle, especially when she'd suffered such terrible treatment at the hands of the unknown killer.

A surge of anger and desperate protectiveness rose within him. Yes, he'd been furious last night—furious with himself for allowing that attack to take place—and he'd taken it out on her. He hoped he hadn't given her a disgust of him.

He thought back over the morning, to the handful of passionate kisses they'd shared. She hadn't *seemed* upset, but you could never tell with women. And Lady Kate was a master at masking her emotions. Witness the iron control she'd shown after the attempt on her life.

There was a light on in the tower room. He scanned the window, half expecting to see her silhouetted there, waiting dreamily for her phantom lover.

At the foot of the stairs, George sat carving a block of wood.

"Go and get dinner and some rest, George. Come back in the morning."

George didn't make any lewd comments, which showed

his respect for Lady Kate. "Right you are, guv. Miss Louisa was here afore, talking to her ladyship. I didn't see no 'arm in letting her up."

"None at all," said Max. He couldn't imagine his sister mentioning the diary. Had she already guessed at the author? He hoped not.

George left with a grunt of thanks, and Max continued up the winding staircase, the sense of anticipation building with each step. He'd do better this time.

He swung open the trapdoor and continued up the stairs. A stab of unease told him to be vigilant; the next instant, something solid swung at his head.

He ducked, then shot through the opening, grappling with his attacker. In no time, he realized his assailant had womanly curves and a soft, fragrant body. He relaxed his grip on Lady Kate's shoulders, then tightened it again when she tried to hit him.

"It's me, Lyle," he barked.

"I know it's you!" she said, pummeling him ineffectually with her hands. Her small fists were trapped between their bodies and felt like no more than butterfly's wings beating against his chest.

She glared up at him. "How *dare* you frighten me like that?"

Surprised, he let her go and she swung a fist at his face, but she was so much smaller than he was, she missed.

Trying not to laugh, he gave up defending himself. He just hoped she wouldn't hurt her knuckles as she settled on his stomach as a target.

Whack! "I'm tired"—thump!—"of being"—thwack!—"a victim! I do not *wish* to stay locked up in a tower like a heroine from some stupid novel!"

She bunched her hands in his waistcoat and glowered up at him like a pugnacious fairy. "Give me a pistol."

"You don't know how to shoot."

"I don't care! Give me one and teach me. There's nothing else to do here anyway. Teach me to fight and I won't feel so—so *damned* helpless!"

She must be laboring under severe emotion to swear like that. He stepped away from her to kick the trapdoor shut. "I'm here to protect you. There's no need—"

Something he suspected was a chamber pot whistled past his head and smashed on the wall behind him.

Max flinched. "Now see here—"

"No! You see here!" She launched some other piece of bric-a-brac at him, but her aim was terrible and she missed again. "I refuse to be a sitting target while you pat me on the head and tell me you know what's best."

She launched into a tirade, brandy eyes flashing fire, her teeth biting off the words.

Max's temper flared. The idea she could defend herself against a paid assassin was ludicrous. Couldn't she see that? Did she think he couldn't protect her himself? Was this her way of punishing him for what happened to her in the bath?

He'd had enough. Gripping her by the wrists, he yanked her towards him. And silenced her the only way he knew.

OH, Lord! Lyle's mouth swallowed her words and ravished her lips until they felt tender and bruised and she couldn't think anymore. Furious as Kate was, something inside her seemed to melt and flow out from her fingertips, down her body. Something warm and liquid and hugely exciting.

She could barely catch her breath, but she drank him in. His arms around her made her feel safe, protected, cherished even. He was so strong and big and hard and everything she wasn't.

She gave a small sigh and sank into the kiss, and when he felt her yield he picked her up as if she weighed nothing at all and carried her to the bed.

Urgent, impatient, he threw her down and came over her, working at the buttons on her bodice with fingers that were too large for their task. Buttons popped and his hand closed over her breast, still covered with her corset and shift.

She gasped at the instant pleasure of his touch. He tugged at her corset, but it laced up the back and the stiff fabric wouldn't yield. He gave a growl of impatience and bent his head. The next instant, she felt his tongue and his lips through layers of fabric, teasing her nipple, his teeth grazing it gently.

A jolt to her loins made her moan and twist her body restlessly. He hadn't even touched her there, but she was mad for him, couldn't wait any longer.

"Oh, please." She writhed beneath him, wishing she had the courage to say what she wanted.

He seemed to know exactly what she needed, because he left off the preliminaries he'd tortured her with the previous night.

Freeing his erection from his trousers, he pushed her skirts up and positioned himself. With one, clear thrust, he was inside her, stretching her to the limit, and she sighed at how right it felt.

She put her hands up to stroke his shoulders and his body trembled. "Oh, God," he panted. "I can't slow down." He kissed her hard on the lips and breathed, "I'll make it up to you, I promise."

She didn't know quite what he meant, but his hips pumped fast and hard, rubbing a place inside her that turned sliding friction to exquisite torment. She rose higher and higher, spinning out of control until her flesh tingled and her bones shattered and showered down in tiny glittering shards.

Her whole body convulsed around him. Seconds later, he gave a guttural groan and collapsed on top of her.

She was raw and sore. She couldn't breathe, but she loved the weight of him, the feel of his hard body against her soft one, pressing her into the mattress. When he rolled away to lie next to her, she didn't want him to go. But she couldn't find the words to tell him.

She lay there, sparkling under her skin, euphoria flooding her body, and he said, "Oh, God. I'm sorry."

The shock was like a dash of icy water in the face. A sick sense of inevitability washed over her. Why had she thought it might be different with Lyle?

Staring at the silk canopy overhead, she found her voice. "What do you mean?"

"I didn't think. I . . ." She glanced at him and saw his Adam's apple move, as if he swallowed past a lump in his throat. "I treated you like a common—" He took a deep breath, rubbing his palms down his face, not looking at her. "It won't happen again."

She would never forgive him for that. For those few minutes, she'd been caught up in his passion. Abandoned herself to her own desire as she'd never done before. And the result had been sublime.

Until he apologized. Until he made her feel like a whore.

"I'd like you to go now," she whispered. She flung her forearm across her face, feeling the hectic heat on her brow, suddenly aware of the damp stickiness between her thighs. All tawdry and sullied now.

*A true lady wouldn't . . .* She screwed her eyes shut to block out Hector's voice.

Lyle seemed to hesitate, as if he wanted to say something, but apparently thought better of it. He adjusted his breeches—he hadn't even taken his coat off, she now realized, or his boots—and launched himself from the bed.

"I'll be downstairs if you need me."

She wouldn't. The room could be burning down around

her before she'd ask for his help. She made herself speak, though her voice came out painfully cracked. "Don't come in again without knocking or I'll brain you with that chair."

That ought to have made her feel better, but she just wanted to curl up and die.

She could feel his gaze boring into her. "I give you my word it won't happen again."

The trapdoor closed quietly behind him. Kate rolled onto her side and let the tears fall.

# Twelve

*I dreamed that Hector found us. In flagrante delicto, bodies entwined. Shocked delight.*

*Hector has never seen me naked before . . .*

LOUISA dismissed her maid and sat at her dressing table, staring into her reflection, as if she could find the secrets of her soul there.

Before that diary came into her life, she'd not been satisfied, nor content, but she'd endured. She'd maintained her poise, and though she ached inside for what she could never have, she hadn't allowed her pain to show through her cheerful demeanor.

But when she read the diary, it became so true and real to her that her carefully constructed façade started cracking like old plaster. And every time Jardine appeared, another part of her veneer flaked away.

What did he want? Why did he persist in tormenting her when he must know there was no hope for them if he continued in his present way of life? How could she make him leave her alone?

A movement in the looking glass caught her eye. She

gasped, but before she could turn, large gloved hands settled on her shoulders, holding her in place.

"I said I would follow you."

Her hand trembled as she brought it up to her throat. She met his dark eyes in the glass.

"How did you—" No. It was pointless asking how he'd gained entrance to her bedchamber. Jardine could move like the wind. No locked door could keep him out.

At least he hadn't made a scene this time. If Max found out . . .

"What took you so long?" she managed.

He snorted a laugh and gave her shoulders a quick squeeze. "That's my girl. I had business to attend to or I would have been hard on your heels. With your permission?" He drew up a chair and straddled it, keeping just behind her and to her right.

She watched him in the glass. His dark eyes glittered in the candlelight, an almost manic expression beneath those devilish black brows. The hairs on the back of her neck stood to attention. Her breath came faster, though after that first caress, he hadn't touched her again. She reached for a pot of cold cream and clenched her hand around it, trying to anchor herself.

Jardine pulled a sheaf of paper from his waistcoat. Her eyes widened as she recognized the hand. The diary!

She shouldn't have done it, but she couldn't resist making a copy of the translation for herself.

"Oh, God!" She choked.

"Yes, I really think you must explain this, my dear," purred Jardine, flinging the pages onto her dresser in a gesture that coupled disdain with banked fury. "I haven't read all of it. To be frank, it turned my stomach in parts. Your prose is a little too florid for my taste, but I caught the general gist."

He thought *she'd* written it. That the encounters in the diary were real. "No! You don't unders—"

He reached forward and swung her about by the shoulders. She'd never been afraid of him before but now she saw the trained killer stripped bare of all his aristocratic polish.

"His name, if you please."

She fought for courage. "So you can challenge him?"

"So I can kill him. Very slowly." Jardine flashed white teeth. "If I can't have you, I'll be damned if some limp cock of a smooth-talking bastard will have you, either. Good Lord, woman! Have you no discrimination?"

She couldn't tell him this was Kate's diary, but then again, how could she admit to writing such things? If only she hadn't given in to weakness and made that copy!

"Let go of me." She wrenched away from him. "The man in the diary is imaginary. I made him up! If you can't see that, then you've syllabub for brains, you idiot!"

Jardine's brows snapped together. "You . . ." Light broke over his devilish features and the hint of a smile. "Why?"

She stared at him, wondering if he could ever understand why a woman might weave these fantasies. Men were so free.

*Because I need someone. Because I'm so lonely sometimes I think I'll shrivel and die. Because no matter how much you want me, you won't ever stay.*

But all she said was, "I don't know why." She gathered the pages and crushed them between her hands, wishing she'd a fire to burn them in. "I was mad, I think."

As she crumpled those pages, she felt cold. And more alone than she'd ever felt before.

"Come here."

She swallowed. "No."

His voice deepened. "Don't tell me you don't want me. All these years . . ."

She'd never understood why he still wanted her, came after her time and again. She was no beauty. By contrast, he had everything—looks, fortune, position. He could have any woman he wanted. Why did he keep returning to her?

"You know I can't." Her voice broke. "You know why! And it's your fault. It's in your power to change but you won't do it. And then you hound me like this! I can't stand it anymore, Marcus. If you cared for me at all, you wouldn't—"

He plucked her off her chair, banded his arms around her, and crushed her mouth with his. Her body, her mind, her soul, flew to him instantly. It was not wise, it was everything she'd vowed she would never do. She'd never leave herself vulnerable to him again.

Louisa wrenched her head to the side, panting as if she'd run a mile. He buried his face in her hair, kissing her throat, seducing her in every way.

But she whispered, "No." And then she said, "No!" And gave him a forceful shove. Her whole body clamored with longing, but she couldn't let him closer after successfully keeping her distance all this time. She couldn't let him love her, knowing that at the end of it, there would only be good-byes.

"Why do you do this to me?" she cried, taking in his stormy expression, the deep sensuality of that skillful mouth. "What do you want from me?"

An arrested look came over his face. Then he turned, running a hand through his hair. "I don't know." Chest heaving, he looked back at her, as a starving man might look at a feast. "I only know I want you."

Her heart had broken so many times. One more fissure snaked through it. "But not enough," she whispered.

She gripped her hands together and tried to still the tremor in her voice. "If you care for me at all, you will stay away."

He gave an ugly crack of laughter. "Oh, I care. And I'll find a way to have you, m'dear. You can count on it."

She gazed at him steadily, summoning all her strength. "Go," she said quietly. "Your empty promises carry no weight with me."

Pain flashed across his face, but so swiftly she might have imagined it. "We might have parted ways, but I never surrendered the right to watch over you." He pointed at her. "Remember that."

He turned and left by the window, as silently as he'd arrived.

Louisa shivered. To have Jardine watch over her was far more dangerous than anything else that might threaten her.

But she'd won this battle. At least, for now, he was gone.

MAX stared into the dregs of his tankard. It was late. He couldn't be bothered reaching for his timepiece, but judging by how much he'd drunk, it must be close to midnight.

He was blessed with a remarkably hard head, but it was time to get back and relieve George. After the debacle with Lady Kate, he definitely craved something stronger, but he'd stayed with ale. A man needed his wits about him when Lady Kate was around.

Besides her more obvious charms, what he chiefly admired about her was her wit, her poise, that desperate courage that drove her to blackmail to defend her brother.

And now that someone had made an attempt on her life, did she cower in the corner? Not she! She'd nearly brained him with a chamber pot, insisted on learning to defend herself. Well, perhaps there were a few things he could teach her if it would make her feel more secure.

His mind darkened. What if she refused to speak to him after what he'd done? It wasn't rape. She hadn't once said no or tried to stop him. He hadn't been so far gone he couldn't tell the difference between a willing woman and one who didn't want him. But—

A sudden hush fell over the taproom. Max looked up. Jardine stood in the doorway watching him, a cynical twist to his mouth.

The patrons resumed talking, but in whispers, which probably meant they were gossiping about this newcomer in their midst. Apparently oblivious to the stir he caused, Jardine ordered a tankard of home-brewed and made his way to join Max.

"Evening, Your Grace," said Jardine, steel in his tone. "I didn't know you were in the vicinity."

"Or else you might have stayed away?" Max raised his brows. "You're not following me, by any chance?"

Jardine sat side-on, with his forearm resting along the table, black-booted legs stretched out before him and crossed at the ankles.

He appeared at his ease, but he surveyed the room in that instinctive way they all did, watching for trouble, mapping out the exit routes. "Now, why would I do that, old fellow? I have utter confidence in you." He paused. "You might be interested to know that Lady Kate's solicitor has been making a small noise at the Home Office about Lady Kate's disappearance."

Max straightened. "The devil he is!"

"Oh, no need to trouble yourself, dear fellow. I made certain he was fed that tale about the sick aunt. I doubt he believes it, but he's been brought to acknowledge he'll do the lady's reputation no favors if he makes a hue and cry." Jardine sipped his ale. "Have you made any progress with Lady Kate's literary offerings?"

The swift change of subject startled Max. He almost reacted, but then he remembered which literary offerings Jardine meant. Jardine could have no idea of the erotic fantasies that had tormented Max's every moment since he'd read them that afternoon.

He marshaled his wits. He needed to try to throw Jardine off the scent. "Are you so certain the memoirs exist? She might have fabricated the entire thing."

"I've read the first chapter," said Jardine.

"Yes, but perhaps there isn't any more," said Max, and the idea seemed less far-fetched than he might have thought. "What, exactly, was in that first chapter?"

Jardine waved a hand. "Oh, it was all rather ephemeral. Nothing damaging per se. Mostly hints and innuendo about what was to come. The lady's instructions were to publish it in the event of her disappearance or demise, but as I have the only copy and you have the lady, we are safe for the time being."

"Did you get a sense of what we might expect when the rest comes to light?" said Max.

Jardine took a sip of ale. "Reading between the lines, I'd say Lady Kate knows a great deal that might fluster our esteemed members of Parliament, but there was no indication of any major revelation in the offing. I could be quite wrong on that score, though." He met Max's eyes. "I want those memoirs. It's time Faulkner had his congé." He frowned. "I'm thinking of giving up fieldwork."

"My God, could you survive?" mocked Max.

"As head of operations, very well, I imagine," said Jardine, staring before him contemplatively. He cocked an eyebrow. "Did you never wish to settle down while you were in service, Lyle?"

"To what? Marriage?" Max shrugged. "Our line of work doesn't mix with marital bliss. Can't say I was ever tempted, no."

"But now you are free to do as you wish. You are a duke. You can have any woman you want."

Max thought of Lady Kate. "But things are never that simple, are they?"

Jardine's features hardened, and the devilish look deepened as he flicked a piece of lint from his sleeve. "No, my dear fellow. That they are not."

"MESSAGE for you, guv." George stepped out of the darkness to join Max in his vigil.

Max took the screw of paper and smoothed it out. "Who brought it?"

"Young lad Perry," said George. "Said you told him where you was heading."

George's disapproval was palpable.

Max sighed. "You've never liked Perry, have you, George? What do you have against him?"

"Nothing specific, as you might say," said George, shrugging. "Don't like the cut of his jib."

Max smiled to himself. Perhaps a little jealousy might be at work here. Perry had been something of a protégé of Max's, ever since that incident with the boy's father. He'd been pathetically grateful for his rescue . . .

Max read the letter by the chancy light of his lantern. "Good news," he said quietly. "Holt has agreed to talk."

"Ah, guv, you're a clever cull and no mistake. You knew he'd talk if he thought his sister was in danger."

"Yes. A masterstroke." Max couldn't help feeling bitter at the necessity. So many lies he'd told her.

Folding the letter, he put it in his pocket. "I'll need to go to London. We can't free the vicar until we're certain he's given us the right information."

He closed his eyes momentarily. He hated to leave matters with Kate still in shreds but he needed to go to London and get this business over with. Perhaps it would give her time to forgive him.

He dismissed George and sat down to plan.

Or at least he tried, but his mind kept flipping back to Kate.

Despite his best intentions, he'd ravished her like some rutting beast up there. If only she'd looked vulnerable and delicate when he'd arrived, he might have been able to rein in this fierce passion he'd conceived for her. But she'd spat fire at him, thrown things at him! He'd wager the elegant Lady Kate had never lost her temper like that before.

Looking back, how could he have resisted her? That diary had him so worked up he couldn't see straight, and then she'd pummeled him and shouted at him . . .

And he could have sworn she'd . . . If he didn't know better, he'd think she might have . . . No. His lips twisted. That was his masculine pride rewriting history. She couldn't possibly have come in such a fast and furious encounter. Not a woman who preferred her men slow and gentle, like that phantom lover. Hell, he wished the man was real, so he could hunt him down and punch his daylights out.

But he couldn't fight an ideal. Could he ever be that man for her?

He glanced upwards, wishing his sight could penetrate the floorboards. Did she sleep? Or was she in as much turmoil as he was? He hated to think of her huddled in bed, perhaps weeping at his brutish behavior.

She wouldn't want him to see her like that. But the fact remained that he needed to talk to her. If he left, if the men he hunted turned out to be as desperate as he suspected, he might never see her again.

He wouldn't tell her that, of course. He'd have to trust Jardine to look after her if something happened to him. Jardine had given his word, and he'd do it, too. Despite his vagaries, the man was solid as a rock when the worst came to pass and his honor was unimpeachable. Romney was a good man in a fight, but he was about to become a father. Jardine was better. He had no emotional ties and his ruthlessness was legendary.

Max stepped outside the tower and whistled the particular tune he and George had devised as a signal years ago. Once again, his gaze lifted to the floor above.

He needed to tell her good-bye.

HE knocked this time.

Kate pressed her fingertips to her temples in an attempt to massage away an incipient headache. She wanted to tell Lyle to leave her be, but if he refused to go she wouldn't win that fight. Better to remain dignified if possible.

So she dragged herself off the bed and straightened her gown as best she could. "Come in."

The faint hope that her visitor was Lady Louisa, or perhaps even Lyle's taciturn manservant, died as that familiar dark head emerged through the trapdoor.

He quirked an eyebrow, humor playing about his mouth. "No missiles this time?"

"Well, you did knock." She tried to keep her voice light, her tone utterly polite. "Did you leave something behind?"

He looked at her for a long moment. "So that's how it will be between us."

She glanced away, fingering the bedpost. "How else could it be?"

He expelled a sharp breath. She could tell he wanted to shake her until her teeth rattled, and the worst part was, she wanted his hands on her, in anger, in passion—any way he chose. Longed for it, in spite of herself.

His restraint was almost palpable. Through tight lips, he said,"I must go to London for a few days."

She couldn't suppress a derisive snort. He was running away. Typical man! Why couldn't she ever rely on anyone, least of all the men in her life?

"And leave me unprotected?" She let a faint undercurrent of sarcasm run through her voice. She refused to betray her fear. She wouldn't beg him to take care of her.

He glanced at the shards of china that still lay scattered on the floor, and his mouth twitched upwards at the corners. "You'll have to improve your aim, won't you? But you needn't worry. George will guard you, and there's my cousin Romney, too. This is his house. I'll be as quick as I can."

She licked her lips. "I could come with you. I might be useful."

"You would be very much in the way," he said bluntly. "And I want you to do something for me while I'm gone. Think about who might want to kill you. What were you going to write in those memoirs of yours?"

"No one but you even knows about the memoirs. How could that be the motive?"

He hesitated. "I'm afraid that's not the case. You said you made sure you had insurance in case something happened to you. A former colleague of mine at the Home Office paid your solicitor a visit."

"Oh, no," she whispered. "He did not hurt poor Mr. Crouch?"

"No. But you may be sure that the Home Office has read that first chapter of your memoirs and knows all about your little scheme." As he said it, he wondered if it were true. If he were gunning for the top job, it was likely Jardine had kept the memoirs to himself.

Still, Kate needed to know the gravity of the case. He didn't spare her. "Where that information might have leaked is anyone's guess. If a government minister or some other associate of yours has taken your threats to heart, they might well want you eliminated."

Kate turned cold. She'd never meant matters to go this far. She would never actually carry out her threat to publish those memoirs, but still, she couldn't admit that to Lyle.

She pressed her fingertips to her throbbing temple. "I—I can't think at the moment. I'll have to go through everything in my mind."

"What about your diary? May I fetch it for you while I'm in London? That might give us a clue."

Kate hesitated. Could she trust him? It seemed she had little choice. "There is no diary. I made it up."

He scrutinized her face for a moment, as if to divine the truth. Then he nodded. "I thought as much. Well, needless to say, I'd rather you didn't commit any more of these charming anecdotes to paper, but think about it, all the same. What's the most damaging thing you know about someone in a position of power?"

"But I don't know anyone who would kill—"

"You never know what someone's capable of until they're driven to it. Let me be the judge of that."

She shivered. An acquaintance—perhaps even a friend—might be the killer? That made it so much worse.

Her hands shook. She gripped them together in her lap. "What about my brother?"

"He's the reason I'm going to London."

Kate's head jerked up. "He has agreed to give evidence? How can that be? They haven't hurt him, have they?"

"Of course not," he said, frowning. "I told you I had methods of persuasion. Your brother has seen sense and has agreed to tell us where those rebels are hiding. If his information proves correct, he will be released."

Kate narrowed her eyes. "There's something you're not telling me. I don't believe Stephen would agree to betray his principles like that."

His expression was unreadable. "That remains to be seen. I'll know more when I get to London. In the meantime, you have your assignment. And for God's sake, don't write anything down."

"What do you take me for? Of course I won't."

Lyle took a step towards her, then stopped. "Good-bye, then." He gave her a strained smile and turned to leave.

She didn't want him to go. Playing for time, she said

quickly, "Am I allowed visitors while I'm here? What about fresh air? May I not walk in the gardens?"

He turned back. "You may see Louisa. And Fanny, too, if she cares to brave the staircase. But I don't think it's wise to go outside—you'll be an exposed target. No one can save you from a chance bullet. There are too many places the killer could hide here. If you crave exercise, take a turn in the barn."

She glanced out the window to where the barn stood, only a few feet from the tower, and made a face.

His expression softened. "It's only for a few days, my dear. I'll be back as soon as I can."

She took her courage in her hands. "And then what?"

He looked at her speculatively, then his gaze ran down her body with an intimacy that brought a flush to her cheeks. He walked over to her, with that strong, fluid confidence that always characterized him.

She braced herself, knowing that if he kissed her she'd beg him to stay.

But his hands clenched into fists, as if with the effort of keeping them to himself. He looked down at her with a faint, rueful smile. "I'd give anything—" He stopped and sighed. "But there's no time now to do things properly. Will you wait for me? I swear I'll make it up to you for what happened here tonight."

What could she do except nod mutely, miserably aware that he completely misunderstood her reaction to that torrid encounter? She couldn't tell him how she really felt. She couldn't bear to see that same look of disgust on his face as she'd seen so many times on Hector's.

Why couldn't she be a normal woman with normal appetites and desires? One who didn't have this embarrassing, rampant passion coursing through her veins? Why couldn't she be delicate and disinterested, the way men expected her to be?

As if he couldn't help himself, Lyle bent to kiss her, and she fought the urge to press closer, to run her hands over his big shoulders and down his chest.

A shudder ran through her, and on a groan, he deepened the kiss, stroking into her with his tongue and the pulse beat in her brain until he tore his mouth free.

"My God, woman, but you bewitch me," he breathed. Running his hand through his hair, he turned away. "Every time, I mean to be gentle and yet every time—"

"Don't," she said quietly.

He looked like he might argue, but after a pause, he nodded. "No, you're right, I have to go. But we *will* sort this out when I return."

Suddenly, she wondered what danger he might face on the trail of those rebels. She'd been so caught up in her own concerns she'd scarcely thought about the job he had to do.

"Be careful," she said. "I know it's quite redundant to say that, but I . . . I shouldn't like it if anything were to happen to you."

He made a noise deep in his throat that sounded like a cross between a cough and a growl. "I can take care of myself. If anything happens to me, I've made provision for your protection."

She couldn't help but smile at his assumption that her only use for him was as a bodyguard. "That was very thoughtful of you," she said gravely.

He looked about him. "Do you have everything you need? I've sent to London for your maid to join you here. She should arrive tomorrow, but if you require, er, assistance, perhaps I could—"

Firmly, she shook her head. "I think we both know where that would lead." And she couldn't bear him to apologize again. "I shall do very well by myself tonight, but I would like someone to help me dress in the morning if a maid might be sent."

He nodded. "I'll see to it." Again, he hesitated. "Good-bye, Lady Kate."

Smiling, she stood on tiptoe. She stroked his jaw, with its faint evening stubble, and kissed his cheek.

"Good-bye."

# Thirteen

*He kissed me in the strangest place today. I was not quite sure I liked it at first . . .*

"It will be the end of an era after this case, won't it, Your Grace?"

Stuck in a carriage with Perry on the way to London, Max had been enjoying a rather pleasant daydream, one that featured Kate in various states of undress.

Reluctantly, he dragged his mind back to the present and opened one eye. He'd given up asking the boy to stop calling him "Your Grace," so he said, "Yes, I suppose it will. For me, at any rate." *And I couldn't be happier.*

Lit by a magnificent sunrise, Perry's youthful face glowed, and his gold hair formed a bright halo around his head. Angelic. For the hundredth time, Max wondered how Perry would survive if he continued his present work. Couldn't Faulkner see the boy was soft?

"I, also, feel the need for change," said Perry, nonchalantly. "Perhaps I might take a position as secretary to a great man."

"Oh, yes?" Max tipped his hat forward and closed his

eyes again. He guessed what was coming. There didn't seem any tactful way to avoid it.

"I could even become a steward, perhaps."

Max didn't open his eyes, but he felt the intensity of Perry's stare. Willing him to offer. Well, he wouldn't. The boy needed to stand on his own two feet. Hanging on Max's coattails wasn't good for him, and none of the gentle hints Max had given him over the years seemed to have sunk in. A clean break seemed the only alternative.

"Do—do you know of such a position, Your Grace?"

"No, not at present, but give me time to make enquiries. I might be able to find you a position." Gently, he added, "With one of my friends."

A gasp came from the other side of the carriage. Max glanced at Perry from beneath his hat brim without appearing to do so. Where before the boy's face had been flushed with a rosy spot of color on each cheek, now his face was white to the lips. The startling blue eyes blazed with pain.

The sight shocked Max. Small things about Perry had given him moments of unease over the years, but recently, the boy worried him more and more. A little hero worship for his mentor was natural in a young man, especially when that mentor had saved him from a terrible existence. But this conversation was the first inkling Max had received of how far matters had advanced.

How the hell was he going to handle it?

Quite simply, he didn't know. All he knew was that he needed to tread carefully. Until he could work out the best approach, he would pretend he hadn't noticed the savage agony in Perry's expression.

Best to change the subject. "Perry, I'm glad we had this chance to talk. I need you to do something for me," he said. He made a lot of work out of opening his eyes and setting his hat back at the correct angle, letting Perry compose himself.

Glancing out the window, Max added, "Strictly speaking, it's not official Home Office business, but I hope you will assist me as a favor."

The boy swallowed painfully. "I'd walk on hot coals for you, Your Grace, you know that. What do you want me to do?"

Max exhaled the breath he'd been holding in anticipation. He'd averted a scene—for the moment, anyway.

"I need to know who hired a man to assassinate Lady Kate Fairchild," Max said. "Ask in all the usual haunts. Seven Dials is a good place to start."

"Yes, sir!" The old enthusiasm flooded back into the boy's tone.

"Oh, and Perry?"

"Yes?"

Max regarded him steadily. "Be discreet, won't you? I don't want to be fishing your body out of the Thames."

The younger man flushed and muttered something, kicking the seat in front of him. Max let this truculence pass. He was far more concerned about the boy's earlier reaction.

The feeling of unease hadn't abated when they reached London. Max instructed the coachman to drive straight to Upper Wimpole Street, dropping Perry at his lodgings on the way.

Perry alighted and looked back into the carriage. "I'll get onto that assignment right away, Your Grace."

"Thank you, but I doubt you'll find any of the likely suspects up at this hour. Begin tonight, and I'll expect a report first thing tomorrow morning."

He tapped on the roof, and Perry hastily shut the door before the carriage sprang forward.

Filing the problem of Perry away for later, Max looked ahead to his forthcoming interview with Stephen Holt.

In a quixotic mood, Max had ordered the vicar's removal from prison. Holt was still under arrest, but now he cooled his heels in a bedchamber at a private house, a jail far more comfortable than the rat-infested hole he'd endured in Newgate.

Despite the man's courage and undoubted altruism, Max felt little sympathy for the vicar. Holt concealed the whereabouts of renegades who'd perpetrated a dastardly crime. For all Max cared, the vicar could rot in jail. He'd only relented because of Kate.

Max squared his shoulders, shrugging off a twinge of embarrassment. The decision to move Holt made logical sense, after all. The unpleasant surroundings of prison hadn't placed the slightest dent in the vicar's resolve. Only the news that Max held Kate had made her brother agree to this meeting.

Max jogged up the stairs and nodded to the guard outside the vicar's door. He hoped Holt was grateful for the clemency he'd been shown and fearful enough for his sister that he would talk. This had better not be a waste of time.

There were two men in the chamber, sitting at a plain wooden table playing cards.

An ill-assorted pair. Holt, a big bear of a man with rumpled, curly hair and an earthy manner that belied his calling. The other, Max recognized instantly. It was Ives, the spindleshanked villain he'd terrorized on Lady Kate's terrace.

Max frowned. He'd agreed to allow Holt a manservant during his incarceration, but he hadn't expected Ives to fill the role.

Holt looked up, and his generally benign expression darkened. He did not stand, a pointed lack of respect. "Your Grace. What an unexpected honor." He cocked his head at his companion. "Ives, you may leave us."

Max lifted a sardonic eyebrow as Ives shuffled from the room. "Strange company you keep."

"Isn't it?" said Holt pleasantly. "Won't you sit down?"

Max took Ives's chair and flicked over his cards. "A winning hand."

"No doubt. He cheats," said the vicar.

"Fortunate I came in when I did, then."

The vicar shrugged. "I don't play for money, so winning or losing is of complete indifference to me. Frankly, it's more interesting to see how soon I can detect the sleight of hand."

He leaned forward, and someone other than Max might have been intimidated by the menace in his attitude. "But enough of these pleasantries, my lord duke. I know what you've come for and I'm prepared to give it to you." Holt's square jaw hardened. "For my sister's sake."

He stared Max straight in the eye. "She'd better be unharmed, or I might forget that I'm a man of God and beat the living daylights out of you."

Max grunted. Holt might have a few pounds on him but fighting for survival tended to hone one's skills more than gentle sparring in Jackson's Boxing Saloon. "You are welcome to try," he said dryly. "But to answer your question, your sister *has* been harmed, but not by me."

Holt's sandy brows slammed together. "Harmed? What happened to her?"

Max didn't see the need to sugarcoat it. "She was almost strangled to death." He waited, while Holt exhaled an appalled breath. "Mr. Holt, I assure you, I will find who's responsible and deal with him."

"You mean you don't know?" Holt slammed the table with his open palm. "My sister was in your care and you let her—"

Holt ranted on, but he didn't say anything Max hadn't told himself a thousand times. Every time he saw those welts on Kate's graceful throat he wanted to tear the world apart with his bare hands.

But dwelling on his culpability was counterproductive. He needed to get Holt out of custody, which would ultimately remove the threat to Lady Kate.

When he judged Holt was running out of momentum, he held up his hand. "Your sister tried to save you from prison by threatening to blackmail the government."

"What?" Holt sat back in his chair. "Why would she do such a thing?"

"She was desperate to free you. She didn't seem to think you would act to save yourself."

"No, and if the little fool hadn't interfered, I wouldn't have to," growled Holt. "Strangled!" He swallowed hard, then raised a horror-filled gaze to Max's face. "And—and you've left her, unprotected, to come here?"

"Not unprotected, you may be sure of that," said Max. Though every minute he was away, he chafed to be back with her. "Tell me where Tucker and the others are hiding and I will let you go. Thus, your sister no longer has a reason to blackmail the government and the threat against her will disappear."

Holt's heavy scowl gave him the look of a bad-tempered blacksmith rather than a country vicar. Max saw no need to reassure him. Let him believe the worst and he'd be far more malleable. And who knew? The worst might yet come to pass.

"I told her—no, I begged her—not to get involved."

"She loves you," said Max evenly. "And your sister is not the kind of woman to sit twiddling her thumbs while someone she cares for rots in jail." A strange sense of pride at Kate's courage and resourcefulness struck him. Despite her fragile appearance, the woman was a fighter!

And closer acquaintance with her brother showed the quality ran in the family. Still, Max needed to win this battle at all costs. "You've already said you'll cooperate, so let's stop wringing our hands and get down to business, shall we? Where are these rebels hiding?"

Holt looked close to despair. "Will you not *listen* to me? I swear those men had nothing to do with the fire at Lyle."

"So you've said before. Why should I place any faith in what you believe? Forgive me, but a man of the cloth must always think the best of everyone—"

"—Whereas someone in your line of work must believe the worst."

Max gave a faint smile. "We're so often proven right, you see." He watched Holt closely. "And I wonder what you know about my line of work."

Holt shrugged, but the flicker of his gaze towards the door told Max that Ives might well have been Holt's informant.

Holt shifted restlessly, then rose and paced the room. He stopped at the window and looked out. "They are in the hills. I'll show you." He took a piece of paper from his waistcoat and threw it down on the table. It skittered across the polished surface, and Max stopped it with his hand. He didn't look at what was presumably a map, but immediately folded it and slipped it into his pocket.

"You will release Kate now?" Holt's tone was still belligerent. For a vicar, he had a lot of pride. But pride could be a strength as well as a weakness. Max respected Holt's staunch loyalty, even regretted the necessity of making the vicar bend to his will.

"You will be released when I find the rebels," said Max. "Lady Kate is free to go. I must warn you, however, that she might well choose to remain under my protection. If you know my former line of business, you will agree that I am well suited to that task."

"Save when you let her almost be killed," said Holt. "Save when you left her to come here. And another thing—" Holt swallowed hard, pointing to Max with a finger that trembled slightly. "I'd like to know what arrangements you've made to safeguard Kate's reputation. Has she been alone with you all this time?"

Max was about to launch smoothly into the tale he had concocted about a sick aunt, when he caught himself. It wasn't simply a matter of providing a sop to the gossips. He had, literally and figuratively—and most pleasurably—compromised Lady Kate Fairchild.

A blinding rush of emotion swept through him. So tangled and tumultuous, for a moment he couldn't speak.

How could he have overlooked the practical consequences of those two fast and furious encounters? Because their life-and-death situation had driven society's strictures out of his head? Because he'd been so wrapped up in the feel and scent of her, he hadn't stopped to think? Or because, once again, he'd shown a gently bred lady a truly unforgivable lack of respect?

"Marriage," he murmured. "Marriage. It's the only thing for it."

He spoke more to himself than to Holt, so stunned by the notion that he almost let Holt's enormous fist connect with his nose.

Reflexively, he dodged and leaped up to defend himself, knocking over his chair. At the same time, he wondered if he shouldn't just let Holt beat the tripe out of him. God and the vicar knew he deserved it.

But Holt must have listened to the promptings of his savior, because instead of taking another swing at Max, he swiveled his hips and planted his fist in the wall behind.

Swearing in a very un-Christian manner, Holt shook his hand with a grimace of pain.

"You're right," panted Max, willing Holt to accept his sincerity. "You're absolutely right. I'll marry Lady Kate. You have my word."

Holt roared. "I'd rather see her in the Magdalene than married to you, sir! Get you gone. You have what you came for." He narrowed his eyes. "And you may be sure that once I walk free of here, the only protection my sister will need is mine."

Coolly, Max said, "I think that is a matter for Lady Kate to decide."

Holt's eyes narrowed. "Does she know you're the reason I'm here?"

Suddenly, the tables turned. A chasm yawned beneath Max and the vicar dangled him over it. He cleared his throat. "She does not."

Holt gave a crack of laughter. "And you think she'll accept you after what you did to me?" He shook his head, with a look that was almost pitying. "If that's the case, you don't know my Kate at all."

In the hall, Max paused to take a deep breath. That interview had rattled him more than any job he'd undertaken for the Home Office.

Marriage. Why hadn't it occurred to him before now? And what must Kate think of such cavalier treatment? Would she even agree to wed him?

But another threat hung over Max's head now. Once Holt gained his freedom, there'd be no stopping him from telling Kate all Max had done. Looking back, Max still couldn't regret it. By incarcerating Holt, he'd found the rebels who wreaked such devastation on his family, and justice had fallen within his grasp. His old watchword held true: the end did justify the means.

But now, he needed to move quickly, to secure Kate before she learned the truth. He'd get a special license. Today, if that was humanly possible. Then he'd return to Hove, marry Kate, and continue with her to Derbyshire.

Once they married, they could sort out their problems. They'd have to. They belonged together. Whatever means he used, in time, she'd come to see that he'd done it to secure their ultimate happiness. And she would forgive him.

A step sounded behind him and he pulled himself together. Without looking to see who was there, he snatched his coat and hat from the table and turned to leave, almost stepping on Ives.

"You!" He took a fist full of Ives's coat and righted him,

then bent down to look him in the eye. "What are you doing here?"

The little man smoothed the crumpled lapel of his coat with a careful hand. "I'm employed in the good vicar's service, Your Worship. As his valet."

"Valet?" Max snorted. A likely story. "Surely you can do better than that."

Ives gave him a beatific, gap-toothed smile. "Oh, no, Your Honor. I never thought to look so high as a position in the service of a gentleman like Mr. Holt. But I do have a way of tying a cravat, Your Worship, which my master will vouch for, and that's a fact."

Max pinched the bridge of his nose. He felt like he'd walked into Bedlam. "This is the most arrant load of nonsense I've ever heard. What does a country vicar need with a valet? Much less a disreputable-looking specimen like— Oh, never mind. You'll only tell me another pack of lies and I don't have time to listen."

Outside, he took a deep, calming breath.

*Marriage.* Even as he considered the logistics of rounding up the band of rebels, the word pounded through his brain.

He must propose marriage to Lady Kate.

KATE threw down her embroidery and started up as the trapdoor creaked open. "Thank goodness for you, Louisa! Otherwise, I think I should go mad, cooped up here."

Louisa looked up and smiled as she climbed the final steps and emerged through the trapdoor. There was genuine warmth and empathy in that glowing look. Kate realized, with some surprise, that she'd found a friend.

Three days had passed since Lyle left. Kate took her exercise every morning in the barn with Louisa for company. In fact, besides the time she spent on the frustrating and rather depressing exercise of working out who might be trying to kill her, Kate had passed most of Lyle's absence in Louisa's company. Though they'd seen much of each other, they never ran out of conversation.

On the other hand, Sukey had been distant, preoccupied since her return. The maid was efficient enough and performed her tasks without complaint, but trying to converse with her was like addressing a brick wall.

Kate tilted her head to study her friend. There was an air of excitement about her today.

"You will never guess what I saw nailed to the notice board in the village square." Louisa held up a tattered piece of paper with a flourish. "This!"

Kate laughed at her unwonted exuberance. "Don't keep me in suspense. What is it?"

"A prizefight!" said Louisa, her eyes sparkling.

"A prizefight? What on earth—"

Louisa held up a hand. "No, do but listen. It is a prizefight between *women*." She waited expectantly. But when Kate still gazed at her in puzzlement, she added, "Don't you see? If we watch, we might glean some hints on how you can defend yourself against this assassin."

Kate laughed at the absurdity of it. "But Lyle said I wasn't to leave the tower, not even for a stroll in the shrubbery. And besides, it sounds horrid. Bad enough for those awful, sweaty men to beat each other senseless, but brawling women? How could a female have so little delicacy of mind?"

"Shocking, isn't it?" Louisa shook her head while she scanned the notice. "It says here: 'The women fight in close jackets, short petticoats, coming just below the knee, Holland drawers, white stockings, and pumps." She made a face. "Rather an odd costume. I wonder why it matters what they are wearing."

"I'm sure it matters to the *men* who are watching," said Kate darkly.

"Oh, yes. Aren't men horrid?" Louisa agreed. "But you

know, George has gone off somewhere and this young man, a Mr. Perry, has taken over his watch. I'm sure we could talk our way around him if we tried."

Kate shook her head. "I don't want to give that killer an easy target."

Louisa looked as though she might argue, then her shoulders dropped. She sighed. "I suppose you are right. It still seems unreal to me that you were almost killed."

Touching her neck, which still bore faint bruising, Kate said, "It seems very real to me."

"Well, if you don't mind, I think I will go," Louisa said. "I shall watch and I'll come home and teach you what I've learned. You did say you wanted to learn how to defend yourself, didn't you?"

*Yes, but I wanted Lyle to teach me.* Kate grinned ruefully at that telling revelation. "I did. But you are not to go to that silly thing on my account. You're likely to be molested or worse among such a rowdy mob. And only think of the damage it could do to your reputation if someone found out."

"I shall attend in disguise," said Louisa. "I shall dress as a servant. Sukey can find me something suitable, can't you, Sukey?"

The maid looked up from her darning and nodded. "I'll even come with you, if you like, miss. Two heads are better than one, my dad always says."

"Quite right, too," approved Louisa. "Can you ride, Sukey?"

"No, miss," the girl said with regret.

"Then I'll take you up before me. You have nothing to fear. I know one end of a horse from the other, I believe! I won't let anything happen to you."

Kate rather thought she ought to object to such an outrageous plan, but Louisa seemed determined.

"You are making me wish I could go, too," she said. "And I don't even want to witness this dreadful spectacle."

"Just wait until we return," said Louisa, with a gleam of mischief. "Then we may practice our maneuvers."

THE fight was staged in a field less than a mile from the village. Louisa knew a shortcut through Romney's land, and she and Sukey arrived in short order at an outbuilding adjacent to the field. They concealed the horse there—no serving wench would own such a fine beast—and walked the rest of the way to the venue.

Sukey didn't divulge where she found their costumes, but Louisa was reasonably certain no one would recognize the Duke of Lyle's sister in this brown fustian gown, sturdy boots, and tattered shawl. With another shawl tied over her head to conceal her blond hair, no one would look at her twice.

Louisa paid their entrance fee and was pleased to note that no one paid them the slightest heed as they maneuvered through the throng to find a decent vantage point.

They were a little late, and everyone's attention was focused on the makeshift ring in the center of the crowd.

Louisa wrinkled her nose. As she'd expected, the patrons were far from genteel, and the reek of ale, tobacco, manure, and—strangely—fish assaulted her as they wove in and out. There were quite a few women present, which Sukey remarked upon.

"My gran made a hobby out of watching executions," added the plump little maid, speaking close to Louisa's ear so she could hear above the din. "Some females like that sort of thing."

The ring lay at the bottom of a grassy bowl, a natural amphitheater often used for sporting bouts by the grace of a local farmer. They soon found a vantage point from which they could view the fight.

After a preliminary introduction by a man who used far too much Circassian oil on his crimped brown locks, the championesses themselves swaggered into the ring, to cheers and catcalls from their audience. Louisa drew her shawl forward, obscuring her face as much as possible, and settled in to watch.

The combatants were both strapping women. One, a flaming redhead, big and raw-boned; the other slightly taller, a statuesque figure reminiscent of Boudicca, with long, coarse black hair and an almost masculine cast to her face.

Both of them, Louisa noted, had enormous bosoms.

"Oh, miss. They are showing their legs!" Sukey hissed. "I scarcely know where to look."

Louisa quirked a brow. "Nothing you haven't seen before, is it?"

Sukey pursed her lips. "Seeing it in the presence of *men* is another thing entirely."

Chuckling, Louisa turned her attention to the fight. She needed to concentrate, dissect, and memorize their moves.

While the women baited one another and solicited insults from the crowd, the patrons placed bets on everything from how soon they'd see first blood, to how soon they'd see certain parts of the contestants' anatomy.

After a few minutes of this, Louisa's face was so hot she could have lit a taper with it. This earthy ribaldry was a side of life she'd never encountered before.

A roar went up, and the fight began.

Snarling and calling names, the women circled each other, reminding Louisa of the witches in a production she'd seen of *Macbeth*. The redhead lunged, but instead of striking with her fist, as Louisa expected, she caught hold of Boudicca's hair.

She yanked, and the redhead screamed like a banshee, then pivoted and drove her elbow into Boudicca's midriff. Boudicca let go and countered swiftly, raking her fingernails down the redhead's face.

Blood sprang to the welts on the redhead's cheek. The

crowd cheered and money changed hands. Louisa's stomach commenced a slow churn.

The redhead howled in pain, and Boudicca followed up her triumph by grabbing a fistful of her opponent's stained shift, ripping it from bosom to waist.

The crowd's reaction was deafening. Louisa glimpsed the redhead's enormous breasts swinging free, before she averted her gaze.

Resolutely, she fixed her gaze once more on the ring. Even if this fight wasn't governed by any kind of rules or code of behavior, she might still learn something. When one was fighting for one's life, it was hardly the time to be polite. She made a mental note. *Yank hair. Twist, followed by elbow in stomach.*

As the fight progressed, the women grew wilder, their clothing scantier, but some of the bout showed real skill. The outing had been worth the trouble, after all.

Louisa had almost seen enough, when Sukey nudged her.

"My lady! That man over there, the one that looks like the devil himself. He is staring at you."

# Fourteen

*The intensity grows until I can hardly bear it. One night I hide, but he finds me. Steals me back to his web.*

*And I am like the hapless fly. Bound, wrapped, and devoured whole . . .*

LOUISA paled. It must be Jardine. One swift glance under her lashes to the opposite side of the ring told her she was right. Even in the crowd, she pinpointed him immediately.

"We must go."

She grabbed Sukey's wrist. They moved through the throng, dodging stray hands and suffering rough jostles and a pinch or two.

Louisa restrained her impulse to run. That would attract attention.

Emerging from the press of sweaty bodies, Louisa hustled Sukey towards the exit. She glanced over her shoulder, trying to see if he followed, and ran straight into a masculine chest.

Ignoring her, Jardine reached forward and plucked the shawl off Sukey's head. "Lady Kate, I presume?"

But when he revealed the plump, blue-eyed face and flaxen hair under that shawl, Jardine's eyebrows slammed together.

"That's not Lady Kate." He shot an accusing glance at Louisa.

"I cannot imagine why you thought it would be," she managed to reply. She was afraid. Mortally afraid. Jardine worked for the government. Killed for the government. Could Jardine be the man who had almost killed Lady Kate? The man who hunted her yet?

He took Louisa's arm in a hard grip. "Where is she?"

Sukey opened her mouth, but Louisa pinched her arm. "I don't know who you're talking about."

"Don't play dumb with me, Louisa. Lyle told me to watch her. Is she still in the tower, or is the maid a decoy? Answer me!"

Louisa hesitated in painful indecision. How could she trust him? She knew what he did. He worked for the Home Office. And Lady Kate was in trouble with the government . . .

A look of comprehension swept over his face. "I see."

His dark eyes searched hers, then he stepped back. "Go home, Lady Louisa. It's not safe for you here."

A tray bearing the late luncheon Kate had ordered arrived at three. The young man who guarded her must have stopped the servant at the door, because he delivered the tray himself.

Kate thanked him and gestured for him to set down the tray on a small table by the window. "Where is George today?"

The blue eyes looked straight into hers. The bright intensity of that gaze sent unease creeping down her spine. For some reason she couldn't pinpoint, this young man unsettled her.

"The duke sent for George and ordered me to take his place. My name is Perry," he offered. "Perhaps the duke has spoken of me."

A denial sprang to her tongue, but he seemed so anxious for her answer that she repressed it. "Oh, yes. I believe he did mention your name."

The blue eyes burned brighter. He licked his lips.

She wanted him gone. With this odd young man guarding her she no longer felt quite so safe.

But Lyle must trust the lad, or he wouldn't have sent him to guard her in place of George. Perhaps, behind that almost effeminate appearance reposed a man of extraordinary fighting prowess. Or perhaps he was a crack shot with a pistol?

The thought increased her nervousness.

"Do you work for the Home Office, Mr. Perry?"

He shook his head. "I work for the Duke of Lyle." He seemed to roll the name around his tongue, savoring it in a way that made her stomach roil.

Kate swallowed hard, and an echo of the pain she'd suffered from her semi-strangulation made her press her fingers to her throat. Something about this young man wasn't right. She wished Louisa would return.

"No doubt he is a demanding master," Kate said, trying to strike a lighter note. "I know I go in terror of his disapproval."

An expression very close to a sneer flitted across his face. He turned to the tray, which sat on the table next to his hip. One elegant finger ran lightly along the length of the fruit knife.

*My God!* Kate froze, icy fear rushing through her veins. It couldn't be . . .

But the next moment, he moved away from the table, his expression perfectly benign. She let her shoulders relax. She was jumping at shadows. He was here to protect her. Lyle had sent him.

But she wanted him to go.

"Well, then!" she said brightly, moving towards the trapdoor, hoping to shepherd him in the same direction.

"Thank you for bringing my tray. If there's anything else, I'll be sure to—"

A tall, dark man erupted through the trapdoor and lunged at Perry, grabbing a fistful of the young man's cravat, bringing them nose to nose. "What are you doing here, you little snot?"

Before Kate could react, Louisa stumbled into the room after the newcomer. "Jardine, you beast! Leave him alone."

Kate almost collapsed with relief. "You know this man?" she said to Louisa.

"Unfortunately, yes!" Louisa ripped the shawl from her head and marched up to Jardine, who had been bombarding Perry with short, staccato questions.

When the boy had answered to Jardine's satisfaction, he let him go.

A blaze of hatred flared in Perry's eyes, swiftly veiled by thick golden lashes. Sullenly, he said, "Anyway, I should like to know what you're doing here, Jardine."

"None of your damned business," Jardine flashed back. He narrowed his eyes and spoke through his teeth. "I don't believe for a damned minute that Lyle entrusted his lady to you, and I don't believe George left his post on a whim. So I'm watching you, young Perry. And if you take one step out of line, I'll make you sorry you were born."

Kate wanted to applaud, but Louisa was not impressed. She squared up to Jardine, shoulders heaving, blond hair a wild tangle. Kate wondered if her friend was about to let fly with one of the moves she'd learned at the prizefight.

But Louisa kept her hands to herself. "You've said your piece, my lord. Now leave the poor lad alone and get out. You are not welcome here."

The look that passed between the two of them could have sent the room up in flames.

How fascinating! Kate tried to think of some pleasantry that would rid them of the men so she could have a long talk with Louisa, but Jardine saved her the trouble.

Ironically, he bowed. "I am well aware of that, Lady Louisa. Allow me to remove myself." He collared Perry and pushed him towards the trapdoor. "You first."

Alone with Louisa, Kate said, "So that was the famous marquis."

"Infamous, more like," Louisa replied.

"Louisa, won't you—"

Louisa's face shuttered. "Forgive me, but I don't wish to talk about it."

Kate hesitated, but being a very private person herself, she respected Louisa's unwillingness to discuss the matter. "All right. Where's Sukey?"

"I sent her to change." Louisa glanced to the window. "Ah, good. You have food. I'm famished."

"Yes. Mr. Perry brought it." Kate moved to the table and arranged some fruit and cheese on a plate, which she handed to Louisa.

Kate picked up a piece of apple to nibble and her gaze fell on the fruit knife. Perhaps she'd imagined Mr. Perry's hostility. A lady tended to see threats everywhere when she feared for her life.

When they'd finished their meal, Louisa wiped her fingers on a napkin. "We should practice what I've learned, don't you think? Let's go to the barn."

Kate eyed her with amusement. "Do you mean you want me to scratch your face and pull your hair?"

"Why not?" demanded Louisa. "I imagine such moves would be quite effective if you were fighting for your life."

Clearly, her friend was in a pugnacious frame of mind. Kate raised her hands in mock terror. "I vow, Louisa, I am afraid of you. Be gentle with me, I beg!"

"Oh, pshaw!" Reluctantly, Louisa laughed. "Come on."

They went downstairs and advised Perry of their mission.

"I'll patrol the perimeter," said Perry, bowing. "Ladies, you may depend on me to keep you safe." His words addressed them both, but his gaze fixed on Louisa. He seemed to want to impress her, perhaps because she was Lyle's sister?

Kate thanked him and hurried Louisa on their way. "That young man gives me shivers," she whispered to her friend when they were out of earshot.

"Who, Perry?" Louisa raised her brows in surprise. "Why, he's harmless."

*Then why is he guarding me?* thought Kate. She said no more as they walked the short distance to the barn. Kate found the rich, pungent scent of a working farm oddly calming. It reminded her of the carefree days of her childhood, growing up in Stratham.

Louisa crossed the barn and started up the ladder to the hayloft. When Kate didn't follow, she looked back. "The hay will cushion our fall."

"Oh, dear," said Kate, wishing she'd never started this. "Are we likely to fall, do you think?"

Obediently, she climbed up the rough ladder to the loft, where the hay lay scattered and soft at their feet.

Louisa dusted off her hands and placed them on her hips. "Now. I want you to try to strike me."

"All right." Kate adopted a boxing stance she'd seen her brothers use, elbows bent and fists bunched in front of her face.

Louisa broke into a peal of laughter. "What are you doing?"

"I'm getting ready to strike you."

Still grinning, Louisa said, "Well, go on then."

Kate hesitated. "But what if I hurt you?"

Louisa giggled again, a strangely youthful sound. "Somehow, I doubt you will. Oh, go on! What's the worst that can happen?"

"I might bloody your nose," said Kate. "I don't like the sight of blood."

Louisa rolled her eyes. "Well, what's the good of that? You can't be squeamish if you mean to defend yourself."

"No, you are right," said Kate, remembering the sheer terror of the attack, and also recalling the heat of fury that drove her to throw punches and ornaments alike at Lyle. "If I am in that situation, I think I would be desperate enough not to worry about the sight of a little blood. In the cold light of day, it's different."

"Well, what chance will you have if you don't learn proper techniques?" Louisa said reasonably. "Now, try to hit me and I'll show you how those women deflected the blow." She took hold of Kate's shoulders and moved her bodily. "Come here and face me . . ."

They practiced for about half an hour. Kate had almost mastered breaking free from a hold when she heard voices and footsteps, coming into the barn.

"Shh!" Kate held up her hand. "Who is it?" she whispered to Louisa.

Her friend's eyes widened a little, as if she recognized the newcomers, but she didn't answer and laid a finger to her lips.

A deep, masculine rumble sounded directly beneath them, then a scuffle, followed by feminine scolding.

"Unhand me, sir! I must go along to the dairy and see how the cheese is progressing."

"Fanny, you are pregnant. You should leave the dairy to Mrs. Burton. Take things more gently, m'dear."

There was a wicked giggle and a rustle of fabric. "What, *everything*? But you know I like some things . . . *hard*."

The man gasped. Then he groaned and said in a thick voice, "My dearest devil, you would tempt a saint."

"Well, that certainly leaves you out of the equation, doesn't it, darling?"

Their laughter mingled, then the lady let out a soft shriek. "Ah, I love it when you do that. No, don't stop. Don't stop!"

"We shouldn't," said a ragged deep voice.

*No, you really shouldn't,* agreed Kate silently.

"The doctor said—"

"Hang the doctor!" gasped the woman. "I—ohhhh. Harder. Yes! That's it. Oh, that's so good, Romney, you—"

The lady broke off with a moan, then launched into a series of high, sobbing sighs. The sighs and groans increased their pace, until Kate was ready to slit her throat before she'd listen to any more.

She glanced at Louisa, who had buried her face in her hands. Goodness, if Kate, a widow, was shocked, what must a spinster lady think?

The encounter seemed to go on forever, but in reality, it must have lasted only a few minutes. Both parties seemed equally—and quite vocally—satisfied with the result.

*Good for them,* thought Kate sourly, wondering why she should feel as resentful as she was appalled.

With more breathless endearments and a deal of lewd suggestion that made Kate turn a brighter shade of red than she was already, the couple left the barn. When they moved beyond the shelter of the loft, she glimpsed a large, shaggy gentleman fastening the fall of his trousers as he followed his lady outside.

Louisa still covered her face with her hands. Kate eyed her, somewhat at a loss.

How was one to deal with a situation like this? It wasn't her place to educate her friend about what they'd heard. But was Louisa distressed by the incident? If Kate didn't speak with her, might Louisa wonder, and worry?

Louisa lifted her head, eyes streaming, mouth agape. Oh, no! Kate twisted her hands in indecision. Until Louisa took one look at Kate's face and burst into gales of laughter.

*Laughing!* "I don't see how you could think that was funny," Kate scolded. "I didn't know where to look!"

"Oh, dear. I do apologize." Louisa wiped her eyes and glanced at Kate, then collapsed into another peal of hilarity.

"The look on your face!" she gasped, lying flat out on

her back, shoulders shaking. Her slim hands clutched her midriff. "Oh, I feel ill with holding it in."

When the last gust of merriment subsided, Louisa sighed and shook her head. "They do it all the time."

"I beg your pardon?"

"Our noble hosts—my cousins! Oh, they think they are discreet, but the number of occasions I've overheard Fanny and Romney having, er, relations in odd places . . ." Louisa struggled up on her elbows. "Are you offended? They are married, after all, and they thought they were alone."

Kate realized her mouth was all scrunched up like a prune. She forced herself to relax, even smile a little, but she couldn't bring herself to share Louisa's mirth.

Was she a prude? Kate pondered the subject. She had always prized her virtue, certainly, and taken pride in her constancy. Faced with a disastrous and passionless marriage, many women of her station would have strayed. No one in her circle of acquaintances would have blamed her, as long as she remained discreet.

But the truth was, she'd never been tempted to sin, except between the pages of her diary. And surely, her phantom lover didn't count.

What if Lyle had come to her while Hector was alive? What then?

No. Futile and destructive to think about what-ifs—especially dangerous where Lyle was concerned.

Louisa was still regarding her curiously.

Kate realized she hadn't answered the question. "Offended? No. Shocked, perhaps, but then I am unused to such . . . open displays of affection."

*Particularly from a husband,* she added silently.

She sounded priggish and stiff, she knew. Yet her inability to laugh off the experience wasn't entirely due to disapproval. When she'd heard the lovers' frank exchange, a tendril of envy had unfurled in her heart.

Lady Fanny had been lusty and demanding, and from her husband's reaction, he'd loved every minute of it.

Kate swallowed past the lump in her throat. If Lady Fanny was any indication, then she, Kate, wasn't so unnatural in her desires, after all.

Why couldn't she find such happiness, too?

FUMING at the delay while he kicked his heels waiting for a special license, Max dispensed with the carriage and rode back to Hove. For all he knew, Holt could have sent a message to his sister by now and it would all be for nothing.

He pushed that thought aside. He didn't want to contemplate Kate's reaction when she found out what he'd done. He'd compound his sins by wedding her before she could discover them, but that, too, was something he wouldn't face before he had to. As always, he would do what must be done.

Max clenched his jaw. The one thing he'd promised himself he wouldn't do was make love to Kate before their wedding night. He'd taken advantage of her quite enough as it was. Perhaps, when she discovered the worst, she'd chalk up this gesture to his credit. He thought of her slender, delicate beauty, her warmth, her smile. Resisting her, even for one night, would be punishment of the severest kind.

He'd given himself a head start on the vicar, but he couldn't, in all conscience, marry Kate while continuing to jail her brother. He'd given orders for the vicar's release and hoped that by the time Holt caught up with them, the rebels would be in his custody.

Perhaps, when he brought those men to justice, when he explained the horror of their crime, Kate would see how necessary it had been to treat her brother that way.

He snorted. And pigs might fly. She'd be furious, that was certain. But would she forgive him? He had to believe that in time she would. She must.

He rode to the stables and handed the reins of his gelding over to a groom, too impatient to see her to adhere to his usual habit of rubbing down horses himself.

Without stopping to pay his respects to those inside the house, he strode to the tower and looked up.

Her light was on. If there were any footholds in the smooth stone surface, he'd climb up to her window, as her phantom lover had done.

One must be practical, however, so he chose the stairs, nodding to George as he went past.

"Er, guv?" George's hoarse voice echoed and bounced between the stone walls.

*What now?* "This had better be important."

"Jest thought I oughta tell yer, that young Perry were here today, guarding the ladyship."

Max's brows drew together. "How came that about?"

George patted his stomach. "Something I ate took me real bad. Casting up my accounts all over, I was. They 'ad to carry me orff." He jerked his head. "Young lad Perry offered to take my place. Well, he couldn't have done a worse job than me, I was in no case to do anything but vomit, and I knew Lord Jardine were at hand if anything went wrong, like."

Max clapped him on the shoulder. "You still look ghastly, my friend. Thank you, George. You did the right thing. Go and get some rest."

As he climbed the staircase, anticipation hummed in Max's blood. He was nervous, he realized with surprise. He'd never proposed marriage before. He wasn't entirely sure how one went about it, except for voicing the obvious question. He rather thought a lot of preliminary compliments and palaver went on beforehand, though. A pity the phantom lover hadn't asked for his lady's hand in that diary. Maybe then Max would know how she'd like it done.

He reached the summit and braced himself for his task.

Just in time, he remembered to knock.

There was a pause. Then her voice said, "Come." And he swallowed hard before he pressed his open palm to the trapdoor to lift it up.

KATE was in bed when Lyle came through the trapdoor.

"Oh! I thought you were Louisa."

She scrambled to cover herself with the wrapper that lay on the counterpane, refusing to meet his eye. She wanted to pull the sheet up to her chin. Ludicrous behavior after the intimacy they'd already shared.

Kate's stomach fluttered wildly. She needed to catch her breath, just a little time to assimilate his presence, so unexpected and so powerful.

"In bed already, my lady? You do keep country hours." Lyle advanced towards her, smiling with a very masculine brand of satisfaction. As if she'd arranged herself this way to entice him.

"It's so deadly dull here without"—she cleared her throat awkwardly—"without Louisa, that I might as well go to bed early. Since my only outing each day is to the barn."

Kate had developed the habit of retiring early in the evenings because Louisa kept Fanny company after dinner and Sukey slept in the house.

She'd deemed it unnecessary to subject Sukey to a pallet on the floor in this small room when a bed in the servants' quarters would be far more comfortable. She barely acknowledged, even to herself, that she was happy to dispense with Sukey's chaperonage at night.

Most evenings, Kate read. The other occupation she used to enjoy in moments of solitude—writing in her diary—didn't appeal any more. Not that she had the diary with her. When she returned home, she'd probably destroy it.

She needed to start living again.

He crossed to the bed and took her hand. "I returned as

quickly as I could." His palm was large and warm, with that faint roughness that never failed to intrigue her. *Those hands . . .*

He regarded her gravely. "Your brother has been released."

"Oh, what a relief!" A rush of warmth filled her chest. She smiled at him. "And I have you to thank."

He made a gesture of repudiation, but she shook her head. "No, I know it was your doing, don't deny it. When may I see him?"

He cleared his throat. "Soon. I'll arrange it."

Lyle sat on the bed, as one who had the right—and perhaps he did, at that. "I said we would discuss matters when I returned. Do you remember?"

She nodded, a little wary. He looked serious and a little troubled. Had she become a burden in his mind?

"I've missed you, Kate." He looked down at their hands, turned hers over and bent to kiss her palm. Thrills tingled up her arm, but apprehension quickly swamped the sensation. Something wasn't right.

All she could say was, "Oh."

Why did he not take her in his arms and *show* her how much he'd missed her? This elegant restraint wasn't like him at all.

"I've been thinking about us," he continued. "And I believe—" He met her eyes and drew a deep breath. "Kate, I want you to be my wife." One corner of his mouth quirked upwards, as if he laughed at his own awkwardness. "Will you?"

"Yes." The word was out almost before she heard the question. She'd known, perhaps from the first time they'd made love, that she would marry him if he asked. Even in the heat of passion she wouldn't give herself to a man lightly. That wasn't in her makeup.

She'd enjoyed her independence, but she'd paid the price of loneliness for her autonomy. And although Lyle was occasionally stubborn and a little autocratic, he wouldn't be a tyrannical husband.

Did she love him? She gazed at his dear, strong features with that distinctive break in his nose. She'd ached for him while he was away, thought about him every moment.

*Yes.*

He took her face in his hands and kissed her lips—just one, light touch—and then her cheek.

Kate savored the feel of him—the warmth, the texture of his skin, but he granted her the merest taste.

She wanted more—to lean into his kiss and abandon herself to him, to throw her arms around him and rub her body against his.

He released her and eased away. "I'll let you sleep."

"Don't you—don't you want to stay?" she asked, cringing inwardly at the nervousness that lent a tremor to her voice.

He hesitated, as if he might be persuaded. If only she were more skilled in seduction! But she feared giving him a disgust of her, as she'd done to Hector. Lyle didn't seem like the sort of man to object to such overtures, but then, she'd thought Hector would like them, too. And she'd been so very, very wrong about that.

Glancing down at the night rail she wore, Kate realized she was scarcely dressed for the role of temptress. White lawn embroidered with tiny rosebuds. She looked like a little girl.

"It's not that I don't—" Lyle raised his gaze to the ceiling and breathed heavily out his nose. "I want to, very much, but I promised myself we would wait until we are married."

She wet her lips with her tongue, thinking of his kisses, longing for the confident possession of his touch.

"And when will that be?"

Lyle's gaze fixed on her mouth. His chest rose and fell rapidly. "Tomorrow. Morning. Early. As early as I can find the parson to do the job. I've a special license. I hope that doesn't sound presumptuous, but if you said yes, I wanted to marry you straightaway."

She stared into his face. Was he as unhappy with this arrangement as she? He hadn't moved, but a burning light in his eyes told her she might sway him if she tried.

She threw back the counterpane and slid out of bed. "It will be as you wish, sir. But before you go, might I have a proper goodnight kiss?"

He cleared his throat. "I don't think that would be wise."

She moved towards him and put her hand on his chest. He flinched, but she held it there, regardless.

"I can feel your heartbeat," she whispered.

Holding his gaze, she slid her hand up to his nape and drew him down to her.

"Kiss me, Max," she breathed.

So close. Their only contact was her hand on him, but his heat enveloped her. She could almost feel his lips on hers. Drowning in desire, she closed her eyes, waiting for the descent of his mouth, a rising tide of passion ready to burst forth.

But he was strong. He put his hands on her shoulders and gently set her at a distance.

The magnetic pull between them severed. Her eyes snapped open, disappointment crashing over her like an icy wave. He frowned at her.

"Don't you want me?" she blurted out.

Lyle ran a hand through his hair. "Of course I want you. If I didn't . . . But I made a resolution—a very noble one, I might add—and I want you to respect it."

His expression softened. "You wouldn't respect *me* if I threw away my principles, however sorely tempted I might be."

He turned and started for the trapdoor. "It's best that I go."

"But they are *stupid* principles!" she cried, following him to the steps. "We've *already*—I mean, what is the harm now?"

He turned back. "No, Kate." His expression told her he was adamant.

Kate stopped. She wasn't going to beg. If he wanted to go, let him. She folded her arms and pressed her lips together.

He smiled. "Good girl. I'll see you tomorrow. And I promise you, my love, our wedding night will be all that you desire."

He opened the trapdoor and started down the steps.

"I've half a mind to cry off," she called after him.

He looked up at her, and the devil was in his eyes. "No," he said softly. "You won't do that."

He reached back to shut the trapdoor, and even beneath his coat, she saw the shift of his muscles, the powerful breadth of his chest.

No, Kate sighed. That she definitely would not.

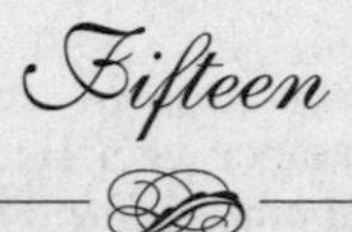

# Fifteen

*He plays my body like the strings of a harp—now a glide, now a strum, now a staccato pluck. Glissandos of pleasure . . .*

KATE became the new Duchess of Lyle without fuss, in Lady Romney's drawing room.

She wore a blue silk gown—blue for loyalty and fidelity—and carried a loose posy of white roses Louisa had picked from the garden. The ceremony proceeded with only four witnesses—Lord Romney and Lady Fanny, Louisa and Sukey.

As Lyle said his vows, Kate thought her heart might burst with happiness. He hadn't said he loved her, but the way he looked at her as he made those sacred promises, so fiercely possessive yet with such latent tenderness in those usually cold gray eyes, she couldn't be mistaken.

She hadn't said the words, either, for that matter. It hardly seemed necessary. She'd never marry without love—real love—again.

How had they fallen in love so quickly? In terms of days and hours, the process had been fast, but their turbulent association, the intensity of the time they'd spent together made it seem an eon since they'd met on the terrace at her house.

However it had happened, she trusted it. After all, the length of her acquaintance with Hector hadn't been proportionate to their happiness. She'd been acquainted with him forever, but as a husband, he'd made her miserable.

She shouldn't think of Hector on such a joyful day. Lyle was hers. After such a turbulent start, it seemed incredible, but it was right.

When the ceremony ended, he raised her hand to his lips, and the gaze that held hers promised so much more.

They parted then, to receive congratulations from Sukey and their hosts, and from Louisa, who kissed Kate's cheek. "I couldn't wish for a better sister."

Kate hugged her. "I'm so happy," she whispered.

Using a gloved knuckle to brush away a tear, Louisa nodded. "So am I. For you."

Sensing something very wrong, Kate squeezed Louisa's hand. "Anytime you wish to talk—"

"Thank you. I'm glad to know it, but please don't concern yourself about me. You must enjoy this day."

Despite their small number, the group managed to make merry. Louisa seemed to have put aside her somber mood and Fanny was in high spirits.

The wedding, Fanny said, had relieved almost unbearable tedium while she awaited her lying-in.

"I want this baby *out*!" she cried outrageously, making Kate gasp and the others chuckle.

Kate took part in the makeshift festivities with enthusiasm, but every other minute, her gaze strayed to Lyle.

She couldn't wait until the evening, when she'd have him to herself.

They'd argued over where their wedding night should be spent. Lyle voted for the superior comfort of his bedchamber, but Kate wanted the tower, with no one near to hear her if she screamed.

By judicious exercise of tact and diplomacy, she won. And she couldn't wait to celebrate her victory.

Finally, twilight gilded the landscape. With Lyle ever vigilant, they walked the short distance from the house to the tower unscathed, with the festive blaze of flambeaux to light their way.

She looked up at the glow in the tower window. Someone must have been there before them to prepare the room. Her prison, where she'd chafed at such close confinement.

Now, she anticipated the isolation with pleasure, because she shared it with Lyle.

In midstep, he bent and swung her up in his arms. She laughed in surprise, giggled like a young girl. She hadn't felt this carefree for years.

He smiled down at her, and she wound her arms around his neck as he strode into the tower.

He moved towards the narrow, winding staircase without a check.

"Oh, no, you can't!" she said, half laughing, but she didn't know his strength.

He carried her up with ease, straight through the open trapdoor. Grinning at her surprise, he bent his head for a slow, lingering kiss before he set her on her feet.

He kicked the trapdoor shut, and the slam made her jump, nerves skittering.

He didn't speak, but gazed at her intently, as if memorizing every feature of her face.

Backing her towards the bed, he kissed her again, slow, gentle, and long. She ran her hands over his big shoulders and felt the tension in them, but his mouth was light on hers, and his soft caresses thrilled her body, filled her with yearning.

*This is nice,* she thought. *Different. No need to rush.*

Still kissing her, his hands moved to the buttons at the back of her gown. Slipping them free one by one, his lips drifted over her cheek.

Hot breath in her ear told her he was panting, impatient as she was, but he held back, exploring her one inch at a time.

And it was lovely, and the melting sensation grew, but she needed him *now*. After his absence, after all the misunderstanding between them, after waiting an agonizing day upon his return, she didn't want to wait any longer. Didn't want to think. She wanted to be swept away.

His lips brushed her pearl-drop earring as he kissed behind her ear. She gasped, and his tongue swiped over her earlobe, making the earring tremble like the rest of her.

He stayed there, teasing and playing, until her gown fell open at the back. She let it slip down her arms and hush to the ground.

Kate stepped out of the puddle of blue silk, moving towards him, sliding her hands upwards to untie his cravat while he ripped off his coat.

As soon as he stood in his shirtsleeves, she let her hands wander over him, feeling the strength in his shoulders and chest. She kneaded the muscles in his back while he kissed her, holding him close enough to feel the hard jut of his erection against her belly, rampant for her as she was eager for him.

Tentatively, she touched him there, cupping her palm over him, anticipating the feel of him, thick and hard inside her. He gasped and jerked, then removed her hand, holding it in his.

"Easy, Kate," he murmured. "I won't last another minute if you do that."

"You don't like it?"

With a ragged laugh, he said, "My innocent, the danger is I'll like it too much." He tilted her face with his hands and kissed her. "Let me take the lead now, darling."

So she did. After all, what did she know of marital relations? And the things he'd done to her at the hunting lodge, and then again here, in this very room, showed he was proficient in the art.

Still, something was missing, and she couldn't pinpoint what. He touched her breast and lightly rubbed her nipple through her shift, and her mind faded as pleasure overtook conscious thought.

*Harder,* she begged silently. But how could she say it? He didn't want her to interfere.

He turned her around to unlace her corset, murmuring a string of endearments and encouragement. She'd never known he could be so talkative. Their previous encounters had been all but silent.

His lips hovered, tantalizingly, over the junction between collarbone and throat, and she shivered, willing him to kiss her there, to bite as he'd promised that first night.

But he seemed to think better of it, perhaps because faint bruising still shadowed the tender skin there, and left the vulnerable spot alone.

*Come back!* But she didn't say it. He knew what he was doing. She ought to relax, stop thinking so much.

And so it went on. A touch here, a caress there. Nothing sustained, everything featherlight and fleeting. By the time they were both naked and lying on the bed she was ready to scream with wanting.

Perhaps that was what he'd had in mind?

"Max," she whispered, but he didn't seem to hear her, intent on nibbling some part of her anatomy. "Max!" she raised her voice and caught his attention.

He looked up, his face a mask of control.

She tugged at his shoulders. "Max, I need you. Please."

It took him a few moments to understand her. He shook his head. "Not yet." And he moved back down her body, kissing around her navel, caressing her hips with those big, rough hands. *Those hands . . .* Her stomach felt fluttery and strange.

And then he moved lower.

"But I—" Kate gasped. He was kissing her . . . down there! Just as her sister Bella had described to her once when she'd drunk a little too much champagne.

Kate had written about such a thing in her diary, but she'd no idea, none at all, because his tongue was doing remarkable things and his fingers rubbed her inside, too, and there was—oh, there was—*something* he did with his lips that just . . . "Ah!"

She convulsed and shuddered on an explosion of pleasure that sent waves of heat and light through her body, right to her fingertips and toes. He kept touching and pressing, rubbing and licking, heightening the sensations, until she moaned helplessly and writhed in restless torment.

When the storm of sensation had passed, he laid his head on her stomach. She opened her eyes and stroked his thick, soft hair with her fingertips.

And with more satisfaction than she usually felt when she lost an argument, she had to admit he'd been right.

*That* had been worth waiting for.

Small tremors still rippled through her when he came over her, bracing himself on his elbows. He positioned himself quickly and eased inside her, moving slowly, inching his way towards her womb.

She watched his face, eager to see his pleasure. But his jaw clenched, his shoulders shook, the tendons in his neck corded with strain. He almost appeared in pain as he moved slowly, so slowly, filling her.

For Kate, the sensations were new and sharp and exquisite. In moments, she clenched and shuddered around him, as if her first orgasm had never ended, just built and built until it exploded again.

She tilted her hips, wanting more of him, allowing him to penetrate deeper. Exhaling a sharp breath, he stroked into her fast and hard, hitting a spot that responded with exquisite pleasure bordering on pain. On a gasp, she wrapped her legs around his hips to take him deeper still, and his whole body stiffened as he broke and convulsed, collapsing on top of her, crushing her in the most satisfying way.

When his tremors finally subsided, he rolled onto his back and ran his hands over his face. "My God, woman. You'll be the death of me."

Smiling, she traced the muscles of his chest with her fingertip. "I can think of less pleasant ways to go."

PERRY sat below the window against the south wall of the tower. He'd trapped a rabbit in the woods and killed it. Skinning the animal slowly, he waited for them to arrive.

He heard the voices, the laughter, the silences as they kissed. And when they reached the top of the stairs, he tortured himself imagining, flayed himself as he'd flayed this small, dumb beast.

The light in the window behind him dimmed. They'd be together now, the duke and . . . and *her*—in bed. Tangled between the sheets. Rising and falling, bodies glowing with sweat.

And with each imagined thrust, Perry stabbed his hunting knife into the rabbit's slack carcass.

"*MY wife.*" Lyle murmured the words in the darkness, holding her hand imprisoned against his chest. It wasn't "I love you" but it was close.

She laid her head on his shoulder. His heart beat steadily now, not the tumultuous gallop as he'd taken her once more.

His slow deliberation tantalized and frustrated her. For the first time, she wondered if there was a difference between the way Lyle treated his mistress and the way he treated his wife.

Of course, she'd never thought of herself as his mistress—such a subservient role, belied by its name. They'd been lovers. Equals, or so she'd thought.

Then why the sudden change? Why did he think she deserved different treatment, now she was his wife?

She remembered him apologizing for their last encounter. He'd been ashamed that he'd treated her like a common trollop. He hadn't said the ugly word, but she'd known what he meant.

Well, perhaps she was a trollop at heart. Because she'd enjoyed every second of that desperate, overwhelming possession.

Now their relationship had been legitimized, would there be no more hot, hard, urgent coupling—only this perfectly pleasant, yet somehow . . . restrained, lovemaking?

She glanced at him, so deep in slumber, so oblivious to her turmoil. The subject was far too delicate to broach without careful consideration.

Perhaps the easiest way to get the message across was not by words. Seduce him. Make *him* so hot for *her*, he abandoned his gentlemanly restraint.

She'd never been good at seduction. Hector's flaccid, difficult performances were testament to that. But for the sake of rekindling that blaze of passion between her and Lyle, she'd swallow her pride and try.

Tomorrow, they left for Lyle Castle and a new life. As good a time as any to put her plan into action.

THE morning dawned clear and bright. Max kissed his sleeping wife's bare shoulder and rose to go for his customary ride.

Riding always helped him think, and he needed to think this morning. Pleasurable as last night was, it had not been . . . entirely satisfying.

As soon as the thought popped into his head, he felt disloyal. But he couldn't shake the impression that all was not right with Kate.

He hadn't asked her about it. That wasn't his way. Action, not conversation, had always been his strength. And the matter was far too sensitive to foul up by saying the wrong thing as he, with his man's insensitivity, was bound to do.

He saddled his horse, a black stallion impatient for his morning run, and mounted. The stallion sidled and pranced, trying to unseat him, the devil, but Max brought him quickly under control.

He guided the stallion out of the stables and set the horse's pace at a walk. He sensed the beast's impatience to gallop, the powerful muscles bunched and ready to stretch. But until they gained open fields, Max reined him in, confining him to a walk.

Frustration radiated from the great beast. He'd not enjoyed a good gallop for days during his master's absence, and he was as hot as he could hold. Max gave a rueful smile. Much as he'd been last night.

He couldn't put his finger on what had gone wrong with Kate. The author of that diary was sensual and responsive. Creative, too, as far as her experience allowed.

Why, then, did he sense a strong reticence in her when they were in bed? She was no schoolroom miss, but a widow of experience. Albeit experience of a staid variety, if he judged the diary correctly.

Perhaps everything had happened too quickly. One minute, he was her captor, the next, her lover, and her husband soon after that. All in the space of a few days.

When the landscape opened to that undulating countryside so typical of the Leicestershire scene, Max loosed the reins and let his mount break into a canter. Soon, the stallion's stride lengthened into a full-blown gallop.

But no matter how fast or hard he rode, Max couldn't escape the niggling feeling that something was wrong. He needed to think, so having shaken the fidgets out of his horse, he turned down a lane and set off at an amble, to see where it would take him.

The scent of spring lay heavily in the air. The sun shone warmly, the breeze was cool, and soon he saw that the trail he'd taken ran along a small stream. He stopped and dismounted to let the stallion drink.

And it was then that the old awareness gripped him.

Someone was watching him.

He narrowed his eyes, scanning the rise of the bank behind him. A flash of movement to his right, behind the fronds of a weeping willow, caught his eye.

Quick as thought, he launched himself through the willow branches and tackled the spy. Overpowering his captive with ease, he rolled the man over, pinned him with one knee and drew his fist back, ready to strike.

Guinea-gold hair and the face of an angel. Blue eyes full of shocked reproach.

Perry.

"Not you again!" Max gave a disgusted snort and got to his feet. "You're going to get yourself killed one day if you keep creeping up on me like that."

Perry sat up. "It's a game I play. I've always played it. Watching you, following you, to see if you'll detect me."

A chill ran down Max's spine. "How often do you play this game?"

"Often enough." Perry kicked the turf with the toe of his boot. "I'm good at surveillance. Everything I know, I've learned from you."

Max stared hard into the distance. He'd meant to have a talk with Perry, and now was his chance. He had a strong feeling this would be an emotional scene, the kind that he usually avoided at all costs.

But Perry was a man now, despite his youthful demeanor. He ought to be treated like one, not mollycoddled like an infant in leading strings. How else was he to learn to stand on his own?

"The duchess and I are leaving for Lyle today," said Max gruffly. "The threat against her has been removed, so she no longer needs protection. And the vicar, Mr. Holt, has divulged the whereabouts of the rebels who committed the arson at Lyle. I shall soon have them under lock and key."

He paused. "It seems that you and I have come to a parting of ways, Perry." He held out his hand.

"No!" Perry burst out, ignoring Max's gesture. "I can't believe that. I cannot believe that after all I've done, you'd leave me—"

Max wanted to shake the boy, but he said, "Now, lad, you knew I wouldn't stay at the Home Office beyond this case. With the dukedom, I have vast responsibilities to attend to. And your feet are firmly planted on the ladder at Whitehall—"

"Hang Whitehall!" Perry flung away, but not before Max saw the glimmer of tears in those startlingly blue eyes. "I only ever wanted to be there because of you."

Oh, Hell. Not tears! Bad enough when women wept all over you, but when a man did . . . Max struggled to conceal his disgust. And he remembered that even when Kate had been strangled half to death she hadn't wept. Not a single tear.

But the root of all this trouble with Perry was that Max had never liked him, not really. He'd been responsible for taking the boy's villainous father away, and a mixture of guilt and duty had made him keep an eye on the lad.

He'd seen the growing attachment, but the hero worship had transformed, somewhere along the way, to an unhealthy obsession. If he'd cared more about the boy he would have thought about the consequences, the damage such devotion might cause. But the truth was, he hadn't cared enough to act.

Perry dashed moisture from his eyes and turned to Max with a look of anguish, his mouth turned down in an ugly shape.

Embarrassed by such raw feeling, Max ignored the emotion and concentrated on the words. “Faulkner thinks you have a future.”

“Faulkner is a pigheaded fool. Jardine will take over, and what will happen to me then? He hates me.”

Unfortunately, that was true. Perceptive of Perry to sense which way the wind blew.

*And what will you do about it, Lyle?* was the unspoken question. For his own peace of mind, he couldn’t offer Perry a position. “Unlikely as that eventuality is, if you should find yourself without employment, you may rely on me. I do not have any positions to fill now, but perhaps one of my friends will have something for you.”

He put his hand on Perry’s heaving shoulder. “Really, Perry, there is no need for despair.”

# Sixteen

*Slow, deep touch. Tension rises. Blood simmers beneath the skin.*

KATE had visited Lyle Castle on a handful of occasions. The families were acquainted and her brother was the incumbent of the parish.

"In fact, I'm more familiar with the place than you are, I daresay," she told Lyle as they took tea upon their arrival. "I've sat in this very chair and mentally refurbished the public rooms, reconfigured the layout of the rooms, ripped out the formal garden beds, and landscaped the park."

He looked down at her, amused. "Entertainments here were that dull?"

Kate grinned back. She loved to make him laugh. How wonderful to see that shadow of trouble fall away, even for a moment. Today, he rode out in search of the rebels who'd set fire to the east wing of this draughty old pile. This morning, she'd made it her mission to take his mind off what promised to be a grim business, indeed.

She arched her brows. "Dull? Need you ask? Dinner parties here were tedious; house parties excruciating. Odiously stiff and formal. The old duke behaved with as much ceremony as if he were the king himself."

Lyle snorted a laugh, his harsh features softening in a way that made her stomach turn over. "No, you wrong the old gentleman. He judged his lineage far more impressive than the king's."

Kate smiled, but she couldn't mistake the edge of bitterness to Lyle's tone.

From what Stephen had let fall, the old duke had been the worst kind of tyrant, the sort of master who'd provoked the uprisings in France. But Lyle would change all that, and Kate would help him. And when they'd seen to the health and welfare of all of their people, when they'd rebuilt the east wing, the seat of the fire, it would be time to transform this cold, gloomy place into a home, to banish painful memories.

This morning, however, she wished to avoid unpleasantness and place no demands on Lyle at all. Concern shadowed his features. He was restless and edgy, prowling the drawing room like a big cat. The last thing she wished was to add to his worries.

Kate turned the subject. "It seems that besides your sister, we are quite alone here. I expected at least two of the aunts to be in residence, but Rimshaw tells me they left for Bath the day before yesterday for their health. Poor dears." She glanced at Lyle. "You say you'd never met the great-aunts before you inherited?"

He made an impatient gesture. "Perhaps one or two. How should I know? There are about a hundred of 'em and they all look the same. Dark, dumpy little women with beady eyes and beaks for noses."

"Hush, someone might hear you," said Kate, her eyes dancing. "Hundreds, indeed! There are *five* sisters, and they are dear souls, all of them. But I must confess I am glad we have the place to ourselves for a bit."

Lyle paused in his pacing and let his gaze stroke her body. "As am I."

Her face heating, Kate rose quickly and crossed to the window. "The gardens are sadly in need of attention," she murmured in a constricted voice. But she didn't see the weed-infested flower beds. She saw the night ahead, when she would finally tell Lyle what she wanted, make him understand.

She imagined them in bed together, between fine linen sheets. The things she would do to him. The things she'd beg him to do to her.

Kate glanced at Lyle over her shoulder. He watched her with a lazy, smug smile on his face, as if he guessed the nature of her musings. She turned back and stared through the window again.

He came up behind her and slid his hands down her arms, murmuring wickedly into her ear, "You blush so delightfully, Kate, one wonders what you are thinking."

A little breathless, she answered, "I fully intend to tell you what I am thinking, but not now." She glanced at him sideways under her lashes, a look filled with sensual promise. "Tonight."

"Tonight?" He pressed closer. "But why wait until then?"

She felt his erection nudge the cleft of her bottom through her gown. He wanted her, and the thought was delicious, novel, utterly thrilling.

His welcoming heat and his strength were so enticing, she almost sank back into him, but quickly, she caught herself. "What if Louisa were to come in?"

Lyle bent his head, and his breath whispered over her skin. "She would go out again." He took her earlobe between his teeth and lightly grazed it, then let go. "Louisa is the soul of discretion."

"The servants, then," she choked, as his hands covered her breasts. "Sir, we stand before a window!"

IGNORING her protests, which grew feebler by the moment, Max let his hands rove her body like marauders, and the more he touched her, the more difficult it was to stop.

"Madness," she breathed, but she didn't pull away.

He ran his finger along the neckline of her bodice, dipping down into the valley of her bosom, then over the enticing swell of her breast, tracing the course outlined by a flimsy muslin ruffle. Drawing her sleeve down, he bent to kiss the shoulder blade he'd bared. She gasped, angling her head to allow him better access.

He trailed kisses along her shoulder, towards her vulnerable throat.

"Someone will hear us," she whispered.

"Not if we're quiet."

"A servant will come."

"Not if we don't ring the bell."

"Someone will see."

"Let them."

He kept nuzzling and kissing her, testing how far he could go before she made him stop. When he ran his tongue over the junction between shoulder and neck, she swayed and threw her head back against his shoulder, protests dying on her softening lips.

He continued to nuzzle her in that sensitive spot, filled with satisfaction at finding a place that made her melt.

Taking ruthless advantage of her distraction, he cupped one of Kate's breasts in his hand, feeling the weight, the firmness, the delectable nipple that peaked and hardened at his touch.

His cock strained at his trousers, and he wished he'd started this in their bedchamber, instead of the principal drawing room in broad daylight with the curtains open. Not that *he* objected to their surroundings, but Kate certainly would if he advanced this any further.

Max all but groaned. Her bottom fitted sweetly into his groin, tormenting him whenever she moved. He wanted to bend her over and throw her skirts up and take her from behind, driving fast and hard, holding her hips while the globes of her pert bottom bumped against him in a frantic rhythm.

And if someone watched them through that window, saw the scandalized bliss on her face, the sheer, spellbound ecstasy on his, all the better. He wanted the world to know that she was his to take, in whatever way he chose.

Max wrenched himself back from the brink of orgasm, panting at the effort of restraint. She shuddered, too, and he realized he'd been rubbing himself against her, imagining these forbidden delights.

Forbidden, because he'd resolved to treat his wife like a lady, with the respect she deserved, the gentleness she craved.

And the strain of it was slowly killing him.

With an iron exercise of will, he stopped, turned her in his arms, and looked down into her face. Her eyes were closed, and her lashes fanned in exotic crescents against her cheekbones. Her lips parted and she swayed into him, tilting her head for a kiss.

Max accepted the mute invitation, willing his member to calm down. He lightened the kiss, slowly pulling away, though every instinct urged him to ravage her mouth and plunder her body without mercy.

Finally, he ended it and lifted her hand to his lips.

"I'm afraid you are right, cautious one. We shouldn't do this here."

Kate opened her eyes, dazed and flushed. "Upstairs, then?"

He gave a shaky laugh and kissed her forehead. "I've stayed too long already. Best if we wait until tonight."

He didn't know whether he could sustain his gentle approach if they adjourned to the bedroom just now. Tonight, he'd follow Romney's advice and take the edge off himself before he went to her. Then, he could seduce her gently, slowly, the way she liked.

The baffled, slightly hurt look on Kate's face made him wince. He'd confused her, which wasn't surprising. Once again, he'd made a mess of something that used not to be so complicated. Bedding gently bred ladies was the very devil.

He plunged a hand through his hair. Lord knew, he wanted more than anything to please her. But he was beginning to wish he'd never read that damned diary in the first place.

MAX was striding down to the stables, his saddle holster slung over his shoulder, when he heard his sister's call.

He turned to see her hurrying in a fluster of muslin skirts down the slope towards him.

Nerves strung taut from anticipating the ordeal ahead, he waited impatiently for her to catch up with him. Besides the pistols, he had a knife in a scabbard strapped to his chest and another in his boot. He was armed to the teeth, in fact, but he hoped there'd be no need to use force. All he intended today was to familiarize himself with the terrain and to locate the rebels' camp. Holt had told him the outlaws numbered five men, but he never trusted anyone's word when his own life was at stake. He'd see for himself how many there were. Five, he, Jardine, and George could manage. Fifteen, and he might need to involve the militia.

"Max." Louisa caught up with him, a little short of breath.

"What is it?" He tried not to show his impatience.

"Before you ride out and leave Kate unprotected, I think you ought to know something."

His brows slammed together. She had all his attention now. "What?"

Her color was deathly and the circles under her eyes showed she hadn't slept. "I—I think Jardine might be the one. The man who is trying to kill her."

"Impossible," said Max. "What makes you think that?"

Louisa seemed to have trouble swallowing. She recited the facts in a low, trembling voice. "He . . . while you were away, Jardine was watching Kate. When I saw him, he interrogated me about her, asked me all sorts of questions about where she was held and who guarded her. When he found Perry with Kate one day, he flew into a rage. I thought he would do the boy an injury, he was so rough with him."

Max shook his head. "No, Louisa. You are barking up the wrong tree."

"How do you know?" she persisted. "Jardine has been skulking around since Kate arrived at Hove. He is a trained killer for the Home Office and someone high up wanted Kate dead. How can you be so sure it wasn't Jardine?"

"Several reasons," said Max. "First of all, if Jardine had wanted to kill Kate, she would have been dead before she left London. And even had she survived to fall into my hands, Jardine would not have made such a clumsy attempt at murdering her at the hunting box. He is too good for that. And third, I asked Jardine to keep an eye on Kate for me while I was gone. He's a scoundrel in a hundred ways, but in this case, utterly reliable."

Louisa put a trembling hand to her chest. He lifted his brows. "Satisfied?"

Slowly, she shook her head. "No. Not at all."

He didn't have time for this, but she was his baby sister, and the devastation in those blue eyes made him ache for her. Well, he didn't think he was wrong to have parted his sister from a ruthless bastard like Jardine all those years ago, but she was a mature woman now, capable of making her own decisions. And he hated to see her so unhappy.

"If you want Jardine, you should have him, Louie," he said quietly.

She started. "Oh! I don't—"

"Yes, you do know what I'm talking about. You've never looked at anyone but him. I might wish you'd settle on a nice, quiet country squire, but it doesn't look like that will ever happen, does it? If you still want Jardine after all these years, I won't stand in your way."

"It's too late," whispered Louisa, her voice low and wretched. "Far, far too late for us now."

"STEPHEN!" Kate flew across the sitting room to greet her brother and found herself enveloped in a tight bear hug.

She freed herself, laughing as she looked up into his plain, snub-nosed face. He looked more like a farm laborer than the son of an earl. "Let me up for air, dear boy! You've never known your own strength, have you? Even when we were children—"

"Never mind that now, love." Stephen released her and turned away. "So you married him," he said in a subdued voice. Suddenly, he smacked a meaty fist into his open hand. "Why didn't you wait? We could have thought of *something* to save your rep—" He broke off, swinging back to face her. "Don't say you are with child!"

Kate stiffened. "I certainly am not!"

Though she might be, after last night. A strange delight spread through her. She would love to have babies with Lyle. But she'd rather die than discuss the subject with her brother, and besides, she'd a notion such a sentiment might send him into an apoplexy. Clearly, he did not approve of this match.

She spoke more calmly. "We simply didn't wish to wait."

"I'll wager," muttered Stephen.

Kate set her hands on her hips. "And what's that supposed to mean? Stephen, I understand you and Lyle have had your differences over those rebels, but if you only knew how happy Lyle has made me, you'd see—"

"No, Kate!" Stephen held up his hand, clearly laboring under severe emotion. "No more." His eyes smoldered under their shaggy brows. "My dear sister, use the brain God gave you! Who do you think put me in prison in the first place? Lyle!"

Instinctively, she shook her head, and kept shaking it as her bright new world crashed around her. It made horrid, perfect sense. All that time, she'd shifted, cajoled, struggled, practically committed treason to get her brother out of prison, when if not for Lyle, Stephen wouldn't have been jailed in the first place.

Oblivious of the shock he'd dealt her, Stephen went on. "And now he will send innocent men to their deaths out of stubborn pride. He won't admit he's wrong."

Her brother continued his tirade, but Kate barely listened.

She'd suspected Lyle had the power to arrange for Stephen's release, should he choose to exercise it. He'd explicitly refused to do so. She'd detested him for that, but her rational self had soon come to understand his side of the story, how desperate he was to find the rebels. And the only lead he'd discovered was Stephen.

But the cold-blooded ruthlessness that allowed a man to throw a country parson into a rat-infested, disease-ridden jail merely to extract information from him appalled her.

How could he have married her, after what he'd done? He hadn't lied outright but by omission. In a way, that was worse.

Stephen clasped her hand with both of his, jerking her back to the present. "Kate, I have someone with me, someone I hope will change Lyle's mind. Would you have your husband fetched, please?"

"He's ridden out," she said numbly. She collected herself enough to ring the bell, and when the butler answered, instructed him to find her husband and request his urgent return. She turned to Stephen. "Someone might catch him at the stables if he hasn't left yet. Who is this man you speak of?"

"The leader of the men who marched on Lyle that day."

"A man accused of setting fire to this house?" Kate's eyes widened. "You brought him here? And left him unattended?"

"He is innocent," Stephen said quietly. "I persuaded him that unlike the former duke, your husband is a reasonable man, and that he will lend an impartial ear to their story."

Kate doubted that was true. For Lyle, everything rode on closing this case and getting on with the next phase of his life. These local men had been the focus of his investigation from the start. Where would he look for the arsonist if those he accused proved their innocence?

Suddenly, she asked, "Why did you tell Lyle where the rebels were?"

Stephen didn't quite meet her eyes. "It was time to bring them out of hiding. They couldn't run forever, and I'm confident that if Lyle will but listen to their side of the story, he will acquit them of wrongdoing. Their greatest mistake when the fire broke out was to run."

He gripped her hands with his big paws. "Will you talk to him, Kate? Will you try to persuade him to see reason?"

She nodded, her thoughts in turmoil. "I will try."

THE footman gave Max the message before he reached the stables.

*Holt was here.* Max almost staggered. He felt winded, as if the servant had driven a fist into his belly instead of delivering his news with all the deference due to a duke.

Kate's brother awaited Max in his library, with the chief

of the rebels in tow. Which meant Kate might already know the truth. Holt must have told her how Max had deceived her. The irate vicar wouldn't keep that news to himself.

Discreetly, the footman cleared his throat, as if to prompt a response. With a start, Max recollected his purpose in coming down to the stables. Clearly, Holt had preempted Max's move to round up the rebels. No need to ride out today, after all.

Barely able to catch enough breath to speak, he sent the footman to call off Jardine and George.

Max didn't immediately return to the house. He looked up, squinting into the sun until his eyes smarted and small, colored lights danced in his vision. Gathering the courage to face her.

Blindly, he turned and set off towards the house. Unprecedented terror pounded in his brain and clenched around his lungs. Now, he'd pay for what he'd done.

He barely considered the stated purpose of Holt's visit. The rebels, here at Lyle Castle? It made no sense, but he couldn't think about that now. He had to find a way to placate his wife, to make her understand. He'd done what had to be done.

But would she forgive him for deceiving her, for marrying her without telling her the truth? He clenched both fists, trying to stave off panic. She *must* forgive him, or there'd be nothing left for him at all.

He reached the stairs to the terrace, feeling as if lead lined his boots. Every step took him closer to disaster and retribution. His heart slammed in his chest.

Max set his hand on the rail and dragged in a shuddering breath. He'd dealt with death and loss and pain and the worst, almost inconceivable cruelties humankind could inflict on one another. He'd performed his job stoically, without hesitation. But his ironclad stomach roiled at the thought of losing Kate. After a scant few days of knowing her, life without his wife had become, quite simply, unthinkable.

But no, she wouldn't leave him. His bright, brave Kate would not take the easy way out. She'd stay, but her pride wouldn't allow her to give him all of herself, the way she had on their wedding night. She'd withhold her joy and passion so he couldn't hurt her again. A heavy price to pay for his cowardice.

Because once you lost someone's trust, you never completely regained it. He'd learned that lesson when his father confessed that his secret gaming obsession had reduced their once wealthy family to penury. Every good thing William Brooke had done throughout Max's childhood and adolescence had been wiped out in an instant, along with the future of all of those his father had professed to love.

Max headed towards the library, where the footman had said the vicar would wait. The servant hadn't mentioned Kate. Would she be there, too, ranged on her brother's side against Max?

But he didn't reach the library. In the hall, Kate blocked his path, her eyes filled with pain.

"I have seen my brother." Her voice echoed in the marble atrium.

He stopped short, and suddenly there wasn't enough air in the draughty hall. All of his previous forebodings raced through his mind. She'd discovered the truth. He'd lose her. She was the most important thing in his life. Christ, he *loved* her!

The realization crashed into him like a runaway stagecoach, leaving him breathless, panicked, and desperate to regain his equilibrium. He needed to argue his case, convince her to forgive him. Convince her to stay.

At the look on her face, his former certainty that she'd remain with him, no matter what he'd done, withered and died. She'd leave. She was his wife until death, but she wouldn't stay with someone like him.

Max knew what it was like to have his trust betrayed. And now he'd turned around and done the same thing to the one person he cared about most in the world.

Kate's eyes burned brightly in her stark, ravaged face. "It was you," she whispered. "*You* sent my brother to jail."

# Seventeen

*In a field in France, poppies drugging pleasure, we couple in the grass beneath a crisp blue sky.*

DON'T *forget the rest,* Max said silently. *I kidnapped you and held you for ransom, though I told you it was for your protection. I stole your diary and read the most intimate secrets of your body and soul. And I used them, too, in every way I could.*

He straightened, clenching his fists, preparing to fight for her with everything he had. It took him two attempts before he found his voice. "Kate," he managed, "at the time, I believed I had no alternative. That fire killed and injured twenty people. Not all of them were family. Some were servants." He breathed in, forcing air into his painful lungs. "Two of them were children."

Her gaze faltered. Tears sprang to those lovely eyes.

When she didn't speak, he went on. "All signs point to those men. Every piece of evidence we have links them with the fire. On top of that, they ran instead of facing their accuser. What else am I to think but that they committed the crime? Your brother admitted he aided and abetted their escape. Forget the sedition charge, Stephen Holt is an accessory to murder."

Kate's lips trembled. She bit down on the lower one until the tender flesh turned white. It tore at his chest to see how valiantly she struggled for control.

He waited, desperately hoping she'd understand.

Finally, she spoke, digging her clenched fist into her chest as if her heart hurt. "Was there no other way you could have persuaded my brother to tell you the truth? Did you have to send him to prison?"

He ran his hand through his hair, then dropped it by his side. "How can I say? There might have been. You know your brother. What do you think?"

She was silent for a moment, her expression grave and troubled. "You lied to me."

"Yes." He sighed. "And there is worse."

Her jaw shifted. Every line in her body grew taut, as if she braced herself.

How difficult it was to hurt her like this! But he needed to make a clean confession, not leave the lie to fester like an open wound.

"When I kidnapped you, it was not for your protection. I held you until your brother gave me the information I wanted. The letter I wrote that first morning was a ransom note. That was my method of persuasion."

Color leached from her face. The pained confusion in her eyes made him long to hold her, but he hadn't earned the right. He couldn't bear her to reject his touch, so he kept his hands fisted at his side.

How could he explain? He wished they might go somewhere more private than this cold, marble entryway, but he needed to say this now or he might never screw up the courage to do it again.

"You suspected I did more than shuffle paper at the Home Office. Well, you were right. They called me 'the Fixer.' No job was too difficult or too dirty for me to handle.

I dealt with the gutter scum, the villainous, and the corrupt. These are men who do not operate within the bounds of the law. To defeat them, sometimes one must play outside the rules."

She held out a hand, as if to ward off his words.

But he had to tell her everything now. "I've been tainted by that world, Kate. To survive there, sentiment cannot play a part. When I jailed your brother, when I kidnapped you, you were just a job to me. It was only later that you became so much more."

He shook his head, marveling at his blindness. "Do you know what my motto has always been? 'The end justifies the means.' I persuaded myself that no good cause would be served by telling you the truth about any of this, that being together was all that mattered. I was a coward. Afraid of losing you." His voice roughened. "More afraid than I've been of anything in my life."

"That's why you wanted to marry so quickly, wasn't it?" she said. "Before I found out."

What he chiefly remembered was a desperate need to make her his and to get inside that lovely body again, without delay. "It certainly wasn't the most compelling reason."

A faint blush stained her cheeks. His heart leaped to see her color return. He scarcely dared to guess what it might mean.

She fluttered a hand. "I don't know what to think."

"I dare not beg you to forgive me just yet," said Max, struggling to keep his voice even, trying not to hope too hard. "I can only promise you that I will never lie to you again."

Soberly, she regarded him. "I daresay we both have our secrets."

Not if she was thinking of her diary. He'd stolen that secret from her. Guilt and shame howled through him like an icy wind. He ought to tell her about that, too, but she didn't look as though she could take much more. Another shocking revelation and her fragile hold on control might snap. He simply couldn't hurt her that much.

But even as he thought it, his better self told him his reasoning was specious.

Max caught her hands in his, an overwhelming sense of longing drowning the objections of his conscience. He wanted her back in his arms, at any cost. He wanted to tell her how much she meant to him, but the words wouldn't come.

When she didn't pull away, hope spiraled delicately inside him, gaining strength until it coiled painfully around his chest. He waited, and the wait seemed like a thousand years.

Finally, she took a deep, shaky breath. "You shouldn't have concealed the truth. But knowing what you'd done wouldn't have made any difference." Her lips twisted in gentle self-mockery. "I don't think anything could stop me loving you."

The relief almost unmanned him. Sick with it, he bowed his head, afraid to touch her in case she evaporated, like a mirage. "I don't deserve you." He looked up and drowned in those brandy-colored eyes. "But I'm presumptuous enough to love you, too."

*Tell her about the diary.*

She smiled and wound her arms around his neck. "Oh, my dear. I know."

MAX was late for the interview with the vicar and Tucker, the rebel leader, but for the best of reasons—he'd been kissing his wife. *His love.*

Feeling extraordinarily well disposed towards the world in general, Max listened to Tucker's story without interruption.

At the end of the tale, Max rested his head against the high back of his leather chair to think.

"You see? It's as I told you," said Holt eagerly. "True, the men did go up to the house to make their demands known to the new duke. They chose a day that was momentous for the entire estate, when the old duke's will was read."

"We hadn't even got there yet when we smelled smoke and the servants raised the alarm," added Tucker.

Max waved a hand to silence them. "Gentlemen, I've heard all this." He picked up a pencil and tapped it on the desk.

"All right," he said slowly. "Suppose I believe you. Where does that leave me?" He bent his gaze on Tucker. "Do you know who set the fire?"

"No, Your Grace."

The answer came readily enough, but Max wasn't convinced. He glared at Tucker under lowered brows, but the man lifted his chin, refusing to be cowed.

Max stifled a frustrated oath. Someone must know something. They always did in small communities like this. But he suspected threats wouldn't do him any good, not with Tucker, and certainly not with Holt. For the moment, he'd let it go.

"If you happen to hear something or remember anything suspicious, let me know."

Holt had a gleam in his eye that Max didn't trust. He was a cunning bastard for a vicar. "Suppose we did know something of interest," said Holt. "Would it be worth our while to disclose it?"

"It would save your friends' necks, if that's what you mean," growled Max. He glowered at Holt for a moment before addressing Tucker. "Very well. What would your men expect in return?"

"They want to come back to work on the estate," said Holt before Tucker could answer. "At a decent wage, mind—not the pauper's allowance the old duke made—and a fair rent."

Max hesitated. Well, what harm would it do? The estate

would have to replace those men otherwise and he believed Tucker's story, damn him. In his line of work, he'd developed sharp instincts about people, and Tucker appeared just the sort of man he'd like to have working for him—honest, dependable, and forthright.

Besides, he needed that information. "Once I've met each of your men and I'm satisfied of their good character, I don't see why not."

Holt beamed and rose from the table to shake Max's hand. "Done!"

"And the information?" Max took a pen and dipped it in ink, trying to conceal his impatience. They'd only ask for more if they knew how anxious he was to hear it.

Tucker spoke. "We—the men and I—think it were this stranger what came about our parts, ooh, mebbe a month afore the trouble started. Name of Hoskins."

*Useless.* Max put down his pen. To these country folk, anyone whose great-grandfather hadn't been born and raised in the district was suspect.

"Young hothead, he was," continued Tucker. "Always wanting to get into fights, looking for trouble. Whenever we talked about taking a stand on wages and rents, this boy would urge full-blown revolt."

Straightening, Max snatched up his pen. There'd been rumors in the Home Office that the spies sent into rural and industrial areas to scent out dissension and unrest were in fact instigating violent insurrection, then informing on the perpetrators and claiming their rewards. No one was certain whether these *agents provocateurs* existed. But perhaps Max had found one.

"And what makes you think this young fellow lit the fire?" said Max, making a note of all he'd been told.

"Well, he were mighty keen on coming with us when we went to see the duke, but on the day, he weren't nowhere to be seen. As far as anyone hereabouts knows, he disappeared that day and never came back."

This sounded like it might lead somewhere. "Can you tell me what he looked like? Height, coloring, and so on?"

The description could easily have fitted any number of young men.

"I could draw 'im for ye, p'raps," said Tucker. "I'm a fair draughtsman, Your Grace."

Max passed him the necessary implements and the man set to work with quick, bold slashes of his pencil. He finished the rough portrait in short order and passed it to Max.

No one Max recognized, unfortunately, but he'd ask around at the Home Office. He sighed. Another trip to London when he needed to be at Lyle. At least this time he could take Kate with him . . .

He slid the portrait into his file and rose to see the men out.

Tucker looked him in the eye and held out his hand. Max shook it without hesitation before he recognized the gesture as a test.

He fixed the man with a no-nonsense stare. "I mean to make changes here, Tucker. Important ones. I trust I'll have your support."

Tucker squinted one eye and cocked his head. "Ye might at that, Your Grace. We'll see."

THE duke's apartments breathed luxury, in contrast with the rest of the shabby, almost Spartan house. Clearly, the old duke hadn't stinted when it came to his own comfort. Kate sat in their private sitting room on the floor by the fire, sipping a glass of brandy. She smiled, running her hand through the thick pile of the Aubusson carpet. The fiery taste of cognac stirred memories of that night at the hunting box, when Lyle had dominated her completely. Now, she waited for him to do it again.

A meeting with his steward had occupied Lyle since shortly after Stephen left. Kate had arranged a light supper to be served them in the library, where they toiled over the estate books. A pity not to dine together on their first night in their new home, but a good master looked after his land and his tenants before he saw to his own comfort. Kate approved of Lyle's dedication.

She cupped the brandy balloon in her palms and swirled the amber liquid around to warm it. Raising her glass silently in a toast to her husband, she took another sip. *Dutch courage*. This time, however, she'd limit her libations to one glass.

Tonight she'd assert herself once and for all. She'd tell Lyle all she desired. She'd make him understand she was no delicate flower. Kate wanted the bold, devastating lover of the hunting lodge, before he'd thought of her as his wife. She wanted to tumble down from the pedestal where he'd set her, straight into his strong, passionate embrace.

The door to Lyle's bedchamber opened and closed, breaking into her thoughts. Lyle?

Kate set down the glass, her heartbeat kicking up a notch. Listening, she heard the murmur of voices. Lyle and his new valet—another trapping of dukedom Max seemed happier without. She'd wait until Dawkins left. And then . . .

It seemed a lifetime later that the valet quitted Max's bedchamber.

Kate waited a few moments. Then quietly, she moved to the doorway and cautiously looked in. No one.

Surely Max couldn't have left, too? Perhaps he'd gone to her bedchamber.

Chuckling at their cross-purpose, Kate moved towards the connecting door on the other side of the chamber. But before she reached it, a sound came from the dressing room. Lyle must still be here, after all.

Kate switched direction and headed in the direction of the sound. What a ridiculously large apartment for one man!

On the threshold, she stopped short, her hand flying to her mouth.

He didn't see her, for his eyes were shut tightly. His dressing gown gaped open, revealing a glimpse of muscled chest and flat abdomen with its sprinkling of dark, coarse hair that arrowed down past his navel. One big hand clenched his erection, moving up the shaft, closing over the head, before gliding back down its length, while the other hand squeezed the base of his member. A dark red flush stained the crests of his cheekbones. His erection was similarly flushed, its tip glistening with moisture as he worked his hand up and down.

Shocked and disoriented, Kate held her breath, unsure what she should do or how she should react. She watched Lyle, appalled, fascinated by the sight of him pleasuring himself. All that male power, the expression of concentration and rapture on his face, was almost unbearably erotic. But as his movements grew faster, her mind finally interpreted what she saw.

*"Lyle!"*

His eyes snapped open. Glazed and bright, it was a moment before they focused on her. "Kate!" Horror flooded his face. "Oh, hell."

He quickly covered himself with his dressing gown and belted it, but the exotic fabric tented where his rampant arousal nudged. "Should've known better than to listen to Romney," he muttered.

"Pardon?" she said, thinking she couldn't have heard right. But he didn't repeat himself. He just looked at her with a strange, agonized hunger that unsettled her even more.

"What are you *doing*?" she burst out. "I mean, I quite see what you were doing." She didn't see *at all.* "Of course, I'm not so naive that I don't know"—*yes, she was, or she had been, until this moment*—"but . . . *why*, Max?"

*Aren't I enough?*

He opened his mouth, then shut it and ran his hand through his hair. "Oh, hell," he said again. He took her arm and guided her back to his bedchamber.

When they stood next to the bed facing each other, Lyle gripped the bedpost and half turned away from her, his hand flexing and tightening around the carved wood. He seemed painfully embarrassed at what had occurred, hardly knowing where to begin to explain.

But she couldn't let him off this time. Why would he feel the need to do that to himself when she was there, in the next room, ready and waiting? A sick sense of foreboding filled her. Was there something wrong with her?

Suddenly, she wondered if she could bear to hear the answer to that question. Perhaps he did this for the same reason Hector had stopped coming to her bed. Perhaps, like Hector, he couldn't maintain his . . . hardness for very long unless he gave himself assistance? Perhaps she simply didn't excite him enough? Had she been too bold in their previous encounters? She'd tried so hard to be quiet and submissive, to let him take the lead.

His color still high, Lyle finally spoke. "Kate, I don't know how to wrap this in fine linen, so I'll just say it. When a man desires a woman as much as I desire you, sometimes he will, er, achieve orgasm before the lady is ready. That is unsatisfying for both parties. Sometimes, the man gives himself an orgasm first, so that he can pleasure his lady without, er, finishing prematurely." He hesitated. "You prefer things slow and gentle, and sometimes, my—my need is so overwhelming that I can't go slowly. I had to . . . do *that* so I could please you. Does that make sense?"

Relief broke inside her. How could any woman mind that her husband desired her too much for his self-control? But what was this about her preferences? Where had he come by that idea? "Frankly, I think it's the most arrant nonsense I've ever heard! I don't *want* you to hold back with me. When did I ever give you the impression I desired such restraint?"

For a moment, he looked thunderstruck. Nostrils flared, he strode to a chest of drawers and drew out a book. He flung it in the air, and it fell with a flutter of pages onto the bed.

One glance told her what it was. Her heart lurched. "My diary?" She launched herself at the bed and snatched up the small book. "You stole my diary? And you *read* it!" The most wretched humiliation swamped her. She sat on the bed, hugging the diary to her. "Why?"

Lyle sighed. "I thought it was your political diary."

She gave him a blank look. What was he talking about? She felt sick.

"When you were going to threaten Sidmouth you said you'd base your memoirs on a diary," he explained.

Kate passed a weary hand over her eyes. "Oh. That diary. But that diary doesn't exist."

"So you told me. Still, I believed it did exist when I stole it from your house."

"And you read it," said Kate, slowly shaking her head. Hot waves of shame surged through her anew. Dully, she said, "I didn't know you were fluent in the Italian tongue."

He made a grim attempt at a smile. "There are so many responses I could make to that, but I'll hold my peace."

"This isn't funny, sir!" Kate threw down the diary and launched off the bed to pace. It wasn't simply that he'd discovered her secret longings, her deepest thoughts. Embarrassment, and the sense of violation, she could bear. But it seemed he'd cross any line to get what he wanted. Could she live with a man whose sense of honor was so skewed?

Trembling with hurt and fury, she rounded on him. "What next will you tell me? First you incarcerate my brother, then you kidnap me and hold me to ransom. And now you've read my diary. The first two you explained. You were doing your duty. I hope you won't try to tell me reading my private . . . imaginings—" She huffed a breath. "I hope you won't try to tell me that was part of your duty also. Is there *nothing* you won't do to get your own way?"

The ravaged expression on his face told her there was

more. Her stomach heaved and turned over. She gripped the bedpost and set her jaw. She was strong. She'd come through so much. She could bear this.

"What is it? Max, if you don't tell me everything now—"

He held up a hand to stop her. "Louisa has read the diary, too. She translated it for me. I didn't know what it was until she finished."

*"Louisa!"* she said. "Louisa has read that—that nonsense?"

"Not nonsense," he said quietly. "Many parts were lyrical, beautiful even. I was moved by what you wrote. And aroused."

Kate knew he meant it as a compliment but the mere thought of him reading that diary sent another suffocating wave of humiliation through her. That he'd enjoyed it only made it worse. If she'd written it for him, she might have reveled in the knowledge, but she hadn't. She'd written it solely for herself. And Louisa! Oh, dear Heaven, what must she *think*?

She fixed him with a pained gaze. "Does Louisa know I wrote it?"

"I haven't discussed it with her, but she has probably guessed."

Kate plucked at the counterpane. Fresh recollections of things she'd written rained on her like arrows, piercing her flesh. She bunched a fistful of fabric in her hand, forcing down the urge to scream, to release the humiliation building inside. How she wished she'd burned that stupid book!

But her embarrassment paled beside the gravity of what Max had done. Would he even understand why she was so upset? She forced herself to meet his gaze. "Reading my diary—and worse, using the knowledge you gained in your dealings with me—don't you see how wrong that was?"

His face had turned to granite, but those gray eyes, usually so cool, burned into hers. "It was wrong. Very wrong.

I knew as soon as I'd read the first page." He swallowed hard. "I'm sorry."

He'd admitted his fault and apologized, but still, it wasn't enough. "Yet, even tonight, you acted on the information my diary contained. If I hadn't caught you doing"—she made a sweeping gesture with her hand—"*that*, would you have told me the truth? And you hustled me into marriage, knowing you'd deceived me on all these points. What if I didn't forgive you so easily, or at all? Did you even consider that?"

"I did," he answered, cutting his gaze away. "I took a calculated risk."

She gave a cry of disbelief. "Oh, yes! What was that motto of yours? 'The end justifies the means.' How very apt!"

In two strides, Lyle reached her. He caught her to him, wrapping his arms around her. Something wild and desperate in his eyes called to her, even as she tried to resist. Her treacherous body responded, instantly, fiercely, and she struggled to quell the excitement that thrummed through her veins. She needed to fight for their future, not melt like an ice sculpture under the sun's blaze.

She tried to push him away, but it was like trying to move a granite boulder. With a ragged sigh, he released her, but his hands slid up to frame her face in a gesture so tender her heart gave a painful twinge. "Kate, I told you what I am—what I've been. When I took that job for the Home Office I was desperate for money—five mouths to feed and debts to pay . . . There was no room in that existence for decency and honor." His thumb caressed her lips. "But all that will change now. I love you."

She didn't doubt his sincerity. His eyes spoke of his love as clearly as his words. His deep voice throbbed with it. The power of that love, the nearness of him almost swayed her, almost convinced her to put this incident out of her mind. But he'd loved her and still he'd taken unfair advantage. How could she trust him not to repeat his behavior?

His hands slid down to linger on her arms. "Kate. Don't—don't leave me. We can sort this out." His voice was hoarse with emotion. "Just give me another chance."

Kate forced down answering tears. "But how will I know?" she whispered. "How will I know whether you've changed until it's too late?" She shivered, digging her toes into the carpet's thick, soft pile for some vestige of comfort. "Let's not speak of this any more. I—I want to be alone for a while. I need time to think."

Lyle gripped her wrist, his face pale and taut with anguish. "That's no way to resolve this. I won't let you go."

She gave a broken laugh. "Will you lock me in a tower? Are you going to *make* me believe things will be different?"

He flinched. The deep hurt in his eyes was almost too much for her to bear. Her soul ached for him. She wanted to wrap her arms around him and tell him all would be well, as one told a frightened child during a thunderstorm. But on this, she couldn't compromise. For the sake of their future happiness, she couldn't give in now.

Max must have seen the resolution in her face. Slowly, he detached his fingers from around her wrist and turned away.

MAX heard the pad of her bare feet cross the carpeted floor, the soft clicks as the communicating door opened and closed.

She was gone. His guts twisted with the feeling she'd never truly come back, just as he'd feared when she'd confronted him in the hall that afternoon. A fierce, sobbing pain burned in his chest. His throat tightened until he could barely breathe.

He gripped the bedpost, head bowed, eyes closed, struggling to force down the most powerful sense of loss he'd known since his father had died, unforgiven, by his elder son.

Had he truly forgotten what it was to be a gentleman, a man of honor and integrity? He'd considered his Home Office persona to be like armor he donned to do battle with the villains of the London underworld, trappings he'd discard once he put that existence behind him.

But he'd been mistaken. Kate had the right of it. Jailing her brother, kidnapping her, and holding her to ransom—those pieces of ruthlessness could be excused because he'd performed them in execution of his duty. He'd vowed to find those rebels and punish them. He hadn't known her and loved her when he'd used such underhanded tactics to achieve his goal.

Reading the diary, using the information he gleaned there, was different. As soon as he'd realized what the diary contained he should have burned the translation and found a way to return the original to its rightful place. But by then, he'd been so enmeshed in that world of passion and sensuality he'd barely considered the ethics of what he did. Later, he'd been so desperate to please her, he'd ignored his own culpability.

An ugly realization, that. He'd chafed against the necessary evils of his work, never dreaming he'd adapted completely to that existence. He'd assumed he could simply shed that life like an old coat and begin afresh.

Was Kate right? Was it too late for him to change?

Max clenched his jaw. No, it couldn't be too late. But how would he make her see the difference in him? He needed to prove himself worthy of her trust.

The alternative was far too bleak to contemplate.

# Eighteen

*Pleasure is chance and fleeting. Only love endures.*

SUKEY unpacked the last of her ladyship's—no, she corrected herself—*Her Grace's* trunks and sorted the clothes into which must be washed and which aired and ironed.

"The green silk tonight, I think." Sukey hummed to herself as she laid the gown on the counterpane. Just a light press and it would do. The duchess always looked very fine in that shade of green. And the emerald set to go with it. The duke would be proud.

A scratch at the door interrupted her. She looked up, to see one of the upstairs maids bobbing a curtsey, a sly look in her eye.

"Well? What is it, girl?" said Sukey briskly. She wasn't one to forget her exalted position as the duchess's personal maid, and she wouldn't let others forget it, either.

"If you please, Miss Phillips, gentleman aksed me ter give yer this."

The girl held out a screwed-up note. Now Sukey saw the reason for that knowing look.

She ought to refuse to receive notes from strange men. Sukey licked her lips. But this particular man . . .

"Ever so 'andsome, he is," said the girl, speculation bright in her eye. As if to say, *I'll take your place if you're having none.*

*Over my dead body,* Sukey thought and snatched the note. "All right, don't stand there gawking. Off you go!"

She watched until the maid left the bedchamber, then she hurried to shut the door. She thought she'd never see him again, but he'd come back to her. Couldn't stay away.

Her fingers fumbled as she opened the note.

*Meet me behind the laundry at eleven o'clock. Don't fail.*

Well! She wouldn't be meeting him anywhere after a summons like that. No sweet words, not even a civil request!

With a sniff, Sukey slipped the note into her pocket and went about her task.

Of course, she would need to go to the laundry at some stage today. Until she found a laundry maid she could trust, she must oversee the care of all the duchess's intimate garments.

And if she happened to see him while she went about her business, who could cavil at that? She'd ignore him, of course. No more than he deserved for thinking he could call her like a dog to heel.

Unhurriedly, she finished sorting garments and picked up her overflowing basket to take it to the laundry.

A warm glow of anticipation swelled in her chest.

THE day was bright and fresh, flush with birdsong and the scents of spring blossom. Kate failed to appreciate the natural beauty surrounding her as she drove out with Louisa to visit some of Lyle's tenants. She'd rather be in bed with the blinds drawn and the covers pulled over her head.

Duty called, however, and Kate knew she'd do better to occupy herself, instead of dwelling on the disaster her marriage had turned out to be. But despite keeping busy all morning, despair over Lyle mired her thoughts and made her sluggish and irritable. Part of her wished she could simply overlook the incident and get on with her new life. But she couldn't. She needed to know there were some lines of decency and honor Lyle would never cross. She needed to know she could trust him.

The trouble was, she didn't know how he might go about earning her trust. If only she could set him three tasks to prove himself, like the labors of Hercules. If only she might have some guarantee. But it wasn't that simple. Perhaps, in the end, she would need to take his good behavior on faith, but she wasn't ready to do that just yet.

They passed through an avenue of cherry trees, laden with blossom. "Isn't this pretty?" Louisa broke the silence that had gathered and swelled between them since leaving the stables. Her tone was overbright, as if she attempted to jolly Kate along.

Kate tightened the reins, slowing the horse to a walk so Louisa might look her fill.

She didn't quite trust her voice to answer. It had taken all her resolution to face Louisa after Lyle told her his sister had read her diary. She still couldn't meet Louisa's eye.

At least she knew her sister-in-law wouldn't be as shocked by those passionate writings as she might have been. From her reaction to that scene between Lady Fanny and Romney in the barn, it appeared Louisa had liberal views about relations between men and women.

Still, Kate's embarrassment seemed larger than she was. It filled her and spilled over the sides, rising in her throat, choking her.

After a few minutes of attempting to instigate conversation and observing Kate's blushes, Louisa said, "You know, don't you?"

After a slight hesitation, Kate nodded.

"I am sorry! So sorry!" Louisa burst out, distress drawing down her features. "Lyle told me the translation was necessary for his work." She searched Kate's face. "Was it? Necessary, I mean."

"He stole the wrong diary," said Kate flatly.

"Oh. *Oh.*" Louisa hesitated. Then she laid a hand on Kate's knee. "My dear, can you forgive me? I should have done more to protect you. I very nearly refused to give the translation to Max, but he assured me the information was vital to his government work."

Louisa regarded her anxiously. Kate bore her scrutiny until she couldn't stand it any longer. "Don't look at me!" she said in a tight, hard voice. "I'm so ashamed."

Softly, Louisa said, "You should be proud."

Kate dropped her hands and stared at her friend. The gig lurched forward, and she quickly tightened the reins again.

"It's not easy for me to say this," said Louisa, "but since you have had to bear your private thoughts read by strangers, I will tell you something. You could have been writing my life."

Kate's shock must have been evident. Louisa hastened to add, "Oh, I don't mean the, er, liaison part of it. That would be ridiculous. But . . . I've known the pain of loneliness that you described, an ache for companionship that's so strong, it's almost physical. It never would have occurred to me to find solace in writing, but perhaps I will try that one day."

Kate was so moved, she could barely speak. That someone had read her diary and understood! But the despair layered beneath Louisa's words sobered her. "Is there no hope for you, my dear?" she asked quietly. "I assumed you loved someone unsuitable, for a lady with your gifts wouldn't remain unwed for so long if she didn't choose to do so. But the marquis . . ."

"There might have been hope once," Louisa said. She managed a twisted smile. "But no longer. I will not be forgiven. And perhaps it is better that way. I—I would like to have children and my time is running out. I believe I shall settle on a nice man who will be kind to me, and put the . . . rest out of mind."

*If only it were that easy,* thought Kate.

A flurry of movement in the trees ahead made the horse shy. Kate struggled to bring him under control, so occupied with managing beast and vehicle that she didn't see the figures in their path until Louisa's hand clamped like a vise over her forearm.

She looked up, to see Perry standing in the middle of the road, his arm around Sukey's waist. He held a pistol to Sukey's head.

Horror held her motionless while Perry shoved the maid before him, as if to display her. "Duchess!" he shouted. "Your Grace! Step down from the gig, if you please. You, too, Lady Louisa." He gloated while they obeyed. "So glad you could join us."

MAX groaned. His head ached as if someone hacked at it with a blunt meat cleaver. He'd hit the brandy a little hard last night, after she'd left. In this state, he had about as much chance of making head or tail of the estate account books as he had of flying.

*She's leaving me.* Over and over, the words beat a tattoo in his tender brain. Max shoved his hands through his hair and blinked hard as the neat figures in their narrow columns blurred before his eyes.

Though she hadn't left physically, there'd been no trace of his Kate in the polite, coldly correct lady who'd accompanied him at breakfast that morning. The elegant automaton who had answered him readily enough when he spoke to her but cut off every attempt at deeper conversation was not the impetuous, passionate woman he'd fallen in love with.

She withheld herself so he wouldn't hurt her again. The knowledge struck him like a physical blow. She might as well have picked up a fire iron and thrashed him with it. He'd have preferred that, in fact. At least physical hurt didn't last very long. The pain of Kate's withdrawal might never go away.

After that excruciating breakfast, he'd moved through the rest of the morning as if he lived in a nightmare. Every minute slowed until it seemed like a lifetime until he'd see her again. Deciphering the accounts had been a particularly foolish thing to attempt, but he needed something to occupy his mind. Usually, he'd find solace in riding or fencing or punching someone, but he didn't have the heart for it now.

Brandy would befuddle his brain nicely, but it was too early in the day for drink. Besides, he wanted another chance to talk to Kate when she returned from her errands of mercy in the village. Drunken ramblings weren't likely to win him her favor.

His heart lurched and set up a frantic pound in his chest. Every time he thought of what he'd done, the pain he'd caused her, he wanted to cut out his heart and throw it down for her pretty feet to stomp on. He knew he'd made a terrible mistake. Every word she'd uttered sank him further in his own estimation.

But how could he make it up to her? How could he find a way to regain her trust?

That was the devil of it. He was adept at analyzing problems, formulating plans, and acting on them with ruthless speed, but he couldn't begin to devise a solution for the most important conundrum of his life.

A step on the terrace outside made Max turn his head. *Jardine*.

Max grunted and sat back in his chair. "Choose your moments, don't you? What are you doing here?"

Jardine took off his hat, dropped his gloves into it, and set it on the desk. "I'm here because you asked me to come, old man."

How could he have been that stupid? "Did I?" For the life of him, he couldn't recall why. Then he remembered. He'd wanted Jardine's help in the arson case.

Jardine spoke before he could marshal a response. "Thought you'd rid yourself of that puling whelp."

Max blinked. "I beg your pardon? What puling whelp?"

"Perry. Saw him skulking around in the vicinity. Thought you'd given him his marching orders." The devilish brows descended over his bright, dark eyes. "If you haven't, you're a damned fool. Anyone can tell he's infatuated with you."

An odd choice of words. "*Infatuated.* Perry?" The ironic curl to Jardine's mouth made Max uneasy. Suddenly, realization dawned. "You don't mean—"

"My God, Your Grace, did you just come down in the last shower?" Jardine mocked. "You didn't know?"

Impossible! Max dismissed the notion that Perry might . . . "Hero worship," he said stubbornly. "Perry looks up to me as a mentor. A father figure."

"Yes," purred Jardine. "And we know what Perry's father did to him, don't we?" That saturnine smile chilled Max to the bone.

Blowing out a breath, Max straightened in his chair. He'd had no idea. Not the slightest clue. How blind, how stupid he'd been! But he wouldn't allow Jardine to make sport of the lad. "I'll speak to Perry," he said briefly. "But that wasn't why I asked you to come. It's about the fire."

He told Jardine about Tucker's assertions that a stranger had arrived at the estate and stirred up resentment shortly before the day the blaze broke out.

"I'd assumed the existence of these *agents provocateurs* was a myth," he said.

"Not at all." Jardine narrowed his eyes. "The government must be seen to be dealing with unrest. Whether that unrest is genuine or fomented by government spies is neither here nor there. All the more excuse for Sidmouth to maintain the state of emergency and increase the government's powers to unprecedented levels. He's not likely to discourage the practice if it yields benefit."

"So we might be looking for one of us," said Max. "A Home Office Johnny seeking adventure and excitement—and a substantial reward. Someone with something to prove."

Jardine nodded. "That about sums it up."

"Perry," Max said.

"Could be."

Fumbling a little, Max pulled out his file and found the sketch Tucker had drawn. He examined it closely, focusing on lineaments rather than depth of color and features that could be disguised or changed.

Lighten the hair, clothe him appropriately, and remove the beard that covered half his face and that sketch might well be Perry. The eyes should have been unmistakable, but it was a pencil sketch, not a painting, and therefore played down Perry's most distinguishing features.

The revelation hit him like a horse kick to the gut. "Do you know what this means, Jardine?" The horror of it surpassed anything Max could have imagined. His chest squeezed painfully. "It can't be true."

For once, even Jardine's eyes widened in shock. "Deranged." He shook his head. "He killed all those people so that you could be a duke. Such is the extent of his devotion."

It was bizarre, yet chillingly probable. There'd been two men and their sons standing before Max in line for the dukedom. All had attended the reading of the old duke's will. All had died in the fire. *Could* it have been contrivance on Perry's part? Bitter, hot bile surged to Max's throat. He could barely comprehend such warped reasoning, but it made horrible sense.

Max set his jaw and banged his fist on the table. "If it's true, I'll see him hang for this!"

Slowly, Jardine shook his head, and the truth broke over Max like a douse of cold water. Frustration at his powerlessness simmered inside him. "It'll be swept under the carpet, won't it? Faulkner can't afford to let the public know he's planted agents around the country to stir up trouble."

"Oh, you'll find our Perry is well protected," agreed Jardine. "Even if it weren't such a sensitive situation, he won't see the inside of a prison cell, much less swing for it."

Max's mind darkened. "Why is that?"

Jardine regarded him pityingly. "You must know Perry is one of Faulkner's boys."

"Faulkner's—" Max broke off, feeling a fool. Why hadn't he seen the truth? It all made perfect sense. No wonder his objections about Perry had fallen on deaf ears all this time. Faulkner wanted him close. Very close, if Jardine were correct. And Jardine usually was correct in these matters. It also explained Perry's contempt and resentment for Faulkner. Even through his disgust and horror at the crime Perry had perpetrated, a twinge of compassion struck him.

Perry's father had used his son vilely. It seemed Faulkner might have preyed on the vulnerable young man, too. "Unforgivable," he said.

"Yes." Jardine walked to the long window and stared out. "With that history, is it any wonder the lad's half crazed?" Suddenly, he swung back to face Max, dark eyes glittering under devilish brows. "But don't you see, Lyle? We have him now. We have Faulkner by the balls." He made a crushing gesture with his fingers. "Right where we want him."

Coldly, Max said, "I've no interest in your political scheming, Jardine. What will we do about that damned boy?"

Jardine shrugged. "Pack him off to Jamaica or Africa or

some other godforsaken place. If you try to have him arrested, Faulkner will quash the charges before the committal hearing. You won't see him hang in England."

Despite the devastation he'd wrought, Max was no longer sure he wanted to see Perry hang. God, what a tangle!

"Letter arrived for you, Your Grace." Max hadn't even noticed the butler standing in the doorway. With an irrational surge of fear, he snatched up the letter and opened it.

*Your Grace—*
*I have her. Did you think I'd let her take you away?*
*Come to the old theater, alone.*
*I want to kill her while you watch.*

The letter was like a punch to the gut, sucking the air from his lungs. Winded, blinded by rage and terror for Kate, and for Louisa, too, Max simply sat there, clenching that taunting message in his fist.

*Perry had Kate.* The world around Max slowed. His throat tightened and a pulse thumped there. As if his heart blocked the air passage, as if he might choke to death on his fear.

*Move!* A voice inside him bellowed like a sergeant major over the din of his heart and the harsh drag of his breath. The silent bubble that cocooned him for those few seconds burst, and the outside world resumed its normal pace.

Years of conditioning kicked in. A mission. Another mission. A job, that was all. He needed to believe that, or he wouldn't be able to function well enough to defeat Perry. Having just resolved to win back his humanity, he needed to shed it again to save Kate.

Max unlocked a desk drawer, took out his pistols and loaded them, cool deliberation overtaking his mind. His hands deftly manipulated gunpowder, ball, and pistol in practiced, disciplined movements. His hands didn't even shake, though beneath the sheer layer of icy calm, agonized fear coursed like a torrent through his body. This was what he was trained for. He couldn't afford to make a mistake.

"What is it, man?" Jardine's voice finally caught his attention.

Max's voice rasped like a rusty gate. "Perry's got Kate. My sister is with her. God knows what he'll do."

Naked rage swept over Jardine's countenance. "I'll kill him."

"Not if I get there first." Lyle finished loading and stood. "Let's go."

*So much for self-defense,* thought Kate, with an anguished roll of her eyes at Louisa. Despite having three strenuously objecting women to deal with, Perry had managed remarkably well. Lyle would be proud of his protégé.

He'd bound the three of them together by their hands, so they sat like the spokes of a wheel with their backs to one another on the stage of a small, dilapidated theater in the castle grounds.

Perry sat on the edge of the stage between the footlights, crooning to himself as he scored his hand with the tip of his hunting knife.

As the network of red welts built on his palm, Perry set down his knife and rolled up his sleeve. He continued the crisscross pattern further up his arm until it blurred, smeared with his blood.

His face remained eerily serene all the while, not once registering pain. Kate's stomach churned. If he could do that to himself, what horrors might he inflict on her and Louisa and Sukey?

She hadn't imagined the hatred in his eyes when first they'd met. Perry was clearly unhinged, more dangerous than a paid assassin could ever be.

What was he waiting for? Kate wanted to ask, but drawing attention to herself while he was in the mood for cutting into human flesh didn't seem like a good idea.

Then, Louisa slipped a hand free.

Kate's gaze flew to her friend. How had she done it?

With a glance in Perry's direction, Louisa ever so slightly shook her head. "Double-jointed," she mouthed.

Another hand flexed, doubled and compressed, painfully, slowly wriggling free. Kate glanced at Sukey, who seemed to have slipped into a daze of terror. Goodness knew what she'd endured in the lead-up to this event. Kate prayed all three of them would live through this.

Working quickly, silently, with one eye on Perry, Louisa managed to loosen Kate's bonds enough for her to tug her hands out of the rope.

With a jerk of the head, she indicated the unresponsive Sukey. After some difficulty, Louisa eased the rope from her hands, too. What would they do if Sukey couldn't run?

Kate scanned the stage for possible weapons. A thick layer of dust covered everything, but she distinguished some wooden swords standing upright in a box. They'd be no defense to a bullet, but she couldn't let herself worry about that. Perry only had one pistol, which meant one shot. Her lips twisted. *Ever the optimist, Kate.*

A storm of booted footsteps set Kate and Louisa into motion. They launched to their feet and ran for the stage door, dragging Sukey with them, while Perry leaped up, his knife and his bleeding arms forgotten.

Kate had hoped he'd leave them and concentrate on the footsteps coming ever nearer, but she heard him shout at her to stop and the unmistakable click of a pistol being cocked.

She froze, willing the others to get away while they could. "He wants me! Damn you, Louisa. Go!" she roared.

Louisa ignored her, but she shoved the unresisting Sukey into one of the wings, out of sight.

"Turn around, Your Grace." Perry's voice was so calm and pleasant, it sent shivers down her spine.

Slowly, Kate turned.

"Do you see her, Max?"

A deep voice from the shadows. "I see her. Yes."

"You can't win on this one, you little snot rag," came Jardine's voice. "I have you in my sights and if you so much as sneeze in the duchess's direction I'll shoot your damned head off. Understand?"

Lyle walked out onto the open stage unarmed, looking relaxed, as if he were taking a stroll in the park. "The pistol, Perry. Give it to me."

His deep voice was calm, his gaze steady. Kate marveled at his cool composure. But then, he did this sort of thing for a living. She shivered. If she got out of this alive she'd make Lyle promise never to work for the Home Office again.

MAX'S mind slowed; time all but stopped. His pulse beat in his ears.

"You heard Jardine, Perry," he said in an even, soothing voice, as he eased ever closer. They were almost arm's length apart now. Perry seemed to stare through him with those brilliant blue eyes, as if he existed in another realm, perhaps the one inside his sick, befuddled head. Blood stained Perry's shirtsleeves. Had Kate done that?

"Jardine is here. I'm here. You can't win," said Max gently. "Come now, lad. Let's not part as enemies. Give the pistol to me." On the last word, he reached for the gun.

Perry, who'd seemed transfixed while Lyle spoke, shot to awareness at the last second. He yanked the gun out of Max's reach and swung it in Kate's direction. "I'll kill her!" he screamed. "I'll do it! I will!"

Terror lent Max lightning speed. He clamped his hand on Perry's wrist, trying to bear his arm upwards to deflect his aim from Kate.

"Kate, move!" he shouted. "Take cover!"

He didn't know if she'd obeyed. He and Perry scuffled in a desperate clinch. Driving his elbow into Perry's solar plexus, Max twisted one hand free to smash him in the jaw. Perry staggered, a look of shock exploding over his face. His expression switched to accusation, as if he finally realized the truth of Max's allegiance.

With a strangled roar, Perry swiveled his hips and shoulders, wrenching free of Max's grasp in a practiced wrestling move. Max looked around wildly for Kate, but she must have obeyed him for once and hidden behind one of the props on the stage. Louisa had also disappeared.

He switched his attention back to Perry, who had scrambled beyond Max's reach. The boy held his pistol in a slack, dangerous grip. He was volatile. He might try to kill Max next.

Max spread his hands in a placatory gesture, still attempting to end it without bloodshed. But when Perry slowly lifted the pistol with a white, shaking hand, he didn't aim it at Max. He pressed the pistol to his own temple.

"Don't do it." Struggling to keep his tone calm, Max moved forward a pace, gingerly at first.

"What do you care?" jeered Perry, his lips curling in an ugly sneer. "You wouldn't care if I lived or died." His eyes reddened, the pain in them raw and ugly. He began to cry, in wrenching, ragged sobs. Watching for his moment, Max saw Perry's grip on the pistol slackening slightly, his finger lift from the trigger.

That moment of inattention was all Max needed. He launched himself at Perry and knocked his pistol hand away, fighting a grim battle for the weapon.

Perry's manic strength seemed to have trebled, and it was no easy thing to overpower him. As they swayed, locked together in a desperate tussle, a thought flashed across Max's mind, treacherously persuasive. He could let him. He could let Perry end it. If Perry survived this encounter, Faulkner would make sure he wasn't tried for murder. If Perry went free, he would come after Kate again. There was no question about that. While this boy lived, Kate would never be safe. How could he let her future be consumed with fear?

*The end justifies the means.*

A fortnight earlier, he wouldn't have hesitated. *Do it!* said the hardened operative inside him. *What are you waiting for?*

But . . .

He wasn't an operative anymore. A man of honor wouldn't take the simple course, because it wasn't right. He wouldn't let this sick, sad boy die by his own hand.

The resolution lent him a surge of strength. Max locked hands around Perry's wrists, forcing him to point the pistol to the ground. He managed to squeeze the trigger. The gun exploded, and Max used the momentum of the recoil to twist the useless weapon out of Perry's grip.

Jardine materialized in an instant, taking Perry into a painful, incapacitating hold. Still, the boy struggled as much as he could, screaming at Kate. "I'll kill you! I'll do it if it takes me the rest of my days, you bitch!"

Jardine roughly thrust him outside.

Max stood there watching their receding backs, his chest heaving. He stared down at the pistol in his hand. If she didn't come back to him now, he might as well shoot himself.

"Max!" Kate ran out from behind a screen, joy and relief flooding her voice. She hurtled into his arms. He closed them around her and buried his face in her hair.

"I'm so glad you came!" she babbled. "I had a plan, and it might have worked, too, if he'd missed his first shot."

Max tightened his arms around her. "Don't even think about it. My God, woman. You'll be the death of me yet."

She gazed up at him, and his heart turned over at the love that shone in her eyes. "You stopped him. You didn't let him die."

With that simple statement, he realized she'd sensed his struggle in those few seconds when he'd wanted to choose the easy path. Bright, intelligent, intuitive woman that she was, she knew what it had cost him to let Perry go. And despite the kidnapping and attempted murder, Kate's generous heart was glad at Max's choice. She prized his honor and his conscience over revenge for Perry's misdeeds.

How could he be so lucky? After all he'd put her through, Kate loved him still. He tightened his embrace and set his lips to hers.

Louisa ran past them to the stage door. "Where is Jardine taking—"

A gunshot burst through the quiet, obliterating the rest of her sentence.

"Stay here." Max dashed outside, passing Sukey, who cowered in the wings next to the stage. Of course, the women hurried after him. They all stopped short.

Perry lay dead on the grass. Jardine looked on, holding a smoking pistol.

Max quickly gathered Kate and Louisa into his arms and turned their faces into his chest. Sukey sobbed noisily behind them.

Despite his noble intentions, the boy had died anyway. Max couldn't help the wave of relief that flooded him, but there was an equal mixture of guilt. Should he have predicted this? He'd been too caught up in Kate to consider what Jardine meant to do with Perry.

*"No!"* Louisa struggled and broke free.

"Louie, don't—" Max watched Louisa run to Jardine and hit him, pummeling his chest with all her might. "How could you? How *could* you? You've killed him, you murderer!"

With an oath, Jardine gripped her by the shoulders and shook her into silence. "If I had, it would have been a mercy, like shooting a rabid dog. But I didn't kill him, Louisa. He carried a second pistol. He shot himself."

To Max, looking on, the statement bore the ring of truth. There was even a tinge of chagrin in Jardine's tone, as if he were furious with himself for letting it happen. Jardine never made mistakes. But it seemed this time, he had.

Louisa had stopped hitting Jardine, but she jerked from his hold and stepped back, white-lipped and shaking. " I don't believe you," she whispered. "You could have stopped him. You make me sick, do you hear me, Jardine? Sick to my stomach. I want nothing to do with you, ever again."

Jardine's expression was grim as he studied the gun in his hand. He looked up. "I know, Louisa. You made that quite clear when last we met. But we are destined to be together, my love." He flashed her a bitter smile. "And nothing I do and nothing you say will ever change that."

THE door flung open and Kate and Max fell into her bedchamber, kissing so hard and urgently, their teeth clashed together, ripping off each other's garments as fast as they could.

Max kicked the door shut behind them and spun Kate around, cursing under his breath at the waste of time unlacing her stays.

As the corset fell to the floor, he squeezed her breasts through her chemise and bit her neck hard. She shuddered helplessly, almost climaxing there and then, but she needed to feel him, skin to skin, so she stepped out of her petticoat and ripped the chemise over her head.

Max moved away to take off his boots and shed his other clothes. She watched him, coveting every inch of skin, every hard muscle, every scar he revealed. When he was completely naked, she remembered her shoes and stockings.

She turned and set her foot on the stool of her dressing table. As she bent to undo her garter he came up behind her, smoothing his hands over her shoulders and down her back in an entirely possessive way.

"Leave them on," he growled, hot breath in her ear. "I like the way your legs look in them." He tweaked one of the ribbons on her garter, brushing her thigh with his fingertips. "Like a present, waiting to be unwrapped."

She shivered, and he continued to speak explicitly about the things he'd do for her, with her, to her, until she could barely stand for excitement. He urged her to kneel on the stool and she held on to her dressing table for support in a clatter of scent bottles and cosmetics.

But his hands, those big hands, roamed her body, not gently, but hard and demanding, just as she wanted, at least this time. They'd share many quiet, gentle nights in the future. Their recent escape from death made the drive to celebrate life and their love in the most primitive way overpowering.

"Don't be shocked." Lyle dipped his fingers into her soft, wet folds, positioning the head of his erection between her legs from behind. "But I'm going to come inside you now."

Kate shuddered. The idea seemed wicked, decadent, and also strangely thrilling. Intrigued, trusting him completely, she waited, tense with anticipation. His member nudged her entrance, opening her, and the slow slide of his shaft as it forged its way inside, stretching and filling her, made her gasp and grip the dressing table tightly to anchor herself. She closed her eyes, reveling in their closeness, in the sweet agony that rippled through her body as he inched forward.

Involuntarily, her inner muscles gripped him. He gasped and paused, breathing hard.

When he didn't move, when the longing became unbearable, she opened her eyes and saw his reflection in the looking glass, all broad shoulders, muscular chest, and flat, taut stomach. The sight of his big hands splayed so possessively over her hips made her tremble. *Those hands . . .*

How she loved him, loved the feel of him inside her. And she didn't need to hide it any longer. Boldly, Kate met his eyes in the glass. "Please," she whispered.

Holding her gaze in a searing connection that sizzled right to her toes, Lyle gathered himself, then surged home with one powerful thrust, ramming against her womb. She cried out at the potent, sweet mix of pleasure and pain, wanting it to go on and on.

He gripped her hips and stroked a slow, steady rhythm, rubbing an exquisitely sensitive place inside her that made her insides clench, desperate to keep him there as long as she could.

His eyes were shut now, and the expression on his face, not of strain but something close to awe, touched her heart. This was the lover she'd seen in him from the first. This was the man she'd wanted all along.

Bending over her so his body spooned hers, he growled in her ear, "And now, my dear, I'm going to ride you harder than you've ever been ridden before."

And he did, while she watched. And it was glorious.

HOURS later, Max and Kate lay together, naked, sated, and spent.

Kate turned on her side, snuggling her back into the hard, muscled warmth of Lyle's chest. He kissed her shoulder and she sighed. His palm skimmed up her torso and came to rest possessively over her breast.

"There's still one thing I don't understand," Lyle murmured into her hair.

"Really?" she said sleepily. "What's that?"

He squeezed her nipple, sending a jolt of ecstasy through her. "If you like the way I . . . love you, why did you write differently in your diary? Your phantom lover was slow and gentle. Why fantasize about something you didn't really want?"

That question had occurred to her also, and she'd realized there was no simple answer. Kate picked up a lock of her hair that lay spread across the pillow. She pulled it taut and pretended to examine it. Then she gave a small, embarrassed shrug. "I suppose the truth is I didn't know what I wanted. My marriage with Hector was . . . uneasy. Difficult. He did not desire me at all, you see."

The big hand stilled on her breast. "Was he mad?"

A giggle caught in her throat. "No, he just couldn't seem to, er, harden. Down there." She blushed, refusing to meet Lyle's eye. Despite all they'd done together, she still didn't feel comfortable discussing such things.

Lyle grunted. "I assure you, the problem was entirely his. If he said it had anything to do with you, he was a damned liar."

Her chest burned with the knowledge. How like Lyle to cut to the heart of her fear. "H-he said I was too eager, too bold. My wanton behavior disgusted him. He didn't like his wife to behave like a common trollop."

Lyle gave a shout of laughter. "What a cod's head."

Kate nodded, sinking into him, relishing his warmth. "I believe now that he did have a problem, but at the time . . . Well, at the time, I so desperately wanted someone to love. Someone who would be kind."

She turned in his arms to face Lyle and ran her palm over his chest. His gray eyes lit with tenderness, warming her heart. She lowered her voice to a whisper. "I didn't know what real passion was until I met you. I didn't know what I wanted until you gave it to me."

To her delight, a slight flush tinged Lyle's lean cheeks. He tilted her chin and took her mouth in an aching, sweetly carnal kiss.

Lyle's lips drifted to her ear. "To think if it weren't for that diary of yours we could have had this so much sooner," he breathed. Thrills skittered down her spine. He kissed his way down the tender skin of her throat.

"If you hadn't *read* my diary," gasped Kate, arching back.

His palm brushed over her nipple, rolling it to a hard peak, then pinching it with exquisitely judged pressure. "No, I don't regret that. Reading your fantasies was one of the most erotic experiences I've ever had."

Kate pulled back to study him. "Is that true?"

He nodded.

The knowledge didn't seem to trouble her anymore. With a secret smile, she ducked her head to kiss his chest. "Perhaps I shall begin a new diary." She trailed the tip of her tongue along his collarbone, tasting salt and man.

"So that I can read it?" Lightning fast, Max rolled her onto her back, pinning her down with his hips, a wonderful, solid weight.

She reached up to cup his jaw with her hand, imprinting this moment in her mind. "So I can remember nights like this. Always."

Turn the page for a look at the next novel by Christine Wells

*Indecent Proposal*

Coming soon from Berkley Sensation!

## London, 1814

WOULD she see him? She could hardly believe she'd found him at last.

Sick with anticipation, Lady Sarah Cole smoothed her worn gloves, gripped the strings of her reticule tighter, and made herself step down from the hackney cab.

As she emerged from the carriage, the stench of rotting fish assailed her with full force. She almost lost her footing on the uneven cobblestones and stumbled again as a large rat shot across her path, its naked pink tail twitching. Battling rising nausea, Sarah held a lavender-scented handkerchief over her mouth and nose to filter the fetid air.

After a few moments, she decided she'd mastered her uneasy stomach and returned her handkerchief to her reticule. Beneath the brim of her plain straw bonnet, she swept a glance up the street.

Ragged children played some sort of ball game against the crumbling wall of a dilapidated shop front. The tavern on the corner did a brisk, noisy trade, even at this hour.

A hawker pushed his cart and cried his wares, adding to the general commotion. Sarah discerned from his barely intelligible bawl that he was selling cat meat.

She shuddered. It was a depressed, filthy part of London, located a stone's throw from the Billingsgate wharfs. The lady she'd once been wouldn't have dreamed of visiting such a place. She shouldn't have come.

But she'd never admitted defeat when matters grew difficult, and she wouldn't start now. Dismissing the cab driver's warning about the rough neighborhood, Sarah paid him the fare and a little extra and asked him to wait.

She caught up her skirts to keep them clear of the rubbish that lined the street and picked a path to the front door of a tall, grim house. As she inquired the way of a sharp-eyed young girl, she tried not to show her dismay. She'd imagined him in circumstances far better than this.

Sarah thanked the girl and gave her a shilling. Glancing up, she saw a small face shimmer in the grime at a third floor window then disappear. Her pulse jumped. Was it he?

No reason why it should be. Slum lords crammed as many bodies as they could into houses such as this.

Sarah rapped with her gloved fist and the door creaked open, revealing a dim hallway with a row of doors either side of it and a central staircase zigzagging up and up, apparently to the heavens. No one came to ask her business, though the squalls of babies and rowdy voices assailed her, penetrating the thin, mildewed walls.

Hitching her skirts a little higher, Sarah crossed the entry hall and mounted the first of several flights of stairs. Not long now.

How would he look—her husband's bastard son? Would he have Brinsley's eyes, or his riot of curls? Years had passed since she'd wrung her hands over Brinsley's tomcat proclivities, yet her heart stuttered at the thought.

The boy was ten years old, conceived mere months after

she and Brinsley wed. The old pain of betrayal, a pain she thought she'd buried, rose to slap her in the face.

Pausing in her ascent, Sarah absorbed the sting with a clenched jaw, her hand closing like a vise around the worm-eaten banister. She took a deep breath, held it, then slowly let it out. The tawdry circumstances of his birth were not the boy's fault. A child did not deserve to live in poverty merely because his father was a scoundrel. She had sold more perfume than ever, scrimped to save the moderate sum she carried in her reticule. All for him. The child she would never have.

Many stairs later, Sarah found the place she sought. She knocked and waited for what seemed like an eternity. Finally, the door swung open and Sarah came face to face with the boy's mother.

"Maggie Day?" The name was branded on Sarah's heart. The first in a long line of "other" women she'd prefer to know nothing about.

"Aye, that's me." The woman leaned against the doorjamb, her expression wary. She shoved stray wisps of blond hair out of her face with the heel of a grimy hand, revealing a faint echo of former prettiness in her high cheekbones and the vivid blue of her eyes. Those eyes flared when Sarah introduced herself. After a slight hesitation, Maggie shifted aside to let her uninvited guest enter.

This was not a social call. Sarah didn't attempt pleasantries. "I've come about the boy. My . . . husband's son." She couldn't yet give him a name. Brinsley hadn't told her what he was called, and the address she'd found among his unpaid bills and notes of hand named the mother, not the child.

Sarah tried not to betray her anxiety, the strange yearning that had gripped her once the hurt and anger at Brinsley's taunts had subsided. *You're barren . . . Useless, even as a breeder . . . I've already fathered a son.*

She forced down the image of her husband's triumph and focused on the scene before her. A straw pallet lay in one corner, made up with a coarse wool blanket. That and a crudely fashioned chair furnished the tiny room. The place stank of boiled cabbage and rat urine.

"Is he here?" Idiotic question. She saw for herself he was not.

A derisive expression flitted across Maggie's features, but she answered politely enough. "Nah, m'lady. Haven't seen him since before sunup. Goes down to the fish markets early, but after that . . ." She shrugged.

Sarah stared. Didn't she know? The boy was ten years old and his mother didn't know or care where he might be all day?

Jealousy seeped like acid into Sarah's chest. If he were *hers* . . . The corrosive burn spread through her, thickening her throat and pricking behind her eyes. She blinked hard and looked away.

Her gaze snagged on a collection of empty bottles in one corner. Did the woman drink? Sarah bit her lip. It wasn't her business; none of it was. But would Maggie use Sarah's money to clothe and feed the boy, or to buy more gin?

Disappointment flooded her, drowning her one small hope. She'd thought she could soothe her conscience by making this short journey—one small gesture to clean the slate. But not only was her mission flawed—she could not possibly hand her precious coins to such a female—she'd given herself one more problem to solve.

She couldn't compel Brinsley to provide for his love child. The pittance she made selling perfume was not enough to keep her and Brinsley, much less the boy as well.

Equally impossible to leave the child in this situation. Honor and simple Christian charity demanded that she ensure his well-being if her husband, his father, would not.

Something must be done. She saw her duty clearly enough, but what *right* did she have to interfere?

Sarah offered her hand to Maggie, using every ounce of self-control to remain civil and calm. "I should—I should like to come again, if I may. To see him."

"Why yes, m'lady. Of course." Disregarding the outstretched hand, Maggie dipped a curtsy, a calculating gleam in her eye that Sarah did not like.

Sarah dropped her hand. "Shall we say Wednesday, at four?"

She looked up, and saw wariness shade Maggie's face once more.

Sarah reassured her. "The boy will come to no harm from me." Impatiently, she added, "I cannot keep calling him 'boy.' What is his name, if you please?"

Maggie eyed her for a silent moment. "His friends call him Jimmy."

Thanking her, Sarah forced herself to leave the shabby room. When she reached the stairwell, all the turbulent emotion she'd dammed inside her spilled over. *That poor little boy.* How could Brinsley be so heartless towards his own flesh and blood?

She fought against it, but her chest heaved with a great dry sob. Sarah pinched the bridge of her nose, trying to quell the burn behind her eyes. She *refused* to weep like a ninny over a young scamp she didn't even know, one borne to her husband's mistress into the bargain. She was doing her duty. Emotion didn't enter into it. The fat, hot tear that rolled down her cheek was the product of overwrought nerves, that was all.

Sarah opened her reticule to pluck out her handkerchief and stopped with a soft, strangled cry.

Every penny of the money she'd brought was gone.

All the heat of frustration and sorrow drained from her face. But how—? Sarah glanced back in the direction of Maggie's room. No, the woman hadn't approached within a foot of her unwelcome guest during that tense encounter. Unless Maggie was a conjurer, she couldn't be the culprit.

When was the last time she'd seen the money in her reticule? Of course! The ragged child who'd given her directions. A moment's inattention while Sarah scanned the upstairs windows would have been enough for an accomplished pickpocket. What a fool she'd been.

Sarah hurried downstairs, nearly tripping in her haste, and burst out into the street. She looked right and left, but of course the girl had vanished. And what would Sarah do if she found her? She could scarcely accuse her of theft without proof, and she balked at the thought of handing a child over to the tender mercies of the law.

Despair weighted the pit of her stomach like a millstone. All her hard work, gone.

Sarah questioned the hackney driver, but he hadn't noticed the girl.

"Something amiss, ma'am?"

Sarah hesitated. The jarvey's open, pleasant face invited trust, but he had a living to earn. If she admitted she had no money to pay him, would he take her word that she'd obtain it when they reached their destination? Or would he whip up his horse and leave her stranded in this mean, tumbledown street?

"Not at all," she replied, trying to sound confident. "Take me to Tom's Coffeehouse, please." Brinsley was a creature of habit. He was sure to be at Tom's at this hour, smoking and gossiping like an old lady with that fool Rockfort and his other dim-witted cronies.

Sarah gave the jarvey precise directions and suffered agonies while they navigated the crowded London streets. Ridiculous, but she couldn't suppress the fear that the driver would order her to turn out her empty reticule and toss her into the street.

She imagined Brinsley, sprawled in a chair with a tankard

of ale at his elbow, smoking a cigarillo and relaxing with his friends. Bile burned in her throat when she thought of the life of ease he continued to pursue, though they barely scraped enough together each month for rent and food. God forbid he should work for a living. As far as she could tell, he lived largely on credit, and supplemented the small allowance his elder brother paid him with sporadic wins at the gaming tables. But it never seemed to be enough.

Surely he wouldn't begrudge her the cab fare? Though he might relish the blow to her pride if he refused, he wouldn't wish to appear ungenerous in front of his friends.

The hackney pulled to a stop outside the coffeehouse—a rowdy, masculine establishment thick with smoke. Sarah scanned the bow windows that gave out onto the street, but failed to see Brinsley within.

There was nothing for it. She would have to look for him inside. "Wait here, please," Sarah called up to the driver. "I won't be a moment."

"Eh? Now, see here, ma'am—" But in a fair imitation of her mother's haughty bearing, Sarah pretended not to hear and swept across the flagstones, inwardly cringing at the prospect of seeking her husband in a public coffeehouse to beg for money. She prayed he wouldn't make the task more difficult than it needed to be. She detested scenes.

A large hand gripped her elbow, stopping her. She gasped and swung around, to see the hackney driver's reddening face.

She swallowed hard. "Let go of me! I told you, I'll only be a minute."

"And where 'ave I 'eard that before?" scoffed the driver. His hold tightened. "I'll 'ave my money first, ma'am, *if* you please."

Before Sarah could answer, there was a blur of movement and a dull crack. The driver dropped Sarah's elbow with a grunt of pain, cradling his wrist. Sarah turned with a gasp and nearly stumbled. Standing between them, looking down at her with those deep, dark eyes, was the Marquis of Vane.

"Did he hurt you?" He made as if to take her arm to inspect the damage for himself, but she stepped back, evading his frowning scrutiny.

She shook her head, insides clenching, heart knocking against her ribs. There didn't seem enough air in the world to breathe. "A—a misunderstanding, merely. You are very good, but please don't—"

Vane lowered the cane he'd used to break the man's hold and switched his glare to the driver. "If you don't wish to feel this stick across your back, you'd better make yourself scarce."

The jarvey was a thick-set man, but Vane towered over him, all broad chest and big shoulders and pure, masculine power. The driver blanched a little, but he retained enough spirit to mount a case in his defense.

Vane didn't appear to listen, but he didn't stem the flow. In the jarvey's eagerness to explain himself, he described Sarah's excursion in unnecessary detail. He even remarked how upset madam had seemed after visiting that dirty old house off Pudding Lane.

Sarah stiffened, so humiliated she couldn't bring herself to argue. Of all the men in the world who might have come upon her in this predicament, why did it have to be Vane?

His swift glance held a gleam of curiosity. She lifted her chin with proud disdain. She mustn't reveal the slightest hint of weakness. He'd show her no mercy if he sensed how susceptible she was, how fiercely she longed for him in the night. She'd never acted on that yearning, never allowed Vane the slightest liberty, not even a chaste kiss on the cheek. But the shame of lying in her husband's bed while she ached for another man's touch was slowly corroding her soul.

The marquis gave no sign he believed the driver's story,

but when Sarah said nothing to contradict it, he flicked a coin to the jarvey and dismissed him with a nod. Before she could protest, the man was gone.

Vane turned to her. "Come, I'll escort you home."

His low, resonant tone stroked down her spine in a warm velvet caress. A shocking wave of heat rolled through her body, left her trembling from head to toe. It was an effort to stop her voice from shaking like the rest of her. "That won't be necessary, thank you," she managed. "It is but a step." She gripped her hands together. "I haven't the funds with me, I'm afraid, but my husband will reimburse you. If you'd be so good as to find him . . ."

Vane followed her gaze to the coffeehouse and his jaw tightened. "I don't want repayment," he said harshly.

No, of course he didn't. Vane's wealth surpassed most men's dreams. And there was only one thing he'd ever wanted from her. He still wanted it. She knew by the suppressed violence in him, the tension that held his large frame utterly still. As if he needed to exercise restraint over every cell in his body to stop himself from touching her.

Faith, but he was magnificent. His dark hair was cropped brutally short, with no attempt to soften the slightly hawkish nose and sharp cheekbones that stood out from his lean cheeks in high relief. His eyebrows were thick and black and straight. He carried himself like a Roman general, with the grace of an athlete and a habit of command.

Even in the open, bustling street, Sarah felt crowded, oppressed, overwhelmed by him. Her pride refused to let her take a backwards step. But oh, she wanted to. She wanted to run.

All she could do was conceal her fear behind that familiar mask of ice. "Thank you. I'm obliged to you," she said in a colorless tone. She would repay him the minute she could. She dreaded being beholden to him, even for such a negligible sum.

He continued to stand there, waiting, as if he expected

something from her. She wasn't sure what it was, but she knew it was more than she could possibly give. She glanced at the coffeehouse. She needed to get away.

"So cold," breathed Vane. "You are . . . quite the most unfeeling woman I've ever met."

Sarah forced her lips into a thin, cynical smile. How little he knew her. The danger had always been that she felt far, far too much. An excess of sensibility had led to the great downfall of her existence. But she'd learned a hard lesson at the tender age of seventeen. She would never let emotion overtake her good sense again. She'd paid for her impulsive choice every day for the past ten years.

The suffering had increased a hundredfold since she'd met Vane.

They stared at one another without speaking. The everyday world rushed past in a muted blur, as if she and Vane were surrounded by smoked glass. Those compelling dark eyes bore into hers, determined to read her secret yearning, searching for a response.

Her heart gave a mighty surge, as if it would leap from her chest into his. But she'd built a stronghold around her heart from the flotsam of wrecked dreams. That irresponsible organ was in no danger.

The miracle was that she still had a heart at all.

Someone jostled her as they hurried past. The strange bubble of suspended time burst, and the world flooded back, swirling around them. Sarah turned away.

And there, in the bow window of Tom's Coffeehouse, stood Brinsley, her husband.

*Watching.*

THE Marquis of Vane flicked a glance at Brinsley Cole across the card table, betraying no hint of the animosity he felt. Vane was—as ever—in control.

The murmur of hardened gamesters intent on play surrounded them, punctuated by rattles of dice and the clack of a ball skittering around the E & O wheel. Occasionally, a low rumble broke out after a win or a loss, but the object of this hell was serious play, and the general mood was quiet and tense. Even the doxies attending each table knew their charms paled next to the turn of the card, and delayed their lusty propositions until the hand was done.

Vane hardly knew what brought him here tonight. He didn't care the snap of his fingers for games of chance, and still less did he care to bed any of the unappealing women who graced the establishment. Whatever had prompted him to visit Crockford's, he wished he'd ignored the impulse. Then he would not have to suffer Cole's infernal smugness, nor remember with every breath that Cole possessed what Vane desired more than anything in the world.

She was fresh in his mind, a rapid hard pulse in his body, an ache that never quite abated and had flared to burning agony when he'd stood so close to her that afternoon.

He'd wanted to leave as soon as he saw Brinsley Cole already seated at the card tables tonight, but that might have created talk he wished to avoid. So he'd smiled and sat and played cards with a man he'd sooner never lay eyes on again. He doubted he fooled anyone at all.

"And how fares your lady wife, Brinsley?" Rockfort slid a glance at Vane as he dealt the cards.

In spite of himself, Vane tensed. Braced for the reply.

Cole lurched to his feet, spilling a buxom trollop from his lap and a dash of claret down his gold embroidered waistcoat. A sneer crossed his angelic features as he raised his glass for a toast.

"To the Lady Sarah Cole! The woman who can outscold a Billingsgate fishwife, freeze a man's balls off with her frosty green glare, then rate him for failing to pick up after himself. My lords, gentlemen—my damned virago of a wife!"

Cole flourished a bow and drank deep.

The gaming hell faded to oblivion. Vane heard nothing above the roar in his ears. The wild beast inside him raged, wanting to lunge across the table, wrap hands around that slender throat, and choke the life out of Brinsley Cole.

Muscles bunched and aching with the effort of restraint, Vane composed his features into a disinterested mask and picked up his cards. He had no right to defend Lady Sarah against her own husband. If he spoke up, people would assume he was her lover. He glanced around the table. Perhaps they already did. He was famed for getting what he wanted, and he'd wanted Lady Sarah from the second he'd laid eyes on her seven years before.

Everyone, it seemed, waited for him to speak.

Vane raised his glass of burgundy to his lips. He sipped, savored, then set the glass on the table in a precise, controlled movement. Without glancing at his cards, he threw them down. "Gentlemen, I've recalled a pressing engagement. I shall bid you good night."

A murmur skittered around the table as he swept up his winnings. Cole, damn his soul to hell, smirked and waved a hand. "My lord, I'll come with you."

Over the players' heads, Vane sent him a brief, scorching glare. As he turned to leave, he saw Rockfort twitch Cole's sleeve in warning. But despite its porcelain perfection, Cole's skin was thick as elephant hide. He stumbled out in Vane's wake.

The frigid air speared Vane through his greatcoat, but did nothing to cool his blood. Brinsley Cole must be blind or suicidal to follow him into a dark alley. The man begged to be throttled and thrown in the gutter along with the other refuse and scum.

Drawing on his gloves, Vane halted and turned around. "What do you want?"

Brinsley swaggered towards him. "The question, my lord Marquis, is what do *you* want? I'll wager I know the answer."

Vane's sigh fogged the air. "Is this where you try to sell me another of your schemes, Brinsley? Canals in Jamaica, that sort of thing?"

His companion barely seemed to notice the veiled insult. Despite Vane's attempt to distract him, Brinsley knew he was on to something. Vane saw it in the avid light that entered the man's wide, soulful eyes. Brinsley scented a weakness, and he'd worry at Vane like a hound at a wounded stag until he worked out how to turn it to his best advantage.

Finally, Brinsley spoke. "You want my wife," he said softly. "You always have."

Shock ricocheted though Vane's mind. Brinsley knew? He'd always known, it seemed. Had Sarah told her husband of Vane's interest? The idea sliced his chest like a finely honed blade. Suddenly, the past rushed back; events and conversations changed color and shape.

He dragged his mind to the present. He needed to remain calm, keep a cool head for Sarah's sake. He wanted Lady Sarah more than he wanted air to breathe, it was true. Her husband knew it, but what difference did that make? As long as Vane made no admissions, Brinsley could think what he liked.

"If you wish to call me out, name your friends, Cole. Otherwise, shut your filthy little mouth." With one careless finger, he flicked Brinsley's wilted shirt-point. "Go home, man. You are drunk. Worse than that, you are tedious."

"Home. Oh, yes!" Brinsley chortled, enjoying himself now. "What wouldn't you give to be in my shoes, eh? Trotting off home to my tasty little wife. And do you know what I'll do to her when I get—"

Fury ripped through Vane's blood. He slammed Brinsley against the stone wall, pinning him with one hand to his throat. It was all Vane could do not to squeeze the life out of the cur there and then.

"Mercy!" Brinsley's face was mottled red, his eyes bulging and frantic. Vane wished he'd put up some kind of resistance, but the pathetic creature made no move to defend himself, save for a feeble kick at Vane's leather-clad shin.

Damn it, he couldn't fight such a poor specimen, much as he yearned to dispatch him to the hottest fires of hell. Vane released his grip, and Brinsley crumpled to the slimy cobbles, wheezing and coughing, clutching his throat.

Vane waited for him to recover, even lent him a hand to help him up. With a glance of disdain, he stripped off the glove that had made contact with Brinsley's soiled person and tossed it in the gutter. "Now, what were you saying before I so rudely interrupted?"

Brinsley dashed blood from his bit lip. "You want Sarah," he whispered, edging closer. "Badly enough to lose your famous control. That must be worth something." He smiled. "That must be worth quite a lot."

Vane remained silent. He willed himself to ignore Brinsley's jibes, turn his back, and walk away. But he couldn't pretend not to care. He must know what Brinsley planned. Though she was beyond his reach in every way, he needed to assure himself that Sarah would be safe.

Yet, even as those altruistic thoughts crossed his mind, a small echo of honesty forced Vane to admit—Brinsley was right. He wanted Lady Sarah Cole in a way no gentleman of honor should want another man's wife. His passion for her was like a recurring fever, rising again and again to attack him in moments of weakness. No matter how hard he trained and fought and conditioned his body, his soul was hers and always would be. For seven years, the knowledge that this worthless piece of rubbish before him possessed Lady Sarah had torn at Vane with razor-sharp claws.

And now Brinsley offered . . . what, exactly?

"You want her," Brinsley repeated. "You can have her . . . at a price."

Vane sucked in a breath. Disgust and desire clashed inside him. Had he misheard? Brinsley couldn't possibly mean . . .

Though Vane maintained his indifferent expression, even managed to look a trifle bored, the very air around them seemed to thicken with his need.

"Ten thousand pounds. For one night with my wife." Brinsley repeated it, stressed each word. "Ten. Thousand. Pounds."

A red haze swept over Vane's vision. He wanted to tear Brinsley apart with his bare hands. He wanted to leave without dignifying that insane, *indecent* proposal with a response. He wanted to forget Lady Sarah Cole existed, excise her from his mind and heart.

But he couldn't. He couldn't save her from Brinsley's loathsome schemes either. He'd tried. She'd spurned him with her cold, cruel smile. But what if the little weasel took this offer to another man with fewer scruples than Vane? What then?

"I ought to kill you, Cole." Vane kept his voice low, aware that a party of men had left Crockford's and headed their way. "Exterminate you like the vermin you are."

Brinsley didn't even blink. "Ah, but I'm well acquainted with your sort, my lord. And I know you would not kill a man without a fair fight." He fingered his bruised throat, then shrugged. "Call me out if you wish to see Sarah's name dragged through the mud. I won't meet you." His expression darkened. "I married that little bitch, my lord Marquis. Short of bloody murder, I can treat her however I damned well please. So think well before you threaten me, sir, or your sweet Lady Sarah might suffer the consequences."

Blind rage, all the more dangerous for its impotence, threatened to overwhelm every principle Vane held dear. He faced Brinsley in the darkness, panting with the effort of keeping his hands by his sides instead of wrapping them around the little weasel's throat. This time, he wouldn't have the strength to let go.

He'd never killed a man before . . .

Their misted breath clashed and roiled upwards. The moonlight glinted off wet cobbles, threw Brinsley's profile into high relief. The thoughtful poet's brow that hid a conniving, low mind; the noble nose that sniffed out weakness and despair; the sculpted lips that now curled in a self-satisfied sneer.

Damn him to hell. Brinsley knew he had won.

Enter the rich world of historical romance with Berkley Books.
Lynn Kurland
Patricia Potter
Betina Krahn
Jodi Thomas
Anne Gracie
Love is timeless.
penguin.com

M9G0907